GRACE PREVAILING

The Crowning Crescendo:
Season of Miracles
Book 7

RACHAEL C. DUNCAN

CKN Christian Publishing
An Imprint of Wolfpack Publishing
1707 E. Diana Street
Tampa, FL 33609

cknchristianpublishing.com

Paperback ISBN: 978-1-63977-471-5
eBook ISBN: 978-1-63977-470-8
LCCN: 2024945248

NOTE FROM THE AUTHOR

When I began researching for my first novel, I was blown away by the vast array of resources available concerning anything and everything biblical! It was thrilling to discover such a wealth of information regarding topics that have always intrigued me.

Because I write Bible-based novels, please allow me to state this simple disclaimer: The novels I write are categorized as biblical fiction, which means I have taken some literary license in instances where the Bible story itself remains silent, unclear, or disputed. As you can imagine, a *lot* of controversy and differing opinions regarding certain biblical characters, settings, dates, etc. So just a reminder, while based on the biblical narratives, this is indeed a work of fiction.

As I tackled this exciting new project, I sought to honor the Word of God, and then I asked the Lord to help me fill in the blanks in a way that will reach my readers, touch their hearts, draw them closer to Him, and bring these beautiful Bible stories to life, inspiring each reader to dive headfirst into the precious Word of God!

Thank you for purchasing this novel. I hope you are blessed page after page!

GRACE PREVAILING

CHAPTER 1

Leah

Circa A.D. 35, Jerusalem

Ah, Jerusalem. The beloved city. The Holy Land, hailed by the ancients as a city upon a hill, adorned like a chaste virgin bride for an adoring husband, the desire of kings. Here, the renowned and mighty Abraham had placed his only son upon an altar in obedience to Adonai, little knowing the great God of Heaven would stay his hand just before the death blow's unforgiving strike. Here, the legendary giant slayer, King David, had governed God's chosen people from his glittering throne. And here, centuries later, the promised Son of David was brutally slain, nailed to a Roman cross while jealous Jews flung scathing insults and insolent soldiers gambled for His clothing.

Here, the resplendent Temple of God crowned the highest hill, dazzling starry-eyed pilgrims with its radiant majesty. And yet, God's glory had departed from the impressive structure hewn of the finest marble and crowned with shimmering gold. Despite all its lustrous pomp and grandeur, the imposing Temple compound remained perched upon Mount Moriah like a slumbering beast, utterly devoid of the presence of God.

Unrelenting. Stone cold, Leah thought, clutching her trembling hands close to her heart. *Rather like the severe, stern-faced men parading proudly about its echoing marble halls...*

Rather like her brother, a rising star among scholars and learned men. And yet every time his gaze fell upon her, she grew cold inside.

Oh, Jerusalem, you once bore such shining promise. Raising listless eyes to scan the dim horizon washed in the waning golden light of sunset, Leah's thoughts meandered on, unbidden. *And yet you rejected your Messiah, your only hope of glory.*

Jerusalem, the last place she wished to be.

Seated upon an elegantly upholstered Greco-Roman style couch situated on an expensively furnished, high terrace overlooking the shining city, Leah contemplated her impossible situation. She was grateful for this moment of solitude in which to think, to pray, to reflect *without* her overbearing older brother telling her what she could or couldn't believe. Though he was a devoted Pharisee and deeply respected by the religious leaders, Leah suspected that he bordered upon fanatical. She hadn't realized how difficult it would be—leaving her father, mother, and homeland to lodge with a stubborn and haughty older sibling she hardly knew.

She didn't even want to think about the scathing lecture he would surely deliver if he knew what she was considering.

Upon her recent arrival in the holy city, Leah

couldn't help but be intrigued by the strange new sect called the Way. Her brother—like all the important men of the academic and religious community—loathed the movement with his every breath. Curious, she had listened to the preaching of a boisterous fisherman-turned-disciple on the streets of Jerusalem and been pierced to the core of her being.

And now...now she couldn't stop thinking about the Man called Jesus of Nazareth. Nor could she deny the Spirit of God moving upon her heart. The bold, outspoken apostle called Simon Peter had convinced her beyond any shadow of a doubt that the Messiah had, indeed, come.

And He wanted to save her.

Releasing a slow, steadying breath, Leah pondered the gravity of such a decision. Should she choose to join the followers of the Way, the consequences would indeed prove dire...and dangerous. Possibly even deadly.

Lifting her modestly covered head, Leah squared her narrow shoulders, her dark eyes kindling like the great sphere of fire descending upon the western hills. Rising slowly, she lifted slender hands heavenward in a gesture of humility and acceptance.

Come what may, she was ready to take her stand.

***

Mary

Jerusalem

The morning sun crested the Upper City, bathing sprawling stone mansions, palm-dotted lanes, and fashionably paved avenues in vibrant autumn sunshine.

Laden with a heavy basket brimming with freshly baked bread and ripe produce, Mary strolled a colonnaded lane with a cosmopolitan air, her regal head held high, her penetrating but lovely gray eyes absorbing the picturesque beauty of the day.

Alongside her, Mary's handsome sixteen-year-old son, John Mark, matched her swift yet graceful gait, shouldering an even larger basket boasting an impressive assortment of tantalizing baked goods. "You appear as a lady on a mission, Mother," John Mark quipped drolly, indifferent to the three burly armed guards flanking them from behind. "But, of course, I suppose you are."

"We all are," Mary reminded him, eager to reach the squalid prison barracks located near the Roman quarter in the Lower City. "When Jesus returned to His Father in Heaven, He entrusted us with a grave yet joyous assignment."

"It's really something, isn't it?" John Mark mused, his aristocratic features stretching into an easy smile. "Watching it all unfold. When Jesus commanded us to take the gospel to all the nations, I never imagined it would look like this."

"Nor I," Mary agreed solemnly, contemplating all that had transpired since her beloved Lord's ascension. The young church had enjoyed a season of joyful ecstasy after receiving the great commission, and their numbers had grown with speed and alacrity. But the blessed soul harvest was swiftly followed by fierce opposition, which rapidly escalated to harassment, persecution, and imprisonment. Even now, Mary and John Mark were on the way to deliver provisions to incarcerated believers.

Such charity was their only hope for survival, as the prisons refused to supply believers with daily rations. By the grace of God alone, the guards were far too afraid of the power Mary's business ventures wielded over the priests and Temple compound to deny her regular visits, though they attempted to make her visits as difficult as possible. Miraculously, the Lord had recently provided an unexpected way around that, as well.

Slender brows drawing together in dismay, Mary refused to dwell upon the many injustices inflicted upon her brethren. After all, Jesus had warned them that persecution would come. And He would strengthen them amidst trials and tribulations, just as He had promised.

"Do you miss them?" John Mark asked frankly, interrupting her train of thought. "Those who are no longer with us?"

Mary could have asked her son if he referenced the brethren in prison, the believers driven from their homes and forced to flee the city, or worse, the courageous martyrs who had been slain for their faith in Jesus.

But instinctively, she knew John Mark was referring to those who had taken the gospel to other—safer—lands.

"I do miss them," Mary admitted quietly, her cautious gaze sweeping the way before them as they traveled despite the armed guards' watchful awareness. At this early hour, the wealthiest residential precinct remained eerily quiet as surprisingly well-dressed servants of the elite somberly went about their morning tasks in the large outer courts of opulent mansions. Others traversed the colonnaded avenues, having been sent to market or on other errands of importance.

Suddenly realizing that her son awaited a further response, Mary smiled bravely. "But many brothers and sisters have found freedom, safety, and respite beyond Jerusalem's borders," she reminded him. "Most importantly, the gospel has been proclaimed in many lands. For this, we must praise God."

"It's strange," John Mark said in his forthright way, having inherited his mother's frank manner, though his speech was far less polished than hers. "Tabitha now resides in a seaside town with her adopted daughter, Laurel. And Philip and Kelila in distant Samaria. Alexander and his wife, Mara, are far away, reaching his relatives in Tiberias. Not to mention dozens if not hundreds of others who have gone north, south, east, and west, taking the Good News with them."

"Amen," Mary nodded as Daniel, the captain of her household guard, stepped in front of them and escorted them across a broad paved street. "It would seem Saul's intent to crush the church has only granted the gospel wings. The message is being carried all over the empire as more and more believers are driven from Jerusalem."

"I might actually pity the man if he weren't evil to the core." John Mark grinned, receiving a look of correction from his mother. Ignoring it, he plunged ahead. "Despite all his grand efforts to silence the Way, Saul has only succeeded in spreading the Word and aiding us in our mission to reach all nations."

"You must remember," Mary reminded him in her motherly way, "he is not beyond redemption, John Mark."

"Why you insist upon praying for Saul of Tarsus is beyond me,," John Mark laughed in his typical carefree manner. "If you ask me, he's the devil wrapped in human flesh."

"He is deceived by a cruel adversary."

"Did you know Uncle Barnabas prays for him too?"

"It doesn't surprise me." Mary couldn't help but smile at the thought of her warm, compassionate older brother. Widely known as the Son of Encouragement among believers, Mary agreed the title suited him well. He often traveled throughout nearby and distant regions, strengthening and encouraging small pockets of believers now scattered across the empire.

According to her brother's last report, miniature churches were springing up like wildfire, setting the empire ablaze with the light of the gospel.

Hiding a knowing smile, Mary traced Daniel's steps with confidence as they drew nearer and nearer to the common prison, her heart nearly bursting at the thought of all her Savior had already accomplished. And to think—this was only the beginning!

The great commission of Jesus Christ was being carried out like an unstoppable force, driven by the Holy Spirit of God propelling faithful believers!

CHAPTER 2

Tabitha

Joppa

"We need a much larger space to conduct our gatherings with the widows and orphans, Tabitha," Tirzah huffed in her no-nonsense way, appearing to take her frustrations out with the broom she clutched within the nimble fingers of an experienced potter. "Last week, we somehow managed to stuff half the widows and orphans of the entire region in this small house! But should two or three more guests show up, I fear the whole place might self-implode."

Laughing musically, Tabitha acknowledged her friend's rising frustration, spreading several thick mats on the floor of Tirzah's modest home to provide more comfortable seating.

"The Lord knows we need more space," Tabitha reminded her cheerfully, bending to ruffle Laurel's smooth curls while her daughter played with her favorite doll near the old potter's wheel. "He is capable of providing a larger place for us. All in His perfect timing."

Straightening from her frenetic sweeping, Tirzah planted a firm hand on her hip. "And when, exactly, do you suppose that might be?"

"Whenever He sees fit."

"We need it *now*," Tirzah pointed out, propping her broom in a corner and watching with an air of long-suffering as Tabitha dragged the low table out of the way, placing it against the farthest wall. "The women and children spill out into the courtyard and onto the street every time we meet! There are far too many of us to continue gathering here. Surely the Lord desires to reach more people than we can cram into this tiny space."

"I'm sure He does," Tabitha agreed, pausing to meet her friend's pointed gaze. "And I believe He will provide for us."

"Your calm composure is simply maddening," Tirzah quipped ruefully, rolling her expressive hazel-tinged brown eyes. "I know I'm new to the Way, but in my past experience, if I wanted to see *results*, then *I* had to get to work."

"And your work ethic is truly admirable, Tirzah," Tabitha assured her. "You are a perseverant, disciplined worker, and the Lord can use that mightily."

"Now, perhaps?" Tirzah grinned, her eyes twinkling mischievously.

"Perhaps," Tabitha supplied, returning her smile. "But I've discovered that the life of a follower is often a delicate balance of both working and waiting. When God says wait, we wait. And when He assigns us work to do, we must roll up our sleeves and get to work without excuses or delay."

"And now?"

"Now we pray and ask the Lord to show us what to do. If He asks us to wait on Him to provide a suitable meeting place, then we wait. But if He prompts us to locate or inquire about a larger space in which to meet, we get to work."

"And in the meantime?"

"We trust."

"I was afraid you might say that," Tirzah groaned. "How on earth can you speak with such calm, unperturbed assurance?"

"It doesn't come naturally to me," Tabitha told her meaningfully, chuckling. "Trust me. When I first became a believer, I was the most impatient and restless of women. At times, I truly wondered if I was a hopeless cause."

Tirzah gave her a skeptical look.

"It's true," Tabitha insisted. "Even after marrying my husband, I worried and stewed about the future constantly. It led to a bit of tension in our marriage, though Stephanos was unbelievably patient with me." With a faraway look, Tabitha silently thanked the Lord for the time she had shared with her beloved evangelist and the lessons she had gleaned during that bittersweet season of life. "Learning to trust God is a daily process, and it takes time—time and prayer."

"*Lots* of prayer," Tirzah emphasized, muttering under her breath and drawing a small smile of amusement from Tabitha.

"Don't you remember when we first conducted meetings in Ruth's tiny little tenement apartment?" Tabitha reminded her, her bright, hazel-green eyes sparkling.

"Of course I do," Tirzah shot back. "I desperately wished to attend but couldn't stomach the thought of breathing the same air as my mother-in-law."

Hiding a smile, Tabitha noted that Tirzah no longer referred to the brassy old widow woman as her *former* mother-in-law. The two had been sweetly reconciled after both decided to embrace the Way—and on the same day, no less.

"Just when I thought we would *never* find a larger place to meet, the Lord prompted *you* to open your home to us, Tirzah," Tabitha reminded her. "Even before you were a believer. So, you see, He knows how to provide additional space when needed."

"If only the Lord would prompt your *uncle* to extend the same offer I did," Tirzah quipped rather drolly, and the two young widows shared a knowing smile. "Just think—Joram has all that space, dozens upon dozens of empty rooms and grand halls just *begging* to be filled! He knows about your ministry to the women and children here, and yet he refuses to host our gatherings in his enormous home. How hard would it be to offer one room—just one room— to aid the needy? But, no, that will never happen. Not with Joram."

"We've witnessed miracles before," Tabitha reminded Tirzah, her lips tipping mischievously.

"It will be a stone-cold day in Hades before Joram relents."

Sharing a laugh, the women returned their attention to their chores as they readied Tirzah's modest little house for the upcoming gathering.

"Speaking of Joram," Tabitha mentioned casually, her brow wrinkling in concern. "I think he is unwell."

"You always say that," Tirzah said, drawing steaming loaves of flatbread from her glowing kiln and placing them on a wide stone countertop.

"But I think he is getting worse."

"Why do you say that?"

"He seems...weaker," Tabitha tried to explain. Her concern for him was really more of a disturbing premonition than an observation of facts, and she had a difficult time placing her finger on exactly what troubled her. "He looks gaunt to me, and he's losing weight. And he is terribly irritable."

"Joram has always been irritable," Tirzah assured her with an impish grin, fanning at the steam rising from the warm flatbread.

"More so than usual," Tabitha supplied, shaking her head in dismay. "I fear he is declining swiftly, Tirzah, and that worries me. He cannot die without the Lord."

"Well, unfortunately, that's up to him." Tirzah sighed, all too aware of her former employer's stubborn disposition.

Nodding somberly, Tabitha reminded herself—just as she had reminded her friend moments earlier—to *trust*. Jesus desired her uncle's salvation even more than she did. Even so, it was difficult not to grow impatient with the obstinate old businessman. Despite the fact that she had faithfully ministered to him for nearly half a year, he continued to suspiciously monitor her every move, demonstrating grudging respect for her ceaseless energy and work ethic. She was beginning to think the man would refuse to trust her even if she loyally served him for centuries on end.

Much to Tabitha's surprise, little Laurel had recently become determined to win him over as well. The toddler's antics toward the grousing old man often proved entertaining to the entire household staff, and several had taken bets about whether or not the little one would eventually win his affection. Tabitha couldn't help but suspect Laurel was succeeding in her endeavor, despite Joram's ever-present scowl and air of indifference.

Smiling fondly, Tabitha turned to watch her little girl at play. Even with her adopted daughter's traumatic past, Laurel had steadily outgrown her reticence and fits of temper, blossoming into a happy, contented child. Her shyness seemed to be wearing off—at least, around those with whom she was most comfortable—though she remained guarded around newcomers or strangers. Even so, tiny bits of Laurel's endearing personality peeked out now and then, delighting Tabitha to her core. She couldn't wait to watch her daughter grow, eventually maturing into a sweet young woman of God.

Thank You, gracious Father, for Mary's sound parenting advice, Tabitha thought, thankful her former mistress was so faithful to keep in touch by letter. Tabitha never hesitated to ask questions about parenting Laurel, confident Mary would supply practical biblical counsel.

"You look lost in thought," Tirzah remarked, turning to slip another pan of expertly kneaded dough into the kiln.

"I suppose I was for a moment," Tabitha conceded, joining Tirzah in her tidy kitchen space. "I was just thinking about Laurel," she said, speaking softly. "She must be nearing her third year by now. I wish I knew the day of her birth."

"What matters is that she is here *now*—with you," Tirzah reminded her warmly, reaching over the counter to place a comforting hand on Tabitha's shoulder. She was the only friend in Joppa with whom Tabitha had confided Laurel's tragic past. "Your daughter is truly blessed. God selected the perfect mother for her. You love her just as if you'd borne her yourself."

"That, I do." Tabitha smiled faintly. "I can't help but wonder if Laurel remembers her birth mother. If she misses her, longs for her."

"She was very young when her mother passed."

"But was she young enough to forget?"

"Only God knows," Tirzah answered truthfully. "But she loves and trusts you deeply, Tabitha. Imagine the fate she might have known, orphaned and alone at her young age. In His abundant mercy, God led her straight to you."

"I thank Him every day," Tabitha said with great feeling. Though initially she had been hesitant to adopt the tantrum-prone little girl, she couldn't imagine life without Laurel now.

"You know," Tabitha mused, her gaze distant. "At times, I feel terribly incompetent…as a mother, as a witness to my uncle…even to instruct the widows and orphans of this region—"

"*You?* Incompetent?" Tirzah scoffed incredulously. "Absurd."

Laughing in response, Tabitha remembered her former mistress, Mary, making the same confession. Like Tirzah, Tabitha had considered Mary's misgivings positively absurd. After all, Mary was an astute businesswoman, incredibly intelligent, and unbelievably talented. Not only did she risk her life daily hosting church gatherings in her home, but she also ministered to those in prison, oversaw at least half a dozen enterprises, and raised a powerful young man for the Lord. At the time, Tabitha could hardly comprehend all her mistress had accomplished, but Mary had assured her that she, too, felt incompetent, at times. And only by the grace of God did she press on.

As must I, Tabitha reminded herself, helping Tirzah stack the flatbread on a large platter to serve as refreshments for the hungry children soon to arrive.

"Even if you *feel* incompetent," Tirzah continued, neatly arranging the warm loaves on the tray, "God will enable you to fulfill your calling. Just look how mightily He has used you already."

"But the widows and orphans are new to the faith," Tabitha pointed out. "They desperately need good, solid teaching. If only one of the apostles was here to plant a thriving church in Joppa! They are far more experienced and capable than I am."

"But God didn't send one of the apostles, did He?" Tirzah pointed out with annoying logic. "He sent *you.*"

"I suppose you're right," Tabitha conceded wryly.

"Of course I'm right."

"Even so, eventually, we will need a *church* in Joppa, a place where both men and women can gather together with their families," Tabitha murmured, watching as Tirzah turned to retrieve the second pan of steaming loaves from the kiln. "We need a godly man capable of planting a church and instructing the brethren here."

"Why can't *you* do it?"

"The Lord has certainly equipped me to minister

to the women and children of this region," Tabitha said carefully. "But I believe a man of God would be far better suited to plant and establish a church here."

"Don't tell me followers of the Way are as stuffy and closed-minded as the pompous old men in the synagogue," Tirzah huffed, provoked.

"It's not about being stuffy or closed-minded," Tabitha assured her. "I simply wish to honor the call of God on my life. I have no doubt He has led me to minister to the women and children of Joppa. But I wouldn't wish to pursue a calling contrary to the Spirit's leading."

"Well, perhaps the Lord isn't in a hurry to plant a church here, seeing as we only have four believing men in the entire region," Tirzah shrugged. "You seem to be handling the women and children just fine on your own."

"With the Lord's help, and yours," Tabitha said, her eyes sparkling. "You mentioned four believing men. I can only think of three."

"Adam and his ill, aging father," Tirzah reminded her, counting on her fingers. "Simon the tanner. *And* that elderly Pharisee who avoids the synagogue like the plague."

"Ah, yes. The friend of Adam's father. I haven't met him."

"I can hardly believe that Simon the tanner accepted Jesus as the promised Messiah!" Tirzah exclaimed incredulously, stepping back to survey the tray they had neatly arranged together. "I never thought I'd see the day."

"My heart overflows with joy and gratitude every time I think of it," Tabitha smiled, thankful that

Adam had volunteered to mentor the older man in the teachings of Jesus.

"Speaking of godly men..." Tirzah quipped as if reading Tabitha's thoughts. "Why shouldn't *Adam* establish a church here? He's been a believer nearly as long as you have."

"I've broached the subject with him several times," Tabitha admitted. "That man is far too humble," she laughed. "He insists he isn't qualified to lead a church."

"Well..." Tirzah grinned wanly, shaking her head in amusement. "That simply proves that he's the perfect man for the job."

Sharing another mischievous chuckle, the widows resumed their work.

CHAPTER 3

Mary

Jerusalem

The common prison was a seedy place located near the Roman quarter and reserved for the basest of criminals and thieves. Those doomed to confinement within the mildew-covered walls behind the relentless iron gates of the ancient structure knew better than to expect a fair trial—or any trial at all, for that matter. In most cases, a prisoner's fate was sealed the moment the prison gate swung shut behind him with a creaking *thud* of finality.

Mary found it irritating that the religious leaders often invented political charges which they fabricated against believers to land them in more frightening Roman prisons, though she wasn't surprised by their blatant manipulation. Hadn't they employed the same tactics to crucify her Lord? She supposed the high priest hadn't space enough in the small underground holding cell beneath his luxurious estate to house the dozens of believers hauled in each week. Thus, Roman aid became essential to their success.

"Ah, fair morning to you, my lady," a heavyset Roman guard stationed at the intimidating prison entrance declared, waving a fleshy hand in greeting.

"Good day to you, noble Crassus," Mary responded, smiling deeply. She couldn't help but think the cheerful, middle-aged guard appeared sorely out of place stationed before the entrance of a Roman death trap.

"What's that you have there?" Crassus drawled, eyeing their full baskets with obvious interest.

Mary was reminded of a friendly, overfed dog drooling over scraps.

"We have brought more rations for the prisoners," John Mark announced with a wry smile, always entertained by the new guard's obvious infatuation with his beautiful and cultured mother—and even more so, with the tantalizing baked goods prepared by her professional chefs.

"Ah, you feed these no-good prisoners like kings," Crassus declared jovially, his jowls wobbling as he shook his head in mock exasperation. "I'd best be on the lookout now. Before long, men will start turning themselves in just to enjoy this delectable fare!"

"Doubtful, that." John Mark grinned, resisting the urge to slap the good-natured guard on the back. "Despite the lovely accommodations here."

Throwing back his head, Crassus enjoyed a good, long laugh.

"Naturally, we have brought a care package for our favorite prison guard," Mary said with a knowing little smile, producing a bulky wrapped package from her wide-mouthed basket. "I do hope you will enjoy it."

"Don't I always?" The warm package was in the guard's eager hands in a flash.

"Shall we be permitted entrance today, Crassus?" Mary asked warmly, silently thanking Jesus for stationing this unlikely godsend at the gate.

"Be my guests." Crassus grinned with an exaggerated bow and a sweep of his large, armor-clad arm.

Within moments, Mary's personal guards were escorting her and her bemused son through the imposing prison gates, each biting back wide grins of amusement and good humor.

Truly, God is good, Mary thought with a hidden smile.

***

Kelila

Sychar

The previous day had been a whirlwind of arrangements and hasty preparations.

Head spinning, Kelila watched glumly as Philip and Ephraim boarded up their small market stall and its adjoining chamber, her heart aching just a bit. Wiping the sweat from her delicate brow, she cradled her protruding abdomen with a trembling hand, reminding herself to stay calm for the sake of her unborn child.

Philip is leaving without me.

It was a shocking revelation and one Kelila had proven entirely unprepared for.

Even so, Kelila knew she had been called to marry this kind, compassionate evangelist. If the Lord was leading him elsewhere, she must support his sacred calling. And there was no doubt in her mind that the Lord's hand was in this. An angel—wonder of wonders, a real, live *angel*—had appeared to Philip near a bubbling brook, instructing him to take the road going down from Jerusalem to Gaza.

And that was all she knew. Philip had been given no explanation and no further instructions. He was simply expected to obey.

And she, the anxious, doting wife, was to do the same. *Obey.* Trust. And believe that God knew what He was doing.

Oh, God, where are You taking my husband? Kelila's heart cried as faithful Adorina drew alongside her, taking her hand and giving it an encouraging squeeze. *We have done so well in Sychar! Why must Philip move on now?*

And why must *she* remain?

When Philip had returned from his quiet time the previous day, his face aglow after a supernatural encounter with the angel, Kelila had hounded him with questions. Must he leave immediately? Where was his final destination? Would he return to Sychar and resume his current ministry, or send word for her to join him elsewhere on a brand-new mission field?

"Oh, and just in case you've forgotten," Kelila had reminded him pointedly the previous day, cradling her growing abdomen. "We're expecting a child. Will you return before he or she makes his appearance into the world?"

Maddeningly, Philip had proven unable to answer any of her questions. He had simply assured her that the Lord had a plan. And they must obey.

Now, as Philip turned from boarding up her beloved little home, an eager smile stretching his bearded features, Kelila felt hopelessly torn. She hated the idea of him departing without her nearly as much as she hated the prospect of leaving Sychar! Hers was a situation in which she simply couldn't win!

And to make matters worse, Philip had the nerve to be *excited* about his journey! Couldn't he see how her apprehension and the uncertainty enshrouding this mysterious calling was tearing her apart? Didn't he care how she *felt*?

Crossing the quiet street, Philip paused before his pregnant wife, tenderly reaching for her and grasping her arms. "I love you," he told her meaningfully, his gaze traveling fondly over her growing baby bump. "My earnest prayer is that the Lord will bring me home before our child is born."

Blinking back tears, Kelila nodded firmly, attempting to be strong. Despite her fears and doubts, she truly desired to trust the Lord. How often had she fretted in the past, only to later wish she had utilized the time and energy to carry on the Lord's work instead?

And that's what I shall do, she decided, forcing a brave smile for Philip. *I shall carry on the Lord's work here until He calls me elsewhere.*

"Have you received any further instructions from the Lord?" she managed a bit shakily, watching as Ephraim drew alongside Philip and clamped a firm hand on his broad shoulder.

"Nothing yet," Philip replied a bit too easily.

Wasn't he concerned *at all?*

"But I sense this journey will be brief," Philip promised her, cupping her face in his hand. "Which is why it's best for you to stay here in Sychar, Kelila, with Ephraim and Adorina. You needn't travel unnecessarily in your condition. But if God calls me to remain elsewhere for an extended period, I shall send for you, Lord willing."

"When will you know?" Kelila pried, her large brown eyes poignantly hopeful.

"Oh, love. I wish I knew."

You and me both, Kelila thought, a bit peeved. Releasing a tremorous sigh, she resisted the fleshly urge to demand answers from him. *Oh, Lord, why is it so difficult to live by Your Spirit rather than my own stubborn flesh?*

"We must always follow the Spirit's leading," Philip reminded her gently as if sensing her tortured thoughts.

Suppressing her mounting frustration, Kelila resolved to *trust* even if it killed her. Even so, she wasn't thrilled about simply waiting around for the Spirit to reveal His plans to them. She would much prefer to know everything *now.*

"You needn't worry about her safety, Philip," Ephraim assured the evangelist with a solemn nod. "She will be safe lodging with us."

"And we shall have a delightful time together," Adorina put in, her typically serious brown eyes betraying a hint of excitement.

Warmed by her friends' eagerness to host her during Philip's absence, Kelila was reminded that she possessed many blessing for which to be glad. The precious life growing in her womb was certainly at the top of her list. And, of course, this priceless couple whom the Lord had brought into their lives. And the wonderful Samaritan people to whom she was called to serve.

So many blessings, she thought, squaring her shoulders in resolve. *Far too many to sit around moping and feeling sorry for myself, as I am sometimes prone to do!*

"Won't it be wonderful," Adorina asked Kelila, interrupting her thoughts, "to share a home for a time?"

"I must confess," Kelila admitted, "I worry about getting in the way. I certainly wish to do my part during my stay, Adorina."

"Nonsense!" Adorina insisted with a nod of finality. "It is a joy to host you."

Smiling appreciatively, Kelila couldn't help but feel rather like a lumbering beast of burden with her heavy, rounded belly and accompanying clumsiness. She hoped she wouldn't be in the way as she attempted to help Adorina with daily chores and housework. Having always been slender and lithe, her bulging abdomen was rather difficult to adjust to.

"Ephraim," Philip said solemnly, turning to look his friend in the eye. "Thank you for being willing to oversee the church body in my absence."

"It is an honor and a privilege," Ephraim assured him with great feeling.

Turning his attention toward his wife, Philip smiled tenderly. "God will be with you, even in my absence," he promised. "With both of you," he added, his eyes twinkling as he placed a hand over their unborn child. "And He shall go before me on the way, as well."

"You really shouldn't travel alone, Philip—"

"God will protect me."

"Make haste, then." Kelila sighed, closing her eyes as if to shut out the reality of her situation. "Don't tarry along the way, tempting bandits and thieves."

Exchanging a knowing grin with Ephraim, Philip nodded soberly. "No tempting bandits and thieves. You have my word."

Slinging a leather bag over his shoulder, Philip prepared to take his leave.

Throwing her arms around his strong frame, Kelila clung to him, resisting the urge to weep. "Be safe," she whispered as he cupped the back of her head with a firm hand. Laying her head on his shoulder, she added, "I will miss you."

"And I, you. More than you know."

"I love you, Philip."

"I love you, too, dear one," Philip assured her with a gentle kiss.

Reluctantly releasing him, Kelila watched as he turned to travel the dusty village path, contemplating the mysterious words of the heavenly messenger.

Arise and go...

Arise.

Drawing a steadying breath, Kelila resolved to do the same. She, too, would rise to the occasion despite the gnawing uncertainty and her own mounting unease. Not once had the Lord misled them. And He would continue to guide them in the Way of life everlasting.

CHAPTER 4

Mary

Jerusalem

Conversing and laughing quietly, believers shuffled about the large, lamplit Upper Room following a prayer service led by the commanding Simon Peter, Mary's nephew by marriage. It had been a pleasant evening of prayer, Scripture reading, and fellowship despite the crackling intensity of the atmosphere beyond the secure stone walls of Mary's villa.

Intrigued, Mary made a beeline toward an un-assuming young man standing nervously near the broad stairway, clearly wrestling with…something. It had taken a great deal of self-control for her to remain poised in her seat during the prayer meeting when he had emerged at the top of the staircase partway through the service, lingering behind the endless rows of wooden benches where the believers had congregated. Clothed in heavy layers of bland, simple garments—including a shroud-like head covering—it was clear the newcomer didn't wish to advertise his presence to anyone—particularly to potential enemies he might possibly encounter on his way to the meeting.

"Agabus." Mary smiled warmly as she reached him, her luminous gray eyes twinkling with welcome and a hint of mirth. "How brave of you to join us this evening."

Agabus' dark eyes met hers, flickering in annoyance. So much for his clever disguise.

"I must ask you to lower your voice, please," the young Pharisee hissed under his breath, wondering how many of her guests had overheard the use of his name.

"You needn't fear, Agabus," Mary assured him, lowering her dulcet tone to placate him. "None of us wish to give you away."

"One careless slip of the tongue could very well prove ruinous," Agabus told her, his glittering eyes sweeping cautiously about the room. "Possibly even deadly."

"Not nearly so deadly as rejecting the Way Christ has clearly revealed to you."

"He hasn't revealed anything to me," Agabus argued, though his tone was far from convincing. "At least, not personally."

"No?" Mary prompted, her slender brow lifting in question. "Then why are you here? And why do you persist in your questions?"

"This is not about me," Agabus insisted, his voice rising in frustration. When several believers glanced his way, he shifted uncomfortably, pulling his hooded shawl to further obscure his bearded face. "I must speak with you," he finally concluded, his gaze shifting anxiously about the crowded room. "Alone."

"If you wish to speak, then we may speak here."

"For heaven's sake, Mary," Agabus breathed, his frustration mounting.

"Go on," Mary prodded, appearing perfectly composed.

Maddeningly aware of the chatter and movement surrounding them, Agabus took a step closer, so close Mary could smell his spice-scented breath. "I come bearing ill tidings."

"Why doesn't that surprise me?" Mary responded, smiling faintly. "What kind of ill tidings?"

"It's about Saul of Tarsus."

"I see," Mary nodded, her expression sobering beneath her pale blue head covering. "What has he done now?"

"It's what he is about to do," Agabus warned her, his obsidian eyes growing serious. "At this moment, he is attempting to obtain permission to target churches beyond Jerusalem."

"Preposterous," Mary declared, her eyes flashing. "He hasn't the jurisdiction to do so."

"The high priest is seriously considering granting his request," Agabus told her grimly. "Your sect endangers the very office he holds."

"On what grounds will Saul make his arrests?"

"By order of the high priest," Agabus sighed. "I imagine Jewish men and women will be dragged from other provinces by order of the Great Sanhedrin."

"Women, too?" Mary asked, surprised.

"I'm afraid no one is safe," Agabus replied grimly. "Once within the grasp of the high priest and the Sanhedrin here in Jerusalem, I imagine far more serious political charges will be fabricated against the prisoners, resulting in life in prison—possibly even the death penalty."

Releasing a steadying sigh, Mary brushed cool fingertips across her smooth forehead, deep in thought.

"This isn't good, Mary," Agabus warned her, daring yet another step closer. "Up to this point, your friends have been safe beyond our borders. But now, if Saul has his way, they cannot run. They cannot hide. In time, they will be hunted down and exterminated one by one. And their cause shall perish with them."

"Never," Mary said firmly, her eyes flashing. "The gospel will reach the ends of the earth, Agabus. Mark my words."

"There's just no way," Agabus countered, shaking his covered head.

"God has already made a Way," Mary told him, her eyes alight with conviction. "And His name is Jesus. Jesus *is* the Way."

"And shall He descend from the lofty heights of Heaven to aid you in this mad cause?"

"He can move heaven and earth to rescue His own," Mary staunchly replied, her logical mind racing a mile a minute. They must seek the Lord and pray with all their might. They needed a plan, and fast.

Agabus simply watched her, annoyed by his fascination with this fearless woman. Couldn't she see it was only a matter of time? Soon, her entire world would come crashing down around her ears. It was simply time to abandon ship!

"I suppose I should have seen this coming," Mary admitted, concealing her distress for the sake of the smiling believers milling about the Upper Room. There was certainly no need to cause them undue alarm. "Have you any idea what prompted Saul's decision to pursue believers beyond the city?"

"If rumor can be trusted," Agabus explained, his dark eyes flickering with hidden amusement, "Saul has experienced a somewhat inconvenient predicament in his personal life."

"How so?"

"Again, *if* rumor can be trusted, I've heard speculation about his youngest sister from Tarsus. Apparently, a marriage has been arranged for her here in Jerusalem with a prestigious man of the religious order. However..." Agabus' voice trailed off as he weighed the heaviness of the brave young woman's fate. "It would seem she has converted."

"Converted?" Mary repeated blankly, stunned. "Saul's sister is a *believer?*"

"According to popular opinion, yes," Agabus replied, unable to mask the grin teasing his bearded features. "Naturally, Saul is humiliated and enraged."

Mary couldn't help but smile her own amusement, despite her concern for Saul's young sister. What a courageous girl she must be!

"But now," Agabus proceeded, his gaze flickering anxiously about the large chamber and coming to rest almost hesitantly upon the stoic Mary. "Now Saul's hatred has been inflamed against your sect unlike ever before."

Mary met his gaze with clear gray eyes, aware of the danger before them.

"Now..." Agabus added darkly, deeply unsettled. "Now, for Saul, it's personal."

CHAPTER 5

Kelila

Sychar

Seated rather gracelessly with elbows propped on Adorina's wooden table, Kelila battled rising doubts and disappointments. Philip remained heavy on her heart. She hadn't realized how difficult it would be, not knowing where her husband was or even if he fared well.

Night had already fallen, and the autumn air had taken its typical evening chill. Had Philip found adequate shelter for the night? Was he warm? Had he been fed? True, she had meticulously tucked away parched grain, dried fruit, and nuts to serve as unperishable provisions for his journey, but what would happen if he ran out? Had he enough coin to purchase necessaries and proper lodging?

Sighing inwardly, Kelila recalled the many nights she and her husband had shared at this very table, enjoying a meal with their dear Samaritan friends.

In fact, it was here that they had spent their very first night in Sychar. Adorina, bless her hospitable heart, had insisted they stay the night, and Ephraim had readily agreed to help the young evangelist obtain a rental property the following morning.

Oh, how Kelila had resisted such arrangements at the time! Smiling faintly, Kelila wrapped her hands around the warm mug of tea Adorina had kindly provided, remembering how irritated she had felt upon their arrival. She had wished to settle down and build a proper home in the village, not rent a shabby old market stall on the main thoroughfare, hemmed in by lowing beasts and shouting merchants! But now, she couldn't deny that the Lord's hand had been in it. How many hundreds of Samaritans had received Christ since then?

And the Lord's hand is in this, too, she reminded herself with a quiet smile. *I may not relish this particular set of circumstances, but God is moving. He is taking the message of salvation to the ends of the earth.*

"May I join you?"

Glancing up in surprise, Kelila noticed Adorina standing across the table, a warm mug of her own clasped in slender hands.

"It's late," Kelila observed, watching as the young woman took the chair across from her. "I thought you were asleep."

"As *you* should be," Adorina chided with a knowing smile. "You should rest for the sake of the baby."

"The baby is resting enough for both of us," Kelila teased, gingerly placing her hands upon her protruding abdomen. "As for me, I couldn't sleep even if I tried. Why waste the time tossing and turning in bed?"

"Especially when you could be sitting up late, all alone, worrying yourself into a stew?" Adorina grinned, her dark eyes twinkling knowingly.

"Well," Kelila confessed, her animated brown eyes dancing. "It does sound a bit silly when you say it like that."

"You miss him already."

"Dreadfully."

"He'll be all right, Kelila," Adorina promised, reaching across the table to take her hand. "God is with Philip. And with you too."

"I wish He could be with the two of us *together* in one place," she quipped wryly, drawing an understanding smile from Adorina. "I knew Philip was a traveling evangelist. I just always expected to accompany him on all his travels."

"There may be times when a mission requires him to go alone," Adorina reminded her. "Some situations aren't fitting to bring wives along. Others, too dangerous. And still others, unnecessary."

"I suppose you're right."

"Perhaps the Lord has asked you to stay in Sychar because you are so gifted at ministering to the people here."

"Me? Gifted?" Kelila repeated blankly. "Philip is the evangelist, not me."

"But Philip is free to pursue his calling because you have learned to run your household like clockwork. Not only that, but you have won the hearts of my people. Many of them have had very difficult lives, riddled with pain and heartache. Your cheerful outlook and ready smile are like a soothing balm to them."

Kelila stared at Adorina in surprise, touched. Though she did enjoy serving those in need, she hadn't really considered herself a worthy partner for Philip. He was so disciplined, so eloquent, so full of faith and resonating with the power of the Holy Spirit, whereas she often found herself wrestling with anxiety and doubt! She was quite certain Philip never worried about *anything*.

It was a bit exasperating at times.

"When do you think Philip shall return?" Kelila asked, changing the subject. Once, she would have basked in the praise of a friend and sought even more adoration! But the Lord was graciously teaching her the art of humility.

"Whenever the Lord says it's time," Adorina responded with maddening certainty, taking a refined sip of hot tea.

"I wish I could stop worrying about him," Kelila admitted glumly, toying with the clay handle of her mug.

"What worries you so much?"

"I don't know when I shall see him again," she whispered, her large eyes welling with tears.

"I can't imagine he will be gone long," Adorina assured her, always practical. Frustratingly so.

"I think it's the fear of the unknown that's most concerning," Kelila mourned, listlessly dragging her half-empty mug across the table. "He could be gone for weeks. Months. Years, even!"

"Or merely days," Adorina pointed out with annoying logic.

Kelila glanced up at her friend, her eyes doubtful.

"Kelila," Adorina said soberly, squeezing her friend's hand across the table. "The Lord isn't going to do you or Philip any harm. He wants what is best for you. Always."

Eyes brimming with tears, Kelila met her friend's unwavering gaze and wondered about this woman's simple faith. She was so practical, so trusting of her Lord. How did faith come so easily for Adorina—a former outcast—while she, Kelila, an evangelist's wife for heaven's sake, grappled with fears and doubts on a regular basis, often having to drag unruly thoughts into submission!

"Your faith is truly exceptional," Kelila sighed, despising her own weakness. When would she finally learn to cast her cares upon the Lord and simply *trust*, once and for all?

"There's nothing exceptional about it," Adorina amended, taking another thoughtful sip of tea. "Jesus promised to do what is best. Even if we don't particularly relish His assignment here and now, what does it matter? It's not about *here*. This life is fleeting, temporary. It's the hope of Heaven we long for, wait for."

Kelila nodded slowly, wishing she possessed this stalwart woman's resolve.

"Besides," Adorina added a bit ruefully. "When I consider the mess I was in when Jesus found me, I realize I have no cause for dismay now, regardless of what may happen. Clearly, I had no ability to run my own life. It was in shambles the day I met Him, but He rescued me from the sinful quagmire, setting my feet upon the Rock of His salvation. When I consider the fact that eternity in utter perfection awaits me, my concerns vanish and my petty complaints cease."

"I feel somewhat ashamed," Kelila confessed, lowering her gaze in embarrassment. "I am an evangelist's wife, the one sent to proclaim salvation to the Samaritans. I should be ministering to *you*, Adorina. And yet, here you are, ministering to *me* as I wallow in doubt and self-pity."

"Nonsense," Adorina put in stoutly. "You have ministered to me on many occasions. That's what the body of Christ does—we exhort and encourage one another, strengthening each other in moments of weakness. And we all have them—none are exempt."

"Well, *you* seem pretty well grounded to me," Kelila remarked a bit wanly.

"We all have our struggles," Adorina reminded her, her dark eyes taking on a vague, faraway look. "In our fragile human state, where would we be without the grace of God? Had I not met Jesus on that fateful afternoon several years ago, I certainly wouldn't be where I am today."

"And where *would* you be?" Kelila asked her, leaning forward with interest. Though she had long been intrigued by this dusky young woman's striking persona, Adorina seldom spoke of her past—and Kelila certainly hadn't wished to pry. But the soft nighttime candlelight invited secrets and whispered confidences as dancing shadows cast by the crackling hearth painted the broad stone walls.

"Where would I be?" Adorina repeated with an enigmatic smile, crossing slender arms as she leaned back in her wooden chair. "I imagine I would be dead by now, though it's possible I could have hired out my services as an indentured servant, sold myself as a slave…or worse."

Cringing, Kelila wondered what could have possibly transpired in her friend's life to promote such dire circumstances.

"My mother died when I was very young," Adorina explained quietly, toying with the handle of her mug. "I don't remember her well now, but I do recall missing her desperately as a child. My father was not a kind, understanding man like my Ephraim or your Philip. He became embittered after my mother's death and resented the idea of raising a daughter alone. He often told me I was a burden to him."

Kelila's eyes widened in dismay as sympathy for her friend washed over her.

"So I suppose I shouldn't have been surprised when he married me off the moment I was of age," Adorina continued, her firm jaw stiffening slightly at the recollection. "I was betrothed at the age of twelve and married by age thirteen—to a man twice as old as my own father."

"Oh my," Kelila breathed, horrified. "That must have been dreadful!"

"I was utterly sickened at the thought of marrying a perverted old man," Adorina admitted, shaking her head in disgust. "And perverted he was, to the core. I spent several years scheming how to escape that marriage. Eventually, I made the nasty man so miserable he threatened to divorce me—to my great joy and utter relief. Which he did, after what seemed an unbearable length of time."

Kelila shook her head, unable to fathom the nightmare of a confused and broken-hearted thirteen-year-old child.

"My father was furious when I returned to him," Adorina sighed. "He refused to support me financially or to arrange a second marriage for me—not that anyone reputable would have desired me. So I struck out on my own in search of what I thought I wanted."

"And what was that?" Kelila asked her, spellbound.

"A man of my own choosing," Adorina explained with a shake of her head. "But I was a foolish girl. I hadn't the slightest idea how to identify a worthy husband. Rather than seeking a kind man of godly character, I chased after shallow, attractive men. When I found one willing to marry me, I could scarcely believe my luck. He was tall, dark, and handsome...and brutal, I soon discovered."

"Oh no," Kelila whispered, her hands protectively encircling her unborn child as her heart pounded in response to Adorina's troubling testimony.

"To my unspeakable horror, my second husband was far worse than the first," Adorina murmured, her flickering dark eyes betraying hidden scars. "I've never known a man with such a violent temper. I often suffered at his hand amidst his raging tirades."

"Couldn't you turn to your father?" Kelila asked earnestly, her eyes glimmering with tears of sympathy. "Wouldn't he help you?"

"Oh, how I tried," Adorina sighed, her tone laced with bitterness. "I begged him to rescue me, but he refused. He said I was simply getting what I deserved for disgracing him."

"Disgracing him?"

"My divorce humiliated him," Adorina recalled, shaking her head in dismay. "He said I was a shameful daughter and claimed that I ruined his reputation."

"You were but a girl," Kelila objected, protective of her friend. "Only thirteen! Far too young to cope with what your father thrust upon you."

"It didn't matter, not to him," Adorina shrugged, attempting to mask her disillusionment. "He had jumped at the chance to unload an unwanted daughter. He was furious when I tried to come back."

"Oh, Adorina," Kelila whispered, sorrowfully shaking her head. "I'm so sorry."

"All have suffered grief. I am not alone in that," Adorina quickly amended, not wishing to garner pity. "I'm simply telling my story because you asked."

"Forgive me," Kelila apologized. "I didn't mean to pry."

"You didn't," Adorina assured her. "I consider you my closest friend. And if my testimony can strengthen or encourage others, I should not hesitate to share it."

Kelila simply nodded, admiring the Samaritan's quiet faith and resilience.

"After a few miserable months of marriage, I conceived a child," Adorina said, her low alto quavering for the first time. "My husband returned home very drunk one night and his temper was out of control. His abuse resulted in a miscarriage, and I lost the baby."

Tightening her grip upon her own growing abdomen, Kelila's eyes filled with tears.

"The miscarriage was so bad the doctor said I was lucky just to be alive," Adorina continued solemnly. "He also said it was doubtful I would ever bear children of my own."

"Oh, Adorina."

"My husband was furious we lost the baby and refused to acknowledge his fault. His drinking became even more excessive than before. Just a few weeks after my miscarriage, he died in a barroom brawl, and I was relieved."

"I can see why," Kelila confessed, stunned by the horrors her friend had endured. Now she understood the hidden pain reflected in her dark eyes, her brave smile, and her stoic demeanor. Adorina had been through the fire, through the furnace, and yet...God had preserved her.

"After the death of my second husband, I knew better than to ask my father for help," Adorina soberly explained, turning her warm clay mug in wooden fingers. "This time, I sought a gentle, peaceable man to support me. I'm ashamed to say it, but I married again out of sheer necessity, and I simply *used* him. It wasn't fair to him, not at all. He was merely a crutch—until he wearied of my bad humor and left. Number four was tolerable; though he, too, abolished the marriage in less than a year. Sadly, I had allowed grief and disillusionment to embitter me, and I became an angry, contentious woman. I'm shocked the marriage lasted as long as it did."

"But you had been through so much," Kelila reminded her. "Such circumstances would embitter anyone."

"I should have turned to the Lord," Adorina sighed. "Instead, I relied on my own understanding, my own strength. In desperation, I sought happiness in forbidden places. And I fell madly in love with a fun, handsome young man who not only *agreed* to marry me but *wanted to*."

"You must have been so excited!" Kelila enthused, thankful the gruesome tale had taken a turn for the better.

"Oh, yes, I was excited," Adorina said wryly. "Until he left me for another woman a year later."

"Oh, dear," Kelila sighed, shaking her head in dismay.

"Exactly," Adorina chuckled knowingly. "Looking back, I'm surprised I hadn't yet realized how incapable I was of planning my own life, of charting my own course. It seemed every decision I made ended in disaster."

"Is that when you met Jesus?"

"Almost," Adorina nodded, a small smile playing about her lips. "At that point, I was sick of men and swore to never marry again—even if that meant begging on the streets to survive!"

"Perhaps my memory fails me, but I thought you were living with someone when you encountered Jesus," Kelila pointed out, curious.

"Oh, I was," Adorina sighed, ashamed. "He was merely a distracting fling. I lived in his home free of charge, without the restrictions and obligations of marriage. It was wrong, and I knew it."

Kelila gently nodded, encouraging her to go on.

"The fateful day when I trudged up to that village well—in the heat of the day, no less, to avoid the plaguing snickers and condescending stares of my people—I was utterly consumed with guilt," Adorina confessed, her expression distant as she pondered the many mistakes of her past. "I simply couldn't fathom how far I had fallen, how *broken* I had become. I hadn't meant for my life to turn out that way. I certainly wouldn't have chosen that fate. And yet, I couldn't shake the feeling that somehow, I *had* chosen. I had *chosen* misery by refusing to acknowledge a God I knew very little about, but somehow knew existed."

"And then what happened?" Kelila asked, leaning forward on the table, her brown eyes wide with anticipation.

"And then I met a mysterious Man at the village well," Adorina fondly replied, a knowing smile teasing the corners of her lips. "And from that point forward, everything changed. My life has never been the same."

CHAPTER 6

Kelila

Sychar

"What a powerful testimony!" Kelila exclaimed, her own troubles forgotten. "Why don't you share it more often, Adorina?"

Smiling faintly, the Samaritan woman rotated her warm mug in her hands. "I have heard others share their 'testimonies' in a boastful manner, almost as if they are proud about the life they led before meeting Christ. Some even attempt to outdo each other, bragging about who has the most shocking past. But that sickens me."

Kelila nodded slowly, suddenly understanding Adorina's hesitation.

"The last thing I wish to do is to boast about my former sins," Adorina said honestly, her dark brown eyes devoid of guile. "Instead, I want to glorify God by proclaiming *His* power over sin, His majesty. If my testimony can encourage others and the Holy

Spirit moves me to share it, then I shall. Otherwise, I choose to keep silent."

"I imagine that's a wise rule to live by," Kelila chuckled. "When I open my mouth apart from the Spirit's leading, I tend to make a fool of myself."

"We all do," Adorina reassured her with a knowing smile.

"I've heard many accounts about your encounter with Jesus at the well," Kelila said, leaning forward a bit. "What did you think when you first saw Him?"

"What did I think?" Adorina grinned, shaking her head in amusement. "Frankly, I was annoyed when I saw a Jewish man seated by the well. I immediately thought to myself, *Great. Here's a pious Jew just waiting to judge me!* I approached Him battle-ready and armed with bitter cynicism, just as I had learned to approach life in general."

"And then what happened?"

"At first, Jesus simply watched me draw near the well. And not in the manner I was accustomed to being watched—with scathing criticism from the women or lustful interest from the men. Rather, He observed my angry movements with a tenderness and warmth that deeply unsettled me. And then— much to my shock and inner chagrin—He *spoke* to me, requesting of me a drink of water. I must confess, that nettled me."

Kelila laughed, picturing her friend's rising angst during the unlikely and unexpected encounter.

"I cringe now when I consider my reaction," Adorina went on, wincing. "I was filled with bitterness and angry venom, which I flung at Him without the slightest hesitation. It was simply my habit, lashing out at men, at life, at the seeming injustice of it all."

"And how did He respond?"

"With warmth," Adorina smiled, her fathomless brown eyes glistening with a faint sheen of tears. "With kindness. He offered to give me living water, and I nearly laughed in His face. I was quick to point out that He didn't even have His own bucket! How, then, did He intend to provide any water, much less this 'magical' living water of which He spoke? But He listened patiently, a small smile teasing His plain but luminous features. And gently, patiently, He explained what He longed to give me: the water which would become a fountain of water springing up into everlasting life."

"But you still weren't convinced, were you?" Kelila guessed.

"Oh, I was convinced that He was *crazy*—crazy to speak to me in the first place, and crazy to babble on and on about His fanciful living water! Scathingly, I dared Him to share some of His special water so I wouldn't have to trudge back and forth to the village well in the heat of the day! And then, having drawn the water I needed, I hoisted my heavy jar in my arms and prepared to leave. And that's when He spoke again: 'Go, call your husband, and come here.' To which I tersely responded, 'I have no husband.' *And thank God,* I remember thinking silently, my anger seething just beneath the surface. *The last thing on this earth I need is another lousy husband to complicate my misery and add to my increasing list of troubles.* And then Jesus spoke, interrupting my bitter train of thought: 'You have well said, "I have no husband," for you have had five husbands, and the one whom you now have is not your husband; in that you spoke truly.' Kelila, I froze in place, every nerve ending in my body afire with shock... and fear... and wonder... How did this Man *know* me—my past pain and my present predicament? I knew He hadn't spoken with any of the villagers about me. They would have sooner spit in His face than conversed with a Jew."

"You must have been stunned!"

"To the core," Adorina nodded, still thrilling at her unexpected encounter with the King of the universe. "Completely caught off guard, I acknowledged that He must be a prophet and then attempted to change the subject. The last thing I wanted was another long lecture about my life decisions. Casually, I asked about the proper place to worship, since Jews and Samaritans remain divided on this issue, hoping to divert His attention. But His answer pierced my heart: 'The hour is coming, and now is, when the true worshipers will worship the Father in spirit and truth; for the Father is seeking such to worship Him.' I couldn't stop thinking of His words—*in spirit and truth*. There was a simplicity about those words, a purity, a holiness that I craved. For the first time in my life, I realized I needed God. I wanted to know Him, *needed* to know Him. But I didn't know *how*. Fighting tears, I attempted to sound knowledgeable about spiritual things: 'I know that Messiah is coming. When He comes, He will tell us all things.' And suddenly, I was desperate to find Him. Whoever He was, wherever He was, I needed Him. And then Jesus rose, gazing deeply into my eyes. In an authoritative yet quiet tone, He said, 'I who speak to you am He.'"

"Amazing," Kelila breathed, chills claiming her

being. Hearing Adorina's firsthand retelling of a story she'd heard many times before was breathtaking, for she sensed the power of God in every word. God had seen this forsaken woman's misery and tears, and He had gently, lovingly *intervened*.

The same loving God was still intervening in the lives of the lost, the broken, and the hurting, even to this day.

"In that moment, I knew the Messiah had come," Adorina continued, interrupting Kelila's thoughts. "And—wonder of wonders—He'd found me! *Me*—surely the least deserving of all His children." Shaking her head in awe, Adorina delicately swiped away a stray tear. "In an instant, my life made sense. Gone were the days of clawing and scraping to find fulfillment in shallow relationships or earthly pleasures. For the very first time, I had a *purpose*, Kelila. Life had *meaning*. I wasn't simply drifting and floating about in aimless misery at the sheer mercy of chance. I was born to proclaim the Messiah, and I chose to embrace that mission wholeheartedly. As Jesus addressed our people during those blessed days, He remained here in Sychar, and I learned more than I ever thought possible. I realized my seething bitterness, scathing tongue, and stinging sarcasm must cease. And I discovered joy in the Lord unlike anything I'd ever thought possible."

"It's truly a marvelous story," Kelila told her with great feeling. "Just listening, I feel strengthened and encouraged. Truly, God will equip us to carry out His calling—just as He has equipped you to proclaim His salvation to anyone who will listen. We needn't fear when the assignment seems overwhelming, because He will give us the strength we need."

"Amen," Adorina agreed. "Praise God."

"And what happened to you after Jesus departed from Sychar, Adorina? And the man you were living with at the time—what happened to him?"

"Oh, I ended things with him the moment I left the village well," Adorina said firmly. "After meeting Jesus, I was determined to no longer live in sin. And then I spent the next two days at Jesus' feet, drinking in every single word He spoke."

"And that's when you met Ephraim, yes?"

"That's a funny story," Adorina chuckled. "Ephraim was a godly man, eager to serve the Lord even before he met Jesus. I hadn't the slightest idea he'd noticed me out and about. He was a highly respected young man, not the sort to take an interest in the likes of me. Apparently, he was moved with compassion for me, the village outcast. Though he hadn't the slightest romantic interest in me, he began to pray for me—for my healing and restoration. And he was there when I came bounding into the village, carrying on about meeting the Messiah at the well. Ephraim was one of the first to investigate my claim about Jesus and one of the first to believe. He later told me he was deeply moved, watching how desperately I soaked up every word Jesus spoke. And he realized his prayers for me had been answered. By the end of the second day, he knew he wanted to marry me."

"And did he propose?"

"He did," Adorina grinned.

"And?"

"And I turned him down."

"No!"

"At the time, the last thing I wanted was another husband." Adorina laughed, waving off Kelila's shock. "But Ephraim was relentless in his pursuit. Over time, the Lord softened my heart toward him. I realized God was offering me a beautiful gift—a godly husband. Something I once dreamed about but never thought to be possible."

"And then you accepted his proposal?"

"I did," Adorina chuckled. "And, of course, the rest is history."

"And your father?" Kelila persisted, intrigued. "What ever happened to him? Did he, too, accept Christ's message?"

Jaw stiffening slightly, Adorina forced a casual smile. "My father left the village many years ago, long before Jesus met me at the well. I remember feeling relieved when he departed without even bothering to say goodbye. I had been harboring a great deal of resentment against him, and of course, he never wanted a daughter in the first place. We were grossly mismatched and better off without each other. At the time, I thought it was for the best."

"And now?"

"Now I simply pray for him." Adorina sighed, though the intensity of her dark eyes betrayed a deeper inner battle.

"And have you forgiven him his treachery?"

Head coming up sharply, Adorina met her friend's curious gaze. "Well, of course I have."

Sensing Adorina's discomfort with the present subject, Kelila decided to change course. After all, the dear woman had already revealed a lifetime of pain and redemption. It wasn't polite to continue prying into every detail of her personal life.

"Thank you so much for this, Adorina," Kelila

said sincerely. "Your testimony has truly strengthened me. The next time I feel tempted to wallow in self-pity or harbor doubts, I shall remember all the Lord brought you through. My slight troubles pale in comparison."

Adorina nodded in appreciation, though her thoughts appeared to be elsewhere.

Leaning back in her chair, Kelila encircled her unborn child with loving arms, considering all she had learned and realizing she must trust her husband's current assignment—as well as her own—into the hands of her wise, capable Father.

Making a conscience decision to do so, she was at peace.

How strange, Kelila thought, a faint smile playing about the corners of her lips. *When I came to faith, I thought I would never struggle again with fear or doubt. But I am learning that faith is not a one-time decision. It is a conscious, daily decision to place my faith in the goodness of God. To trust His plan for me and those I love.*

Perhaps it was her passionate, larger-than-life personality that so often propelled wild concerns. *After all,* she thought with a knowing little smile, *I do tend to make mountains out of molehills.*

Perhaps by recognizing this about herself, she could learn to harness her doubts and anxieties when they arose, casting her cares upon the Lord Jesus and choosing to walk in faith.

CHAPTER 7

Tabitha

Joppa

"May I ask what you're doing?"

Battling exhaustion, the typically observant Tabitha had missed the hurried footfalls approaching the torchlit court. On all fours, she paused her vigorous scrubbing, rocking back on her heels to face her harried visitor.

"Hello, Eli."

"It is late. Shouldn't you be abed?"

"Yes, I should," Tabitha acknowledged with a rueful smile, swiping back stray honey-colored tresses with a soapy forearm. Despite the autumn chill after nightfall, her forehead was beaded with perspiration, her soiled garments dampened with both sweat and soap suds.

"Then what are you doing out here?" Eli, the cautious overseer of the estate, asked from the doorway, peering reluctantly at the sudsy stone court reserved for the servants' messiest jobs. "And why, pray tell, are you out here scrubbing this court a second time?"

"Joram wasn't satisfied with my first attempt to-day," Tabitha informed him with a wry smile, rolling up fitted sleeves.

"Wasn't satisfied with your work?" Eli repeated blankly. "It was spotless!"

"I thought so, as well."

"What more can you do?"

"I can try again."

"And if it still isn't to his liking?"

"At that point, I suppose there is nothing more I can do," Tabitha acknowledged with a tired smile. "I plan to turn in soon. I've nearly finished."

"You were finished the first time," Eli muttered, surprised by his master's pettiness. Though Eli certainly hadn't approved of Joram's decision to hire his niece in exchange for room and board, he couldn't help but respect the lovely widow's character and work ethic. Though he'd never admit it, he'd grown rather fond of the young woman and her giggling little daughter in spite of himself.

"I appreciate your concern, Eli," Tabitha said with great feeling. There was a time when her presence alone would have aggravated the staid overseer. And yet here he was, checking on her long after he should have retired for the night!

"I'm not concerned," Eli answered quickly, wringing anxious hands. "I'm sure you know what you're doing."

"Oh, I wouldn't be so sure about that." Tabitha laughed, a musical sound that paired well with the autumn night song and the warm crackling of burning torches.

"May I ask, well, ah...ahem, may I ask a rather personal question?" Eli dared, his turbaned head peering cautiously over the threshold.

"Of course you can," Tabitha assured him, exulting inwardly. Eli had proven one of the most difficult citizens of Joppa to win over. Distrusting by nature and easily perturbed, he had remained suspicious about her presence in Joram's mansion for months. Though she prayed for his salvation daily, she didn't seem to be making any visible headway.

"Well," Eli stammered, his eyes roving about the court to ensure that they were alone. "Just when it appeared you were making a bit of progress with your uncle, he clamped down on you twice as hard as before. Now he seems determined to nettle you at every turn, making your work quite challenging and driving you to near exhaustion with his demands. Why is that?"

"Because he is *afraid*," Tabitha answered carefully.

"Afraid of what?"

Considering Eli's honest question, Tabitha wrung out her sea sponge in a large bucket at her elbow, her brows drawn thoughtfully together. "Joram is afraid to open his heart to anyone," she finally said, careful not to disrespect her uncle. "He was desperately hurt when he lost his wife and child. Since then, I believe he has been trying to protect himself from further pain."

"By making *your* life difficult?"

"Hurting people have been known to do strange things," Tabitha acknowledged gently. "When I first lost my husband, I lashed out in anger at the entire world—even toward those I loved most. It was only by the grace of God I was rescued from that trajectory of hurt, bitterness, and rage."

"But Joram could choose the same path, no?"

"As with my case, only by the grace of God,"

Tabitha reminded him humbly. "And up to this point, Joram hasn't been receptive to His mercy."

"May I ask…" Eli faltered, discreetly lowering his tone. "May I ask why…why you put up with it?"

"Because Jesus loves him deeply," Tabitha answered truthfully. "And though Joram nettles me at times, I couldn't bear to see him perish without Christ."

"Christ? Your Rabbi," Eli supplied, shifting uncomfortably. It was no secret the staunch Jew considered her sect ill-informed and bordering blasphemous.

"Yes," Tabitha nodded firmly. "And even if that requires me to suffer a bit of discomfort now, it will all pale when my uncle is welcomed into the heavenly kingdom."

"It's a strange doctrine, yours," Eli confessed, shaking his heavily turbaned head in perplexity. "Most would say life is fleeting and we ought to seek our own happiness."

"It is precisely *because* life is fleeting that we must not live to please ourselves," Tabitha assured him with a knowing smile. "The decisions of our lives are crucial when there is an eternity ahead of us to lose or to gain."

***

Leah

Jerusalem

"Be seated."

Biting back a sharp retort, Leah entered a dim lamplit chamber as one might venture into a lion's den, her heart pounding loudly in her own ears. She couldn't help but feel as if she were about to be on trial, and the thought was disconcerting. Reminding herself that she spoke with her own brother rather than a darkly shrouded member of the Great Sanhedrin brought little comfort. Saul was little more than a stranger to her.

"You requested an audience with me?"

Fleetingly, Leah wondered if it was normal for one to "request an audience" with one's own brother. Growing up, she had known few children beyond the resplendently wealthy neighborhood in which she had been raised. The families dwelling behind breathtaking pillared facades of opulent houses conducted themselves as her own had—with the utmost regard to civility, higher education, and deep reverence for sacred tradition.

"Well?" her brother demanded, impatiently shuffling through the aging parchment scrolls scattered on the surface of his polished desk. "It must be urgent for you to disrupt my valuable time in such a careless manner."

Holding her tongue with great effort, Leah stiffly lowered herself onto one of two claw-armed chairs facing her brother's impressive desk. "It is."

"Well then?"

"It is regarding my betrothal—"

"What of it?"

Tired of being barked at like a fumbling new recruit, Leah straightened in her seat, boldly meeting her brother's gaze. Was it just her imagination, or were his smoldering dark eyes daring her to defy him?

"I wish to contact Father in regard to my betrothal."

"Why?" Saul demanded, instantly suspicious.

"I must ask him to dissolve it."

"*What?*" Pushing back his chair, Saul flung his powerful form to his feet. Planting his hands firmly upon his desk and leaning forward, he spat out, "Absurd!"

"I cannot marry him—"

"Oh, you can. And you will!"

"I sense darkness in his heart."

"Darkness?" Saul sneered, shaking his covered head in derision. "Our father has arranged a marriage for you to one of the wealthiest, most successful, and prestigious scholars of Judea! And you dare suggest darkness in his heart?"

"He is wealthy, yes. And successful by most men's standards," Leah dared, never breaking eye contact with her disgruntled brother. "But what of his character?"

"I can personally vouch for his character," Saul snapped, running a troubled hand over his intricate prayer shawl. "He is a close friend and colleague."

Her brother's promise brought little comfort. Leah assumed that Saul probably considered his own character impeccable, as well. Shuddering slightly, she scanned her surroundings with new awareness, recognizing that the darkened atmosphere of Saul's private office seemed consistent with the inner darkness now haunting his soul. It was as if a strange, unfamiliar presence had pervaded the air, ever watchful and vigilant.

Had her brother always been this way? She couldn't recall.

Once, he had merely been a zealous young student—zealous for the Law, zealous for good works. Somehow, after leaving home to study under the most respected and influential scholars, Saul's zeal had blossomed into driving ambition. Relentlessly, he sought the highest honors, the highest positions. And now? Dropping her own kindling gaze to her lap, Leah released a troubled sigh. His burning ambition had driven him to tottering on the brink of murder.

It was unthinkable, but she hadn't the slightest idea what to do about it. Did their father—himself a devoted Pharisee—know? Would he approve of his son's ambitions, or frown upon him in dismay?

Shaking her head in resignation, Leah realized she wouldn't know. Buried in important religious work and scholarly pursuits, Leah's father was scarcely known to her. She supposed perhaps she knew her brother about as well as she knew her own father.

What had happened to their family?

"As you can see," Saul said coldly, sweeping his elegantly clad arm over the top of his desk, "I have pressing matters to attend. This discussion is over."

"Not for me," Leah said quietly, lifting intense dark eyes to meet her brother's stunned gaze.

Eyes hardening in fury, Saul lowered himself behind his desk, folding his hands in a manner that indicated his burning irritation. "I said, the matter is closed. There is nothing left to discuss."

"But there is," Leah dared, wondering at the boldness of her own speech.

"It would seem your newfound faith has bolstered your courage and sharpened your tongue," Saul drawled caustically, studying her with open disdain.

"I mean no disrespect to you or your colleague, my brother," Leah said slowly, evenly. "But I cannot marry him. And your aid is required to reach Father." Pride burning, Leah sorrowed anew at her inability to read and write. Though the sons of the family were privileged to receive the best education money could buy, the daughters were trained in domestic skills and the art of homemaking. And though she was grateful for the fastidious training she had received and could host an impressive dinner party to arouse the jealousy of the wealthiest aristocrat, such skills couldn't help her now. She needed Saul's help contacting her father, and the thought rankled.

Suddenly, Leah realized what it was that so infuriated her brother and his dark-robed colleagues regarding her newfound Messiah, Jesus of Nazareth. For just as she needed Saul's help to reach her father in Tarsus, the religious leaders had stood between the people and their Father in Heaven for centuries. But Jesus had come to usher in a new and living way—a way in which every man, woman, and child had direct access to God. Jesus' loving sacrifice upon the cross had enabled even "commoners" to approach the Throne of Grace, and thus, a "holy man" was no longer required to act as intercessor between God and men. Jesus' perfect sacrifice had stripped these men of their power, robbing them of their death grip upon the people. No wonder the religious leaders opposed Christ's message with such vigor!

"You are a silly, foolish girl," Saul said coldly, drawing Leah's thoughts back to the present. "Haven't you the slightest idea how many young women long to be in your position? Should you marry Yosef, yours will be a life of wealth, recognition, and prestige."

"Yes," Leah admitted softly. "But far *better is a little with the fear of the Lord, than great treasure with trouble*, and *better is a dinner of herbs where love is, than a fatted calf with hatred.*"

"Don't fling the Proverbs of Solomon at me, you fool," Saul growled, clearly peeved. "If you'd like a contest to see which of us better knows and understands the Scriptures, I'd be happy to oblige you. Besides, you don't even know Yosef. How can you possibly hate him?"

"I don't hate him," Leah assured him. "But given his powerful position in the synagogue, he would certainly hate being married to me, a follower of the Way."

"You are not a follower of the Way!"

"But I am."

"Listen to me," Saul said, leaning forward on his desk, his gaze dangerous. "This is a rebellious phase you are going through, and nothing more. I cannot understand it, as you have always done what you're told—grudgingly perhaps, and certainly with a bit of attitude—but you have done it, nonetheless."

Leah returned his gaze with clear eyes and a calm expression, further nettling him. Something about that look reminded him far too much of Mary of Jerusalem, a constant bur in his side and stench in his nostrils! Saul didn't want to think about that.

"I swear by all the gold of the Temple," he declared, his tone betraying his great angst, "I am convinced you are dabbling in this confounded cult just to spite me."

"In time, perhaps you will see this is not merely a phase, my brother," Leah told him, surprised by the confidence the Holy Spirit had supplied. "This is my life now. And I cannot share my life with someone who vehemently opposes everything I hold dear."

"You listen to me, and listen well," Saul ground out, his tone threatening. "You will *not* disgrace our family in this manner. You have been sent to Jerusalem for the sole purpose of an arranged marriage with a reputable man. And marry him, you will."

For a long, quiet moment laden with heavy tension, brother and sister measured each other's resolve.

Leah was the first to speak, her tone laced with sorrow as she reluctantly changed the subject. "Can the rumors about you be trusted, Saul? Is it true?"

"Is what true?" he fumed, attempting to maintain his air of authority despite his boiling indignation. Whereas some of the noblest and most respected men of the Sanhedrin revered him, his own sister betrayed not the slightest fear of him.

"Are you going to hunt down believers beyond these borders, dragging men and women alike from their homes and families and committing them to prison? Possibly even death?"

"My righteous endeavors are none of your concern," Saul informed her coldly, his eyes flickering with a hint of doubt.

"Righteous endeavors?" Leah repeated, shaking her head in disbelief. "Will your hatred and bloodlust never cease?"

"Enough!" Saul seethed, slamming a closed fist upon his desk. "You are an ignorant young woman and a fool. And I will not rest until every so-called *believer* is dead and rotting in a common grave of twisted, gnarled bones!"

Taken aback, Leah gripped the gilded arms of her chair, intentionally lifting her gaze to meet his. Speaking in a calm, measured tone, she dared, "And shall you kill me, too?"

Leah's question lingered heavily along with the crackling tension in the air, followed by a chilling silence that sent her heart racing ahead like the galloping hooves of a wild steed.

Meeting his sister's gaze with cold, calculating eyes, Saul's hardened mouth formed a grim line as he lifted one arm with a dismissive wave of his golden stylus. "Go. You are dismissed."

Rising with grace and dignity, Leah turned and left her brother's office.

CHAPTER 8

Tabitha

Joppa

Standing outside the impressive, double-door entry of her uncle's private chambers, Tabitha awaited Joram's response after several sturdy knocks. Bearing a heavy tray laden with breakfast fruits and grains, she was puzzled by the lack of her uncle's typically terse command to enter. This had become a tradition of sorts between the two of them—her presenting his Sabbath breakfast on the lovely balcony overlooking the shimmering blue Mediterranean while he glowered and stewed, irritated by her usual request to accompany her to the synagogue for Sabbath service. Not once had he accepted her cheerful invitation, though Tabitha persisted anyway.

Perplexed, Tabitha knocked again, a bit more insistently this time.

"Is everything all right here?"

Glancing over her shoulder, Tabitha saw the

turbaned Eli hurrying down the hall, his tablet and stylus in hand, as usual.

"I do hope so," Tabitha replied, her honey-colored brow etched with worry.

"He has not permitted you to enter?" Eli asked in confusion, drawing alongside her.

"He hasn't responded at all," Tabitha admitted, her stomach churning. It was clear to the entire household that the master's health was declining—at least, it seemed clear to everyone but Joram. He stoutly insisted he was in robust health and vehemently forbade the staff from "fussing over" him. Even so, she couldn't help but worry for him, haunted by the sickening thought of discovering him lifeless in bed or lying prostrate on his office floor...

Privy to her concerns, Eli paused beside Tabitha, giving Joram's door several hard knocks. "Good morning to you, sir," he said loudly, hoping to be heard and acknowledged. "May we enter?"

Silence lingered on in the most disconcerting way.

Exchanging nervous glances, the servants needn't ask what the other was thinking. Taking charge, Eli pushed open the double doors and barreled inside with Tabitha hot on his heels.

"Master?" Eli called out, his voice ringing through the garish bedchamber. "Master, are you well?"

Glancing toward the enormous four-poster canopy bed perched against the furthest wall, Tabitha was relieved to find it empty and unmade. Her uncle must be up and about. Had he somehow slipped from his private chambers unnoticed?

He is probably in hiding, she thought, just a bite snidely, her concerns temporarily eased in her amusement. *He's trying to dodge my weekly Sabbath invitation.*

"Master!"

Eli's anxious cry immediately drew Tabitha's attention toward the balcony as the devoted overseer rushed to his master's side.

Instantly repentant and horror-stricken, Tabitha, too, hastened toward the balcony where her uncle sat slumped on his elegant wrought-iron chair at the breakfast table, his face ashen, his body appearing like a crumpled rag doll. Slamming the breakfast tray on the empty table, she kneeled at his feet beside Eli.

"Oh, thank You, Father," Tabitha breathed, seeing that Joram remained conscious. "Uncle, you are unwell!"

"I'm fine!" Joram snarled, lifting his head with obvious effort. Attempting to straighten in his chair, he winced in the bright early morning sunlight. "And I told you not to call me that!"

"What happened?" Tabitha exclaimed, reaching for his arm.

Slapping her hand away, Joram sat up a bit straighter, gripping the arms of his chair like a lifeline. "I said, *I'm fine!*"

"Master," Eli dared, hovering over him like an anxious mother hen. "Forgive me, but...well, you do not appear to be all right. You look—"

"It was merely a slight fainting spell, nothing more," Joram spat out, his face reddening in his agitation.

"But Master—"

"Enough!" Joram raged, clearly regaining his strength. "I'm not an invalid. Perhaps if breakfast had arrived in a timely manner, I wouldn't have felt so lightheaded!"

Annoyed, Tabitha resisted the urge to slap him with the breakfast tray. After all, she had arrived right on time with his morning meal! Her uncle had simply been too busy endangering his own health to respond to her persistent knocking!

"Now go, both of you!" Joram snarled, turning slowly and painstakingly in his chair to reach for the breakfast table. "Leave me in peace."

"But—"

"Go!" Joram bellowed, halting his niece's anxious protest.

Biting her lower lip, Tabitha considered voicing her usual question. But clearly, her uncle was in in no shape to travel down the hall, much less across town to participate in a synagogue service.

Sensing the direction of his niece's thoughts, Joram's silver brows drew together in disgust. "Don't even ask," he smirked, reaching for a bright piece of fruit and taking a generous bite. "And I don't expect either of you to breathe a word about this little incident to anyone, you hear?"

Glancing at Eli, Tabitha saw that his concern for Joram matched her own.

"Now *go!*"

"Yes, Master." Shoulders slumped slightly in defeat, Eli turned on his heel to depart.

Reluctantly, Tabitha followed suit, leaving her uncle alone on the balcony to glower after them. Though she was convinced he needed medical attention, she knew he would refuse to see a physician with his dying breath.

Lord God, she prayed, closing Joram's double

doors behind her and a very quiet Eli. *Help me be a faithful witness to Joram. He doesn't wish to hear any preaching; thus, my actions must speak for me. But You know how he nettles me, Lord! Help me demonstrate Your love without wavering.*

Exchanging a hopeless glance with Eli, Tabitha released a somewhat tremorous sigh.

I fear there is little time left to reach him.

***

Mary

Jerusalem

"I see you continue attending church meetings in disguise."

Appearing somewhat miffed, Agabus pulled his billowing robes closer about his person, his awkward head covering partially obscuring the lovely, tenacious widow from view.

"Have you considered that perhaps arriving here shrouded in mystery might draw even more attention to yourself, my friend?" Mary pointed out with maddening logic, receiving a look of annoyance from the young Pharisee.

"I shall take my chances," Agabus told her stoutly, his eyes roving nervously about the bright Upper Room as smiling believers clustered together to share farewell pleasantries and warm embraces. "I cannot risk being seen by the religious leaders."

"As you can see," Mary reminded him with a mischievous smile, "the religious leaders haven't particularly arrived here in droves this evening."

"But I could be seen on the way. Or on the way home."

"I see."

"It is doubtful that you do," Agabus muttered in obvious annoyance, torn between fear, frustration, and conviction. "I remain in a rather tenuous position."

"Yes, you've mentioned that," Mary nodded, her eyes twinkling with mischief. "Several times, actually."

"And my situation has not improved," Agabus said in a hushed tone, leaning in a bit closer to be heard above the merry din. "If anything, it has worsened considerably."

"How so?" Mary asked him, interested.

"I suspect that Saul of Tarsus detects my—ah, let's say…fascination—with the Way."

"And why do you suspect such?"

"He watches me with the eyes of a vulture," Agabus murmured, deeply unsettled. "I wouldn't be surprised if he sent spies to my home. Thus, the disguise."

"And you believe that disguise would fool a trained spy?"

"I slip out a back door utilized by the few servants I have recently been privileged to hire," he informed her, appearing somewhat pleased with his own ingenuity. "And I take a very circuitous route."

"Ah, clever."

"You mock me," Agabus remarked, his thick brows knitting together in trepidation.

"Never," Mary promised, touching his heavily robed arm in a pacifying manner. "I wouldn't mock you, my friend. Your situation amuses me—that is all."

"I fail to be amused by my troubles."

"I can understand that," Mary assured him, nodding warmly toward several large families as they departed. "We all have our troubles, Agabus. We all have something to lose. But as I've mentioned several times before, anything we might lose in this life pales in comparison to the victory we gain through Jesus Christ."

"I must be certain of that before doing anything so...so *brash* as joining this forbidden sect."

Mary smiled warmly in response, for it was clear this timid brother was teetering on the brink of the most important decision he would ever make. In recent weeks, she had doubled down on her prayers for him, beseeching the Lord to embolden his heart.

"I must be going," Agabus informed her, stiffly adjusting his garments. "The hour is late."

"Safe travels, Agabus," Mary said meaningfully, her care for the young man evident upon her lovely features. "And do remember that I pray for you without ceasing, that the Lord Jesus will reveal himself to you beyond any shadow of doubt, forever sealing your belief."

"Good evening, my lady." Clearly uncomfortable with the conversation, Agabus turned and descended down the sprawling staircase, eager to return to the familiarity of the coveted house in his prestigious priestly neighborhood and the safety of his academic scrolls.

CHAPTER 9

Leah

Jerusalem

Pacing a darkened, torchlit hall, Leah tried to ignore
the eerie shadows writhing like anguished demons
cast upon the colonnaded marble walls. Knowing
that her scholarly brother was undoubtedly sequestered within his private office at this late hour,
buried beneath piles of cryptic scrolls, she was free
to roam the great house. It was an impressive affair,
though smaller than the opulent mansions of prominent religious leaders. The Judean home belonged
to their father, who in turn had inherited it from
his father. She hadn't the slightest idea how many
ancestors long dead had previously traveled these
frescoed halls. Clearly, her forefathers had deemed it
important to own property in Jerusalem even while
residing in Tarsus or other illustrious cities of the
empire.

Now, her brother, Saul, benefited from their foresight, as he resided in a beautiful house in a wealthy neighborhood nearest the priestly precinct. Within such close proximity to the Temple compound and its goings-on, Saul's work and studies had proven very convenient. She wondered if he would inherit the lovely home when their father passed.

Emerging beneath a pillared entrance, Leah stepped into the quiet gardens adjoining the graceful house. Moonlight washed the late autumn blossoms and rich green foliage in ethereal silver hues, reminding her of the lush, flowering courts of her father's mansion back home. Pausing beneath the inky shadows of the sprawling fronds of towering palms, Leah gingerly placed her hand upon the nearest trunk, lifting her gaze toward the whitewashed moon hovering in a deep velvet sky.

Despite the peace the Holy Spirit had supplied once she accepted Jesus Christ as her Lord and Savior, her heart was heavy and troubled tonight. She feared for her brother, Saul, though she hardly knew him. Even more so, she feared for the believers he intended to hunt down and destroy.

"I feel so alone," she whispered into the gathering darkness, drawing her shawl closer around her shoulders to ward off the night's chill. "Father, in the name of Your precious Son, Jesus, please hear me. I am lost, drifting about and seemingly at the mercy of chance. My brother is determined to exterminate my fellow believers and marry me off to a cold-hearted hypocrite. What can I do? I need help, guidance, mentorship. *Something.*"

Releasing a tremorous breath, Leah hugged the palm's sturdy trunk, wondering at the sensations rising in her chest. Though thoughts of frustration and helplessness sought to claim her entire being, she couldn't deny the hope kindling—burning—in her heart.

"I am new to this," Leah amended softly, her dark eyes searching the heavens as if seeking a sign as she prayed. "Show me what to do, how to live. Guide me in Your truth. Don't let me take the wrong path."

Though her heart rebelled against the idea of praying for the man who seemingly stood between herself and a blessed future, Leah added softly, "And help my brother, Saul. Turn his heart toward You. He is blind, Lord. Help him see." Shaking her head, Leah wondered how Saul—as intelligent as he was—could have possibly missed the truth about Jesus. After all, he had been meticulously trained in the holy texts his entire life, while *she*—a younger daughter considered good for nothing but to someday marry a scholar, bear his children, and further his distinguished lineage—had received table scraps, bits of ancient prophecies and Scriptures here and there as her older brothers were instructed by respected scholars. Occasionally, she learned bits and pieces of Torah proclaimed from the pulpit at the synagogue. But little more than that, though her heart had quietly longed for more. And yet...*she* understood the fulfillment of prophecy, embracing Jesus Christ as the long-awaited Messiah so loudly proclaimed by the prophets of old, while her learned brother, Saul—Gamaliel's star pupil, the envy of his class, his father's pride and joy—had entirely missed it. And not only Saul, but the majority of his Pharisaical brethren clad in regal black and white.

How is it that I—the unlikeliest of all candidates, an uneducated young woman—can see it, while those privileged to study the Word of God have adamantly rejected the Messiah it foretold?

Once again, Leah was reminded of the hardness of the religious leaders' stubborn hearts. And yet, her father and her brother expected her to marry one of them!

Squaring her shoulders in resolve, Leah thanked God she wasn't given to fear. Though she had acquiesced to her stern father's wishes and expectations all her life, a fire had burned within her belly, promising something more.

Well, now I have found it, Leah decided, releasing her grasp on the palm's graceful trunk. *And like the man in the parable of Jesus who discovered great hidden treasure in a field, I, too, am willing to relinquish all that I have to obtain it.*

***

Kelila

Sychar

"I have been considering what you said."

"Um, I say a lot of things. Probably too many things!" Pausing halfway through hanging a damp garment on the line strung in Adorina's blossoming outer court, Kelila glanced sideways at her friend, her expression teasing. "You will have to be a bit more specific, Adorina."

Chuckling lightly, the Samaritan woman reached into the large basket of freshly laundered garments while a persistent breeze teased the dark hair framing her angular features, firm chin, and thoughtful brown eyes. "About my father," she clarified quietly, draping another garment over the line.

"I said something about your father?" Kelila asked blankly, mentally reviewing their most recent conversations—which were many. Several weeks had slipped by since Philip's unexpected departure, and though Kelila missed him desperately, she cherished these precious days spent with her dear sister in Christ and the Samaritan people. Meanwhile, she had done her best to pitch in with the cooking, cleaning, and housework, despite Adorina's incessant fussing and "mothering" over her. Repeatedly, Kelila insisted she was perfectly capable of helping with the chores. "Carrying a baby doesn't render one incapable of anything but lying on a plush couch all day to be waited on hand and foot," was her oft-repeated refrain. Eventually, Adorina had softened just a bit, allowing the evangelist's wife to assist with the lighter chores.

"You asked me about my father a few weeks ago when I shared my testimony with you," Adorina reminded her, her gaze fixed on the damp garments she draped over the line with practiced hands. "You asked me if I had forgiven him."

"Oh, that," Kelila remembered, suddenly feeling a bit uneasy. At the time, Adorina hadn't seemed particularly pleased about her honest question.

"Well, frankly, I'm glad you asked," Adorina confessed, adjusting several fluttering garments Kelila had hurriedly flung over the line in her typical carefree fashion.

"Why is that?" Kelila asked her, puzzled.

"Because..." Adorina sighed, stepping back to survey the neat row of garments flapping smartly in the morning breeze. "Well, I suppose I'm glad you asked because…because…I'm not entirely sure that I have."

"Have *what*?"

"Forgiven him," Adorina said quietly, turning sober eyes upon the lovely young Cyrenian.

Kelila stared at her friend, stunned. After all, Adorina always seemed so…perfect! So *together*. Her faith had been unshakable from the very beginning. She was smart, sensible, and grounded. *Never flighty or impulsive, like me,* Kelila thought a bit ruefully. And yet here she stood with tears in her dark eyes, admitting a painful inner struggle which Kelila never would have guessed.

"I know—it surprised me too," Adorina sighed, shaking her lightly covered head in dismay. "When I met Jesus, He cleansed me of my sins and gave me a new beginning. Honestly, I haven't truly considered my father since then—until now."

"I'm terribly sorry if my prying questions opened old wounds—"

"No, I'm glad we discussed it," Adorina insisted. "Otherwise, I might have remained unaware of the sin in my heart."

"I'm not entirely sure I would call it *sin*," Kelila said, defensive for her friend. "Your father treated you deplorably. His behavior toward you was unthinkable! Surely anyone would harbor ill feelings toward—"

"No, Kelila," Adorina interrupted frankly, her solemn eyes betraying her pain. "I must call it what it is. Sin is *sin*, even if it's uncomfortable to admit. Jesus clearly said, *'If you forgive men their trespasses, your heavenly Father will also forgive you. But if you do not forgive men their trespasses, neither will your Father forgive your trespasses.'* It is a sobering thought."

It was, indeed. Kelila nodded slowly, troubled for her.

"Despite my deep discouragement, I keep remembering something the Apostle John said when he visited us with Simon Peter."

"What did he say?"

"He said that if we confess our sins, God is faithful and just to forgive us our sins and to cleanse us from all unrighteousness."

"Ah, yes," Kelila smiled, warmed by the memory. "I remember that."

"Clearly, I must take this sin before God and ask Him to forgive me, to cleanse me of this anger harbored against my father."

"Well, John was right," Kelila encouraged her with a bright smile. "God is faithful. He will help you through this."

Bending to scoop up the now-empty woven laundry basket, Adorina met her gaze with clear brown eyes. "Jesus forgave *me*, despite my sordid past. How, then, can I deny my father the same kindness? Even so, it won't be easy. I'm not even sure I can do it, Kelila. How can I forgive the man who was supposed to *love* me, but instead loathed my existence and refused to help me when I needed it most?"

"Take it before the Lord," Kelila suggested, wishing she had the answers. "It is truly a hard thing, forgiving someone who has hurt you so deeply. But I've heard Philip say that if we submit to God in obedience, then He will help us to do the impossible."

CHAPTER 10

Leah

Jerusalem

Located before the towering fortress walls of the tetrarch's Upper City luxury palace, the Upper Market was an enormous affair sheltered on three sides by impressive Roman-style arcades boasting endless rows of marble pillars upholding broad walkways and enclosed stone structures. The sprawling market floor seemed to stretch forth endlessly with its sea of merchants' booths and a multitude of bored or eager customers moseying about the vast stores of desirable merchandise. Deeply congested with hawking merchants, scurrying slaves, anxious servants, and impatient patrons, the massive commercial center was the perfect place to get lost in a crowd...which is exactly what Leah desired.

Ambling rather aimlessly about the various market stalls, Leah was glad to have escaped her brother's smoldering, watchful eye. She couldn't help but wonder if he was presently mulling over her fate, deciding whether or not to prosecute her along with the rest.

She certainly wouldn't put it past him—arresting his own sister simply because she disagreed with his theology. The thought nettled, and yet again, she wondered at Jesus' seemingly impossible command to love one's enemies.

"How does your mistress fare on this fine day?" She heard the booming voice of a friendly merchant ringing through the crowd.

Drawn by the robust voice, Leah glanced over her shoulder and saw an elegant seller's booth boasting a mind-boggling array of exotic aromatic spices. The largely built merchant donning an Eastern turban and a wild beard appeared pleased to assist a petite, graceful girl about Leah's own age. Perusing the servant girl's careful selections, he tallied up the cost, to which she readily produced glistening coins and placed them gingerly in his large, open palm.

Turning fully upon the scene, Leah tilted her heavily covered head to one side, strangely drawn by the girl's cheerful laughter and sunny smile as she dialogued with the kindly merchant. Donning simple, unadorned attire and a modest head covering, she appeared quite content in her station, despite her lowly serving status. And by the looks of her purchases, she served a large, robust, and wealthy household. The basket resting upon her slender arm was brimming with bundles of dried herbs and packets of fresh, fragrant spices. But even more lovely than the spices' heady fragrance was the gentle air about the young lady, like a sweet-smelling perfume.

Curious, Leah tentatively approached the seller's stall, hoping the bustling shoppers hovering near the area would shield her from the girl's view. As she drew nearer, the sound of the maidservant's shy but friendly voice caused Leah's heart to leap with bubbling hope. She couldn't help but sense that perhaps... just perhaps... Could this girl be a *believer* in Jesus? Leah sensed the same loving Spirit within the bright young woman, the same Spirit that had first drawn her to Christ.

Attempting to appear casual, Leah ambled even closer, just behind the young woman and the seller's stall. Pretending to browse the merchandise on the seller's table, she was taken aback when the girl finished her exchange with the merchant, spun spritely on her heel, and nearly bumped into her!

"Oh dear, please forgive my carelessness! I didn't see you there."

Staring at the girl in surprise, Leah attempted to return the kind apology, but discovered in dismay that her tongue was sufficiently tied.

"Are you all right?" the girl persisted.

As the kind maidservant studied her with concerned eyes, Leah decided they were definitely the same age, at the very threshold of womanhood, but that was probably the only thing they had in common. This girl was small and delicate, fragile-boned and graceful. Her expressive brown eyes and rosy lips appeared almost too large for her gentle, oval face. Dark curls graced her slender shoulders and framed her face in the most becoming way.

"I suppose I must be going," the maidservant said, mistaking Leah's stunned silence for aloofness. Even so, her eyes remained warm, her voice kind.

"Shalom and good day."

Managing to mumble a rather awkward apology, Leah watched as the maidservant retreated, respectfully picking her way through the harried shoppers bustling in the square. Heart sinking, she felt as if she had relinquished a desperately important opportunity, though she couldn't quite understand why.

No, I will not relent. Dark brows drawing together in determination, Leah made up her mind in a split second. *I will not squander an opportunity that may very well be from the Lord.*

It was decided. She would follow the girl and inquire about the hope she saw shining in those soft brown eyes.

***

Rhoda

Traversing a fashionable, palm-dotted lane, Rhoda clutched her woven basket in anxious hands, wondering if she should break into a dead run or simply continue ambling casually along as if nothing was amiss.

The mystifying girl from the merchant's booth was following her with intentional, purposeful steps. But why? Did she intend harm? Was she mentally unstable or perhaps even dangerous?

Stomach clenching in fear, Rhoda quickened her step, silently beseeching the Lord to guide her safely to Mary's villa.

"Wait!"

Freezing in the middle of the broad walkway

abutting the paved street, Rhoda turned around slowly, confused. The girl had addressed her, and she couldn't ignore her—not with a clear conscience, anyway. Oh, how grateful she was that they were in a busy, open area rather than a secluded alleyway!

"Please. Please wait!"

Puzzled, Rhoda watched as the young woman from the merchant's stall jogged up to her, her jaw set in determination, her dark eyes flashing fire. Studying the girl, Rhoda's heart went out to her, for her sharp features were far too serious and careworn for her tender age. She wore a broad head covering that concealed most of her hair, which was pinned back in a severe fashion. The dark roots peeking out from the veil on her forehead nearly matched the color of a raven's wing. Her inquisitive eyes, framed by stern eyebrows, matched the color of her hair, and dark circles beneath them betrayed many sleepless nights. She wasn't lovely by popular standards, but Rhoda decided that her obvious zeal and fervent determination was rather magnetic. Mysterious and watchful, she spoke with a hint of an accent, indicating that she wasn't a native of Judea.

"Hello," Rhoda offered in reluctant greeting, noting that the girl's garments were expensive and expertly tailored, despite the drabness of the colors—likely selected intentionally to avoid attracting unnecessary attention. "Are you following me?"

Leah's serious brows lifted in surprise, for the maidservant's tone held not even a trace of rudeness or accusation despite the suspicious nature of her approach. "Forgive me," she managed, bowing her head in obvious discomfiture. "But I must ask—that is, I must know...well—"

"Yes?" Rhoda prodded gently, sensing the girl's hesitation. "Are you all right?"

"Yes," Leah answered swiftly, then appeared to reconsider her thoughtless response. "Well, *no*. Well, perhaps. It is too soon to tell."

Rhoda studied her, intrigued but also cautious.

"My name is Leah," the stranger dared, reluctantly lifting her gaze to meet the shy maidservant's.

"Greetings, Leah. I am Rhoda."

"Shalom, Rhoda."

"Shalom." Rhoda smiled, amused by Leah's unusual behavior. "Can I help you with something, friend? I would be happy to assist you in any way—"

"Yes, yes," Leah interrupted her, clearly eager to get the awkward conversation over with. "I must ask you—are you… well, are you…"

"Am I what?" Rhoda asked blankly, puzzled.

Appearing to steel herself for Rhoda's reaction, Leah straightened, meeting her gaze with burning intensity. "Are you a follower of Jesus of Nazareth?"

Rhoda stared at the bold young woman in surprise.

"I know it's none of my business," Leah plowed ahead, anxiously wringing her hands. "But I just sensed it, watching you at the seller's booth—"

"You can ask me anything you wish, Leah," Rhoda quickly assured her, hoping to set her at ease. "I am happy to answer your questions."

Now it was Leah's turn to stare in amazement.

"And, yes, I believe Jesus is the Messiah, the Son of the Living God."

"God be praised," Leah murmured, her heart pounding a steady song of relief in her chest.

"And you?" Rhoda asked warmly, reaching out to

touch her arm. "Do you believe?"

"I do," Leah assured her, nodding vehemently. "With all my heart."

"Amen." Rhoda smiled, already sensing a comradeship with the brave young woman. "It was very courageous of you to seek me out, Leah. Believers are not particularly safe in this city."

"Tell me about it," Leah muttered, her expression tightening as she considered her hate-crazed brother, Saul.

"Have you a place of refuge, Leah?"

Since tears were considered a sign of weakness in her family, Leah seldom shed one. However, Rhoda's earnest question invoked emotions deep inside that threatened to crumble her firm resolve. Steeling herself against the sorrow flooding her heart, Leah answered honestly, "I abide with my older brother. He is not a believer."

"I see," Rhoda nodded in understanding. "And I imagine he hasn't permitted you to attend any local church gatherings?"

"He would come unglued should I even suggest it."

"I don't wish to place you in any danger, Leah," Rhoda said, her brown eyes sweeping the perimeter as if she half-expected the girl's fury-stricken brother to materialize out of thin air. "But you are welcome to join us in prayer and worship any time. We meet each evening in my mistress's home and study the teachings of our Lord Jesus."

"That is exactly what I need," Leah told her, mentally calculating what her punishment might prove to be should her brother ever find out. "And where is this place you meet? Who is your mistress?"

"My lady is Mary of Jerusalem," Rhoda informed her proudly.

"Mary of Jerusalem!" Leah declared in shock, startling the shy maid.

"Yes," Rhoda supplied somewhat hesitantly. "Do you know of her?"

"I believe the entire region knows of your lady," Leah quickly amended, hoping she hadn't unwittingly planted a seed of suspicion in Rhoda's mind. If Rhoda or any of the believers found out that her brother was the notorious Saul of Tarsus, she would surely be barred from fellowship. "She is a courageous woman."

"That, she is," Rhoda agreed fondly. "Will you join our service this evening, Leah?"

Knitting her brows together in dismay, Leah battled contrary emotions. How desperately she longed to *learn*, to meet with like-minded believers and grow in her faith! She was quite certain she couldn't do it alone. And hadn't she *just* prayed, asking the Lord to lead her to those who could help? In His gracious love, the Lord had answered her petition.

Even so, if Saul *ever* discovered she was fraternizing with Mary of Jerusalem—his archnemesis—he would kill her. Should she do such a thing, the shred of mercy Saul currently harbored toward his little sister would certainly be forever destroyed. And yet despite that unwelcome fact, she found herself responding with confidence, "Yes, Rhoda. I will join you."

"Wonderful!" Rhoda beamed, pleased for her. "Then I shall see you this evening at my lady's estate."

"Perhaps..." Leah dared, dropping her gaze in embarrassment. "Well, perhaps—if it isn't too much to ask—you can help show me the Way. I desperately want to follow Jesus. I just don't know how or even where to begin."

Smiling with all the warmth in the world, Rhoda nodded her agreement. "I would consider it a great honor and privilege to walk beside you on your journey."

CHAPTER 11

Kelila

Sychar

A faint chill arrived along with the wintry month of Kislev, promising a festive holiday season as the Feast of Lights drew near.

If only the Samaritans kept the Feast of Lights! Kelila mourned inwardly, lifting a flickering candle as she gazed out the latticed window in the guestroom in which she had resided alone for nearly six weeks now. Feeling unusually homesick for Jerusalem and those she had left behind, Kelila gazed into the gathering darkness of dusk, imagining the preparations her Jewish family and friends must have been making as they happily prepared to usher in the ever-glorious Feast of Dedication.

Oh, what fun she'd had when she lived with her sister Candace, her brother-in-law Simon, and their two young boys celebrating the Feast of Lights in Jerusalem! How the entire house had glowed beneath the light of dozens of cheerfully burning lamps and flickering candles! How the aroma of fresh baked goods and tantalizing sweets had filled the air!

Fleetingly, Kelila considered suggesting to Adorina that they celebrate the feast in Sychar. What fun it would be to light dozens upon dozens of candles, to gather around a crackling fire at night to commemorate the dazzling feats of heroes and kings, and to bake all manner of sweet delicacies to enjoy! Even so, she quickly thought better of suggesting such a thing. After all, she didn't wish to offend these wonderful people. Why would the Samaritans be interested in observing a feast that commemorated the cleansing of a Temple they were forbidden to enter upon the pain of death?

But, oh, how she would miss the bright festivities this year! Nearly as much as she missed Philip. And her relatives back home.

Sighing wistfully, Kelila placed her candle on the window ledge and cradled her protruding abdomen, wondering when this child would make his or her appearance into the world. According to her somewhat tenuous calculations, she was somewhere around her sixth month. Her womb had stretched considerably since Philip's departure as the child within her rounded belly continued making his or her presence known. How she longed to share these sweet moments with her husband as the precious little one grew within her womb. Wouldn't he love to see her now?

Will he return before my time comes? Kelila wondered, blinking back unwanted tears. *Lord, I know You are using him to further Your kingdom, but I need him too. Is it selfish to ask You to bring us back together before this child is born?*

After crossing the room, Kelila lowered herself rather painstakingly onto the overstuffed sleeping pallet Adorina had generously provided. Leaning her back against the wall, she closed her eyes, one hand nestled protectively on her belly. Moments like these were when she felt most tempted to slump back into her old pattern of willful self-pity. Thankfully, the Holy Spirit of God was faithful to remind her to resist the carnal urge.

In addition to that nagging temptation, it felt odd watching Adorina's husband, Ephraim, so easily assuming Philip's role among the Samaritan church, especially as they began meeting in his home. Why was it so difficult watching another man oversee the sacred work her husband had begun in Sychar? She knew it was what Philip would have wanted. He certainly wouldn't wish for the infant church to fall apart or go astray without godly leadership, and Kelila could think of no better man to oversee it than Ephraim. Still, watching him address the believers each day made her miss her husband even more.

But Philip has warned me against a spirit of jealousy or competition on many occasions, Kelila reminded herself. *We are not to harbor such feelings against our fellow workers in Christ. This is the Lord's work—not Philip's or Ephraim's or anyone else's. And we must work together as the body of Christ—united in thought and deed—to fulfill His purposes on the earth.*

Folding her hands over her bulging belly, Kelila resolved to surrender her emotions to God rather than allowing herself to be carried away by them. After all, He knew what He was doing in Jerusalem, and in Samaria, even unto the ends of the earth.

Even so, she couldn't help but pray for Philip's soon return.

***

Rhoda

Jerusalem

"Who's your friend, Rhoda?"

Heart pounding at the sound of her beloved's voice, Rhoda swiveled around in surprise to discover herself face to face with John Mark's laughing, teasing eyes.

"Oh," Rhoda murmured, her hand fluttering to her heart. "You startled me, John Mark."

"I did, didn't I?" he grinned, drawing alongside her as believers milled about the Upper Room, awaiting the commencement of the evening prayer service. "I suppose it's a habit of mine."

"Startling me?"

"I rather enjoy it."

Blushing deeply, Rhoda redirected her gaze—and her thoughts—to safer subjects. The large, glowing chamber was filling rapidly with earnest men, women, and children eager to participate in prayer and worship. She was pleased to see their numbers growing despite the fierce persecution they faced.

"So?" John Mark prodded, his broad shoulders brushing against hers as he leaned in to whisper secretively, "Who is she?"

"Leah?" Rhoda asked, following his gaze toward the serious young woman across the room and wondering why her young master had this maddening effect on her! Attempting to slow her rapidly beating heart, she knew her girlish feelings for John Mark were impossible, utterly preposterous. But how on earth would she ever subdue them?

"Her name is Leah?"

"Yes," Rhoda nodded, feeling even more shy than usual in the presence of her handsome young master. Across the room, Leah stood beside Mary, hanging upon her every word with rapt attention as the graceful widow warmly addressed a group of believing women near the speaker's platform. The girl had been attending church meetings for several weeks now, and to Rhoda's great relief, her initial nervousness seemed to have worn off—for the most part. Leah seemed overwhelmed with gratitude to be considered part of this body of Christ. In awe of Mary and touched by the believers' kindness, she was rapidly growing in faith and knowledge of the Scriptures.

"My mother said you invited her to join us," John Mark continued, his curiosity piqued. "Why?"

"Because she was struggling to keep the faith alone," Rhoda quickly informed him, aching anew for the girl. "I can't imagine doing such a thing. She must be a very strong young woman."

"We have many strong women among us," John Mark teased, playfully bumping her with his shoulder.

Sensing his hidden compliment, Rhoda was perplexed. She certainly didn't consider *herself* a strong woman. Now Mary—*she* was the embodiment of a strong woman, for she had faced opposition head on and overcome it, despite the sudden death of her husband, scathing threats from the Sanhedrin, and the loss of respect from the religious and academic communities. And her dear friend Tabitha—*she* was a strong woman, plowing headfirst into the mission field immediately following her husband's tragic martyrdom. And Candace, bravely crossing the Great Sea with her husband and two young sons to reach lost relatives in Cyrene. Even the free-spirited Kelila, who had bravely followed her evangelist husband to the hostile region of Samaria. In fact, Rhoda could think of many believing women who could easily be considered such. But *her*, Rhoda—*strong*? She had always been shy, even timid. She preferred to be seen and not heard—*Well, preferably, neither seen nor heard,* she thought with a small smile. She was happy to serve others in silence, her quiet smile resonating the inner peace she enjoyed in Christ.

"So Leah's family doesn't believe? None of them?" John Mark pressed, interrupting her private thoughts.

Daring a peek at his dancing brown eyes, Rhoda wondered if he was truly interested in the present topic or simply making conversation. "I know very little about her family," Rhoda admitted. "She seems rather reserved. I know she lives with an older brother, but he doesn't believe."

"And the rest of her family?"

"They aren't here."

"What do you mean? Are they dead?"

"Oh, no," Rhoda quickly amended. "But they don't live in Jerusalem."

"Where are they from, then?"

"Leah said she grew up in a large, thriving city," Rhoda replied, crinkling her brow as she attempted to recall the small bits and pieces she had learned in recent weeks. "Somewhere in the region of Cilicia, I think."

"Which city in Cilicia?"

"She didn't say."

"Interesting."

Glancing sideways at him, Rhoda wondered at his tone.

"But her brother is here in Jerusalem, and he doesn't believe?" John Mark reiterated, clearly thinking it over.

"That's right."

"I suppose that could prove dangerous for us."

"Many among us abide with unbelieving family members," Rhoda pointed out, feeling a bit defensive for her new friend.

"That's true," John Mark agreed, acknowledging her argument with a small shrug. "As always, I suppose we must trust God to protect us. The Holy Spirit must have led her here for a reason."

As if sensing their topic of conversation, Leah glanced toward them, a question in her dark eyes.

"Will you please excuse me?" Rhoda asked meekly. "I should see how she's doing."

"By all means," John Mark quipped drolly, though his teasing eyes failed to mask his keen disappointment as he watched her go.

CHAPTER 12

Leah

Jerusalem

Leah was relieved when Rhoda joined her among the group of talking women, her compassionate brown eyes filled with warmth.

"How do you fare this evening, my friend?"

"I am glad to be here," Leah answered honestly, respectfully lowering her tone so she wouldn't interrupt Mary's conversation with the women. "I saw you talking with that young man over there. Who is he?"

"John Mark?" Rhoda asked, blushing in a telltale manner that thoroughly amused the observant Leah. "He lives here. He is my master—Mary's son."

"I see," Leah nodded, her respect for the dashing young man deepening the moment she learned he belonged to Mary's family.

"He was just asking about you, as well," Rhoda smiled. "I can introduce you to him if—"

"What was he asking about me?" Leah asked

abruptly, surprising Rhoda.

"Oh," Rhoda stammered, confused by her reaction. "He simply asked your name. He hasn't had the opportunity to speak with you yet."

"That's all?" Leah asked, attempting to squelch her rising angst. "My name?" It was crucial that *no one* here learned about her family connections. She couldn't bear to be thrown out of fellowship with these wonderful believers! And if they discovered who her brother was, she wouldn't blame them if they never spoke to her again.

"He may have asked about your family," Rhoda ventured slowly, feeling strangely unsettled. "Why?"

"What did you tell him?"

"I told him I thought you were a very courageous young woman, choosing to follow Jesus even when the rest of your family rejected Him."

"Courageous?" Leah sighed, looking away with a hint of bitterness. "I am far from it."

Rhoda simply studied her, perplexed by the girl's suspicion and inner turmoil.

Recognizing her error too late, Leah pursed her lips in frustration. "I was just curious, that's all," she said quickly, deciding she'd best change the subject—and soon. She could only hope she hadn't blundered beyond repair. After all, Rhoda seemed to see the best in everyone despite their circumstances. "John Mark is quite handsome. Are you promised to him?"

"*Promised to him?*" Rhoda gasped, covering her mouth in shock. "Heavens, no!"

"No?" Leah asked, lifting a knowing brow. "It is obvious you have feelings for him. And he, for you."

"I am far too young to be betrothed," Rhoda rushed ahead in a breathless whisper, praying no one was within earshot of their embarrassing dialogue. "Besides, John Mark is the son of the wealthiest woman in Jerusalem. Heaven forbid he marry an orphaned servant girl like me!"

"Why not?" Leah rushed ahead, fascinated by Rhoda's horror. "It would be his honor and privilege to marry a godly young woman like you."

"I wouldn't dare entertain such thoughts!"

"But haven't you?" Leah pressed, her previous anxiety forgotten in their lively debate. "Your eyes light up in his presence."

"It is an honor to serve a godly master."

"Ah, and is that the only reason you blush from head to toe each time he enters the room?"

"Leah, please," Rhoda begged, growing pale. "I would be mortified should anyone overhear this conversation."

"Ah, I understand," Leah nodded solemnly, thankful the attention had been diverted from her own situation. "We needn't discuss it. Even so, he has eyes for you alone. Surely you know that."

"That's...well, that's preposterous," Rhoda argued rather lamely, stunned by Leah's observation. "Like I said, I am far too young to entertain thoughts of betrothal and marriage. It isn't helpful, fitting, or proper at this time."

"No," Leah sadly agreed. "I suppose it isn't." What she wouldn't give to be in Rhoda's position, even if she was only a servant.! If only her overzealous brother shared Rhoda's modest views about marriage! For soon, she would be expected to marry a complete stranger—a man who detested all she held dear.

The troubling thought threatened to snatch the peace she so enjoyed about the Upper Room, so Leah promptly cast it aside. She would worry about it later. Perhaps the Lord would help her strategize a plan against it. But oh, how she wished she could share her dilemma with Rhoda. Even more so, with the wise Mary! Surely the believers would have sound counsel for her. But how could she possibly do so without revealing far more than she intended?

"We should find a place to sit," Rhoda invited, jarring Leah's tumultuous thoughts back to the present moment. "Peter and John are approaching the platform, which means the service is about to begin."

Nodding faintly, Leah followed Rhoda to a bench near the front where Mary often sat with John Mark. She was about to take her seat beside the kind maidservant when a familiar face emerged at the top of the marble stairway across the room. Though the young man appeared enshrouded in far too many layers of heavy clothing, Leah recognized the eyes instantly—dark and searching, burning in intensity.

"I know him," she hissed, grasping Rhoda's slender wrist.

Perplexed, Rhoda turned to study the cloaked figure to whom Leah was referring.

"That man is a *Pharisee*," Leah insisted, her dark eyes flashing indignantly. "He shouldn't be here."

"My lady knows him and speaks with him often," Rhoda quickly assured her, wondering how on earth Leah knew he was a Pharisee. He had an unusual name... What was it? Ag—Aga—Something that began with an *Ag*, but she couldn't recall it. "He isn't a threat to us."

"Every Pharisee in Jerusalem is a threat to us."

"Not *every* one of them," Rhoda quickly reminded her, puzzled yet again by the girl's obvious alarm.

"Many former Pharisees have accepted Jesus as Savior and joined our ranks."

"And has *he*?"

"Not yet," Rhoda answered honestly, her heart going out to the anxious young scholar. "But my lady believes he will, and soon."

Tentatively, Leah lowered herself onto the bench beside Rhoda, carefully adjusting her shawl and head covering. She couldn't risk being recognized by the religious scholar. She had glimpsed that particular Pharisee traversing the Temple's pillared halls often—not to mention, visiting her own brother's house on several occasions! Should he catch a glimpse of her face, would he remember her? She could only hope not.

Releasing a tremorous sigh, she prayed fervently that she would blend in with the sea of modestly covered women taking their places among the long wooden benches.

Despite her rising alarm, she couldn't help but wonder if Saul knew that one of his trusted confidants had begun attending the meetings hosted by his greatest nemesis.

***

Tabitha

Joppa

"What, pray tell, are you up to *now*?"

Busily tidying the reception hall, Tabitha glanced over her shoulder when a befuddled Eli slipped beneath a lavishly curtained entrance, anxiously clutching his writing tablet close to his chest. A few feet away, her little girl, Laurel, played happily with wooden blocks on a plush Persian rug with Tirzah seated comfortably beside her, watching her antics with a fond smile.

"Now, now, Eli," Tirzah spoke up, always ready to playfully taunt the rigid overseer. "You needn't get your little turban in a wad. Tabitha is merely readying the house for the Feast of Dedication."

"The Feast of Dedication…" Eli murmured, his voice trailing off in concern as he clutched his tablet even closer in obvious angst. "Miss Tabitha, you know as well as I that my lord refuses to observe the feast days!"

"So far, yes," Tabitha acknowledged with a rueful smile, hopping off a small step ladder she had utilized to string thick garlands of elegant local greenery on the walls. "But he celebrated them once, years ago. Before tragedy struck and he lost—"

"Ah, ah, ah!" Eli warned her, a rigid forefinger aimed at her in emphasis. "We are forbidden to discuss it."

"And I wouldn't discuss the death of Joram's wife and child with *him* unless he so desired," Tabitha assured Eli. "But my Aunt Penny was a gracious, godly woman. Wouldn't she have desired us to reach her stubborn husband? And how better to stir one's interest in the great God of Heaven than to get lost in the wonder and mystery of His sacred feasts?"

"She did love the feasts and holy days," Eli mused, his eyes somewhat wistful and distant. Quickly recognizing his blunder, he shook himself out of his reverie. "But Lady Peninah is no longer here with us," he announced firmly, clutching nervously at his tablet. "And the master certainly wouldn't wish to make a fuss about any particular day, feast or not. He will be positively furious should we defy him in this way."

"I wouldn't dare defy a direct order, Eli," Tabitha went on with a good-natured smile, stepping back to examine her work. "But Joram hasn't forbidden *me* to celebrate the feasts. Besides, this is the Feast of Dedication. Since this festival is more patriotic than religious in nature, observing it may prove less offensive to Joram."

"That is doubtful..." Eli muttered, wearily massaging his forehead.

Ignoring him, Tabitha swept up an armload of candles, her bright hazel-green eyes assessing the large chamber. "Won't this reception hall look positively radiant filled with blazing candles?"

"Blazing candles?" Eli sputtered, slamming aside his tablet and hurrying to catch up with her as she placed several of varying sizes upon a broad, marble-topped stand near the vestibule leading to the entrance. "The master will not hear of it!"

"And why not?" Tirzah demanded, enjoying their little debate from her place beside young Laurel. "Has he something against candles? Or is it the happiness, camaraderie, and cheer he most detests?"

"Tirzah, please," Eli groaned, peering nervously down the corridor leading toward Joram's office and praying his master wouldn't emerge from the shadows. "You aren't helping."

Tirzah merely grinned, clearly amused by his frantic expression.

"Come now, Eli! Won't it be exciting to celebrate the feast?" Tabitha asked him, as if oblivious to his mounting angst. Moving swiftly, she arranged several more candles atop gilded tables, stands, and shelves, humming softly as she worked.

"Wait!" Pausing mid-step, Eli sniffed the air, his features tightening in dismay. "Is that... Do I smell pastries and sweet fruit preserves?"

"Indeed," Tabitha nodded, smiling broadly. "I've asked Martha to help prepare some customary sweetmeats to usher in the feast."

"For heaven's sake!" Eli moaned, shaking his head in despair.

"Lighten up, Eli," Tirzah teased, helping Laurel build a rather impressive tower with the wooden blocks. "Joram will get over it. Besides, it isn't lawful for Jewish men to flay their servants alive. So you've no cause for concern."

"How comforting."

"Eli," Tabitha explained, pausing amid her preparations to meet his gaze with warmth. "I believe this may be one small way to show my uncle we care. One can learn so much about the God we serve through the feasts He ordained. And though the Feast of Lights came about after the Law was written, there is still much to be discovered about our great God in this celebration. Do you understand?"

"I understand," Eli grumbled, snatching up his tablet and preparing to take his leave. "Even so, I cannot approve."

"And I understand that, too," Tabitha assured him without criticism.

"And when you say we can learn much about *God* by observing feast days, I do hope you aren't referring to your crucified Prophet," he went on disapprovingly, vehemently shaking his head. "You wouldn't wish to make a heretic of your own uncle, would you?"

"Of course not," Tabitha said quickly, drawing a sigh of relief from the harried overseer. "I wish to make him a *believer*."

"Oh, for heaven's sake—"

"You can't speak on this matter, Eli," Tirzah inserted stoutly, drawing a look of annoyance from the turbaned steward. "You haven't even bothered to examine Tabitha's claims about Jesus."

"I wouldn't dare," Eli hissed, lowering his voice in fear. "To do so reeks of blasphemy!"

"Since when is studying the Scriptures considered blasphemy?" Tirzah challenged.

"Since your strange little sect began fabricating claims about a dead Man and contorting the Holy Scriptures to do so!"

Sensing a full-blown argument in the making, Tabitha quickly interrupted the heated discussion. "May I send for you if I need any assistance with the preparations, Eli?" she asked innocently, changing the subject.

"I have no desire to participate in this madness!"

"Suit yourself," Tirzah shot back, receiving a slight look of correction from her friend.

"I do hope you know what you're doing, Miss Tabitha," Eli muttered, fluttering from the room with long robes trailing like the feathers of an agitated bird. "I, for one, don't wish to be involved."

"Don't look at me like that," Tirzah grumped once Eli had fled the scene. "How can I hold my tongue when Eli acts all pompous and conceited?"

"He isn't pompous, nor conceited," Tabitha assured her, turning to retrieve more garlands she had draped over an elegant, upholstered couch. "He is devoted to the religion of his fathers, that's all. And he is afraid."

"Afraid of what?"

"Afraid he may offend the God he's served faithfully all his life."

"By accepting His *Son*?" Tirzah gaped, annoyed.

"You know as well as I how the religious leaders instruct our people—they swear God has no son but Israel," Tabitha reminded her. "They saw Jesus as an ordinary man. His claims of divinity both shocked and outraged them."

"But Eli places his trust in the pompous old men at the synagogue rather than God," Tirzah pointed out. "He must seek the Scriptures rather than the sages if he intends to discover the truth."

"And we must pray for that continually," Tabitha said softly, longing for the nervous steward to find his salvation in Christ. "The Holy Spirit will continue to woo him. Eventually, he will see the truth. I believe that."

"How can you be so sure?"

"*You* did, didn't you?" Tabitha grinned, placing the last candle on a table.

Knock, knock, knock!

"Now who could that be?" Tirzah mused aloud, exchanging a look of surprise with Tabitha as several unexpected raps on the door rang through the reception hall.

"The sentry must have permitted a guest to enter the outer court," Tabitha supplied, confused. The guard posted at the gate was nearly as crotchety and uninviting as his master, Joram. Tabitha supposed whoever had managed to gain entrance must have proven persuasive indeed!

"Well, I suppose I'd best answer that," Tabitha decided, as Eli had vanished from sight and was most likely in hiding. "Will you wait with Laurel, Tirzah?"

"Of course."

Slipping into the elegantly frescoed vestibule, Tabitha reached for the broad handles of imposing double doors. Pulling them open with a bit of effort, her jaw dropped in utter shock at the sight meeting her wide, hazel-green eyes.

"Philip?" she gasped, her heart nearly stopping at the sight of her late-husband's closest friend and partner in ministry.

"Greetings, dear sister!" the young evangelist beamed, arms outstretched, the sunlight streaming into the outer court bathing his frame in an almost heavenly light. "Praise our gracious Father that we meet again!"

CHAPTER 13

Agabus

Jerusalem

Trembling deep inside, Agabus drew a calming breath as he stood upon the impressive threshold of a man he had once deeply respected.

A man he had now come to fear.

A stone-faced manservant met him at the door, ushering him into a darkened vestibule, dimly lit by smoldering hanging lamps. "This way," the servant said tersely, his obsidian eyes flickering slightly.

Agabus wished he could read the burly servant's thoughts. Something about his sober manner was disquieting, to say the least. Did the servant expect to witness the demise of an indecisive young Pharisee at the iron fist of his master?

Following the simply clad manservant down a dark, pillared corridor, Agabus drew another breath, this one even more tremorous than the first. Silently, he tried to prepare himself for what might lie ahead. But how was one to do so when they hadn't the slightest idea what dangers they faced?

Even so, he was quite certain his defection had been discovered. Someone had ratted him out, he had no doubt. And the consequences would prove severe, indeed. Possibly even fatal.

With a swift nod, the manservant paused at a wide stone entryway, indicating the room his guest should enter, before vanishing down the torchlit labyrinth of halls by which they had come.

Sending an emergency prayer heavenward, Agabus stepped into the dimly lit office as one might enter a dragon's den. Every nerve ending afire with caution, he quickly assessed the darkened chamber.

Saul of Tarsus was seated behind his desk, his shadowy silhouette eerily reminiscent of a bird of prey perched upon a rocky ledge, his chiseled profile barely discernible in the dimly lit chamber. Lifting his bearded chin, the Pharisee met Agabus' gaze with the cunning eyes of a predator.

Agabus caught his breath at the sight. He couldn't move. He couldn't speak. Ridiculously grateful for the flowing tallith masking the growing beads of sweat upon his brow, he steeled himself against the death sentence that was sure to come.

"You must be wondering why I summoned you here at this late hour," Saul mused in his characteristically deep voice, stroking his neatly cropped beard in a manner somewhat akin to that of his former mentor, Gamaliel, the most respected member of the Great Sanhedrin.

Inwardly cursing his own cowardice, Agabus merely nodded, unable to form words of response.

"Come," Saul gestured impatiently, failing to set

the younger student at ease. "Be seated."

Crossing the room on wooden legs, Agabus slowly lowered himself onto one of the upholstered chairs facing Saul's massive desk, gripping the gilded arms like a lifeline. Fortunately, the gathering darkness sheltered his white knuckled grasp.

"I summoned you," Saul continued, his tone bordering upon dramatic, "because I have news that might prove of great interest to you."

"News?" Breathing a sigh of relief, Agabus tried to remember he wasn't out of the woods yet. Saul was a crafty one, and he mustn't lower his guard.

"Indeed," Saul responded with a dip of his elaborately covered head. "I have been granted permission to change the world, Agabus. To right every wrong that wretched, self-proclaimed Prophet inflicted upon our nation and our people."

"Sir?" Agabus blinked, perplexed, though he needn't ask of which Prophet the Pharisee spoke.

"As you know, the detestable sect called the Way is spreading like a foul, contagious disease, sinking its talons into outlying regions and beyond," Saul explained, his eyes glowing with a deep-seated hatred that unsettled Agabus to the core. "And like any cancerous tumor, this sect must be cut out. Utterly obliterated."

Agabus could only stare, barely breathing, his grip tightening on the arms of his chair.

"But the Lord has not forsaken me, for I will triumph over these foes," Saul murmured, and Agabus found it rather difficult to reconcile the just and loving God of Heaven with this Pharisee's murderous reputation. "I have obtained permission to marshal an entourage to track down believers outside of

Jerusalem. Together, we will drag them back to the city in chains to be sentenced to their doom."

His insides growing cold, Agabus wondered if he looked as pale as he felt.

"We must demonstrate force to the highest degree, Agabus," Saul declared, his fist pounding the desk for greater emphasis. "We mustn't harbor the slightest shred of tolerance toward this poisonous sect, none whatsoever. And I have made it my aim to ensure that these wretched, so-called *believers* will never be safe again—not here, not anywhere else. I have obtained permission from the high priest to launch my first attack upon believers in Damascus."

Instinctively, Agabus knew he must find Mary. The church must be warned of Saul's dangerous plans, and fast! He could scarcely believe Saul had actually obtained permission to use force beyond the holy city. Frankly, he hadn't expected the Pharisee to receive such approval.

"I shall depart immediately after the Feast of Dedication," Saul was saying, drawing Agabus' thoughts back to the disturbing conversation. "And you, Agabus, shall join me."

Join me? Saul's words struck him like a punch in the gut. Straightening in his chair, Agabus frantically resisted the panic rising in his chest. How could he—a pacifying, peace-loving man by nature—possibly assist Saul in this bloodthirsty, godforsaken mission? Not only that, but he had grown to respect the believers in Jerusalem. They were kind, charitable, honorable people. Worse—even with all his scholarly knowledge and religious upbringing, he couldn't *prove* that they were wrong about Jesus, their Messiah.

How could he possibly come against their brothers and sisters with a clear conscience?

"Agabus?" Saul commanded, his smoldering eyes pinning the anxious young man in place. "Say something!"

"You...you wish for *me* to join you?" Agabus managed, his voice sounding high-pitched in his own ears.

"That *is* what I said, isn't it?" Saul smirked, folding well-shaped hands atop his desk. The powerful hands of a brawler, not the gentle hands of a holy man.

"But..." Agabus protested, still flabbergasted by the suggestion. "But...*me*? Why me?"

"Do you object?" Saul demanded, his dark eyes narrowing in sudden suspicion. "I chose you—along with several brilliant scholars—to accompany me because you show unusual promise in your studies and your understanding of the Torah, among other sacred texts. You will do well, Agabus, and you will rise in position and standing—*if* you follow the right leader. Follow *me*, and I assure you, you won't regret your decision."

Follow Me. Recalling the famous invitation of a humble Galilean Carpenter, Agabus was further unsettled by Saul's offer. The eyes of the Carpenter had conveyed warmth and light, peace and promise. And yet the eyes of the cloaked Pharisee before him kindled with darkness, hatred, and animosity. Shifting uncomfortably in his chair, Agabus swallowed hard, wondering how in the world to respond without invoking his own death sentence.

"Well?" Saul demanded angrily, his impatience flaring. "Your floundering indecision does not become you! I am offering you the world. What more can I give? What is it that you *want*, Agabus?"

Gazing into the flaming eyes of the church's most notorious enemy, Agabus realized this was, indeed, a test. Perhaps Saul had sensed his faltering faith, his mounting interest in the Way. Perhaps his very life depended upon his willingness to accompany Saul on this mission.

"Well?" Saul bellowed, throwing himself to his feet and nearly sending his throne-like chair toppling behind him. "What do you want?"

Tears stinging his eyes, Agabus lowered his head. "I want the will of God," he whispered, and he meant it. Wholeheartedly. But was he too anxious, too fainthearted, to embrace it?

"Good," Saul breathed, folding powerful arms over his chest as he towered over the frightened young Pharisee. "Then we want the same thing."

Agabus lifted his head, stunned. Surely Saul didn't believe that. Did he?

"If it's the will of God you seek, then you shall accompany me on this journey to Damascus."

"And if I decline?" Agabus dared, drawing upon the faint flicker of courage kindling in his chest.

"Ah, I'm afraid you have no choice in the matter," Saul informed him, his eyes glowing with wicked satisfaction. "You see, I have here paperwork from the desk of the great Caiaphas himself. He, too, agreed with the list of colleagues I have compiled to accompany me on this journey." Thrusting the parchment across the desk, Saul waved it before him, tempting him to take it.

Trembling, Agabus reached across the desk, tentatively accepting the parchment documentation.

Eyes quickly scanning the contents, he saw his name in bold script, along with those ordered to accompany the zealous Pharisee upon his death mission to uproot the church of God.

The bold seal of the malevolent high priest was unmistakable.

His entire being growing cold as stone, Agabus lifted his gaze toward Saul, who stood watching him with grim amusement. Snatching the papers away from him, Saul rolled them back up and placed them upon his desk with a slow smile of triumph.

"Damascus is only the beginning," he said, the lamplight casting writhing shadows across his hardened jawline. "First, Jerusalem. Then, Damascus. And soon, all the world."

Agabus could only stare, his stomach churning like the waves of a deep and troubled sea.

"This, my cowardly friend, is only the beginning," Saul announced coldly, crossing the room to pause before an elegantly latticed window. Silver moonlight poured through the graceful latticework, bathing his features in a disturbing otherworldly glow. "I shall be the one to end this madness. *I* shall become the man responsible for the extinction of the wretched Way. And it's only a matter of time."

CHAPTER 14

Kelila

Sychar

The twenty-fifth day of the long-awaited month of Kislev dawned cold and clear, with slate gray skies and a brisk though not unpleasant breeze.

It felt odd, awakening to the Jewish Feast of Lights as if to any other day. The small house on Sychar's main thoroughfare remained eerily dim and still even as the sun came up. There were no cheerfully burning candles to announce the commencement of the holiday, no festive lamps gracing the walls and windowsills. The warm and cozy fragrance of fresh bread and tantalizing baked goods remained glaringly absent. Neither did the frenzied scampering of tiny feet meet Kelila's ears as it had in the home of her sister, Candace, when her small nephews had giggled and shouted out their glee even before sunup, noisily alerting their parents to dawn's impending arrival.

Attempting to shrug off her swelling disappointment, Kelila rose laboriously from her sleeping pallet, cradling her bulging belly.

At least I have you to keep me company, little one, she thought, aching all over for her still-absent husband. How many weeks had he been gone, anyway? She was beginning to wonder if she would ever see the man again!

Now, don't be unfair about this, she chided herself inwardly, crossing the narrow guest room to a small stand housing a pitcher, basin, and washrag. Delicately cleansing her face and hands, she tried to remind herself that Philip's long absence was no choice of his own. He was merely carrying out the calling of a traveling evangelist, in obedience to God. She should be proud of him, not peeved.

Which was far easier said than done, especially on a dreary winter day in the heart of Samaria when one was forced to ignore the festivities and cheer of a very special holiday, one near and dear to her heart.

Sighing, she dressed as quickly as her added "cargo" would allow, reminding herself it was far more important to deny oneself the pleasures of a holiday than to cause hurt or offense. The Feast of Lights commemorated the purging of the Temple in Jerusalem—a place Samaritans were strictly forbidden to go. It would be rude and unseemly to mention the feast to them.

At least I have plenty to keep me busy today, she thought rather glumly. She had promised to spend the day assisting an elderly, infirm couple on the outskirts of town. She always enjoyed the old woman's lively chatter and her husband's silent annoyance. *Perhaps on the way home, I'll visit the young widow whose four children have recently suffered miserable colds.* If the young woman allowed, she would prepare some warm broth for the weakened children, allowing the mother a moment of much-needed rest.

After combing and smoothing her cascading ebony tresses, Kelila reached for her warmest shawl. She would swallow a quick breakfast of gruel before bidding Adorina farewell and departing for the day.

***

Mary

Jerusalem

"My lady, I must speak with you. It is urgent."

Turning on the balcony in surprise, Mary found herself face to face with a nearly distraught Agabus.

"Agabus, my friend," she said in greeting, exchanging looks of concern with her older brother, Barnabas. It was a delight to have him with her to lead the upcoming prayer service ushering in the Feast of Dedication. The entire house was ablaze with shining candles in readiness for the feast at sunset. Even the balcony upon which they stood was draped with festive greenery and boasted tall standing lamps already ablaze with light. She hoped Agabus didn't bear ill tidings which would mar their joy nor the excitement of the believers eager to hear about Barnabas' recent travels and the progress of new churches in outlying regions. "You have arrived early—what a lovely surprise! Now what has transpired to render your countenance so?"

"Good evening, Barnabas," Agabus added quickly, almost an afterthought. "I am glad you're here. You should know, too."

"Know what, my troubled brother?" Barnabas asked cheerfully, reaching out to steady the anxious young man. "What has happened?"

"I have word…" Agabus managed, the waning sunlight casting his features in tragic shadow. "Word about… about Saul of Tarsus."

"Ah," Barnabas acknowledged, his tone concealing any true concerns. "And what is our misguided brother up to these days?"

"Even more mischief, I'm afraid," Agabus conceded, nervously wringing his hands as he spoke. Lowering his gaze, he felt the intensity of Mary's eyes upon him. "I regret to say he has accomplished what he set out to do. He has obtained permission from the high priest to uproot the churches in outlying regions. He plans to depart for Damascus after the feast, intending to raid the local church and drag the believers back in chains."

Exchanging a distressed look with her brother, Mary reached for the railing to steady herself.

"I'm stunned the high priest has granted this request," Barnabas said frankly, shaking his head in sadness.

"And I, as well," Agabus admitted, his dark eyes bleak.

"You have previously shared concerns about this," Mary sighed, her gray eyes troubled. "I have prayed long and hard against it. And yet, God has seen fit to permit it. There must be a reason."

"What possible good can come from this?" Agabus stared at her, incredulous. "Saul's rampage in

Damascus may provide some temporary relief for the believers here in Jerusalem during his absence. But ultimately, he has been granted permission to terrorize the church on a far greater scale. Other cities will be targeted. Damascus is only the beginning—he said so himself."

"Someone must warn the believers in Damascus," Mary spoke up, concerned for her unsuspecting brothers and sisters in the Syrian province. "Barnabas, what can we do—"

"I will set out at dawn," he promised her, squeezing her hand. "I can warn the believers there of Saul's upcoming arrival."

"But, Barnabas," she protested. "If you are in Damascus when Saul arrives to *capture* believers—"

"God will protect me," he reminded her, amused by the look of utter shock on the face of the young Pharisee beside him.

"And if you are arrested?"

"Then God will sustain me."

"Oh, Barnabas."

"I can stay with my good friend, Ananias. He is a committed follower of Christ and will gladly welcome a visit from me, along with news about the church here in Jerusalem."

"I find it unlikely he will welcome the tidings you shall bring this time," Agabus muttered, feeling self-conscious in the face of Barnabas' unwavering courage.

"When will Saul depart?" Mary asked him, mentally calculating a plan of action. "You said after the feast."

"Ten days hence."

"Then if you leave for Damascus at dawn, Barnabas, you shall have plenty of time to warn the believers there." Mary sighed, secretly wishing someone other than her brother was carrying out the dangerous mission. Even so, she knew the Lord would go before her brother, paving the way.

"There is something else," Agabus confessed, his dark eyes welling with regret and apprehension.

"What is it?" Mary asked, steeling herself for another unexpected blow.

"I have been ordered to accompany Saul on the road to Damascus."

"You?" Mary stared at Agabus in disbelief. "But why?"

"Perhaps it is a test," Agabus sighed, staring down at his own nervously shuffling feet. "Perhaps he senses my interest in the Way."

"I see," Mary nodded, exchanging knowing looks with her brother. "And this is Saul's way of testing your loyalty, yes?"

"I imagine so."

"And what will you do?"

"I cannot disregard a direct order from the high priest, Mary," Agabus hissed, deeply troubled.

"This could prove dangerous for you, Agabus."

"Trust me, I know."

"We shall pray for you without ceasing," Mary told him, graciously overlooking his vacillating courage. "For your safety, but most importantly, for your soul. May Jesus reveal Himself to you as Messiah in an unmistakable way, Agabus. May you be staggered by His power and driven to your knees. For this, I shall constantly pray."

Blinking in surprise, Agabus swallowed hard. Her words proved a bit unsettling, as he wasn't entirely sure he wished to be driven to his knees. Even so, he found solace in her great faith, somehow.

He could only hope she had enough for both of them.

CHAPTER 15

Kelila

Sychar

The sun was setting like a smoldering ball of flame, casting slate-colored shadows upon the gently rolling Samaritan hills, as Kelila listlessly traveled the main thoroughfare toward the humble house of her gracious host and hostess. Overhead, heavy gray cloud cover attempted to obscure the sun's final rays, rendering the early evening gloomy and dim. The chill breeze rustling through the streets whipped at Kelila's shawl in the most pestilent way, tempting her toward irritation.

It had been a long, wearying day, though she felt good about the assistance she had provided for the elderly couple, the young widow, and her children. The Lord had supplied ample opportunities to serve today, for which she was grateful.

Slipping past the creaking gate and entering Adorina's verdant outer court, Kelila attempted to shake the homesickness still vying for her attention. She couldn't help but wonder how her sister, Candace, was ushering in the Feast of Lights with her delightful young family. There was surely much joy, laughter, and merriment involved, not to mention a delectable feast spread upon the brightly lit table as tantalizing baked goods turned golden in her trusty clay oven.

Speaking of baked goods... Crinkling her nose, Kelila wondered at the utterly delightful aroma wafting upon the wintry breeze. Perhaps she was merely desperate, but she was almost certain she smelled pastries stuffed with sweet fruit preserves.

And then the door swung open before her as cheerful light spilled into the outer court, emanating brightly from within the house and showcasing Adorina's tall, slender silhouette upon the threshold.

"Welcome to the commencement of the Feast of Lights, dear sister!" Adorina smiled, ushering her inside with a broad sweep of her arm.

Stunned beyond belief, Kelila's mouth dropped open as she was drawn inside by eager hands and surrounded by dozens of their dearest friends and fellow Samaritan believers. With enthusiasm, giggling children threw open the shutters, allowing the light of the house to spill into the outer court and the dusty streets. The cheery atmosphere was aflame with brightly burning light, and centered upon the feast-laden table was an elegantly wrought menorah waiting to be lit.

"Greetings, dear sister," Ephraim boomed, draping an arm around his beaming wife's shoulders. Gazing heavenward, he recited for all to hear, "Gracious God, *we thank You for the miracles, for the re-*

demption, for the mighty deeds, for the saving acts, and for the wonders which You have wrought for our ancestors in those days, at this time." Beaming toward those crowded in his house, his gaze came to rest warmly upon Kelila. "Did I say it correctly?"

Recognizing the familiar words oft recited during the feast, Kelila could only nod through her stream of happy tears. "Yes!" She laughed, shaking her head in amazement. "Yes, you did!"

"I learned many profound and wise words reserved for this special celebration," Ephraim went on, and the attention of every Samaritan crammed into the packed little house came to rest expectantly upon him. "But the words that most affected me were these: *You made a great and holy name for Yourself in Your world, and effected a great deliverance and redemption for Your people Israel to this very day.* Brothers and sisters, these words were indeed fulfilled by the arrival of Jesus Christ, the true Light of the world! What a joy it is to celebrate the marvels He has wrought, the great name He has established for Himself upon the earth, and the deliverance and redemption His shed blood has provided once and for all."

"This is lovely, truly lovely," Kelila breathed, her tear-filled eyes traveling over the sea of warm faces, the feast spread upon the table, and the brightly burning candles gracing the entire house. "But I thought Samaritans didn't celebrate the Feast of Lights?"

"Neither do Jews associate with Samaritans," Adorina pointed out. "And yet, that didn't stop you and Philip."

Cradling the growing child in her womb, Kelila

struggled against tears of gratitude...toward her faithful God, and toward these precious people to whom she had been called.

"This is but a small way in which we can say *thank you*," Adorina explained, stepping forward and taking Kelila's hands in hers. "Thank you, Kelila, for breaking down the barriers between Samaritan and Jew. Thank you for the love and service you have so graciously provided from the moment you arrived. And no matter where the Lord may lead you, you will always be in our hearts."

Blinking back tears, Kelila wondered if it was possible for one to feel any more blessed than she.

***

Painstakingly, Kelila lowered herself onto her straw pallet, utterly exhausted but glowing with happiness. Smiling dreamily, she leaned her back against the wall, fondly cradling her bulging baby bump.

She couldn't imagine a more perfect night. Celebrating the Feast of Lights with her dear Samaritan friends had proven far more special than she could have imagined. She couldn't believe they had surprised her so. She certainly hadn't expected half the village to be crammed into Ephraim's tiny house, awaiting her return! The kindness and warmth of these wonderful people filled her heart with gratitude, her eyes with tears of thanksgiving.

Oh, Lord, how blessed I am! Thank You, Lord. Thank You for leading me to these dear, sweet people!

"Kelila? May we speak with you a moment?"

Glancing up in surprise, Kelila saw Adorina

and Ephraim emerging from the narrow doorway. Something about their manner and expressions sent off warning bells in her mind—not to mention the fact that they were both joining her in her own private quarters far past the usual time to retire.

"Ephraim, Adorina," Kelila beamed, bolstering her brightest smile despite her unease. She certainly didn't wish to appear ungrateful. "I cannot thank you enough for this night. I was touched beyond words."

Exchanging slightly pained expressions, husband and wife acknowledged her thanks with gracious smiles. Settling next to Kelila on her pallet, Adorina touched her shoulder in appreciation as Ephraim dragged a wooden stool a bit closer and sat down, a parchment letter in hand.

Instantly suspicious, Kelila's eyes came to rest upon the telltale letter. "What is that?"

"We thought it best to share this news *after* the celebration," Adorina explained softly, squeezing her hand in a motherly fashion. "We have received word from Philip."

"Oh?" Kelila asked, her delicate brows lifting in surprise. Peeved, she couldn't help but wonder why Philip had written *them* rather than *her*! But then she saw their troubled expressions, her heart dropping in the most unpleasant manner. "What is it? Is he all right?"

"Oh, he's fine," Adorina promptly assured her, sensing her alarm. "Philip is doing well."

Apparently not well enough to inform *her* directly! Attempting to dismiss her annoyance, Kelila asked pointedly, "Is he coming home?"

Adorina looked to her husband, her eyes glittering with a faint sheen of tears.

Kelila's pounding heart dropped even further in her chest.

"Kelila," Ephraim said gently, his eyes encouraging his wife to be strong. "Philip wrote to us because he didn't wish for you to be caught off guard by an abrupt change in plans."

"Change in plans?"

"The Lord has guided Philip's steps throughout his travels. He has ministered in many Samaritan cities. In this letter, he describes an incredible encounter with a powerful Ethiopian eunuch on the road from Jerusalem to Gaza. Apparently, the man possesses great authority, working directly for the Ethiopian queen. Ironically, her name is Candace. Isn't that your sister's name, as well?"

"It is," Kelila acknowledged with a hint of suspicion, wondering if Ephraim was attempting to distract her from troubles at hand.

"Apparently, the eunuch was struggling to understand a Messianic prophecy in the scroll of Isaiah," Ephraim explained. "By God's grace, Philip preached the message of salvation and the man believed. He was baptized on the road, right then and there."

Kelila knew she should be ecstatic about the salvation of a lost soul—not to mention the fact that the Ethiopian would surely carry the gospel back to his homeland—and yet she was so anxious about the contents of Philip's letter she could scarcely comprehend the victory.

Sensing her anxiety, Ephraim decided to get straight to the point. "Kelila," he said gently, carefully. "Philip has requested you join him in Joppa. Right away."

"Joppa?" she repeated incredulously. "Why?"

"Only the Lord knows, I imagine," Ephraim supplied with annoying logic. "But to Joppa you must go. And soon."

"But when will we return to Sychar?" Kelila asked, sensing Adorina's sharp intake of breath beside her. "Surely Philip is eager to return home!"

"I'm afraid your work in Sychar has drawn to a close, Kelila," Ephraim said, his features etched with sorrow. "But Philip promises you shall return to visit us. Often."

Your work in Sychar has drawn to a close. Thankful she was sitting down, Kelila bowed her head, warm tears dropping on her lap. *Oh God,* her heart cried, riddled with pain. *You led us here. I learned to love it here. Why must we leave? Why?*

"I know this must be hard for you," Ephraim sympathized, his kind eyes welling with sorrow. "It's hard for us, too. We love you and Philip like family."

"And we *are* family," Adorina put in firmly, taking Kelila's arm. "We will always be family, even when miles apart."

Nodding her bowed head, Kelila fought for composure. She didn't wish to make a fool of herself before these staunch heroes of faith, and yet… yet her heart was crushed. How could she bear to leave this place? These precious people?

Amidst her shock, it suddenly occurred to her that Adorina—her dear friend and sister in Christ— wouldn't be there when her child was born, wouldn't hold the newborn baby in her arms. The sobs overtook her then, threatening to overcome her.

Oh, the price of obedience! The cost of carrying one's cross wasn't cheap.

But it's worth it, she reminded herself, despite her gnawing pain. *It is worth it, isn't it, Lord?*

"Be strong in the Lord, dear sister," Ephraim exhorted her, rolling up the letter and placing it in the folds of his robe. "He will go before you. He will pave the way."

Accepting Adorina's teary embrace, Kelila had no doubt the Lord would pave the way.

But could He ease the pain gripping her heart?

Long after Adorina and Ephraim had turned in for the night, Kelila lay awake, blinking back stinging tears and begging God for strength. And somehow, the peace of God enveloped her like a warm blanket, promising hope. Joy. Eternity.

Dragging in a calming breath, Kelila made up her mind. She would not resist the will of God, not this time. Hadn't she learned her lesson by now? Hadn't she learned that God knew best?

Sweet Jesus, You left Heaven for me, she prayed, rolling onto her side and gazing out the latticed window as silver moonlight streamed within, bathing her face in light. *Knowing this, surely I can leave this place for You.*

CHAPTER 16

Tabitha

Joppa

"Absolutely not! This is outrageous!"

Resisting the urge to cringe when Joram's closed fist slammed hard upon his desk, Tabitha bit her lower lip, casting a look of apology toward Tirzah and Philip. The three stood before Joram's massive office desk long after sunset, having requested an audience with him via the ever-reluctant Eli. Clearly, Joram hadn't been in any hurry to see them. Now, as Tabitha observed her uncle's red-faced reaction, she wondered if she had made a terrible blunder by approaching him. It seemed just about everything she said or did infuriated her irritable relative, despite her constant overtures of kindness and mercy.

"Forgive me if my request has caused you undue frustration, my lord," Tabitha said, striving for calm. "But Philip has traveled a very long way. Last night, he slept in a makeshift tent outside—"

"That is no concern of mine!"

"And he is in desperate need of lodging," she finished calmly, meeting his steely gaze with clear, unperturbed eyes. "The hour is already late, and Philip is a dear friend. Though he stubbornly insisted upon making his own camp rather than trouble you, I must humbly ask your permission to offer him one of your empty suites during his stay. It disturbs me for him to be sleeping outdoors in a city foreign to him."

"This is a private home, not a public inn!" Joram stormed, measuring the mild-mannered evangelist with a hint of discomfiture. "And I certainly do not recall granting you permission to receive an out-of-town guest!" he added, glaring pointedly at his niece.

"Tabitha had no knowledge of my coming," Philip interjected in his kind, easy manner, his tranquil smile clearly unsettling the old man. "Please forgive my intrusion, my lord. I shall willingly locate accommodations elsewhere."

"The lodging in these parts caters to crass, seafaring men—gamblers, drunkards, and the like," Tirzah interrupted with a cool look of accusation reserved for Joram. "I wouldn't wish that upon any guest of mine!"

"Well, then, you'd best be glad he isn't a guest of yours," Joram seethed, visibly annoyed.

Attempting to curb her impatience, Tabitha mentally scrambled for a solution. The thought of a hardworking evangelist sleeping on the hard ground after weeks of difficult travel was unthinkable!

"As previously mentioned, I am perfectly capable of setting up my own camp," Philip assured them cheerfully, receiving looks of disappointment from the women and one of disbelief from Joram. "Thank you, nonetheless, sir. I appreciate your time. I'll be on my way."

"That truly isn't necessary," Tirzah huffed, her hospitable nature crying out against the injustice and shattering Joram's short-lived sense of relief. "Any friend of Tabitha's is a friend of mine and thus, I count you as a friend, Philip. And though I recognize it would be inappropriate for you to lodge with me at this time, you may stay in my home once your wife joins you here in Joppa. I have plenty of room for both of you."

"We wouldn't wish to impose, Tirzah—"

"It's no imposition," Tirzah insisted stoutly, receiving a look of relief from Tabitha. "I insist. In fact, you can stay there *now*," she added, her tone boding no argument. "It's late, and you needn't struggle to make camp in the dark of night. I shall stay here with Tabitha until your wife arrives—"

"Oh no, you won't!" Joram declared, his red face contorting in keen displeasure. "I will *not* have a meddlesome potter woman constantly underfoot! You won't be sleeping under my roof!"

"Tabitha serves you in exchange for her room and board," Tirzah huffed, unintimidated by Joram's tirade. "Thus, whomever she welcomes into that miserable little hole you've provided is entirely up to her!"

"I will not have you invading my peace all the night long," Joram snapped in mounting perturbation. "Is it not enough I must put up with you all throughout the day? Even now, my house is aflame with candles I did not order nor approve, and that for a foolish feast I do not observe!"

Crossing her arms, Tirzah offered him a smug little smile in response.

"*Fine*," Joram growled, lowering himself onto his chair and snatching up an elegant stylus. Annoyed by Tirzah's suggestion, he tapped it on the desk in agitation. "The evangelist can stay, but only until his wife joins him. *Then* I expect him to relocate to your miserable little hut, Tirzah, the moment his wife arrives."

"Thank you kindly, your graciousness," Tirzah responded with a sarcastic little curtsy.

Exchanging a knowing look with Philip, Tabitha hid her smile at the lively young widow's spunk. It would seem she had succeeded in outsmarting the irritable Joram once again.!

"Truly, thank you, my lord, from the bottom of my heart," Tabitha quickly amended, her expression warning Tirzah against further antics. "I am honored by your willingness to help us."

"And I, as well," Philip put in with great feeling. Extending his hand across the desk, he smiled broadly at the irritable businessman. "Thank you, sir, for your hospitality."

Ignoring the kind gesture, Joram lifted a stack of parchment paperwork from his desk, shuffling through it in obvious dismissal. "Now go. All of you," he ordered, his lips twisting in derision. "Leave me here in peace."

***

Kelila

Sychar

Nearly the entire village gathered in the main square to see Kelila off, wearing broad smiles despite the tears glistening in many of their eyes. All were happy to see her carrying on the Lord's work, though they assured her they would miss her and Philip. Desperately.

"Be strong in the Lord, every single one of you," Kelila exhorted them, mustering up her bravest smile. Standing just beyond the beloved little market stall—a place she once despised but had grown to cherish—she hoisted her pack a bit higher on her back, her dark eyes traveling over the sea of dear, shining faces before her. "Though Philip couldn't be here today, he beseeched us to extend his heartfelt greetings to all of you. And he promises we shall visit you again as soon as the Lord permits."

Cheers of excitement and approval rippled through the crowd as the women and children hurried toward her, surrounding her, anxious for final embraces. Wrapping her arms around those who clustered about her, Kelila resisted the tears burning her eyes. She would be brave for these kind, hospitable people, determined to lavish them with hope and promise rather than sadness.

"All right, everyone," Ephraim announced, shouting above the din. "We'd best allow our dear sister to depart. She is losing hours of precious daylight, and her husband anxiously awaits her arrival in Joppa."

As Ephraim and Adorina drew before her, Kelila took the hands of her dearest friend—a woman who would undoubtedly be remembered throughout the pages of history. But to her, she would always be a sister, a friend, a confidante. "I shall never forget the moment we met," Kelila said, laughing through her tears.

"There at the well," Adorina smiled, shaking her

head in amusement. "Both of us wondering what on earth to do next. And yet the Lord had it planned all along."

"As He always does," Kelila murmured, reminding herself as much as anyone else.

"Even now," Ephraim assured her, giving his wife's shoulder a gentle squeeze. "God has great things in store for you and Philip."

"And for you," Kelila reminded him. "And for this village. Philip has appointed you to oversee this precious little flock, Ephraim." Swallowing hard, Kelila entrusted these dear people into the hands of God—and this capable, steadfast leader. "I couldn't imagine a worthier man for the job."

"I can only thank God that Philip has enough faith in me for the both of us," Ephraim admitted ruefully, drawing a smile from both women. "But God will guide this church. He has from the very beginning."

"Indeed." Adorina nodded her agreement.

"Thank you for arranging a safe group for me to travel along with," Kelila said with great feeling. A few paces away, a donkey brayed impatiently, reminding her she had little time left in Sychar.

"It's the least I can do," Ephraim told her. "You and Philip have done so much for us."

"Only by God's grace, I assure you." Kelila laughed, remembering her doubts, hesitation, and downright defiance upon their arrival in Samaria. "Thank Him for His abundant mercy!"

When Adorina gathered her in motherly arms, Kelila held her back, resisting stubborn tears. "I will pray for you every day," she promised.

"And I, for you."

"Don't forget to send me letters!"

"And you, as well!"

"God be with you," Ephraim told her firmly, drawing his trembling wife close.

With one last look upon the sea of Samaritan faces she had learned to love like family, Kelila adjusted the pack on her back and turned to join the entourage of merchants and families waiting to depart, their beasts of burden saddled and prancing about impatiently, eager to be off.

Oh, God, be with them! she cried inwardly, her heart breaking in her chest. *Bind our hearts together even when we are apart. Nothing can separate us from Your love, nor the love You have granted us for each other.*

Gracious Father, help us to remember that.

***

Mary

Jerusalem

"A burden must weigh heavily upon your heart to prompt a visit at this late hour on the eve of your departure."

Turning cautiously, Agabus faced the enigmatic widow standing before him, a lamp in her hand, her waist-length brown hair tied in a simple braid and partially masked by a sheer, pale blue shawl. Even in the darkest hours of night, she appeared poised, graceful, lovely. At peace.

What he wouldn't give for even the smallest portion, the faintest whisper, of that perfect peace!

Frankly, it was maddening—the unshakable tranquility of Mary and her hunted sect. Didn't they recognize the danger they faced? Hadn't they the slightest fear of death? Torture? Life imprisonment?

And yet, he—bordering wealthy, successful, secure in his coveted position—battled a constant state of anxiety and depression. It was as if he sunk deeper and deeper into a miry pit of fear and uncertainty with every passing day.

With an anxious sweep of his surroundings, Agabus noted the vacant benches of an empty Upper Room. Mounted candles and hanging lamps burned faintly, vaguely lighting the vast chamber. Despite the deepening shadows and absence of graciously smiling believers, Agabus noted the peace about the room—as if the fervent prayers of the saints had somehow consecrated or hallowed the meeting space. Each time he stood within these walls, he was aware of a keen though unsettling sense of *belonging*, a burning desire to *stay*. To abide with these earnest, kindhearted people. To inquire about the crucified Savior whom they sought to imitate in thought, word, and deed.

And yet, the consequences of such an action frightened him to his very core.

"Have you come in search of truth?" Mary asked him, shaking Agabus from his disturbing reverie.

"I have come in search of…help," Agabus admitted hoarsely, his dark eyes welling with apprehension.

"Our help comes from the Lord."

"The Lord," Agabus repeated dully, crossing his arms behind his back. "And if Jesus is Lord?"

"Then you must confess it," Mary told him without missing a beat. "You must believe, repent, and walk in the Way."

"And yet, here I am, sent to accompany Saul to destroy those who embrace that very doctrine—upon the morrow."

"It's not too late to recant, to turn."

"And what of my life, then? I shall be put to death without question."

"And welcomed into life everlasting."

"You sound so...so *certain*!" Agabus groaned, balling his hand into a desperate fist. "But how can you know, Mary? How can you be so sure? What if I embrace this Messiah of yours, only to be put to death? If you are wrong, I shall be judged most harshly by the God of our Fathers for dabbling in forbidden doctrine!"

"And if I am right?"

"If you are right..." Agabus shook his head, followed by a long, dismal pause. "If you are right, then I am doomed. Destined for destruction."

"But you needn't be."

Agabus groaned in frustration, his hand passing anxiously over his billowing prayer shawl as he paced back and forth.

Mary simply watched him, praying silently. Though unaware, Agabus stood upon the threshold of eternal life...or condemnation. The slightest tipping of the scales might propel him rapidly to either side. And yet, she knew a mounting peace, an assurance, that all would be well.

Despite Saul's hateful mission.

Despite Barnabas' dangerous undertaking in Damascus, warning the believers.

And despite Agabus' glaring cowardice.

"Agabus." She spoke with great conviction, her

luminous gray eyes promising peace and purpose. "I have told you before, and I shall tell you again. I am praying for you without ceasing, that—"

"I know, I know," Agabus interrupted tersely, appearing almost comical in his agitation as he paced about the Upper Room in his trailing robes. "You're praying that God will reveal Jesus as Lord to me, beyond any shadow of doubt. *I know.*"

"And He will."

"But *how?*"

"We must wait and see."

Agabus halted his mad pacing, staring at her in glaring exasperation.

"Until then, Agabus, go in peace. And may the Lord be with you."

Deeply troubled, Agabus turned and strode past her without a word. With a final, poignant glance over his shoulder, he disappeared down the gaping stairwell, his dark robes fluttering behind him.

Mary watched him go with a calm, bemused smile, thankful her guards had permitted him entrance despite the lateness of the hour. The Holy Spirit was undoubtedly at work in him, tugging at his heart, patiently drawing him.

Surely it was only a matter of time. Soon—perhaps very soon—the wavering Agabus would be forced to choose a side, to take his stand.

CHAPTER 17

Leah

Jerusalem

The hour was late—far past midnight. And yet, the lamps continued to burn in Saul's private office, casting disturbing shadows upon the richly uphol-stered furniture and the wooden shelves lined with parchment scrolls.

Heart pounding like a blacksmith's hammer upon searing, red-hot metal, Leah gathered her courage and stepped into the faintly lit chamber, feeling somewhat like the courageous Esther standing before the fearsome king of Persia, unsummoned.

She had expected to find her brother seated be-hind his massive desk, poring over ancient parch-ment scrolls, as usual. Instead, he stood poised be-fore an elegantly latticed window, silver moonlight streaming upon his face and faintly illuminating his harsh, uncompromising, bearded profile.

"You shouldn't be here."

Saul's terse admonition was far from encouraging. Steeling herself against the scathing rebuke sure to come, Leah dared another step, deeply unsettled by the darkened atmosphere of her brother's office—almost as if they weren't alone. As if someone—something—lurked within the shadows, monitoring her brother's every move.

"It is late," Saul flung at her, refusing to honor her with a second glance. "Why are you here?"

"I must ask you to reconsider your journey, my brother."

Saul's only response was a cruel, humorless laugh.

"You plan to leave for Damascus within a matter of hours," Leah spoke quietly but firmly. "Don't do it, my brother. I beg you."

Slowly craning his neck, Saul cast a disdainful glance toward her, strangely unsettled by her earnest plea. Her entrance was like the opposite of a solar eclipse. Rather than gathering shadows, light seemed to emanate from her form, dispelling the darkness of his chamber—as if dark forces fled at the mere sight of her. Pursing his lips, Saul dismissed his thoughts as utterly ridiculous, preposterous! After all, *he* was a respected leader within the holiest community on earth, and she was an ignorant, misguided young woman dazzled by the fascinating myths of a blasphemous religious sect. Probably just to spite him.

He refused to be cowed by an errant little sister.

"What you are about to do..." Leah spoke again, her voice low. "How can you persecute the church of God?"

"The church of God?" he smirked, finally turning to face her. "The *Temple* is the church of God! Israel, His son. You are a foolish and gullible woman. And I will not be counted among those who forsake the one, true God for cheap religious fancies."

"But you have already forsaken Him," Leah reminded him, wondering if her life was about to end. "We, the believers in Jesus, *are* the Temple of God because the Holy Spirit has taken up residence in us. We, the church, have become His hands, His feet, on earth. My brother, by attacking *us*, you, in turn, attack *Him*—the one true God."

"Blasphemy," Saul breathed, his dark eyes forming two narrow slits. "I implore you, Sister, cease this worthless babbling or I swear I shall silence you myself!"

"I have no doubt you will," Leah declared boldly, her dark eyes flashing. "Or at least, you shall try. But in the end, God will prevail."

"He will, indeed," Saul told her, his eyes glowing like burning coals. "And we shall see upon whom His favor rests."

"And what if God stops you in your tracks, my brother? What shall you do then?"

Saul stared at her, strangely unsettled, seething.

"I fear for you, my brother," Leah told him, her dark eyes guileless in the light of his burning lamps. "I fear for your safety. Worse, I fear for your soul."

Saul could only stare, every nerve ending alive with fury. Resisting the burning urge to strike her, Saul turned away, shaking in rage. This young sister whom he knew so little about had the makings of a young Mary of Jerusalem, and it greatly disturbed him. He couldn't help but wonder if their father knew. Perhaps he should write to him, warning him of the potential disgrace this girl could wreak upon their reputable family. But then it was highly likely his father would blame *him* for the girl's defection. After all, she was in his care, his keeping, here in

Jerusalem. His father would demand to know how she had been exposed to the teachings of a foul, blasphemous sect upon his watch.

Furious, Saul wondered how he had gotten himself into this impossible situation. He certainly had no desire to oversee the betrothal of a rebellious, starry-eyed young woman. He didn't need this, not now!

"Please, Saul. I only ask that you reconsider—"

"*Enough*," he commanded, his tone dangerous. "I've heard enough. And I will not have you distracting me upon the eve of the most important mission of my entire career."

Leah watched him intently, her dark eyes troubled.

"You are a shame and a disgrace to our family, our people, and our nation," Saul spat, hatred kindling in his cruel gaze. "You have no right to speak of such matters, nor do you know your place."

Leah only waited, determined to hold her tongue as she had learned to do from Mary, who often reminded her that Jesus, when reviled, did not revile in return.

"I leave for Damascus at dawn," Saul informed her gruffly. "There, I swear to you, I shall accomplish my purposes. And when I return, we shall seal your betrothal. You will marry Yosef, and you will do it gladly. You will not shame this family and all we have worked so hard to achieve. Until then, you had best resign yourself to your fate."

"The blood of the saints shall be on your hands and on your head, Saul. May God have mercy on your soul." Without another word, Leah turned and left the office, her gait matching the determined strides he'd seen so often utilized by Mary of Jerusalem.

The blood of the saints shall be on your hands and on your head. Hairs standing on end at the back of his neck, Saul attempted to banish the indescribable fear gripping his heart. Annoyed he was so impacted by the ridiculous arguments of a foolish girl, he stormed behind his desk, falling dismally onto his large, throne-like chair. Gripping the gilded arms, he closed his eyes, attempting to gather his peace.

And yet troubling images danced across the tortured recesses of his mind—a dying evangelist upon his knees, beseeching God to forgive his tormentors.

And the burning intensity in the hazel-green eyes of a beautiful young widow standing before her husband's grave, a tiny child upon her hip, and her maddening words of dismissal as she stole quietly past him…

I forgive you, Saul.

May God have mercy on your soul…

Gripping his head in his hands, Saul feared he would have far better luck banishing his pounding headache than the troubling memories that plagued him.

***

Kelila

Joppa

Dusk was falling rapidly as Kelila drew near the palatial mansion which, in his letter, Philip had instructed her to locate upon her arrival in the bustling port city of Joppa. Washed in the warm golden hues of sunset, the seaside town was utterly breathtaking with quaint cobbled walks, towering stone walls graced with green ivy tendrils, Grecian urns overflowing with verdant plants and blooming shrubs, and shimmering ocean views.

Cradling her bulging baby bump with tired hands, Kelila was thankful the breathtaking scenery provided a temporary distraction from her aching, swelling feet and screaming lower back. Appreciation for the mother of their blessed Lord, Mary, swelled within her as she considered the hard travel the strong but gentle woman had endured journeying from Nazareth to Bethlehem near the time of her delivery. The poor woman had been even further along than she was, and Kelila wondered how on earth Mary had endured.

Grateful for the presence of the two burly manservants sent by the Samaritan caravan to ensure her safe arrival, Kelila watched as one approached an armed guard, boldly requesting to see Philip, the evangelist.

In awe, Kelila glanced up at the monumental affair before them with its towering walls, iron gates, flowering gardens, and large stone courts. To think, Philip was lodging *here*! At least, she assumed he was. Why else would he have directed her to come here? She wondered who owned the impressive estate, supposing it must be a believer if Philip was accepted here. Fleetingly, she thought of her friend, Tabitha, who had left Jerusalem to minister to her wealthy uncle in this very city. Was it too much to hope that Tabitha still remained in Joppa? For all Kelila knew, the lovely young widow had long since won her uncle to the Lord and returned to Jerusalem.

Unexpectedly, a commotion erupted in the outer

court just beyond the iron gates, drawing Kelila from her hopeful thoughts. Confused, the armed guard cast a look of annoyance over his broad shoulder as two excited young women—one with a toddler on her hip—burst through the wide double doors of the opulent manor, racing across the broad court with wide smiles and shining eyes.

"Tabitha!" Kelila cried, her eyes welling with tears of sheer joy. "Tabitha, it's me—Kelila!"

"Of course it's you!" Tabitha laughed, hurrying past the disgruntled guard as he grudgingly opened the gate for them. "Look at you! Philip told us you were with child, but to see you so big and round—" Laughing and crying together, the women threw their arms around each other, chuckling heartily when the baby in Kelila's womb pressed mightily against Tabitha's smothering embrace.

"And little Laurel—just look at you!" Kelila cried, tears streaming down her face as she pinched the little girl's cheek. "My, you're growing up fast!"

Grinning shyly, the toddler turned her face away, hiding it on her mother's shoulder.

"Kelila, this is my dear friend, Tirzah," Tabitha beamed, taking the arm of the attractive woman beside her and drawing her forward. "She, too, is a believer."

Returning Tirzah's ready smile, Kelila guessed the woman to be at least ten years her senior, and yet her vibrant features remained youthful as ever. With large hazel-brown eyes, richly colored brown hair, and sideswept bangs framing high cheekbones and a firm jawline, her face and form were arresting, conveying both beauty and intelligence.

"You must be the owner of this fine mansion,"

Kelila exclaimed, confused when both women burst into a fit of giggles at her unexpected remark.

"If only!" Tirzah laughed, exchanging another look of amusement with a grinning Tabitha. "This place belongs to Joram, Tabitha's uncle."

"*This* is your uncle's estate?" Kelila gasped, dumbfounded.

"It is," Tabitha nodded, entertained by Kelila's gaping reaction. "Didn't Philip tell you in his letter?"

"Philip's letter of instruction arrived in Sychar even before he arrived in Joppa," she laughed, her weariness seeping away in her gladness to be surrounded by friends once again. "He directed me to locate the largest manor by the sea once I reached Joppa and to inquire of a man named Joram."

"Clever Philip," Tabitha chuckled, lowering her daughter as the girl scrambled to be free. Watching as Laurel scurried happily into the outer court beyond the gates, Tabitha returned her attention to the travel-weary evangelist's wife. "He must have remembered me telling him about my uncle's estate before I left Jerusalem, and he had the faith to believe he would be welcomed here."

"Welcomed? Only because *you* were here," Tirzah put in stoutly, drawing a look of surprise from Kelila.

"Sadly, my uncle hasn't accepted Jesus as Lord," Tabitha explained, warmed by Kelila's look of genuine sympathy. "He isn't very receptive toward strangers...or relatives. Or anyone, really, for that matter."

"I see," Kelila laughed, understanding. "I'm just glad Philip found you when he arrived, Tabitha. Speaking of which...where is he?"

"Ah, about that..." Tirzah grinned, exchanging another knowing look with Tabitha. "We have been anxiously awaiting your arrival. We knew you should be making an appearance any day now."

"And Philip anxiously awaits you at Tirzah's house," Tabitha revealed, her hazel-green eyes twinkling with excitement. "You and he shall abide there, since my uncle wasn't willing to host you, I regret to say."

"It will be an honor to abide with you, Tirzah," Kelila told her newest sister with great feeling. Suddenly remembering the manservants waiting patiently at the gate, Kelila wheeled around in distress. "Forgive me, both of you, for leaving you standing there!"

The young men exchanged rueful smiles, having rather enjoyed the happy exchange after many days of grueling travel.

"Thank you so very much for escorting me here," Kelila told them, the appreciation evident in her tone. "You needn't wait around on me any longer now. Please, feel free to rejoin your caravan."

After exchanging brief farewells, the manservants left with little ceremony, glad to have accomplished the task assigned.

"Now come along," Tirzah exclaimed, offering her hand. "My home is but a short distance from here. We've arranged for a mule-drawn cart to take us, so you needn't wear out your tired feet even a moment longer."

"You have thought of everything!" Kelila declared, touched. "Thank you, truly."

Having been led to a modest, mule-drawn cart, Kelila was surprised when Tabitha held back as

Tirzah slipped comfortably onto the driver's seat. "Aren't you coming along, Tabitha?"

"I abide with my daughter at Joram's estate," she explained, her bright eyes promising to see her soon.

"Oh, how delightful!" Kelila exclaimed, clasping her hands. "How grand to dwell in a seaside manor in Joppa! Your chambers must be breathtaking."

"Only if you consider a tiny, windowless stone storage chamber breathtaking," Tirzah harrumphed, receiving a questioning look from Kelila.

"Never mind that," Tabitha smiled, waving aside Tirzah's sarcasm. "But we shall meet again tomorrow, after you've had the chance to recover from your long journey, Kelila. I can tell you more then."

"I cannot thank the two of you enough," Kelila said meaningfully, her gaze traveling between the two beaming women. "I was quite nervous about venturing to a new, unfamiliar place, but you have welcomed me with open arms. I cannot wait to sit down with you both and have a nice, long chat! Tabitha, I hoped you were still in Joppa, but I didn't know for sure. You must tell me *everything*—all about your experiences here! And, Tirzah, I want to learn all about you and your story, as well! My, we have a lot of catching up to do, don't we?"

"*After* you get some rest," Tabitha laughed merrily, her luminous eyes twinkling. "Now go! Greet your husband and show him how much you've missed him."

"Oh, shall I ever," Kelila exclaimed as Tirzah took the reins and expertly directed the mule toward the cobbled street.

Stepping up onto the curb, Tabitha watched them go, a faint sheen of tears glistening in her soft eyes.

Though she wouldn't dare douse Kelila's bubbling happiness, seeing Philip again ——her late husband's closest friend—standing upon Joram's threshold, beaming his joy and larger than life, had hurt just a little. She couldn't help but wonder how differently her life would have unfolded had Stephanos survived. Would she—like Kelila—be carrying the child of her beloved? Would they have raised a loving family together, training their little ones in the way of the Lord? How might they have partnered together in sharing the gospel with the world?

Purposefully blinking back stubborn tears, Tabitha resolved—once again—not to dwell on the painful past or nagging *what-ifs*. After all, God was in control. He had *good* plans for her, plans that would further His blessed kingdom, resulting in the salvation of the world.

She was privileged to participate, privileged to be counted among the children of God.

Turning on her heel, Tabitha left to join her shy but happy little daughter—her husband's parting gift to her.

CHAPTER 18

Kelila

Joppa

Heart aflutter with nerves, Kelila tentatively followed her hostess through the narrow stone court encircling the quaint little house which Tirzah called home. The sun was setting rapidly, casting the delightful village in mysterious shadows. Even so, warm light spilled from the windows of the small house and shone from the roof enclosed with low walls, lighting their way.

Suddenly nervous, Kelila wondered what it would be like to see Philip again. How long had he been gone, anyway? The weeks without him had ticked by at a snail's pace, nearly driving her to distraction. How desperately she had missed him, vacillating between annoyance at his prolonged absence and wishful longing for him! But now—standing in the softly lit court with her beloved just beyond the door looming before her—she could hardly wait to see him, though she wondered what he would think of her bulging belly. She was quite certain it had tripled in size since he had departed from Sychar! A bit self-conscious, she cradled her rounded baby bump with trembling hands.

Just think, she thought, perturbed. *We have been apart for nearly three months, and now I shall greet him looking like a beached whale upon the coast!* She could hardly remember what she had looked like before, with a perfectly slender waistline and an enviable, hourglass figure. *I suppose those days are over—at least for now,* she thought, her lips tipping in amusement. *This little one has surely seen to that.*

Squaring her shoulders, Kelila attempted to dismiss her steadily mounting self-consciousness. Within mere moments, she and Philip would be together again—that's what mattered. And she was determined to make the most of their time together. After all, it was entirely possible the Lord might call the evangelist away again. And she wanted to savor every moment she had with her husband.

"Welcome to my home, Kelila," Tirzah announced with a dramatic sweep of her arm, drawing Kelila's attention back to the daunting present moment. "And my home is your home, so long as you remain here in Joppa," she added meaningfully. "It is a privilege to host you. Now…are you ready to see your husband?"

As if in response, the door swung open on creaky hinges, seemingly of its own accord. And there stood her dear Philip, smiling broadly, his strong, sturdy form engulfing the entirety of Tirzah's narrow threshold.

"Philip!" Kelila cried, a sob catching in her throat.

Just the sight of him was enough to reduce her to tears, reminding her how very much she had missed him and how grateful she was to have him.

"My love!" Philip grinned, eagerly gathering her in strong arms.

Weeping on his shoulder, Kelila attempted to steady her fragile emotions. After all, Tirzah looked on with a wide smile, and Kelila didn't wish to be taken for a blubbering fool!

"Just look at you!" Philip exclaimed, drawing back and taking her hands in his, his warm brown eyes traveling fondly over her bulging belly.

"I know," Kelila nearly groaned, her color deepening in embarrassment. "I look—"

"*Beautiful*," Philip declared, his tone boding no argument as his eyes shone with pride. "The loveliest I have ever seen you."

"What?" Kelila exclaimed, stunned.

"You are a sight for sore eyes, my darling," Philip told her, gathering her to himself once again. "Our little one is surely making his presence known, isn't he?"

"Or *hers*," Kelila corrected him, her eyes gleaming with mischief. Though she wouldn't admit it to Philip or anyone else, she was secretly hoping for a little girl. What fun it would be to raise a daughter, to dress her in sweet little garments and braid her long tresses!

"Yes, or *hers*," Philip agreed gently, his eyes flickering with emotion as he tucked a stray strand of raven-black hair behind his wife's ear. "Either way, we shall welcome him or her with open arms. Oh, how I've missed you, beloved."

"And I, you," Kelila assured him, blushing slightly

when he bent to kiss her smooth forehead.

"I suppose it's now time to make myself scarce," Tirzah quipped good-naturedly, slipping past them and entering the cheerful home aflame with dozens of flickering candles. "Come in, come in! Make yourselves at home. As for me, I shall be spending a cozy evening on the rooftop beneath the stars. But, please, don't hesitate to find me if you need anything."

"On the roof?" Kelila repeated incredulously, following her husband and Tirzah into the comfortable little house. "But you can't! At nightfall, there will be a terrible chill in the air—"

"Nonsense!" Tirzah chided, crossing the room to stoke the fire in the kiln. "I'm a hardy potter woman, after all. The fresh air will do me a world of good!"

"But, Tirzah—"

"I insist!" Tirzah put in stoutly, turning toward the tantalizing spread of dried fruit and nuts, freshly baked bread, and seasoned fish which she had lovingly prepared for the young couple. "Now come, enjoy a meal together. Should you need anything at all, you know where to find me." With that, Tirzah left the small house, closing the door firmly behind her.

Kelila turned wide eyes upon her husband, Philip, dismayed. "She has been so kind to us, Philip. Too kind! She cannot spend the night on the roof!"

"Tabitha and I both tried to dissuade her, but she's a stubborn one," Philip laughed, shaking his head in amusement. "That woman has some serious spunk."

"So I noticed! But how can we ever repay her?"

"By making the most of our time in her home, her city," Philip told her, drawing her close and taking her hands in his. "The Lord has important work for us to do here, Kelila. And Tirzah shall be part of it."

"Joppa is simply breathtaking, Philip," Kelila exclaimed, awed by the beauty of the quaint seaport town. "I wouldn't mind settling down here, you know."

Laughing softly, Philip brushed her rosy cheek with the back of his knuckles. "You look radiant, my darling. I'd say the seaside suits you well."

"How long shall we remain here, Philip? Should we begin searching for a place to stay?" she asked, somewhat hopeful that perhaps, here, the Lord would allow them to establish a home of their own.

"I sense our time in Joppa shall be brief," Philip responded honestly, and Kelila was forced to swallow her disappointment once again. "But take heart, beloved. I believe this season of traveling evangelism is drawing to a close. Perhaps, soon, the Lord will show us where He would have us abide."

Heart leaping inside her chest, Kelila bit back the floodgate of questions bursting forth from her innermost being! For now, she would choose to be content in this calling, this mission, this present moment, this sacred time alone with the man she loved.

Draping her arms over his broad shoulders and clasping her hands behind his neck, she met his warm gaze, her own playful. "I'm just thankful the Lord brought us back together again. I missed you quite a bit while you were gone, believe it or not."

"Did you?" Philip teased, tapping the tip of her nose.

"More than you know," Kelila confessed. Standing on tiptoes, she grinned rather impishly, planting a firm kiss on his mouth and tingling with joy in the presence of her beloved.

***

Tabitha

The next morning was a whirlwind of excitement and preparations. Tabitha could scarcely believe that a beloved leader from Jerusalem had come to preach the gospel in this breathtaking, bustling city she had grown to love and cherish. The widows she had befriended were strong, hardy women—both young and old. They possessed grace, dignity, and grit, trusting the Lord to provide for their children despite apparent helplessness and daunting circumstances. Wouldn't they be thrilled to hear the teachings of one who had walked with Jesus when He was on the earth, a member of the famous Seventy sent out to minister in the name of Christ and a former deacon of the Jerusalem church!

"There aren't words enough to describe my joy now that you and Philip are here," Tabitha confided, strolling alongside Kelila on a quaint, cobbled lane boasting tall stone walls strewn with delicate ivy. Towering palms lined the way, their verdant fronds swaying in the brisk morning breezes.

"Oh, we are overjoyed, as well," Kelila declared with great feeling, cradling her baby bump in loving hands. "When I learned our next destination was Joppa, all I could think about was finding you, Tabitha! I could only pray you would still be here."

Tabitha smiled in response, glad the bright, cheery evangelist's wife had agreed to accompany her to the tenements by the sea to spread word about Philip's arrival and impending sermon, while Tirzah and her mother-in-law, Ruth, prepared Tirzah's small home for as many guests as possible.

"Wasn't it cute when Laurel offered to 'help' Tirzah bake fresh bread for the guests?" Kelila grinned, drawing another smile from Tabitha. "I was almost tempted to stay just to watch her 'assist'!"

"Laurel is an excellent helper. She adores breadmaking, though it isn't her strongest point," Tabitha chuckled fondly. "She spends hours in the kitchen with Martha—the head cook at my uncle's estate—pestering her with all manner of questions about cooking and baking. But Martha, bless her dear old soul, enjoys every moment of it."

"I can imagine," Kelila beamed, tickled by the toddler's enthusiasm to participate in the day's excitement. "Your Laurel is a precious girl. I imagine I could learn quite a bit from you about this whole parenting thing."

"You have a good head on your shoulders and, most importantly, the Holy Spirit to guide you," Tabitha pointed out. "You will be a wonderful mother."

"It's daunting to even consider it—you know, being a mother," Kelila confessed, her large brown eyes wide. "I can be so flighty, even careless at times. Frankly, I don't feel capable at all."

"You needn't feel incapable," Tabitha assured her, wishing she had far better counsel to offer, but she was brand-new at being a mother herself. *If only Mary was here to soothe and advise,* she thought for the umpteenth time. "Focus on the most important thing, which is training your child in the way of the

Lord. When in doubt, always reference the Word of God. And seek the counsel of those who walk in obedience, those bearing worthy fruit in their endeavors."

"You've changed," Kelila observed, pausing mid-stride to study her friend from Jerusalem. "You've always been on fire for the Lord, Tabitha. But there's a quiet strength, a maturity about you, that wasn't there before."

"I suppose tragedy and hardship have a way of forcing one to grow up," Tabitha remarked with a wry smile. "There are times when the old fire flares, and I struggle to keep my composure or hold my tongue. But thank God the Holy Spirit is working on me, smoothing out the rough edges."

"And I trust the 'old fire' is still there," Kelila observed with a knowing smile. "It must be for you to have so boldly upended your entire life and relocated to an unfamiliar city, reaching dozens of women and children for Christ, and putting up with that pompous uncle of yours! Even so, it seems the Lord is refining you, redirecting your zeal and determination to be used for His glory. Your life is a testament to the power and grace of God, Tabitha."

"I can only thank the Lord for that. *I* certainly had nothing to do with it."

"But you have been obedient, have you not?"

Tabitha only smiled.

"This is such a nice walk, isn't it?" Kelila exclaimed, sensing that perhaps her friend would prefer a change of subject. The young widow rarely talked about herself and seemed far more comfortable focusing on others. "What a beautiful place this is. You and Laurel must enjoy living here!"

"I do, though at times, I miss Jerusalem desperately—especially my brothers and sisters there. You know, Mary. Rhoda. Your sister, Candace…"

"I understand that. Though Sychar was wonderful, I felt the same."

"Philip has told us incredible things about your time with the Samaritans. The Lord worked mightily through you, Kelila."

"As you previously stated, *I* certainly had nothing to do with it!" Kelila declared emphatically, and both women shared a laugh. "That was the Holy Spirit at work."

Tabitha couldn't help but smile, grateful for Kelila's sparkling presence. The young woman had proven remarkably entertaining from the moment she had arrived on the scene in Jerusalem, shocking her sister Candace and instantly snagging the attention of a particularly shy deacon…

"Now, tell me all about your time here in Joppa," Kelila exclaimed, looping her arm through Tabitha's in a sisterly fashion. "Philip has already updated you about *our* ministry in Sychar, but I want to hear all about *yours* here in Joppa! Tell me about your uncle—Joram, yes? Have you made any headway there?"

"Very little," Tabitha admitted ruefully. "Frankly, when I left Jerusalem, I had my own ideas about what the Lord would do here in Joppa. I suppose I shouldn't be surprised that He had an entirely different set of plans than I did."

"Meaning?"

"Well, I thought I would arrive here and promptly win my uncle to the Lord, but Joram stoutly refused the gospel from the very beginning, even forbidding me to speak of it again."

"Oh, Tabitha, I'm so sorry."

"You needn't be," Tabitha quickly assured her. "Instead, the Lord led me to countless widows and orphans who desperately needed Him. Their hearts were open to the gospel from the very start, and it has been an absolute joy to instruct them, watching them grow in faith each day."

"Rather like your ministry to the widows and orphans in Jerusalem at the Synagogue of the Freedmen!"

"Yes, very much like that."

"And your uncle—do you think he will ever come around?"

"I hope and pray that he will," Tabitha admitted. "I do believe his animosity toward me has eased a bit since my arrival. And though Joram would never admit it, he trusts me. He knows I care about him and will do right by him."

"It sounds like your love for him has proven a far greater witness than a mere sermon ever could."

"It's the best I can do, and I ask God for strength to reach him daily. Joram doesn't make it particularly easy."

"I can see that!"

"Even so, I can't help but mourn the fact that his heart remains closed to Christ's message. At first, I'd wondered if the Lord planned to reach him, inspiring him to open his home to be used by the believers here, as Mary has done in Jerusalem. His mansion is the perfect place to host a local church, after all."

"Isn't it tempting, at times, to question the Lord's distribution of gifts?" Kelila teased, her brown eyes dancing. "Why couldn't *Tirzah* own the giant mansion and *Joram*, the small cottage? Then we would have the perfect place to host church gatherings!"

"I suppose that's why God reminds us that His ways aren't our ways," Tabitha quipped, a wry smile tipping her lips.

"Clearly!"

"Even so, I'm thankful Tirzah has so graciously opened her home to us. Otherwise, we wouldn't have a place to meet at all."

"Once word spreads about Philip's arrival, do you suppose Tirzah's home will be large enough to host everyone?" Kelila asked, her delicate brow wrinkling in deep thought.

"Frankly, that's what I'm concerned about," Tabitha confessed. "We scarcely fit *now*, and that's just the widows and orphans gathering. Even then, we spill out into the courtyard and onto the street. I'm just not quite sure how to make this work."

Cresting a gentle hill, the women paused as the glittering waters of the Mediterranean loomed upon the horizon, perfectly dazzling beneath the sun's benevolent rays.

"It really steals your breath away, doesn't it?" Kelila mused, tilting her head as her gaze swept across the panoramic view.

"It does," Tabitha agreed, sobering at the wondrous beauty of God's creation. "I never tire of this view. Never."

"Tabitha, *that's it*!" Kelila exclaimed, grabbing her friend's shoulders in a rush of unbridled excitement. "That's our answer!"

"Our answer?" Tabitha repeated blankly, wondering if her friend had gone mad. "Our answer to what?"

"We'll meet *there*—on the shore, by the sea! Philip can instruct the people by the sea!"

Speechless, Tabitha turned to scan the marvelous view once again as gentle azure waves lapped against white sandy beaches with snowy gulls soaring majestically overhead, releasing their plaintive cries.

"Tell me it isn't the perfect idea," Kelila challenged, her brown eyes dancing with glee.

"It's…it *is* perfect," Tabitha agreed, shaking her head in awe. "Why didn't I think of it months ago?" What better location to reveal the Living Water than upon tranquil shores, surrounded by the marvelous beauty of God's design? Hadn't her Lord oft instructed His followers from a fisherman's vessel upon the sea, docked near the crowded shore?

"See?" Kelila beamed, thrilling at the exciting prospect of prayer, worship, and godly instruction alongside gently lapping waves. "The Lord has provided an answer. Another problem solved!"

"Indeed," Tabitha smiled in agreement, warmed and encouraged by Kelila's enthusiasm.

"Come," Kelila declared, taking her friend's arm and nearly dragging her along the cobbled way. "We must hurry and spread the word! Philip's instruction will begin soon."

Laughing merrily, Tabitha picked up speed. Relishing the task at hand, the two young women hurried down the picturesque lane, their countenances alight with eager anticipation.

CHAPTER 19

Tabitha

Joppa

"My, this part of town is nothing like your uncle's opulent neighborhood!" Kelila gasped as she and Tabitha finally reached the docks flanking the aging seaside tenements. "I had forgotten the hustle and bustle of such a port."

Chuckling her acknowledgment, Tabitha paused in front of a wide, cobbled street passing before the towering apartment buildings, watching as numerous carts rattled by, the drovers shouting impatiently at their lumbering beasts while harried, half-clothed slaves hurried across the road, their bare arms laden with heavy burdens. Massive ships with billowing sails slumbered at the ancient docks like sleeping giants, while muscular menservants swiftly emptied and loaded heavy cargo and well-dressed shipmasters looked on with crossed arms and an air of skepticism. Overhead, majestic gulls dipped and swayed, crying out their dismay at the frenzied scene below as droves of humanity scurried about like so many ants, all anxious to accomplish their purposes.

"So many boats! Droves of them!" Kelila declared, her gaze traveling toward the docks cluttered with monstrous cargo ships and gently bobbing fishing vessels. "Every imaginable kind!" Tearing her gaze away with a bit of effort, she glanced toward the shoddy tenements towering precariously heavenward and observed, "I've never seen tenements in such close proximity to a port and surrounding markets. The poor tenants must not have even a moment's peace!"

"I'd imagine not," Tabitha sighed. "Tirzah's mother-in-law, Ruth, lives here and insists one eventually grows accustomed to the deafening cacophony of the docks, though Tirzah teases that the old widow has merely become hard of hearing."

"This kind of ruckus would render *anyone* hard of hearing!"

"I imagine so," Tabitha nodded, smiling faintly. Taking a deep breath, she braced herself for crossing the busy street. "Say a prayer and follow me," she teased.

Laughing merrily, Kelila followed Tabitha's lead as she crossed the street with the caution of one skirting a seething volcano, for ox carts and mule-drawn wagons clattered by with alarming speed and regularity. A simple misstep could easily result in disaster.

"Well, good morning to you!"

Relieved to have made it across the street unscathed, the glowing mother-to-be glanced up in surprise at the sound of an unfamiliar, masculine voice calling out a cheerful greeting. She realized the voice belonged to a surprisingly handsome young merchant stationed dutifully behind a fruit vendor's stall.

"This must be the famous Kelila I've been hearing so much about!" the young man decided, his features stretching in a broad grin.

"Good morning, Adam," Tabitha responded lightly, guiding her confused friend toward the market stall—one of dozens lining the lower level of the ramshackle apartment structure.

Blinking her surprise, Kelila drew before the neatly organized booth with its own bright canopy and sturdy wooden stand. With a slight pang to her heart, she was reminded of the familiar little market stall in Sychar with its faded canopy, empty barrels, crooked shelves, and tall jars of meticulously potted herbs lovingly planted by her dear friend, Adorina.

"Kelila, this is Adam," Tabitha explained, interrupting Kelila's poignant thoughts and gesturing toward the grinning, well-built young man standing behind the seller's booth. "He is a dear friend and fellow believer."

"Greetings," Adam addressed Kelila warmly. "I have already met your husband Philip, and I look forward to his teaching later this morning."

"We're glad you can attend," Kelila responded brightly, studying him with a curious expression. "Are you one of Tabitha's recent converts?" she teased.

"Adam was already a believer when I arrived in Joppa," Tabitha quickly supplied, embarrassed by Kelila's obvious interest regarding her relationship with the handsome young man. "If you can believe it, it was actually Barnabas who first shared the gospel with Adam."

"Barnabas?" Kelila repeated, puzzled. "Is he here, too?"

"He visited once amidst his many travels," Adam explained, delightfully entertained by Kelila's reaction. "Even before Tabitha arrived. His testimony was compelling. I was, first, intrigued; later, converted."

"Amazing!"

"Adam's father is also a believer," Tabitha added.

"I would love to meet him, as well!" Kelila exclaimed. "I do hope he can join us for Philip's teaching."

"Sadly, my father is confined to his bed," Adam revealed, his hazel-flecked brown eyes betraying hidden pain. "But I assure you, I shall relay your husband's teachings the moment I return home to him."

"What a shame," Kelila sighed, her deepest sympathy evident in her tone. "I'm so sorry, Adam."

"You needn't be. Despite his infirmities, Father remains in good spirits," Adam assured her. "His body is weak, but his faith is strong."

"Praise God for that!"

"Indeed."

"I suppose we'd best find the widows now and announce the good news about Philip's sermon," Tabitha inserted, tactfully changing the subject. "Adam, Kelila and I plan to go door to door upstairs, spreading the word to the women and children residing here. As for the local men, may I count on you to spread the word? I believe their response shall prove far more receptive if the invitation is issued by a fellow man, someone they respect."

"I'm not so sure about that. I imagine it'd be difficult for any man to deny an earnest request from the two of you."

"Adam!" Tabitha breathed, blushing slightly as Kelila laughed merrily.

"But I will gladly spread the word," Adam promised, his brown eyes sparkling with humor. "When and where shall I instruct them to go?"

"When—just before midday. And where—by the sea, upon the quiet stretch of shore nearest Joram's estate," Tabitha quickly informed him.

"By the sea? What a delightful place to host a service."

Kelila shot Tabitha a triumphant grin.

"All right, then," Adam chuckled, casually removing his vendor's apron and tossing it aside. "I'll get right to work recruiting men to attend Philip's service. Prepare yourselves for quite a crowd, ladies."

"Oh, we will," Kelila informed him. "The more, the merrier!"

"Thank you, Adam, truly," Tabitha added, her tone and expression heartfelt.

"It's my deepest pleasure."

Turning to enter the narrow vestibule sheltering the first flight of steep stone steps, Tabitha was caught off guard when Kelila froze in place, whirling around to face the kindly merchant as he prepared to take his leave.

"Adam?"

Turning his head, Adam awaited the expectant mother's inquiry with an amused smile.

"Is your father able to receive visitors?"

Tabitha turned to look at Kelila, her lips parted in surprise.

"He is, indeed," Adam responded lightly. "Father loves guests."

"Then Philip shall come to *him* later today, after he has finished his sermon," Kelila stated with an air of finality. "Your father needn't miss out simply because he is confined to his bed!"

"Now, we wouldn't wish to impose upon your husband's time, Kelila," Adam said quickly. "He has far more important matters to consider—"

"I insist," Kelila put in stoutly, waving a forefinger with a hint of mischief. "The matter is settled. Philip shall pay your father a visit this evening."

"And he will be most grateful, as will I," Adam assured her, the warmth of his expression conveying his deep gratitude. "We will eagerly await his visit."

"Until later then. Good day!" Flashing her winning smile, Kelila grasped a speechless Tabitha's arm, nearly dragging her into the vestibule and up the first flight of stairs.

***

"He likes you. You know that, right?"

Emerging at the top of the final flight of stone stairs and stepping into a darkened corridor, Tabitha paused to gape at her exuberant friend in wide-eyed confusion. "What?"

"Adam. He likes you!"

"Adam likes *everyone*," Tabitha responded a bit more tersely than she intended, certain Kelila couldn't possibly be implying…

"Don't pretend you don't know what I mean,"

Kelila said pointedly, pausing to offer her friend a playful poke on the shoulder. "He looks at you as one might gaze upon a stunning work of art!"

"Don't be ridiculous, and please, lower your tone," Tabitha hissed, her cheeks warming in humiliation. "Adam is a fellow believer, and nothing more. He treats *everyone* with kindness and respect. I assure you, he relates to me no differently than he would to anyone else."

"Ah, and I suppose Adam will gaze longingly into Philip's eyes, as well, when we visit his house this evening?"

"*Kelila!*"

"It's true," Kelila shot back, undeterred. "I do believe he's smitten."

"Well, even if that's the case—which it *isn't*—Adam would never act upon his feelings," Tabitha insisted, perturbed.

"And why is that?"

"Because he thinks I am married."

"*What?*" Now it was Kelila's turn to stand, gawking, amid the dimly lit corridor.

"Adam thinks that I'm a married woman—"

"I heard you the first time," Kelila shot back, sounding appalled. "But why on earth does he think that?"

"I think he assumed I had a husband when we met," Tabitha said, feeling somewhat defensive and a slight twinge of conscience. "I suppose because I have a daughter and the financial means to assist the orphans and widows here, he just thought—"

"So he simply *assumed* you have a husband, and you failed to set him straight?" Kelila demanded, her dark eyes narrowing in suspicion.

"Why would I?" Tabitha exclaimed, feeling increasingly uncomfortable with the course of their conversation. "It would seem terribly inappropriate to march right up to a handsome young bachelor and announce the fact that I'm unmarried.!"

"So you think he's handsome?" Kelila grinned.

"Kelila, for heaven's sake! I'm simply trying to make a point."

"Oh, you've made a point, all right," she teased, laughing heartily at the widow's mounting consternation.

"Has anyone ever told you that you can be positively exasperating, at times?"

"On occasion," Kelila grinned impishly, her brown eyes sparkling with fun. "But mostly, my irresistible charm outweighs the rest."

"Let's just forget about this foolish talk," Tabitha muttered, strolling up to a decrepit wooden door placed in the wall—one of many lining the ridiculously narrow corridor. "We're wasting time with idle babbling when we should be spreading word about Philip's upcoming sermon."

"One last question, then I shall leave you alone," Kelila promised, flouncing alongside her with a mischievous grin. "Do you suppose Adam shall remain forever oblivious to the fact that you don't have a husband? He's bound to figure it out sooner or later, after all."

"I *do* have a husband, Kelila. In life and in death, Stephanos will forever be my husband, my beloved." Heart pounding in dismay, Tabitha squared her shoulders, intentionally avoiding her friend's penetrating gaze. "And when Jesus returns to take us home, we shall be together again—Stephanos and

I—as if we were never apart."

"I'm sorry, Tabitha," Kelila offered gently after a moment of lingering, awkward silence had passed. Recognizing she had struck a nerve, she added softly, "I didn't mean to tease."

"You needn't apologize." Tabitha sighed, regretting the terse manner in which she had addressed her dear sister in Christ. "My tone was harsh. Forgive me."

"There's nothing to forgive," Kelila insisted, offering her friend's shoulder a comforting squeeze. In thoughtful silence, she watched as the striking young widow reached out to knock firmly on the door before them.

Standing stiffly beside an uncharacteristically subdued Kelila, Tabitha bit her lower lip in consternation. Awaiting a response from the other side of the door, she wished she could erase the conversation that had passed between them. For the truth was, Kelila's prying questions had unsettled her far more deeply than she cared to admit. She couldn't imagine sharing her life intimately with another man—not after losing her beloved Stephanos. And yet, if she revealed her widowhood to Adam, she risked losing his friendship—and his respect. Both of which had become strangely, unsettlingly important to her. But how would he feel when he eventually discovered that she had allowed him to believe a falsehood about her marital status? Would he be disappointed in her? Angry, even?

Or, worse, would he then feel free to pursue her, to explore the possibility of something more than just a friendship? Groaning inwardly, Tabitha realized she would then be placed in the exceedingly awkward position of having to reject his affections.

Releasing a sigh of frustration, Tabitha pushed such troubling thoughts far from her mind and focused on the matter at hand.

CHAPTER 20

Tabitha

Joppa

The sun traveled high overhead as throngs of eager men, women, and children flocked to the seashore, their expressions betraying both curiosity and anticipation. Standing near the front of the swiftly growing crowd, Tabitha anxiously awaited the commencement of Philip's sermon, her pulse quickening as the time drew near. With a hint of amusement, she suppressed a knowing smile, watching as Kelila fussed over her husband, adjusting his tunic and brushing her slender fingers through his hair.

Releasing a wistful sigh, Tabitha remembered what it was like to fuss over her own husband. With a sharp pang to her heart, she realized how much she missed it.

The musical sound of a child's laughter drew her back to the present moment, scattering reticent thoughts. With a small smile, Tabitha watched as Tirzah hoisted a giggling Laurel high into the air. Squealing her delight, the little girl waved her cherished doll in feverish exuberance. Apparently, the excitement in the air was contagious.

Scanning the rapidly growing crowd, Tabitha was stunned by the town's response to Philip's simple invitation! Hordes of men, women, and children had flocked to the sandy beach, chattering enthusiastically about the upcoming sermon. Fleetingly, Tabitha wondered if these people had come seeking truth or merely a fascinating diversion from the drudgery of day-to-day living. Undoubtedly, some were sincere in their quest for truth, while others were simply curious.

Lifting her gaze heavenward, Tabitha closed her eyes, her face bathed in sunlight. Despite the brisk morning air, the sun's gentle rays warmed the sand beneath her sandaled feet, reflecting off the glittering sea in the most pleasant way. Overhead, billowing clouds drifted lazily across a pale blue sky, seeming to be in no particular hurry.

Thank You, Lord, for this perfect day, her heart whispered in thanksgiving. *You have provided a beautiful location for Philip to share Your blessed gospel of love. Please, Father, soften their hearts, making them receptive to Your truth.*

Smiling faintly, Tabitha gloried in the prospect of Philip establishing a church in Joppa. She certainly hadn't felt qualified to do so on her own. And while she had thoroughly enjoyed instructing the women and children, she was overjoyed that the local men might prove receptive to the gospel now.

As if confirming her thoughts, Tabitha spotted Adam and Simon joining the fringes of the crowd. With a hidden smile, Tabitha noted that the wide-open space and fresh sea air proved abundantly helpful dispersing the repugnant odor lingering about the burly tanner's person. That fact alone was a blessed relief.

Swiftly spotting the lovely young widow, Adam flashed Tabitha a broad smile.

Cheeks warming in embarrassment, Tabitha offered a faint nod of acknowledgment, praying Kelila's prying eyes were directed elsewhere. Turning her gaze toward Philip, Tabitha saw that he appeared ready to address the gathering.

"It's time," Kelila exclaimed, excitedly joining Tabitha and Tirzah near the front of the crowd.

"Indeed, it is," Tirzah jovially agreed, amused by Kelila's bubbling enthusiasm.

"Greetings!" Philip declared in a booming voice, drawing a hearty response from the waiting crowd. "It is an honor to meet with you today."

To Tabitha's great amazement, the gathering responded with cheers, shouts of greeting, and wild applause. Exchanging hopeful looks with Kelila and Tirzah, Tabitha pinched her daughter's rosy cheek as the little girl clung to the beaming potter woman, both fascinated and apprehensive about the crowd's swelling response.

"The message I share with you today is unlike any you have ever heard, nor shall ever hear again," Philip announced, his warm brown eyes traveling fondly over the crowd. "It is the message of Jesus Christ, the Son of God, the true and living water."

Heart springing into her throat, Tabitha bowed her head, praying fervently for revival.

***

Joram

On a gracefully suspended balcony overlooking the glittering azure waters of the Great Sea, a lone man stood grasping the intricate wrought iron railing, his knuckles whitening as his grip tightened painfully upon the cool bars. Lips tightening in dismay, old Joram's cold eyes narrowed in indignation as he strained to see the distant shoreline just beyond towering city walls. Silver brows furrowing in rising anger, he seethed inwardly as hordes of citizens swarmed the sandy beach, closing in upon the barely discernible form of a quiet yet good-natured evangelist.

For the love of all that's just and good! he thought, inexplicably peeved. That stubborn, headstrong niece of his was about to single-handedly destroy the peace of an entire city!

Upper lip curling in derision, Joram wondered what could be done to stop the growing madness. Why couldn't Tabitha simply live and let live, rather than setting out to corrupt every Jew in the nation with her strange, heretical beliefs? Why concern herself with the plight of strangers, spending hours slaving over her sewing and piecing together quality garments for ungrateful riffraff?

With an unwelcome stab of conscience, Joram

was reminded of another beautiful woman from his painful past—a woman who could not rest until the needs of every man, woman, and child within reach were met.

A woman so very much like this kindhearted, strong-willed niece.

Scowling deeply, Joram turned sharply on his heel and left the balcony.

***

Tabitha

Kneeling quietly beside her sleeping little daughter, Tabitha leaned forward to brush the girl's silky curls back from her forehead. Though the sun hadn't yet set, the toddler was exhausted from all the excitement of the day, having spent hours on the beach during Philip's powerful sermon, breathing in the invigorating sea air and absorbing the thrilling sights and sounds surrounding them.

"Knock, knock! Anyone home?"

Glancing up, Tabitha smiled welcomingly when Kelila poked her head through the door, her ebony ringlets cascading about her shoulders like a silky waterfall. "May I come in?"

"Of course," Tabitha responded quietly, grateful Kelila had lowered her typically exuberant tone since her daughter was sleeping soundly.

"Tirzah told me I could find you here," Kelila explained, gingerly entering the cramped chamber and painstakingly attempting to lower herself onto the floor beside Tabitha.

"Please, be seated on the cot there by the wall,"

Tabitha offered graciously, hiding a small smile. "Even if you did manage to get down here with me, I'm not sure we'd get you back up again!"

"Sadly true," Kelila chuckled wryly, cradling her rounded belly. "I'm not as agile these days."

Tabitha managed a smile, suffering a slight pang in her heart in Kelila's sparkling presence. Observing the Cyrenian woman's beautifully rounded baby bump, Tabitha found it was difficult to keep her mind from wandering to thoughts of sorrow and self-pity. *I will never know what it is to carry the child of my beloved in my womb,* flitted across her mind for the umpteenth time since Kelila's arrival, further dampening her spirits. That tender dream had perished forever along with her husband.

Swiftly recognizing the dangerous direction of her thoughts, Tabitha rose to help Kelila as she lowered herself onto the stiff cot. Gently taking her friend's elbow, Tabitha couldn't help but smile as Kelila began her slow descent.

"Good heavens!" Kelila laughed merrily, coloring slightly in embarrassment once she was finally settled on the cot. "I feel as though I possess the grace of a lumbering ox these days."

"Nonsense," Tabitha chided, seating herself beside Kelila on the cot. "You're lovely."

Kelila's pointed expression indicated that she strongly disagreed.

"Now, how on earth did you gain entrance here?" Tabitha asked her, amused. "Joram's guards are relentless. And Eli—the overseer—wouldn't dare disregard my uncle's wishes."

"I like him," Kelila decided, turning to look at Tabitha.

"Who? Eli?"

"Yes. Somehow, I convinced the guards to let me in. Eli met me in the outer court, wringing his hands and looking nervous, as always. But when I told him I had come to see you, his demeanor changed and he told me how to locate your room. I think he has a soft spot for you, Tabitha."

"Our relationship is certainly improving." Tabitha smiled, recalling those early days when Eli had been convinced she simply couldn't be trusted. Though he remained rigidly close-minded regarding the Way, over time he had become an ally, of sorts, in Joram's house. She could only pray he would eventually accept Jesus as Lord.

"So *this* is the lodging your uncle provided for you," Kelila observed, her dark eyes scanning the bare stone chamber in obvious disapproval. "Tabitha, this simply won't do.!"

"But why not?"

"It's far too small for a growing child! And you haven't even a window to let in a bit of fresh air—"

"Nonsense," Tabitha cut in, gratified by her friend's concern. "From what I've heard, you and Philip spent months living in a dilapidated old market stall! So I think Laurel and I can manage here. Besides, we spend very little time in this room. Most often, we are moving about the mansion accomplishing our chores, or visiting the orphans and widows."

Kelila crossed her arms, unconvinced.

"Philip's sermon today was exceptional," Tabitha told her, intentionally changing the subject. "It touched my heart to see so many of the locals gladly receiving Jesus and His salvation."

"Oh, mine too!" Kelila exclaimed, her bright eyes conveying her joy. "The light of the gospel has shone upon this city. You must be thrilled, Tabitha."

"Truly, beyond words."

"And I, as well!" Lowering her gaze, Kelila anxiously twirled a long strand of curly dark hair, clearly a bit apprehensive about the subject she intended to broach. Lifting her gaze, she met Tabitha's with both sincerity and regret. "But, Tabitha, I haven't come to discuss Philip's sermon today."

"No?" Tabitha inquired, instantly on guard.

"No." Releasing a long, self-deprecating sigh, Kelila added solemnly, "I owe you an apology."

"An apology?" Tabitha repeated, surprised. "Whatever about?"

"I shouldn't have teased you about your friendship with Adam," she sighed, looking away in remorse. "It was only in fun, but I realize now it was thoughtless and insensitive to speak that way. You lost your husband to senseless violence, and I can't imagine how painful it must have been for you—and still is. Forgive me, Tabitha, if in my carelessness I rubbed salt on an open wound."

"I know you meant nothing by it," Tabitha answered quietly, wondering why she felt so uncomfortable discussing this subject with Kelila. Even now, she would like nothing better than to bid her friend farewell to spend the remainder of the evening alone, nursing her sadness and confusion.

But that would be displeasing to the Lord, she reminded herself, sitting up a bit straighter in her resolve. *These feelings I have right now—thoughts of fear and confusion—are not of God. Ours is a God of peace, while chaos, disorder, and confusion are from the evil one. Perhaps it's time to evaluate these contrary feelings, rather than simply ignoring them and hoping they will go away on their own.*

"It's clear to me you remain deeply in love with Stephanos," Kelila was saying, reminding Tabitha that their discomfiting conversation remained unfinished. "And it would be just awful if I made you feel awkward or self-conscious around Adam. He is a godly man and an ally in the faith, and you—not to mention, the church here—will need him, so please don't push him away on my account! Forgive me for so grossly misinterpreting the signals passing between you two."

"Perhaps you weren't so wrong in your assessment," Tabitha managed quietly, staring dully at her own hands folded numbly in her lap.

Kelila stared at her friend in surprise, hesitant to breathe a word lest she shatter Tabitha's sense of safety and confidence.

"Perhaps..." she sighed, shaking her head in disappointment. "Perhaps I became defensive when you started asking me questions about Adam because of my feelings toward him. They're a bit confusing," she confessed, releasing another wobbly sigh. "Adam is a kind, caring, godly man. When first we met, I was instantly reminded of my dear Stephanos."

Kelila nodded gently, allowing her friend the freedom to speak in her own way, at her own pace, without judgment.

"The fact is, it's impossible *not* to feel drawn to Adam," she sighed, wondering if Kelila could hear her heart pounding in her chest. "Everyone adores him, even crusty old men like Simon the tanner. He's just a wonderful person, full of the Holy Spirit and good deeds."

Kelila nodded again. Though she'd just met the young merchant, she agreed with Tabitha's assessment of him.

"So, perhaps, when you hinted that I might be interested in Adam, I felt guilty—disloyal to Stephanos, somehow. You see, when my husband died, part of my heart perished with him. I was certain I couldn't possibly love another man the way I loved him, with such fierce devotion. And I didn't want to."

"I can understand that," Kelila assured her meaningfully.

"Even now, the thought of marrying another man breaks my heart," Tabitha confessed brokenly, her voice catching.

Reaching out, Kelila touched her friend's trembling shoulder in a motherly manner, offering it a gentle squeeze.

"I just feel...confused," Tabitha admitted a bit roughly, regaining her composure. "I suppose I must ask the Lord to help me through this unexpected season of doubt."

"Again, I understand," Kelila assured her, her expression indicating her sincerity. After a long, solemn pause, Kelila added a bit hesitantly, "Tabitha, may I ask an honest question?"

"Don't you always?"

"Have you completely ruled out the possibility of a second marriage?" Kelila dared, carefully gauging her friend's reaction. "Will you live the remainder of your days as a widow, without a husband? Without a family of your own?"

"I *do* have a family," Tabitha quickly reminded her. "I have Laurel. And I have the body of Christ."

"I only ask because I want you to be happy," Kelila said softly.

"The allusion of supreme happiness can be very deceptive," Tabitha explained slowly, carefully, her brow furrowed in deep thought. "And the world's notion of happiness is misleading, filling our heads with notions of passion, romance, and *happily ever afters*. Sadly, we've been convinced that ultimate bliss lies in finding *true love*. And by *true love*, I am referring to the worldly notion—the idea that we can derive supreme happiness from another person. But, Kelila, we can't."

Thoughtfully tilting her head to one side, Kelila waited expectantly for Tabitha to go on.

"I'm certainly not arguing against marriage, for it is a gift from God. I'm simply saying that God calls some to remain single, some to marry, and still others to widowhood. Each season of life is a gift to be embraced and used for the glory of God."

"And you believe God wants you to remain a widow?"

"Regretfully, I realize that I've failed to seek Him in this matter," Tabitha confessed, shaking her head in dismay. "Perhaps that's why I've felt so confused lately. When I lost Stephanos, I made up my mind I would *never* marry again. I didn't even bother to consult the Lord about it; I simply made up my mind. But God wants me to seek Him in *all* things, and I have failed miserably to do so in this instance. The key is to embrace His will in every aspect of life, but how could I possibly do so if I haven't sought His guidance in this area? So perhaps our little misunderstanding this morning was a blessing in disguise, Kelila, for it has prompted me to seek the

Lord in this."

"Well, at least some good has come from over-using my big mouth," Kelila decided with a wobbly smile.

"On the contrary, I'm grateful you spoke up," Tabitha told her, feeling better already. "If you sensed any undercurrents between Adam and me, then perhaps I must evaluate the way I am conducting myself. I certainly wouldn't wish to mislead anyone or give a man the wrong idea, nor do I want to be a woman of mixed messages. Until the Lord reveals His will for my future, I must remain content in this season."

"Spoken like a very wise woman who knows what she is about," Kelila stated with a playful poke to the shoulder.

"Well, I haven't the slightest idea, but thankfully, the Lord does," Tabitha admitted with a wry smile.

"On that note, I must depart," Kelila announced, rising from the low cot with quite a bit of help from Tabitha. "Philip and I must keep our promise to visit Adam's father this evening."

"Don't you mean *your* promise?" Tabitha teased.

"Well, yes.," Kelila grinned with a wave of her hand. "But Philip was glad I offered. He, too, had planned to visit Adam's father when the occasion presented itself. Would you like to come along?"

"As much as I'd love to, I must stay and see to my chores," Tabitha told her with a gracious smile. "Having spent a lovely afternoon by the sea, I'm running a bit behind and my uncle will have my head if my assignments are neglected."

"Best of luck to you, then," Kelila chuckled. "Besides, your little one might not take kindly to being awakened after such a long day."

"Well, probably not," Tabitha agreed, smiling fondly at the sweet little bundle slumbering contentedly on her straw mat.

Exchanging warm embraces, the women bid each other whispered farewells.

With a tired smile, Tabitha watched as Kelila slipped out the door and into the corridor, a bounce in her step despite the added weight of her unborn child. Leaning against the doorpost, Tabitha closed her eyes, thanking God for bringing an important matter to her attention.

Your will, Lord, as always. You know what is best.

CHAPTER 21

Tabitha

Joppa

"May I…ahem, well…may I have a word with you, Miss Tabitha?"

Rocking back on her heels, Tabitha set aside the dirty rag with which she had been scrubbing the broad tiles of the reception hall, tiredly running the back of her hand across her forehead to smooth the damp tendrils of golden hair clinging to her face.

"Good evening, Eli," she greeted him, hoping she looked far less weary than she felt.

"You are working late tonight," Eli observed, gathering his nerve to broach a subject that appeared to weigh heavily on his mind.

"I am a bit behind on my chores," she confessed, ringing out the washrag and draping it over the side of her soap bucket. "I spent the afternoon at the shore, listening to Philip's sermon."

"Yes, yes. The master was none too happy about

that."

Tabitha lifted a brow, amused. Had Joram said something about her absence?

"May I, well, may I ask a question of you?"

"Always," Tabitha assured him, preparing to rise. "What troubles you, Eli?"

"No, no. You needn't rise on my account," Eli insisted, holding up a hand and appearing regretful to have interrupted her work. "This will only take a moment."

Tabitha looked up at him with large, questioning eyes, her curiosity outweighing her exhaustion.

"That boisterous young lady who came to visit you—she mentioned that her husband plans to visit the house of an invalid tonight, the father of a young man named Adam," Eli rushed ahead, clutching his writing tablet as if it were a lifeline.

"Yes," Tabitha nodded, wondering how any of this information concerned the flustered overseer. "Why?"

"Would that happen to be Josiah, whose son Adam currently minds his father's market stall by the docks?"

"Why, yes," Tabitha supplied, surprised by Eli's unexpected knowledge. "Wait. Did you say *his father's* market stall?"

Now it was Eli's turn to blink in surprise. "Why, yes. Didn't you know?"

"I thought the booth belonged to Adam. Isn't that his trade?"

"Oh, no. Heavens, no. Adam was a promising student of the Law, very involved in the study of the Pentateuch and such. I believe his desire was to fight for the rights of the poor, the voiceless, the oppressed."

"Adam wished to become a doctor of the Law? To defend the defenseless?" she repeated in shock.

"Precisely. He seemed to believe that influential men in prominent political and religious roles often take advantage of those without proper knowledge of the Law and the Scriptures. He wished to reintroduce this knowledge to commoners, insisting therein lies their freedom and happiness. As you can imagine, his interpretation of Torah vastly contradicted that of our esteemed religious leaders."

"So what happened?" Tabitha asked in surprise, her heart pounding in her chest. "Why did he so drastically change course?"

"His father became deathly ill," Eli supplied, his countenance falling. "So Adam took over his father's business to support him. Without Adam's help, Josiah would have surely lost the business and come to ruin."

"So Adam laid aside his dreams to care for his father," Tabitha realized, heart aching just a bit. It was so like Adam—setting aside his own desires for the sake of others. And he did so with a kind word and cheerful smile for all he encountered, despite his keen disappointment.

"Adam makes a decent living by the docks, so it isn't all bad," Eli quickly amended. "Far more than he would have made aiding the needy and the oppressed, who would undoubtedly prove unable to adequately compensate him for his time. Not only that, his theology isn't in keeping with that of the religious leaders', and I doubt they would have allowed him to practice his version of the Law of Moses for long."

"I can imagine," Tabitha murmured indignantly, her mind racing. Try as she might, she just couldn't envision the strong young man donning a lawyer's stern garments! Nor could she imagine him buried within the dark stone confines of the stuffy old synagogue, immersed in the study of the Law!

"Eli, how do you know so much about Adam?" Tabitha asked slowly, confused. "Are you a relation of his?"

"No, no. His father and I were boyhood friends," Eli confessed, lowering his gaze but failing to mask the regret in his eyes.

"*Were?*" Tabitha prodded gently. "What came between you?"

"After Josiah accepted a false religion and became an apostate, I was forced to distance myself or else be banned from the synagogue."

"You know about Josiah's faith in Jesus?"

"The whole town knows about it! Josiah attempted to win the religious leaders, but as you can imagine, it didn't go very well."

"And he was banned from the synagogue?"

"Only after he refused to recant his blasphemous doctrine."

Shaking her head sadly, Tabitha suddenly realized what Adam had meant that day at the market stall, when he had revealed his faith to her. He had cautioned her that such a faith would indeed prove risky—possibly even dangerous—in Joppa.

At the time, she hadn't realized he had been speaking from experience!

Poor Adam! It would seem his father had been cast from the synagogue for believing in Jesus. Not only that, old Josiah had lost all his friends and the respect of his neighbors. And, very likely, Adam's dream of practicing law had been dashed to pieces, as well. Even if the elders remained unaware of Adam's faith—which was highly unlikely—they wouldn't dare allow the son of a "heretic" to interpret the Law of Moses in their town and local synagogue."

"Perhaps now you can understand why I have cautioned you to keep your strange ideas to yourself when attending synagogue services," Eli muttered, wringing his hands in his nervous manner. "The religious leaders have pronounced him cursed, and the wasting illness he now suffers is undoubtedly punishment for his dangerous apostasy."

"Surely you don't believe that," Tabitha said, rising slowly to meet his gaze head on. "Josiah's illness has nothing to do with his faith in Jesus. On the contrary, his faith is upholding him during this trying season of life."

"Unless he recants, Josiah will perish in his sins," Eli repeated almost mechanically, avoiding Tabitha's gaze and clutching his tablet like a shield. "The religious leaders have pronounced it so."

"The religious leaders are *wrong*."

Tension crackled heavily in the air as silence lingered between them, almost like the strange sensation one experiences before a severe lightning storm.

"I suppose we shall see about that," Eli finally dared, clearly torn between the testimony of the courageous young woman before him and the dark omens pronounced by religious leaders.

"Yes," Tabitha nodded, attempting to curb her righteous anger toward those who had plagued so many with foolish superstitions and paralyzing fears. "Yes, indeed. We shall."

***

Kelila

Joppa

Wandering rather aimlessly about the small, lamplit central chamber of Adam's father's modest but tidy home, Kelila wondered if perhaps she shouldn't have come. Upon hers and Philip's arrival, Adam had swiftly answered the door, greeting them warmly and ushering them inside with hospitable enthusiasm. However, they had scarcely crossed the threshold when Philip had straightened, his countenance alighting with recognition and eager expectation. Instantly intrigued, Kelila was about to question her husband when he promptly cut short all pleasantries and asked to see Josiah, Adam's father, immediately.

"Of course, of course," Adam had responded, looking a bit surprised. "His good friend, Phineas, is sitting with him now, upstairs. And he is eager to meet you, as well."

"Wait here, beloved," Philip had gently instructed Kelila, and she couldn't help but feel a stab of disappointment—and annoyance—at his command. "We won't be long," he added, tossing her a playful wink.

Without further ado, Adam had led Philip up a steep, dimly lit flight of steps, apparently toward his father's sick room, leaving Kelila to stand, confused, near the threshold.

We won't be long, ha! Kelila thought, peeved by Philip's unlikely assurance. The evangelist was famously long-winded! What if he spoke with Adam's father late into the night? *But I suppose it wouldn't be appropriate for me to enter another man's bedchamber, even if it is his sickroom,* she decided, wondering what to do with herself in the time being.

I should have stayed with Tirzah, she thought in consternation, aimlessly meandering about the modestly furnished living space. *That would have proven far more palatable. We could be relaxing before the crackling kiln in her lovely little home, enjoying a warm mug of tea and chatting about anything and everything. But now I must simply stand here and wait—for hours, perhaps!*

Listlessly tracing the wide mouth of the stone water jar near the door, Kelila couldn't help but admire Adam's work ethic. The water supply was filled to the brim. Not only did he labor long hours at the docks, six days a week, but he seemed to keep a very neat and orderly home, as well. Clearly, his father was unable to keep house, being confined to his sickbed, which left all the chores to Adam.

It must be difficult for them, without a woman to help nurse Adam's father and tend to the home, Kelila thought sadly. She had learned through Tirzah that Josiah's wife had passed away over ten years ago. After her death, the merchant had remained a widower, cheerful and hardworking, until his sickness eventually rendered him an invalid.

An unexpected clatter of tumbling pots and pans jerked Kelila's attention toward the small kitchen area, where she was startled by the appearance of a rotund, middle-aged woman sporting a dirty apron, messy brown hair sticking out from a slipshod cap, and a sour temper.

"For the love of—" the woman sputtered, bending to retrieve the armload of pots and pans she had dropped in her careless haste. "For heaven's sake!"

Confused, Kelila drew a bit closer to the kitchen, somewhat relieved that the stone counter stood between her and the less-than-friendly woman gathering up dented cookware.

"What in Israel—" the woman declared, straightening at the unexpected sight of a young woman standing near the threshold. "Who are you?" she demanded brusquely. "How did you get in?"

"I am a friend of Adam's," Kelila stammered, protectively placing a hand on her bulging abdomen. "My husband is visiting Josiah, upstairs. And you? Have you been here all this time?"

"Just came in that back door there," the woman grumped, motioning toward the narrow exit just behind her. Clearly irritated by Kelila's presence, she studied the dusky foreigner with unveiled distaste and snapped, "You're not from around here, are you?"

"I'm not," Kelila answered with a rueful grin. "My husband and I are here visiting friends."

"Your husband..." the woman muttered, shoving wayward brown hair from her eyes. "Would he happen to be the meddlesome evangelist stirring up all the ruckus around here?"

"One and the same," Kelila replied, amused. "I take it you haven't yet attended one of his services?"

"Wouldn't dare."

"And why not?"

"I don't need me some new brand of religion that'll surely kindle the wrath of all the important people around here," the woman huffed, turning her attention toward the waning light of the cookfire. Impatiently, she began stoking the low flames, muttering under her breath as she coaxed it back to life.

"You must be a friend or relative of Adam and Josiah," Kelila surmised, merely for the sake of making conversation. She didn't relish the idea of simply standing there in awkward silence while the ill-tempered woman bustled about the small cook space.

"Neither one," the woman responded tersely, stacking pots and pans rather haphazardly on the stone counter. "I'm Ida, a neighbor. Adam hired me to do the laundry and keep house—only twice a week. He handles most of the chores around here."

"He's a handy fellow," Kelila quipped, confused by Adam's choice of a housekeeper. Sharp-tongued and foul-tempered, Ida was nothing like her kind-hearted, good-natured employer. "How long have you been working for him?"

"Since his father became an invalid," Ida responded with little grace. "It's a downright wonder that man is still living. I've seen plenty others with the same sickness pass within a matter of weeks or months of getting ill. They waste away, little by little, until the sickness consumes them."

"What exactly is it that ails him?" Kelila asked, realizing she knew very little about Josiah's situation.

"Heaven only knows," Ida shrugged, haphazardly ladling fresh water into a large metal pot. "Most everyone around these parts believes the man was struck down by God Himself, after he embraced some foolish religious doctrine."

"I see," Kelila nodded, deeply saddened. It was bad enough to be sick unto death; how much worse to be disowned by one's entire village and deemed a heretic, an outcast. Poor Josiah!

"What?" Ida snapped, her shrewd black eyes blinking in suspicion. "You disagree?"

"I do," Kelila responded, uncowed by the housekeeper's groundless challenge.

"Well, that shows how much *you* know."

"If Josiah was forsaken by his friends and neighbors, then why are *you* here working for him?" Kelila asked pointedly, ignoring the woman's sarcasm and presenting a challenge of her own.

"Money is money, and I'll take a little extra wherever I can get it," Ida grumped, turning to suspend the full kettle over the crackling fire. "I'll take an outcast's coins the same as a reputable man's."

"Hmm."

"Don't get me wrong," Ida muttered, turning around to face her and wiping damp hands on her smudged apron. "Josiah has a good heart; he's just misguided. And his foolish religious ideas may cost him his life."

"On the contrary," Kelila shot back, joining the woman in the kitchen and placing her hands on the wide stone counter between them. "Josiah's faith in Jesus is the doorway to everlasting life. Sickness may ravage the body, but it cannot destroy the soul of one redeemed by the blood of Christ."

"Ah, you believe in that nonsense, as well!"

"With all my heart."

"Well, best of luck to you, then," Ida harrumphed,

reaching for a wooden spoon and bending to stir the dried lentils soaking in the kettle. "But I'll tell you this—only God can heal that man. And I fear his newfound *Savior*—this Jesus, the One whom Josiah ranted and raved about in the synagogue—shall leave him sorely disappointed."

Crossing her arms in disgust, Kelila resisted the urge to snap at the pompous little woman and her faithless proclamation. After all, what kind of witness would that be? Bowing her head, she decided to pray instead.

For it would seem this bitter woman was in far greater need of healing than her bedridden benefactor.

***

Philip

Philip gazed down upon the shriveled, wasted shell of a man who once must have been strong and robust, like his son. But despite Josiah's apparent illness, his eyes remained clear and alert, his smile weak but ready. He was a tall man, with shoulders far too broad for his emaciated form. His curly graying hair and beard were neatly trimmed—clearly Adam's tender doing.

After warmly drawing the evangelist into the room, Phineas, Josiah's devoted friend and a former Pharisee, stepped back respectfully, anxious to hear whatever words of comfort the young man might have to offer.

Smiling warmly upon the fading merchant, Philip knelt beside his sickbed, placing strong, well-shaped hands over the thin, withered hands of Adam's father.

"Ah, the famous Philip," the older man rasped, painstakingly turning his head to exchange knowing smiles with Adam and Phineas. "Thank you for this."

"It is my honor and privilege to meet with you," Philip assured him, humbled by the merchant's humility and courage in the face of death. "Josiah, I've been told you believe Jesus is, indeed, the Son of God."

"Jesus Christ, Son of God, Savior of the world."

"Amen.," Philip nodded, his entire being filling with joy as the Holy Spirit welled within him, guiding his thoughts, directing his actions. "I have but one question for you, Josiah; and this, from our Lord. Not from me."

"Anything," Josiah managed weakly, struggling to squeeze Philip's strong hand.

"Josiah," Philip declared, rising slowly to his feet. "Do you want to be well?"

The room grew instantly still as the men within the small chamber became startingly aware of the powerful presence of God. Adam and Phineas exchanged looks of awe, wondering if they were about to witness the kind of miracle they had only heard about.

Lifting a hand as one with great authority, Philip spoke in a tone that nearly shook the small chamber in which they stood.

"In the name of Jesus Christ, the Son of God, be healed!"

CHAPTER 22

Kelila

Joppa

Ida nearly dropped another neat stack of cookpots as an unexpected commotion erupted upstairs. Heart springing into her throat, Kelila exchanged a questioning look with the harried housekeeper as an explosion of hearty shouts, uproarious laughter, and even dancing feet met their ears.

"What in heaven—" Ida declared as the sound of pounding feet came crashing down the darkened staircase. And then Josiah emerged from the shadows, bounding down the stairs with the explosive energy of a young boy, with Philip, Adam, and Phineas not far behind him.

Releasing an earth-shattering scream, Ida failed to keep the stack of pots in her grasp this time. The entire stack clattered loudly to the ground as her hands flew to her mouth in wide-eyed fear.

"Greetings, our dear little housekeeper!" Josiah

boomed, taking the plump woman and lifting her off her feet. Swinging her several rounds about the kitchen, he placed her back on her feet, seemingly oblivious to her screams of utter terror. "I am healed!" Josiah cried, tears of joy streaming down his face and into his beard. "I am restored!"

Exchanging a knowing look with Philip, Kelila's eyes glistened with happy tears as she realized the miracle God had wrought on behalf of Adam's faithful father. Adam and Phineas flanked the evangelist on either side, grinning ear to ear.

"But… but…*what?* How…how did you do it?" Ida stammered, pressing herself flat against the furthest wall as she eyed the calm evangelist in obvious fear.

"*I* did nothing," Philip assured her. "Josiah was healed in the name of Jesus Christ, the Son of God."

"Praise be to God," Josiah declared, his brown eyes sparkling with ethereal light. "And blessed be the name of His Son forever and ever!"

"See?" Kelila told Ida with an impish little grin. "It would seem Josiah's newfound Savior hasn't disappointed him, after all!"

***

Leah

Jerusalem

"Leah? Are you all right?"

Jerking her attention toward the sweet young woman standing before her, Leah covered her heart with one hand, deeply troubled. "Rhoda," she said dully, looking away. "You startled me."

Gazing with deep concern upon the stern-faced girl hunched over on the bench, Rhoda noted Leah's bent shoulders, her troubled dark eyes, and the way her slender fingers toyed with the shawl she clutched almost desperately about her narrow frame, as if she wished to vanish into the warm, comforting folds of the simple garment.

"You don't look well," Rhoda stated honestly, her large brown eyes softening.

"I suppose..." Leah sighed, her voice trailing off in dismay. "I suppose that's because I am *not* well."

"Shall I find Mary?" Rhoda asked, appearing further concerned for her.

"No, no. Please, don't do that."

Glancing anxiously about the Upper Room, Rhoda watched as fellow believers ascended the stairway, their tones reverently hushed as they greeted one another and found their respective benches before the service would commence. Though she thought it best to locate her mistress, she chose to honor Leah's request. Lowering herself onto the bench beside the distressed young woman, Rhoda touched her shoulder. "What troubles you, Leah? How can I help?"

Lifting her head, Leah met her gaze, her own burning with shame.

Puzzled, Rhoda wondered about her friend's guilt-ridden expression, her heart picking up speed as a strange premonition settled over her.

Something was wrong, terribly wrong.

"Leah?"

Looking away, Leah lowered her head, releasing a tremulous sigh. Torn between plaguing guilt and rising fear, she realized she could no longer keep her identity a secret. How could she worship with these wonderful people when her own brother was on the road at that very moment, determined to hunt down their fellow believers?

I should have found a way to stop him, she thought, plagued by doubt. *Surely there was something I could have done to stop him. Surely, something...*

"Leah? You can tell me, whatever it is," Rhoda assured her, her eyes so kind and patient Leah was further pained by her failure to intervene on behalf of the believers in Damascus. It felt wrong to keep silent now, wrong to hold her tongue.

Rhoda deserved to know who she, Leah, really was. The entire congregation deserved to know. After all the love and acceptance they had lavished upon her, she owed them that simple courtesy. She owed them the *truth.*

Closing her eyes tightly, Leah clenched her fist, praying she would not be banished from this precious gathering for the sins of her older brother.

"Rhoda," Leah breathed, sensing her new friend's apprehension. "I haven't been entirely honest with you."

"Honest?" Rhoda repeated, perplexed. "Honest about what?"

"About my identity," Leah whispered, her color deepening in shame. "About who I am."

Heart fluttering like a trapped bird, Rhoda studied her friend with anxious eyes, uncertain about where the conversation was headed.

"As you know, I am not from Jerusalem," Leah confessed, her heart pounding frantically in her chest. "I hail from Tarsus of Cilicia. My father sent me here to stay with my brother, who is acting on my father's behalf to arrange a marriage for me—a marriage with a very prestigious and highly respected religious scholar. This man—he isn't a believer."

Rhoda nodded slowly, wondering why Leah felt guilty about any of that. It was perfectly natural for a father to want the very best for his daughter, after all. And Leah's father, an unbeliever himself, wouldn't understand the importance of selecting a believing husband for his faith-filled daughter. But none of that was Leah's fault; on the contrary, the situation was entirely out of her control.

"But that's not the worst part, Rhoda," Leah persisted, her dark eyes boring into her friend's like two fiery coals. "My brother…" she paused, steeling herself for the worst confession of all. "My brother is Saul of Tarsus, and at this very moment, he travels the road to Damascus. There, he intends to destroy all followers of the Way."

Rhoda's heart sprang into her throat, beating wildly. Sensing herself recoiling from Saul's sister—Saul's *sister*, for heaven's sake—Rhoda attempted to remain calm, at ease. She didn't wish to make a scene, nor did she want Leah to regret her painful honesty.

What have I done? Rhoda thought, her eyes frantically scanning the raised platform before them for any sign of her mistress. Had she unwittingly ushered a dangerous deceiver into their midst?

Covering her face with her hands, Leah shook her head in shame. "Oh, Rhoda. I'm so sorry. I should have told you. I should have told all of you."

Rhoda attempted to steady herself and calm her racing heart. After all, it wasn't entirely impossible that Leah was sincere in her faith, and she certainly didn't wish to scare or shame the new believer—if her conversion was, indeed, genuine. And though Rhoda wasn't the least bit surprised that Saul intended to obliterate the believers of Damascus—Agabus had already revealed that terrible truth—she was far more overcome by Leah's shocking revelation regarding her identity. To be sharing a bench with the *sister* of a blood-crazed killer—the man bent upon the torture and destruction of those she loved—was unnerving, to say the least.

Forcing herself to remain calm, Rhoda studied the anxious young woman beside her, pondering the severity of Leah's shocking confession. Had Saul planted her in their midst with cruel intent? Did she share his kindling hatred toward the believers? Perhaps the girl was a skilled double agent, working for her brother all while feigning sympathy toward the church...

"I'm so sorry I wasn't entirely truthful with you," Leah apologized earnestly, her voice barely above a whisper. "But I was so ashamed. I was afraid that... that if anyone knew about my brother, I would be cast out. I couldn't bear to be cut off from God's people. Please, Rhoda. Please, forgive me."

Biting her lower lip, Rhoda studied the penitent young woman before her and saw true grief and sincere repentance etched upon her every feature. Suddenly welling with sympathy for the distraught girl, Rhoda took her hand. "You needn't apologize," she said quickly, offering her trembling hand a gentle squeeze. "On the contrary, you are quite courageous coming here despite your brother's unwavering stance against the Way."

"Then...you're not mad at me?"

"Of course not," Rhoda declared with great feeling, wondering what—if anything—should be done about Leah's confession. "I understand why you were nervous to tell us. And surely the others will understand, as well."

"Oh, Rhoda, I do hope so."

"They *will.*"

"But what about my brother, Saul? And the believers of Damascus? What can be done about this?" Leah persisted, her obsidian eyes welling with desperation. "How can we stop him, Rhoda? What can we do?"

"We can *pray.*"

Startled, both girls turned on the bench to see Mary seated calmly behind them, her graceful hands folded in her lap, her gray eyes sparkling with warmth and understanding.

How does she do that? Rhoda thought with an admiring smile. It seemed her lady always appeared right when and where she was most needed.!

"Then... then you heard everything?" Leah whispered, clearly dismayed.

"Enough to know that you are a very brave girl, Leah," Mary assured her, leaning forward to place a steadying hand upon the girl's shoulder. "Now, let us speak with the congregation. I believe it's time we begin praying for that poor, lost brother of yours in earnest."

CHAPTER 23

Saul of Tarsus

On the Road to Damascus

Dusk was swiftly falling upon the straggling entourage of travelers, hemmed in by serious-looking hired guards brandishing far more serious-looking spears. Shielding his eyes from the staggering rays of the setting sun, Saul grimaced, watching the dark-robed men of his entourage with scorn.

They're soft, he thought, irked beyond measure. *Every last one of them.*

Painstakingly, Saul had selected promising young men who excelled in their studies to aid him on this important journey, little considering the fact that these diligent scholars were accustomed to being sequestered in luxurious homes, donning soft garments and seated behind elegant desks.

Clearly, several days of hard travel had posed a rude awakening for them.

Tightly clenching his jaw, Saul marveled at the incompetency of his comrades. He daily buffeted

his body into submission, partaking of the most nu-
tritious foods and exercising his solid muscles with
uncompromising regularity. But these boys—for
they could hardly be called *men*, in his opinion—
were so absorbed in scholastic pursuits that they
had neglected the care and strengthening of their
physical bodies.

And the miserable fools were slowing him down.
It was unacceptable! And now—*now* he must squander yet another night lodging in a shoddy, age-old
caravanserai scarcely fit for a measly pauper, much
less Judea's finest! He could see it just up ahead,
cresting a brown, sun-scorched hill. Even the relief
of cooler months had failed to restore the long-dead
greenery of the sunbaked promontory and the
surrounding area. The landscape was less than impressive, in his own estimation, further souring his
mood. Nothing but acres of bare farmland, dotted
here and there with a dead, dry tree.

*At this pace, we'll never reach the caravanserai
before nightfall,* he thought, peeved. It was far more
difficult setting up camp after dark.

Steeling himself against his own burning indignation, Saul quickened his pace, wondering if the
professional armed guards resented the tedious
pace as much as he did. How much longer until
the splendid gates and towering walls of ancient
Damascus loomed into view? A seasoned traveler
might complete the journey from Jerusalem to Damascus in two weeks or less. But at this rate, he'd
consider himself lucky to reach the ancient city
before the new year commenced! Even with a slew
of expensive, mule-drawn carriages, a professional guide, and the most highly trained guards that
money—and Caiaphas—could buy, the entourage

proceeded at a snail's pace.

And a crippled snail, at that, Saul seethed, disgusted. His colleagues were utterly pathetic. The fact that they were losing precious time didn't seem to disturb them in the least. Suddenly drawn by angry shouts far from the road, Saul pulled himself from his brooding reverie to identify the commotion. He was surprised to see an ox pulling—or rather, *refusing* to pull—a plow in a large field just off the dusty road. Several dirtily clad farmers had gathered round the stubborn beast, enjoying a good laugh at the owner's expense.

The owner didn't seem to find the ox's behavior particularly funny.

With an air of boredom, Saul folded strong arms in front of his chest, a smirk tipping his lips at the farmer's obvious chagrin toward the defiant creature. Exasperated, he shouted at the stubborn animal in rage, wielding a sharp, dangerous-looking goad by which he slashed at the legs of the powerful beast to urge him in the right direction.

Heart pounding dully in his chest, Saul felt strangely rooted in place, glued to the pitiful scene even as the lavish, mule-drawn carriages of his colleagues passed him by and faded into the background. Stroking his bearded chin in grim amusement, Saul wondered at the ox's indignation. Surely the beast recognized he wouldn't have his way in the end! Ultimately, he must submit to the will of his master or risk his own destruction.

Unable to tear his gaze from the powerful beast as it reared its head and lowed in furious protest against its master, Saul shook his head in condescension as the scoffing farmers scattered like mice, spooked by the ox's violent outburst. Oddly disturbed, he watched as the fierce black creature lunged backward, kicking violently against the goad and cutting himself deeply.

Uncharacteristically moved by the scene, Saul realized in dismay that he sympathized with the poor ox. For like the bleeding, raging animal before him, his violent efforts and stubborn resistance against the Way had proven futile thus far.

I am but one man, he thought, resenting his apathetic colleagues with every fiber of his being. Adorned in fine, soft robes, these young religious scholars oft boasted of their passion for the Law— until they were required to take action to defend it.

How am I to single-handedly overthrow this wicked religion which spreads like dangerous wild-fire? How am I to do this alone?

Saul was certain he had done everything in his power to uproot the growing church. And yet, when ten believers were swiftly silenced, twenty more sprang up in their place. And now so-called *churches* were cropping up not only in Judea and Galilee, but in all the surrounding regions.

How was he to crush this seemingly unstoppable force with his own human limitations?

Attempting to curb his wrath, Saul closed his eyes. Strangely enough, it was the face of the dead evangelist that filled his conscious mind as a conversation shared long ago surfaced in his memory.

"As long as I draw breath, I will refute your sacrilegious claims," Saul had threatened the maddening evangelist called Stephanos. *"Of this you can be certain—you will indeed be silenced, just as your so-called Christ was blotted from this life when the Romans nailed Him to a wretched cross."*

Stephanos hadn't seemed the least bit concerned

about Saul's pompous threat. Instead, he had merely smiled, unsettling the seething Pharisee far more than Saul cared to admit.

"Ah, but the Romans didn't know our God overcomes evil with good, dear brother," Stephanos had replied in his easy way. *"By nailing Jesus to the cross, they unwittingly participated in God's grand plan for the redemption of all mankind. And by your own stubborn resistance, you may find yourself doing that very thing."*

Clenching his fists at his sides, Saul was tempted to curse the day he was born. He had been certain Stephanos's death would put an end to the evangelist's self-righteous preaching. And yet, it was as if the dead man's words haunted Saul from beyond the grave, plaguing his sleepless nights and torturous waking hours.

Even worse than before.

By nailing Jesus to the cross, they unwittingly participated in God's grand plan for the redemption of all mankind. And by your own stubborn resistance, you may find yourself doing that very thing...

Gritting his teeth, Saul turned his attention from the ox, determined to cast the disturbing incident—and the evangelist's troubling words—far from his mind.

***

Tabitha

Joppa

"This is a bad idea."

Holding back a smile, Tabitha calmly acknowledged Eli's concern with a simple observation. "Joram allows you an hour to sup and to rest at midday, does he not? Surely you are free to utilize your own time as you see fit."

"But if the master learns I have chosen to fraternize with heretics and apostates—"

Suppressing a laugh, Tabitha paused on the road, gently touching the overseer's arm. "It will be fine, Eli. Joram needn't know your whereabouts every hour of the day."

"And yet, somehow he *does*."

"You worry too much."

"And you, not nearly enough!"

Smiling, Tabitha resumed her easy gait. She was nearly bursting at the seams, thinking of the surprise that awaited Eli at Tirzah's house. She knew that Tirzah, Philip, and Kelila were just as excited as she was as they awaited her arrival.

"The master will find it suspicious that we left the house together," Eli went on, stepping aside as a mule-drawn cart clattered by them on the bustling avenue. "And you know he doesn't like it when you leave your daughter in Martha's care."

"Joram is bedded down for his afternoon nap and shall be none the wiser."

"Or so you think!"

"Calm down, Eli. Everything will be fine."

"But I must ask why you have insisted that I accompany you to visit your troublemaking friend. You know as well as I that the master disapproves of her!"

"Deep down, I imagine Joram is relatively fond of Tirzah."

"That is doubtful."

Tabitha only grinned.

"Couldn't we have simply spoken with her before she left Joram's estate for the day? And why this dreadful air of mystery?" Eli persisted, losing his nerve as Tirzah's quaint little house loomed into view. "Why not simply tell me what is afoot?"

"Now where's the fun in that, Eli?"

"I am not interested in *fun*."

"But everyone likes surprises!"

"I detest them."

"Don't worry," Tabitha assured him as they reached Tirzah's low gate. "Trust me, you will be happy I brought you here today." Opening the latch, she fondly recalled the last time she had stood in this outer court with Eli—the day Joram had sent his flustered overseer to "retrieve" her after she had been turned away at the door. How could she have possibly known that this exasperating fellow servant would soon become dear to her heart? If only he, too, could be counted as a brother in Christ! But as of now, Eli stoutly refused to consider Jesus' claims of Messiahship, so concerned was he about losing credibility at the synagogue—the very life-blood of his religion.

Pausing before the door, Tabitha indulged in a small smile of anticipation. Perhaps, after today, that would change...

"This whole ordeal is risky and quite perplexing—" Eli was saying as the door swung open unexpectedly, surprising them both.

Halting mid-sentence, Eli stood, spellbound, his jaw dropping in disbelief at the shocking sight that met his wide eyes.

"Greetings, my dear old friend!" declared a fully

restored Josiah, larger than life, standing boldly on the threshold and grinning broadly.

Staggering backward in fearful amazement, Eli's eyes grew round beneath his bright turban as he stared at the shining faces of the believers surrounding Josiah—Philip and Kelila, Adam and Phineas, and Tirzah grinning mischievously—all eager to witness the reaction of the typically stern overseer.

"Jo—Jo—Josiah," Eli stammered as Tabitha drew alongside him, steadying him by the elbow. "You're... you are well!"

"I am *healed*," Josiah boomed, stretching out his arms in emphasis.

"Healed..." Eli repeated dumbly, unnerved. "But... but *how*? You were at death's door! No one—*no one*—expected you to recover!"

Exchanging knowing looks with his fellow believers, Josiah ushered his former boyhood friend nearer the door. "Come," he invited, his lusty voice confirming his health and vigor. "Honor me by sharing a meal with us, my friend. And allow me to tell you all about it."

CHAPTER 24

Tabitha

Joppa

Much to Tabitha's disappointment, it was a silent and rather awkward retreat from Tirzah's house back to Joram's resplendent estate.

Eli had not appreciated Josiah's glowing report about his healing in the name of Jesus, the "dead troublemaker" whom the stringent overseer had long since deemed a heretic and a rabblerouser. Adam's father had scarcely completed his joyous testimony of restoration when Eli had risen stiffly from his mat at the table, adjusting his turban with an air of perturbation.

"A wild tale," he had stated, red-faced in his attempt to conceal his mounting angst...and fear. "But I must be off. I haven't time to dilly dally around the table all afternoon when there is work to be done at my master's estate."

Heart sinking, Tabitha had glanced around the

table at her brothers and sisters in Christ. While Philip, Kelila, Adam, and Phineas appeared deeply saddened by Eli's rejection, both Josiah and Tirzah looked shocked and even slightly indignant.

"Jesus *healed* me, Eli," Josiah had declared, rising and grasping his former friend by stiff shoulders. "Surely you wish to learn more about Him now!"

"A dead rabbi cannot heal a man," Eli told him, his eyes shifting in discomfiture.

"I couldn't agree more," Josiah had assured him, nodding vigorously. "Thus, you have proven my point. Jesus Christ is *alive*, friend! He is alive and restoring our broken nation and our broken bodies to this very day! Can't you see it?"

"I really must be going," Eli had answered stiffly, grasping at his intricate overcoat as if wishing to disappear within the elaborate folds. "Good day, everyone."

"Come on, Eli!" Tirzah had declared in exasperation, determined to get a word in before Eli fled the scene. "I've always known you to be stubborn, but surely you're not blind!"

"Nor am I a fool."

Tirzah had opened her mouth to retort, but a gentle look from Philip had stilled her tongue, though grudgingly.

Surprised and saddened by Eli's unexpected reaction, Tabitha had watched as Philip rose amicably from the table, firmly grasping the overseer's cold, trembling hand. "It was an honor to sup with you today, Eli," he smiled, his tone full of warmth and assurance. "I hope we can speak again."

Muttering something under his breath, Eli had hastily withdrawn his hand from the evangelist's and made a beeline for the door.

"Wait. I shall come with you." Exchanging knowing looks with the fellow believers around the table, Tabitha had risen gracefully, sensing it best to walk home with the disgruntled servant. She didn't wish for him to feel betrayed nor abandoned. Sensing the sympathetic eyes of her friends upon her as she crossed the room behind the swiftly retreating servant, she gently closed the door behind them. Even as they crossed the outer court, Eli spoke not a word to her, though Tabitha decided no words were truly necessary. The rigid back he presented to her spoke volumes.

Deeply discouraged, Tabitha was comforted knowing that her fellow believers had undoubtedly grasped hands to pray fervently for Eli's salvation the moment the door had shut behind them.

The typically short walk to Joram's mansion dragged on for what felt like an eternity. The heavy silence lingering in the air between them was disheartening, especially when Tabitha had expected Eli to be amazed by the miraculous healing of an old friend. Instead, he seemed further closed to the truth, even more deeply troubled.

"I apologize if we made you feel uncomfortable, Eli," Tabitha finally said as Joram's impressive gates loomed into view, armed sentries on either side of the entrance. "I didn't wish to upset you."

"You set me up."

Stunned, Tabitha froze along the path near her uncle's towering ivy-strewn stone walls. "I had no intention—"

"Regardless of your intent, that's how it felt," Eli shot back forthrightly. "You led me into...into...into a *trap*, a den of lions!"

"How so?" Tabitha asked him, sincerely seeking to understand.

"What did you suppose?" he asked her, wheeling around to face her. "That I would see my boyhood friend restored to health, be astounded by the so-called miracle, and be converted on the spot?"

"Well, I certainly hoped," Tabitha admitted with a rueful smile.

"Then I shall tell you as I told that troublesome potter woman friend of yours—I am not a fool!"

"Of course not."

"And I will not be fooled by a clever deception."

"A clever deception?" Tabitha repeated, shocked. "You saw Josiah yourself! He is healed, through and through!"

"He recovered from a long illness. That is no miracle, in my estimation."

"But you *yourself* said Josiah was at death's door," Tabitha reminded him, amazed. "How can you say his healing wasn't a miracle?"

"Occasionally, sick people get well. Such was the case with Josiah."

"Surely you know that isn't true—"

"I know that I could find myself in a world of trouble should I follow your path of blind belief," Eli sighed, shaking his head in defeat. "I cannot risk it."

"If only you knew what was *truly* at risk, Eli—"

"I do not wish to discuss this any longer," he cut in nervously, wringing his hands. "I respect your decision to choose your own religion, Miss Tabitha. And I must ask that you respect my right to do the same."

Tabitha nodded miserably, wanting to cry. "I

never meant to upset you, Eli. I only arranged the meeting with Josiah because I care about you."

"Well, you certainly have an odd way of showing it."

Dismally, Tabitha watched as Eli turned on his heel and hurried past the armed guards posted at the gate, his bright red turban bobbing along with his harried steps.

Well, that couldn't have possibly gone any worse, she thought, peeved. Sighing deeply, she couldn't help but feel as she had on that fateful day when she'd stood outside her uncle's manor for the first time, the door slammed soundly in her face.

How she wished she possessed the wisdom and tact of her late husband. Her beloved Stephanos would have known how to reach this impossible man! Stephanos had never been perceived as pushy or insensitive to another's beliefs.

Oh, Lord, I never intended to make Eli feel cornered at Tirzah's house. I only wished for him to see Your hand at work.

Patience, beloved. I know what I AM doing. Rest in that. Rest in Me.

Placing a steadying hand against the wall, Tabitha closed her eyes, attempting to rest in the Lord's promises, as instructed.

Even so, Father, what will it take for that man to come to his senses? How much more of a miracle could he possibly ask for?

Trust Me. I have a plan. You'll see.

Sighing, Tabitha resumed her anxious steps. After all, there were chores to be done, and she certainly hadn't time to mope and stew about her present failure.

She could only hope she hadn't damaged Eli's trust beyond repair.

***

"Where have you been?"

Halting mid-step, Tabitha turned to see Joram seated in a garishly upholstered chair in the reception hall's sitting area, his countenance stern. Though his stance appeared relaxed and casual, she sensed he was merely poised as a viper calmly waiting to strike.

Resisting her own impatience, Tabitha forced a seraphic smile she was far from feeling. After all, she was eager to check on her daughter after returning from Tirzah's and finish her chores for the day. And after her disappointing experience with Eli, the last thing she wanted was an interrogation from her pretentious uncle.

"Are you going deaf?" Joram groused, his eyes narrowing in suspicion. Sizing up his niece like a cat with a doomed mouse, he commanded haughtily, "I asked where you have been, and I expect an answer!"

"I have just returned from Tirzah's house," Tabitha answered honestly, balking inwardly at his imperious tone. At the present, she hadn't the slightest inclination to put up with Joram's loathsome condescension. It hadn't been a particularly pleasant afternoon, thus far.

Lord Jesus, help me!

"Returning from Tirzah's?" Joram dared her, a silver brow lifting in derision. "Then you weren't carousing on the beach again with your irresponsible young friends?"

Carousing on the beach with irresponsible young friends? she thought, sorely tempted to defend herself. *That's a fine way to say, Worshiping God with fellow believers!* Nettled, Tabitha carefully concealed her annoyance. "No, I wasn't at the beach. Surely you know that. You can see Philip's gatherings from your balcony."

Glaring at her, Joram's face reddened at the implication of her remark. "I have far more important things to do than spy upon your worthless rallies from my balcony!"

Smiling sweetly, Tabitha denied the urge to confront his blatant lie. *Now if only he could also hear Philip's sermons from that great distance, as well!* she thought, peeved. *That might actually do him some good.*

"I think it's time we had a little chat, the two of us," Joram stated, his tone menacing as he gestured toward the empty chair facing his.

"How nice," Tabitha chimed, taking the seat before him with a practiced air of anticipation. "We do need to spend more time together," she teased.

"This discussion is not about exchanging empty pleasantries!" Joram argued, perturbed. "I am displeased with this arrangement and disgusted by the way you conduct yourself."

Tabitha remained seated calmly in her chair, hands folded in her lap, her demeanor tranquil despite her raging inner turbulence. Though she would have liked nothing better than to lash out and defend herself against Joram's groundless accusations, she had walked with the Lord long enough to recognize the danger of surrendering to one's emotions, and she determined to steel herself against them. Right now, the Lord had presented yet another opportunity to witness to this angry uncle, to minister peace.

Appearing somewhat surprised by his niece's calm capitulation, Joram leaned forward in his chair, his brows knitting together in dismay. "Why are you here?"

"Because you asked me to sit down," Tabitha offered, an impish little grin teasing the corners of her lips.

"Don't play games with me! You know what I mean."

"You won't like my answer."

"Then try me!"

Studying her uncle's flaming countenance, Tabitha nodded slowly, praying for wisdom in her response. "I am here because God led me to Joppa," she replied.

"Ah, a vague, insouciant explanation that tells me nothing at all."

"When Jesus ascended to His Father in Heaven, He commanded His followers to take His gospel to all nations. We knew we would be scattered, sent to deliver the message of salvation all over the world," Tabitha explained. "At the time, none of us knew where would be sent. Well, God has sent me here. To Joppa."

"A fine excuse to take advantage of a wealthy relative, living a privileged lifestyle in a seaside town with friends!"

"A privileged lifestyle?" Tabitha repeated, stunned. "Forgive my boldness, my lord, but perhaps you should take a closer look at the situation. I work grueling hours for you in exchange for a very small storage space adjoining the servants' quarters. My spare time—which is sparse, to be sure—is utilized ministering to the poverty-stricken widows and orphans of this region. Most nights, I fall into bed bone-weary, only to rise less than five or six hours later to begin again. I'm not entirely sure your assessment of a 'privileged lifestyle' is entirely accurate."

"And am I supposed to feel sorry for you?" Joram demanded harshly, grasping the gilded arms of his chair with white-knuckled fists. "Your situation is far better than most widows can boast!"

"And I wouldn't disagree," Tabitha answered humbly. "Daily, I see young widows with little children, desperately poor. Many haven't the slightest clue if or when they may have their next meal. Some of them are homeless, hungry, and cold. I am grateful, my lord, for this roof over my head. I am exceedingly grateful for your employment. The Lord has met my every need, and I have no complaint."

"The *Lord* has met your needs?" Joram challenged. "From how I see it, *I* have provided this roof over your head. *I* have seen to your needs."

"By the Lord's gracious will, yes, you have provided a place for me to work and to lodge. And I am very thankful."

"Are you?" Joram drawled with a sardonic lift of his brow. "Why, then, do you consider it your right to come and go as you please? Have I not made myself clear? I expect you to remain on the premises and work like any other servant would be expected to do! Just because we are...well, some might consider us kin...that does not give you the right to do as you please!"

"We are more than kin. I am your niece, the daughter of your only sister," she reminded him gently.

"And what is that to me?" Joram huffed. "Am I to harbor fondness or leniency toward you simply because we happen to be related?"

Tabitha only smiled.

"Now, have I made myself clear?" Joram persisted, leaning forward in his chair. "You are not to leave the premises for any reason unless you have first obtained permission from me."

"I beg your pardon, my lord, but that was not our agreement."

"Excuse me?"

"According to our initial arrangement, I would work for you in exchange for room and board. At the time, you presented me a very detailed list of tasks to perform each day, agreeing that I would be free to come and go as needed if my chores were accomplished."

"And you consider it acceptable to take advantage of my generosity?"

"Of course not," Tabitha affirmed, reminding herself to remain patient despite her frustration with Joram and his unhealthy need to control others. "Today, I shared lunch with friends during the hour you allow us servants to dine or to rest at midday. Do you consider that taking advantage?"

"This is not an isolated incident!" Joram argued, his color deepening in anger. "You seem to consider this town your own to do with as you see fit. You plant yourself right in the middle of other people's business without a second thought! And I haven't the patience nor the stomach for busybodies."

"I can see you are upset—"

"Upset is an understatement!"

A lingering moment laden with crackling tension passed between them as the uncle measured his niece, clearly at his wit's end.

"If you have become displeased with this arrangement, I can seek employment and living quarters elsewhere," Tabitha finally spoke, willing to keep her word. "This is your house, my lord, and I don't wish to cause you distress."

"No?" Joram challenged, his face reddening as his temper flared. "What an interesting thing to say, when all you cause me is *distress*! You are a contentious, discontented woman, stirring up trouble in my household and in this town! Soon the authorities will take notice of your radical religious gatherings and put an end to all this nonsense."

"Ours are peaceful gatherings, my lord. We haven't caused any harm nor any trouble to anyone—"

"But trouble will come! Mark my words," he threatened, leaning back in his chair and breathing heavily. "Indeed, trouble will come. When it does, you won't even know what hit you."

"Is that a threat?" Tabitha asked him quietly, meeting his angry gaze with calm, clear eyes.

"It is a promise. That I assure you."

Tabitha returned his gaze, her own laden with sorrow...and pity.

"What?" Joram ground out, clenching the arms of his chair. "Why are you looking at me like that?"

"My heart breaks for you," Tabitha answered truthfully, wondering if she had finally discovered someone beyond the Lord's redemptive reach. "You have so very much, and yet, you are so full of bitterness and hatred that you cannot enjoy it—not even for a moment."

"I don't need nor want your pity!" Joram shouted, attempting to stand but falling limply back into his chair, red-faced and breathless. "I have far more than you'll ever have."

"On the contrary," Tabitha said softly. "I have everything I need in Christ."

Joram's only response was a condescending sneer.

"You don't look well," Tabitha observed quietly, watching as the color drained steadily from her uncle's face. Was he about to experience another bizarre fainting spell? "Are you—"

"It's none of your concern!"

Nodding in resignation, Tabitha rose slowly, pausing briefly before her uncle, now crumpled uncomfortably in his chair. "Despite our differences, my lord, you are dear to me and I care deeply about you. Though you haven't made it easy, I do love you. And no amount of threatening or raging on your part will change that."

Joram gazed up at her with something akin to awe, though his eyes quickly hardened in his usual manner along with his rigid jawline, concealing his surprise at Tabitha's heartfelt and vulnerable confession.

"Nonetheless," Tabitha continued, folding her hands humbly before her, "I cannot strive to please you at the expense of pleasing God. If my presence has become too burdensome, I shall depart, though sorrowfully, and with tears for you."

Joram only glared, working his jaw impatiently back and forth as if attempting to maintain his composure.

"In the meantime, I shall finish my chores," Tabitha informed him, turning to leave. "Please consider my words. And if you wish for me to leave, just say the word and I shall do so."

"Just get back to work," Joram growled, rubbing his aching head in agitation.

Offering a slight bow of respect, Tabitha slipped from the room, thankful to have escaped the presence of her inexorable relative.

Hurrying toward the kitchen and her waiting daughter, Tabitha silently thanked the Lord for helping her keep her peace and maintain her witness in the face of Joram's bitter animosity.

CHAPTER 25

Agabus

On the Road to Damascus

The first twinkling stars were just appearing upon the rose-colored horizon when the exhausted band of travelers straggled into the paved court of an ancient, crumbling caravanserai.

Grimacing, Agabus brushed aside the sheer curtains of the enclosed carriage's window, observing the dilapidated old structure ahead with distaste. He, who was accustomed to comfortable nights in his own plush canopy bed, didn't appreciate the seedy accommodations this journey had afforded, not in the least.! The rural inns long established upon dusty country roads were often poorly maintained, and like this one, boasted crumbling, colonnaded walls surrounding a wide-open inner court. Only the most basic of necessities were provided, such as a well or fountain to provide water for the animals and weary travelers, and fodder for beasts of burden.

Wrinkling his nose, Agabus was disgusted by the idea of drinking the same water undoubtedly utilized for the beasts of burden, laundry, and bathing. For the love of all that was holy and good, when would this dreadful excursion end?

Releasing the elegant curtain, Agabus watched listlessly as it fluttered back into place, concealing the undesirable view. Leaning his head back, he attempted to relax in his jostling seat, dreading yet another long night in which he would be expected to share sleeping space with man and beast alike on the cold, hard ground.

**

Agabus couldn't sleep.

And somehow, he knew this cursed restlessness had absolutely nothing to do with the hard, uncompromising ground upon which he tossed and turned, the penetrating desert chill, the lowing of anxious beasts, nor the threat of bandits—or worse, Zealots—descending upon them in the night. No, his was a mental anguish, a raw gripping fear, that so disturbed his entire being—and his sleep. Or lack thereof.

Sighing irritably, Agabus covered his head with his expensive tunic, wishing he could shut out the cacophony of the lowing beasts of burden and the unsettling hum of the desert night song. Thoughts of Mary, Barnabas, and the believers of Jerusalem crowded his mind, further disturbing him.

Were they praying for him right now? Somehow, he sensed that, perhaps, they were.

Squeezing his eyes tightly shut, Agabus gripped

his temples with his hands, attempting to drown out the heavy *clank, clank, clank* of the unforgiving iron chains jostling in the mule-drawn wagon on the road. He heard them even now, long after the disturbing refrain had ceased, for the clanking had accompanied them the entire journey, reminding him of Saul's hate-driven mission.

Anxiously, Agabus wondered if he could bear the cries of the prisoners as the cold shackles were clamped upon their ankles and wrists. He knew those arrested would be expected to travel the entire distance back to Jerusalem on foot—at least one hundred and fifty miles, by his own estimation—shackled together like prisoners of war, driven by the stinging whip. Neither the women or children, the elderly or the infirm, would be spared this grueling humiliation.

Some would undoubtedly perish along the way.

Rolling over once again, Agabus cast aside his tunic and rose a bit shakily, his stomach twisting in knots.

He wasn't cut out for this. He was a religious *scholar*, for heaven's sake! A man of peace.

And what if Saul was wrong? What if God was against them?

Stepping around his snoring colleagues—all of them bedded down for the night—Agabus wandered aimlessly about the old inn, pausing thoughtfully beneath the colonnades overlooking the darkened horizon. Placing a trembling hand upon the arched stone wall, Agabus gazed into the distance, mesmerized by the starry sky suspended over miles of countryside washed in late night shadows.

"Adonai in Heaven," he whispered, his gaze fixed

upon the glistening stars. "What am I to do?"

His earnest plea was met by stony silence. Sighing, he supposed he shouldn't be surprised. What had he expected, anyway? A ringing response from the God of the universe, spanning the gap between righteous heaven and sinful earth?

Shaking his head in disappointment, Agabus leaned heavily against the wall. Were it not for the fierce armed sentries posted on all four corners of the age-old structure, Agabus would have been tempted to venture out into the night, lost in thought and prayer. However, he had no desire to be mistaken for a bandit or intruder by one of their overzealous guards wielding dangerously pointed spears. He supposed he would be far safer within the walls of the inn, sheltered beneath the deeply arced colonnades.

His thoughts were interrupted when the sound of hushed, barely discernible whisperings met his ears, floating upon the wind. Stiffening, Agabus' gaze swept the scene, coming to rest upon the still form of a brawny man standing just beyond the walls of the caravanserai.

Groaning inwardly, Agabus knew that resolute form could belong to no other than Saul of Tarsus, the mastermind behind this dreadful mission. Annoyed, Agabus watched as Saul folded powerful arms over his chest, his tense form barely discernible in the rising darkness.

Nettled, Agabus considered Saul's glowering countenance upon this journey. The Pharisee had gazed upon the other young men with unveiled loathing and condescension. Somehow, Saul, their leader, hadn't seemed the least bit daunted by the hard travel. But then again, Saul wasn't built like the others. Unfortunately, the man was built to last. Lean, hard, and athletic, he immersed himself daily in rigorous exercises for both the body and mind. His training was impressive and quite expansive.

Wryly, Agabus conceded that his own academic training certainly hadn't prepared him for the rigors of hard travel. Ruefully, he wondered if his aching bones and muscles would ever be the same again—*if* he survived this journey, which was questionable in his opinion.

At that moment, the cloud cover broke unexpectedly, releasing a stream of silver moonlight that slanted across the powerful form of Saul, still deep in prayerful meditation.

Daring a closer look, Agabus noted the firm set of the Pharisee's jaw, the hardness of his eyes, and his uncompromising stance.

Stunned, Agabus realized that Saul's countenance appeared strangely, inexplicably *troubled*. Almost despairing.

How odd, Agabus thought, further unsettled by this shocking revelation. Was Saul having second thoughts?

Exceedingly anxious and unwilling to have his intrusive presence betrayed by the glaring moonlight, Agabus turned swiftly on his heel to return to his miserable sleeping space. He didn't even want to think about the verbal lashing he would receive, should Saul discover him standing there, staring. The man was famous for his raging outbursts, and Agabus hadn't the slightest desire to be on the receiving end of one.

Carefully picking his way through the courtyard

of snoring Pharisees and scholars—who appeared far less dignified in their present state, he decided—Agabus lowered himself upon the wrinkled mantle still spread upon the cold flagstones, resigning himself to yet another sleepless night laden with fear and dread.

***

Ananias

Damascus

Rap, rap. Rap, rap, rap!

"What on earth—" Adjusting his disheveled night cap, old Ananias of Damascus sat up in bed, his heart pounding in time with the overzealous fist beating upon his front door.

Rap, rap. Rap! Rap! RAP!

"I am coming, I am coming!" Ananias murmured groggily, wondering what sort of catastrophe awaited him on the other side of the door. It was the middle of the night, for heaven's sake! Surely the persistent visitor had come bearing bad news... or worse, evil intent.

Slipping from his warm bed and hurrying down a darkened corridor, Ananias stumbled over a low stool, stumping his toe in the process. Further chagrined, he snatched a hanging lamp from the wall as he approached the door, bracing himself for whatever might await him on the other side.

"I said, I'm coming!" he grumbled loudly, throwing aside the latch and swinging the door open wide. Lifting his lamp high, his eyes widened in surprise.

"Barnabas!" he declared, stunned by the sight of his good friend from Jerusalem, a fellow believer. "For heaven's sake, man! You scared this old soul nigh to death! To what, may I ask, do I owe the pleasure?"

"Greetings, my dear brother," Barnabas grinned, his light brown eyes twinkling with fun...and mischief.

"Tell me, what is going on?" Ananias demanded, suddenly nervous.

"Pardon the intrusion," Barnabas quipped with another easy smile. "But things are about to get interesting, my friend. And I thought you should be the first to know."

CHAPTER 26

Tabitha

Joppa

I should rise. There is work to be done, and plenty of it.

Sighing, Tabitha gazed up at the darkened ceiling, watching the faint, flickering shadows cast by the oil lamp on her bedside table.

It was early—too early—and the rest of the household undoubtedly slumbered on, to remain in bed for several hours yet. But Tabitha knew she must see to her chores now if she was to have time to devote to her daughter in the afternoon and evening. And Philip had requested that she join him, Kelila, Adam, his father Josiah, and Phineas, the former Pharisee, at Tirzah's house later that evening for a special update. She certainly didn't wish to miss that. But first, the chores must be done.

Most mornings, Tabitha rose from her bed with energy and zeal, pondering the possibilities that lay ahead. But this morning was different, for the failures of the previous day weighed heavily on her heart and mind. It was almost tempting to acknowledge the enemy's taunting refrain of *What's the point of even trying? Why continue on as you do? You work your fingers to the bone in Joram's house, serving these ungrateful people, and still they won't believe. Why not return to Jerusalem, where you are loved and appreciated? Why keep groveling at your uncle's feet, allowing him to walk all over you?*

"No," Tabitha spoke aloud, pulling herself up to a sitting position. "This is the day the Lord has made, and I will rejoice and be glad in it." How many times had her beloved Stephanos reminded her of this in the past? Swallowing the unexpected lump forming in her throat, Tabitha tossed aside her worn blanket, resolving, "I *will* rejoice and be glad in it."

Dressing quietly so she wouldn't disturb her sleeping daughter, Tabitha couldn't help but wonder why so many in Joppa had gladly received Christ, while her own uncle and those in her household stoutly refused the hope of the gospel. It didn't seem right, and she wondered if perhaps she had failed miserably in her attempts at evangelism. Perhaps she simply wasn't gifted in that area.

Reaching for her comb, Tabitha dragged it through her long honey-colored tresses, attempting to overcome her feelings of despair. *Perhaps I am a complete and utter failure,* she thought, disheartened. *If I were a better witness, a better evangelist, then surely those of my own household would believe.*

A prophet is not without honor except in his own country, among his own relatives, and in his own house... Setting aside her comb, Tabitha squared her shoulders determinedly as the tragic words of

Jesus surfaced in her memory. He, too, had been rejected by members of His own family and deemed a blasphemer by those of His hometown. Jesus was a *perfect* Man, His witness and testimony flawless, and *still* they refused to believe! So, too, had the family of her departed husband rejected Christ, and Stephanos was the most brilliant evangelist she had ever known. It was not until after his death that his mother, Daphne, had finally seen the truth, though his father, Amal, denied the gospel to this very day. It was certainly no fault of Stephanos' that his father refused to believe.

I suppose those closest to you can see your quirks, flaws, and imperfections, Tabitha realized, swiftly braiding her long hair with nimble fingers and slipping a simple covering over her head. *And many will use these human weaknesses against us, as an excuse to deny the Way— despite the fact that there is no perfect human witness, excepting Jesus during His time on earth.*

Reaching for an apron and securing it around her slender waist, Tabitha's thoughts traveled on. *But I suppose this is why it's all the more important to walk by the Spirit, denying one's own flesh,* she decided, bending to kiss her daughter's forehead and preparing to leave. *Unbelievers are watching everything we do. Many of them wish to discredit us, merely to justify stubborn unbelief. But we must walk by the Spirit as best we can. Only by God's grace can we witness faithfully.*

Slipping out of her room and into the dimly lit corridor, Tabitha mulled over her tasks for the day, contemplating which to tackle first. She hoped Eli wouldn't continue avoiding her like the plague. The walk home from Tirzah's and the remainder of the previous day had been painfully uncomfortable. She certainly didn't relish another day of stilted conversation with him, followed by an air of long-suffering and stony silence.

Taking a turn, she slipped into the servants' washroom to splash cold water upon her face, praying as she did so.

Lord, I was so certain that Josiah's miraculous healing would at least prompt Eli to consider the Way, she prayed, gracefully drying her face with a towel. Setting it aside, she gazed into the cheap mirror hanging upon the wall, most likely installed by and for the female staff. Though her reflection was blurry at best, she supposed it was better than nothing at all.

That is how I feel, she thought, tilting her head to one side and watching as her reflection followed suit. *Everything is so muddled, so blurred. I long to see the final end, and yet the outcome remains hazy at best. Will Joram ever believe, Father? And what about Eli, and Martha, and Jonas? My fellow servants are so concerned about risking the wrath of the religious leaders that they fail to see what is at stake! They are wonderful people, Lord, so why can't they believe? What will it take to win them?*

Sighing, Tabitha turned and left the washroom. She had wasted enough time mulling over the dreaded *whys*. She supposed she'd best leave the future in God's hands.

That's where it belonged, anyway.

***

Suppressing a tremorous sigh, Tabitha pressed herself against the cold stone wall encircling Tirzah's shadowed outer court later that evening, her heart pounding in her chest. Overhead, the darkened sky glistened with shimmering stars, an arced evening moon slicing through the heavens like the silver blade of a reaper's scythe. As a wintry breeze rustled through the courtyard, Tabitha gathered her shawl beneath her chin, the frail fabric bunching in her trembling fingers.

Creak!

Tabitha turned her head as the front door opened on groaning old hinges, followed by a soft *thud* as it closed behind the emerging form of Kelila, an understanding smile lighting her features.

"I saw you slip out while Philip was addressing everyone," Kelila told her, drawing alongside her and gently touching her wrist. "Are you all right?"

"It's simply a lot to take in," Tabitha answered after a long pause. "I wasn't expecting him to announce that you must leave Joppa so soon. Must you really depart at first light? Can't you stay just a little longer?"

"It seems sudden, I know," Kelila agreed, lowering graceful hands to cradle her bulging belly. "I was surprised as well when Philip told me this morning."

"The Lord has called him elsewhere? So soon?"

"Caesarea Maritima," Kelila supplied softly, reluctant eyes betraying her unease in the glowing torchlight.

"Caesarea Maritima?" Tabitha repeated incredulously, stunned. "But why would God send you to a predominately Gentile city?"

"Not only Gentiles reside there," Kelila pointed out. "Many wealthy, sophisticated Jews abide in Caesarea."

"A handful, perhaps. Certainly not enough to make any headway with the gospel," Tabitha argued, her despair overriding a twinge of conscience. "You will be ridiculously outnumbered, Kelila."

"Perhaps. Even so, the Lord has called us to make disciples of *all* nations," she told her, reminding herself as well. "And that includes the Gentiles of Caesarea and beyond."

"I know," Tabitha nodded miserably. "I simply worry for you, abiding in a dangerous, pagan city," she added, considering the thriving Roman metropolis dominating the Mediterranean coast between Joppa and Tyre. "You're aware it functions as the home base for the governor, Pontius Pilate?"

"Philip told me."

Tabitha would have liked to disclose the fact that the governor's wife, Lady Procula, was a believer, but decided against it. Both she and Mary had promised to protect the noblewoman's identity. But perhaps, with the evangelist's arrival, the gospel would explode in the chief port of Roman Palestine, urging the dignified woman to break her silence.

"At least we will be close," Kelila offered, interrupting Tabitha's scattered thoughts. "I think it's but a few days' journey from Caesarea Maritima to Joppa, even with a little one in tow," she added with a wry smile, glancing down at her rounded belly.

"I must confess, I was hoping for a longer stay," Tabitha sighed, honestly meeting her friend's gaze. "It has been wonderful having you here. And so many have received Christ since your arrival. I fear the enthusiasm may dwindle at Philip's departure. How can we go on without a grounded, godly leader?"

"First, you have the Holy Spirit to lead the church in Joppa. And that is more than enough," Kelila reminded her. "But you will not be bereft of godly leadership, either. That's why Philip appointed deacons tonight to oversee the church in his absence. And finer men he could not have found."

Color deepening, Tabitha abhorred the way her insides twisted in apprehension at Kelila's reminder. Seated on a bench with Laurel in Tirzah's house, she had watched, alarmed, as Philip had anointed Adam, his father Josiah, and their faithful friend, Phineas, to lead and oversee the growing church of Joppa.

"You don't seem pleased," Kelila observed, wondering if Tabitha disapproved of Philip's choice of deacons. "What are your concerns?"

"My concerns?" Tabitha repeated, buying some time. How much should she tell her friend? Perhaps her apprehension was silly, ungrounded. Perhaps she was merely borrowing trouble.

"Do you think Philip should have chosen others to be deacons, rather than Adam, Josiah, or Phineas?"

"Oh, no," Tabitha quickly assured her, her color slightly deepening. "They are worthy men, completely devoted to Christ and the furtherance of the gospel. It's just, well…" Releasing another shaky breath, Tabitha decided to be frank. "Kelila, I lost Stephanos to a hate-crazed mob after he was appointed as a deacon in the Jerusalem church, because wicked men like Saul of Tarsus were threatened by his message."

Kelila simply nodded, waiting for her to continue.

"I guess what I'm trying to say is… Well, I deeply respect Adam and Josiah. And though I know very little about Phineas, he, too, is a wonderful man.

The thought of losing them to bitter enemies... it frightens me. And Josiah having just received healing—has he been saved from death only to be preyed upon by wicked religious leaders?"

"Ah, I see," Kelila affirmed, suddenly understanding. "You fear losing them just as you lost your husband."

"Yes," Tabitha nodded miserably, tears springing to her eyes. "Deacons are never safe."

"Perhaps not by the world's standards," Kelila ventured cautiously, carefully gauging her friend's reaction. "But when a man is appointed to serve as a deacon by the will of God, then he is in the safest place he can be—in the center of His will. Do you suppose a man would be any safer living in disobedience, apart from God's protection?"

"No," Tabitha sighed, shaking her head in dismay. "I suppose not."

"Then place these men in God's hands," Kelila encouraged her, playfully squeezing her arm. "They'll be far safer there than anywhere else."

"I'll try to remember that," Tabitha promised, wishing her wayward feelings matched her friend's staunch conviction. "I think we all go through difficult seasons, times when it's far easier to doubt than trust. But if I cling to God's promises, I know He will guide me through this."

"You've been through so much," Kelila said, admiring Tabitha's strength and resolve. "It's only natural to have doubts, at times. But you're right—God won't fail you. He will help you, even now. Even when it feels like your efforts are futile, or when it's tempting to turn back toward home and all that's safe and familiar."

"I know you're right," Tabitha nodded, shivering slightly in the chill breeze. Hugging herself with slender arms, she added, "Although I'm not sure there's anything safe about Jerusalem, right now!"

"Well, you make a good point," Kelila laughed.

"I shall be praying for you, Kelila, as you and Philip travel to Caesarea," Tabitha promised. "Although I would be less than honest if I said I wasn't hoping you would stay long enough for me to meet your precious little one."

"Oh, same," Kelila said with great feeling. "But perhaps the Lord will arrange a meeting between us soon."

"I do hope so."

"Besides, it will be at least another month, maybe even two, before this little one makes his or her appearance into the world."

"We'll see about that," Tabitha grinned. "I've heard babies have a way of showing up whenever they see fit."

"So I've heard," Kelila groaned, shaking her head in consternation.

"Well, I suppose we should return to the others," Tabitha decided, grateful for Kelila's kindness and exhortation. "Thank you for finding me here."

"I knew something was wrong when you stepped out. You would have done the same for me!"

"I will miss these talks of ours."

"And I, as well," Kelila assured her. "But know this—not a day shall pass without Philip and me lifting you up in prayer. Try not to fret about the unknown. God has good plans in store for you. Now all you must do is leave the future in His capable hands."

CHAPTER 27

Tabitha

Joppa

Going about her chores the following day, Tabitha mourned the fact that Philip and Kelila had departed for Caesarea Maritima. She knew she would miss them greatly. Philip's gentle yet powerful guidance had proven more assuring than she could have possibly imagined. And it had been so comforting to be in the presence of fellow believers from Jerusalem, her beloved home. After bidding the evangelist and his wife farewell, homesickness had washed over her entire being so powerfully she almost couldn't bear it.

But we have not been left without able leadership, even with Philip's departure, she reminded herself as she scoured the frescoed walls of the upstairs corridor connecting the many bedchambers of Joram's mansion. *Philip has chosen worthy men to govern the little church here. And by God's grace, the church in Joppa will grow just as it has in Jerusalem, Sychar, and beyond.*

Drawn by the silvery sound of her daughter's happy laughter, Tabitha glanced over her shoulder, pleased. Faithful Tirzah was seated on the hallway floor with Laurel, the two of them stacking wooden blocks rather precariously.

"Look, Mama, look!" Laurel squealed in delight. "A tower!"

"It is, indeed," Tabitha laughed, exchanging knowing looks with Tirzah. "Although with one or two more blocks, that tower may collapse like the crumbling walls of Jericho."

Giggling, Laurel reached for another wooden block, her teasing brown eyes daring Tirzah to stop her from tempting fate.

"Miss Tabitha! Miss Tabitha!"

Surprised, Tabitha turned around as Eli barreled down the hall, nearly colliding into Laurel's knee-high block tower. Halting suddenly, he shot a rather pointed look toward Tirzah, who returned his annoyed expression with fiery challenge.

"Really, Tirzah, must you clutter the entire hall? People must pass through!"

"Heaven forbid you merely step over it or go around," Tirzah shot back, never missing an opportunity to nettle the uptight overseer.

"For heaven's sake—"

"Is something wrong, Eli?" Tabitha interrupted, setting aside her scrub cloth. She was shocked that Eli had approached her since he seemed to be avoiding her like the plague. Until now.

"It's the master," Eli sputtered, appearing anxious and somewhat disheveled with his turban slightly askance.

"Has something happened?" Tabitha asked, instantly concerned. "Is Joram all right?"

"He's worked himself into a tizzy, and I fear for his health," Eli admitted, ringing his hands and looking bereft without his tablet. "At the moment, he is raging like a madman. I have been unable to pacify him, and the others won't dare go near him in his present state.!"

"Why is he so upset?"

"He was supposed to meet with an investor from Greece, a silent partner of sorts, next week," Eli rushed to explain. "Apparently, my lord just received word that the investor's visit has been delayed, possibly even cancelled. The master is quite upset about it."

"I see," Tabitha nodded. "But what can I do, Eli? I have no means of changing the investor's mind."

"No, but perhaps you can soothe your uncle's," Eli dared, his eyes hopeful.

"I tend to have the opposite effect on him," Tabitha pointed out with a skeptical lift of her brow.

"Though he will never admit it, the master respects you," Eli rushed ahead, stunning Tabitha to her core. "Your presence alone may help curb his wrath."

"I am flattered, Eli, but that is doubtful—"

"These fits of rage are not safe for the master's health," Eli insisted anxiously. "Please, for all our sakes, *try* to calm him down!"

Tabitha glanced at Tirzah, a question in her eyes.

"I'll stay with Laurel," Tirzah assured her as the toddler placed the final block on the tower, toppling it over with a loud crash followed by a chorus of delighted giggles. "You go. And be careful."

"Thank you, Tirzah," Tabitha said with great feeling, turning toward Joram's frantic overseer. "All right, Eli, let's go. I shall follow your lead."

***

Approaching Joram's private office, Tabitha and Eli exchanged looks of alarm as the sound of shattering glass rang through the corridor, followed by Joram's furious shouts and the echo of pounding feet rapidly pacing the floor.

Springing into action, Tabitha parted the curtains sheltering the office entryway and darted inside, leaving Eli to cower and quake in the corridor.

Covering her mouth, Tabitha suppressed a gasp of horror. The office was in shambles. Shards of pottery and broken glass carpeted the floor. Plush chairs were overturned and the contents of Joram's desk had apparently clattered to the floor with one furious sweep of his arm.

Turning on his heel, Joram approached her like an angry bull, his red eyes nearly bulging. "Get out!" he screamed, pointing an accusing finger toward the entry she had used. "Get out! I did not summon you!"

Praying silently, Tabitha held her ground as her uncle drew before her, breathing hot, threatening puffs of air onto her face.

"I said, *GET OUT!*"

"You must calm yourself, my lord," Tabitha said firmly, immediately noticing the blue veins bulging in his neck and forehead. "Your health is at stake."

"As is yours, should you fail to obey my command!"

"Please, take a seat," Tabitha instructed gently,

ignoring his obvious threat and gesturing toward the throne-like chair behind his desk. Thankfully, he had failed to overturn the monstrosity.

"I will not!" Joram raged, turning on his heel and pacing like a caged beast. "You have no right to order me about!"

"Your entire staff is cowering in fear of you," Tabitha told him, watching as his steps grew increasingly unstable. "Please, take a moment to compose yourself. I shall prepare a cold compress and—"

"You will do no such thing!" Joram shouted, his lips curling in derision. "I don't want your help!"

"I can see that, but you may need it, my lord."

"I don't need anything from you!"

"May I ask why an investor's delay would arouse such unprecedented fury?" Tabitha dared, watching as Joram froze across from her, his bloodshot hazel-green eyes pinning her in place.

"That is none of your concern!"

"My concern is for your welfare."

"Perhaps you should consider your own!"

"Forgive me, my lord, but no business meeting is worth this toll on your health." *And sanity,* she wished to add, but wisely held her tongue. "Already, you have more money than you could possibly spend in a lifetime. Why all the fuss over one unnecessary investor? Surely you needn't bother with such things!"

"Since when did you become my financial advisor?" he sneered, his words oddly slurred as he stumbled on his feet.

"Are you all right, my lord?" Tabitha asked, her heart increasing its incessant pounding. She feared another fainting spell was on the way.

Wincing, Joram grasped his forehead in both

hands, mumbling incoherently.

"My lord?"

Abruptly, Joram crashed to the ground, broken pottery crunching beneath him as his limp body landed upon the jagged shards with a sickening *thud.*

Crying out in horror, Tabitha ran to him, kneeling beside him and cradling his head on her lap. "My lord? My lord, please! Speak to me!"

Joram lay still as stone, his face and lips growing ghostly pale.

"Eli!" Tabitha shouted, tears coursing down her cheeks. "Eli, hurry!"

Having heard the unexpected crash, the overseer plowed through the curtained entrance, gasping in sheer panic at the sight of his master sprawled on the ground, lifeless and still.

"Summon a doctor at once," Tabitha commanded, pressing trembling fingers beneath her uncle's jawline.

"Right away," Eli sputtered, turning to flee the dreadful scene.

Oh, praise our merciful God, she thought, detecting a very weak pulse. *He isn't dead!*

Clenching her eyes shut, Tabitha struggled against her tears as Eli hurried off, beseeching the Lord on behalf of her uncle.

Please, Father, grant him one more chance.

***

"As previously stated, there is nothing more to be done for him."

Clenching her fists in frustration, Tabitha met the physician's patronizing gaze head-on, undeterred by his pompous and condescending manner. "Surely there is *something*—"

"There isn't."

"You are reputed as a skilled physician," Tabitha argued, her gaze flitting toward the motionless form of her uncle, now peacefully reposed on his massive four-poster bed. "Have I hired you to do *nothing*? Shall you earn a fine wage merely to pronounce doom?"

"And what would you have me do, young lady?" the physician dared her, lifting his leather bag from Joram's bedside, crossing the large chamber, and pausing near the door where poor Eli stood, anxiously wringing his hands. "His symptoms indicate an obstruction or reduction of blood supply to the brain—indeed, a very serious matter. Note the drooping nature of the left side of his face and body. With such cases, the most probable outcome is for the patient to suffer another similar incident—possibly several such incidents—until he succumbs to death."

"Will he awaken before that?" Tabitha demanded, slightly hopeful.

"It's unlikely, but not entirely impossible."

Tabitha exchanged knowing looks with Eli, her heart breaking inside her chest. "For many months, Joram has suffered strange bouts of weakness, even fainting spells—paralyzed by headaches one moment, then raving in fury the next. All along, I have known something wasn't right, but I never suspected..." Shaking her head in despair, Tabitha regained her composure with a bit of effort. "Had I known it was this serious—"

"If this man's reputation can be trusted, there is little you could have done for him," the doctor suggested snidely. "This type of illness seems to prey upon men of Joram's disposition."

Resisting the urge to glare at the haughty doctor, Tabitha suddenly recognized why Joram had lost all faith in physicians while seeking a cure for his beloved wife, Peninah. Most likely, all had proven every bit as callous and unhelpful as this one.

"What can I do for him in the meantime?" Tabitha finally sighed, sensing the doctor's impatience.

"Keep him comfortable," he replied matter-of-factly, his tone devoid of the slightest trace of human empathy. "Leave the balcony doors open as they are now to allow for fresh air and circulation. And should he arouse—by some unlikely miracle—feed him broth, if he'll take it."

Releasing a long, slow sigh, Tabitha nodded. "I will do as you say."

"I must be going," the doctor informed her gracelessly. "Where shall I collect my payment for the examination?"

Sorely tempted to disregard her Christlike witness and give the insolent doctor the tongue-lashing he deserved, Tabitha somehow held her peace. Turning toward Eli, she said calmly, "Eli will show you out and see that you receive proper compensation."

With a curt nod, the doctor turned on his heel, following the anxious overseer from the room.

With another despairing sigh, Tabitha tentatively approached her uncle's bed, her heart throbbing dully in her chest. Drawing a rather garish-looking chair next to the bedside, she lowered herself slowly, woodenly, onto the cushioned seat. She was grateful Tirzah had promised to stay with Laurel as long as needed. Now, she was free to minister to her uncle. Though she would pray ceaselessly for a miracle, she wanted to be with him should he take his final breath.

Gently touching his forehead with the back of her hand, she was troubled by the feverish heat upon his skin. As soon as Eli returned, she would ask him to fetch a cold compress. Though she wished to do so herself, she couldn't bear to leave him alone in his present state.

Clasping her hands tightly in her lap, Tabitha watched as Joram's chest rose slowly, painstakingly, with each labored breath he drew, wondering if she should attempt to locate a physician in a neighboring town. Joppa's only medic had proven entirely unhelpful, and she feared others might very well be the same.

If only I knew how to find Luke, she thought, remembering the kindly Gentile physician who had cheerfully and gladly rendered aid to the Jerusalem church on many occasions. She supposed she could write to Mary, inquiring about Luke's current location. Even so, she recognized that the chances of reaching him in time to save her uncle were slim.

Closing her eyes, Tabitha bowed her head, resolve welling up inside her even as despair threatened to overtake her.

"This is not the end," she spoke into the deafening silence, her tone resonating with determination. "Jesus Christ is Lord," she added firmly, imagining that dark spirits must be writhing at her faith-filled declaration.

Lifting her head high, she spoke with great conviction, unwilling to lose heart. "And this is not the end. It *cannot* be the end."

CHAPTER 28

Leah

Jerusalem

The lamps of the Upper Room were dim as Leah bowed her head, twisting her hands nervously in her lap. Her head covering slipped forward slightly, and she shoved it back in agitation, her frustration and anxiety mounting.

"Do not lose heart."

Glancing up in surprise, Leah saw Mary standing calmly before her, a trusting smile touching the corners of her graceful mouth.

"I am trying to be strong," Leah explained miserably, hating the disbelief reflected in her own voice. "Trying to trust the Lord."

"May I sit with you?" Mary asked her, extending a gentle hand toward her.

"Yes," Leah nodded, thankful for Mary's strengthening presence as she took her place on the bench beside her. "Please."

"We have been fasting and praying for three days now on behalf of your brother, Saul," Mary reminded her, her gray eyes alight with... Was it *hope*? Anticipation?

Leah gave the lovely widow a questioning stare, wondering at the warmth reflected in her eyes. "Your brother, Barnabas, is already in Damascus. And my brother, Saul, is on the way," Leah murmured, squinting, deep in thought, as she contemplated impossible things. "My brother wants to *kill* your brother, and yet here we are, sharing a bench together, bound by cords of love."

"It is truly remarkable, isn't it?" Mary smiled, touching the girl's cold hand. "Our God has a way of breaking down barriers of separation, doesn't He?"

"It's one of the things that first drew me," Leah confessed. "But, Mary, I am so ashamed. My brother has caused such horrendous pain for all of you, such inexplicable suffering for so many—"

"But *you* are not responsible for your brother's sins," Mary told her firmly. "Saul is accountable to God."

"But if I had been better, stronger, more persuasive, then perhaps I could have convinced him—"

"No," Mary interrupted gently, willing the troubled girl to meet her reassuring gaze. "You have served the Lord faithfully, Leah, doing the best you can. You cannot force another person—not even a family member—to repent, to obey. Even so, God is still in control, even now. He is working behind the scenes, even when we cannot see Him or feel Him. Even when we are afraid."

"I just wish I had more faith..." Leah sighed, her voice trailing off in despair. Bolstering her waning resolve, she started over. "Mary, I want to believe that God is at work in my brother's heart. I want to believe that he isn't beyond redemption. But when I consider all that Saul has done, the great sins he has committed against God and against the brethren, I recognize how impractical it is to hope for change."

"And you believe our God is only capable of working *practical* miracles?" Mary asked her with a knowing smile.

"Well, no," Leah blushed, ashamed of her lack of faith. "But a change of heart for Saul seems very unlikely at this point. He has strayed so far from God, so far from holiness and love. Besides, God grants all of us free will. And I'm afraid my brother has utilized his own free will to choose hatred and destruction."

"It is true God grants us free will, the power of *choice*," Mary agreed, nodding thoughtfully. "However, God is the master of touching our circumstances and gaining our attention. I have prayed fervently for your brother for many years. And I believe that God can reach him."

Dropping her gaze to her lap, Leah closed her eyes, the whispered prayers of a hundred fervent saints rising all around her like a heavenly chorus. Most of them had remained in the Upper Room for days on end, fasting and praying with single-minded determination. Expecting and believing a miracle. Interceding for her brother, Saul.

Why, then, couldn't she believe? Where was her faith?

"Just remember," Mary said, touching Leah's knee in a motherly fashion. "Our God is a consuming fire. Death could not hold Him, nor could the grave keep

Him within its dark confines. Knowing this, what chance does one angry Pharisee stand against the everlasting God?"

***

Agabus

On the Road to Damascus

Rumored as one of the oldest cities on earth, Damascus, a thriving metropolitan community sheltered by the snow-capped mountains bordering Syria and Lebanon, prospered under Roman supervision. Three major trade routes branched forth from the commercial city, both fueling and satisfying the Romans' lust for exotic luxuries of the East. With the exception of two main roads splitting the city—the Decumanus Maximus, simply dubbed Straight Street, running east to west, and the Cardo running north to south—Damascus boasted an extremely confusing array of narrow, haphazardly twisting and turning streets and alleyways, tightly lined with ancient stone buildings and colorful awnings crowning chaotic open-air bazaars. Corralled by a narrow stone channel, a thundering river eventually split and spread across the fertile green plains of Damascus before vanishing unassumingly into the quiet desert marshes surrounding the barren hills encircling the city of towering palms.

Agabus' entire being flooded with relief as he caught his first fleeting glimpse of the age-old city up ahead, with its sea of flat-roofed stone houses and verdant plains surrounded by soaring fortress walls boasting seven lofty gates.

It was truly a remarkable city. Had he not suffered weeks of miserable, grueling travel, Agabus might have been fascinated by its rich history and charming attractions.

Staggering painstakingly alongside a mule-drawn wagon, Agabus contemplated climbing back into his luxurious covered chariot. He couldn't decide which was worse—plodding along the road on aching feet and trembling legs, or jostling mercilessly in the carriage. He was convinced that every bone in his body had somehow shifted out of joint during the miserable excursion.

Grimacing in discomfort, Agabus forced himself to plant one expensively sandaled foot in front of the other, struggling to keep a steady pace. Up ahead, Saul led the straggling entourage, appearing far more like the grim-faced guards wielding spears than his frustrated, travel-weary associates. Gritting his teeth, Agabus leaned into the stubborn loathing washing over him, relishing it. He couldn't help but fantasize about all manner of disasters that might possibly befall Saul of Tarsus. In his opinion, the ruthless Pharisee was no better than an overgrown bully, forcing others to aid him in his wicked conquests.

Squinting against the blinding rays of the midday sun, Agabus shielded his eyes, attempting to gauge the time. They had been traveling hard since before dawn. Based on the position of the radiant ball of flame, he decided it must be about noon.

Would they reach Damascus before nightfall? If so, what kind of accommodations had Saul arranged for them in the city? He could only hope the lodging in Damascus would prove far better than the lousy caravanserais along the way. And, should God be merciful, he would soon locate a decent shop in the city to replace his filthy, travel-worn garments and sandals. His cherished robes were in a pitiful state—soiled, wrinkled, and torn in several places. Worse than that, he was convinced he reeked of animal stench and sweat. He had always prided himself on his flawless hygiene and respectable appearance. Now, he was entirely unpresentable, and the thought galled.

He had never been more desperate for a proper cleansing in the ritual baths and a fresh change of clothes in his entire life.

Clenching his fists, Agabus plodded onward, bemoaning his very existence. He didn't even want to think about what Saul planned to do once they entered the city. How many innocent men, women, and children would soon suffer at his hand? He could only hope and pray that Mary's brother, Barnabas, had succeeded in warning the local church of Saul's sinister intent. Perhaps they were all in hiding by now, safe from Saul's cruel aim.

Great God in Heaven, how did I get myself into this mess? All he'd ever wanted was to serve God, to study His Law and aid others in their desire to do so. But it would seem his dream had been forever lost, trampled under the feet of men like Saul.

***

Mary

Jerusalem

Mary awakened with a start.

Kneeling on the floor of the Upper Room, her

hands clasped upon the bench beside her, Mary realized she must have drifted off to sleep amidst her fervent prayers. She had slept very little in recent days, so engaged was she in the spiritual battle at hand. Glancing quietly about the room, she saw groups of believers huddled together, their heads bowed and hands clasped together as they prayed for the believers in Damascus and for the enemy of their faith, Saul of Tarsus.

Glancing over her shoulder, Mary saw Leah and Rhoda sitting together on a nearby bench, their foreheads touching as they grasped hands and prayed fervently for Leah's violent brother. Smiling faintly, Mary couldn't help but be touched by the sweet picture of two young women seeking the Lord in earnest. Close by, her son, John Mark, was praying with his mentor, Simon Peter, and several young men.

A quiet breeze drifted through the open windows, rustling the fluttering curtains and whispering its way through the tranquil chamber. Gently touching her cheek, Mary wondered at the wind's gentle caress, like a tender kiss from Heaven or the faintest stirrings of the Holy Spirit.

It is time.

Heart pounding, Mary instantly recognized the voice of her Shepherd. But what was He telling her? Were their earnest prayers of many years about to reach fruition? Rising to her feet, Mary crossed the room, pausing before Simon Peter. Respectfully taking his arm, she drew him aside, her gray eyes burning with zeal.

Simon Peter took one look at his wife's beloved aunt and *knew.*

"This is it?" he asked her, his dark eyes reflecting the fire and excitement in Mary's own.

"It is."

Breaking into a wide grin, the former fisherman clapped his hands energetically, startling many in the room. "Attention, everyone!" he shouted, drawing looks of wonderment and confusion from the brethren. "Please, gather around! Clasp the hand of the person beside you as we form one unbroken circle of prayer and petition before God. The Holy Spirit is at work! I can feel it." Exchanging another knowing look with Mary, he received a firm nod of affirmation from the graceful woman, further bolstering his excitement. "It's time to pray unlike we ever have before!"

CHAPTER 29

Agabus

On the Road to Damascus

Agabus froze mid-step, instantly on the alert.

A wintry breeze rustled through the straggling caravan, teasing the weary scholars' black and white garments and tugging at their stately headdresses. Up ahead, a large mule snorted in agitation, and his four-legged comrades followed suit, stamping their hooves in alarm.

Unbidden, Agabus' heart rate picked up speed as the armed guards exchanged cautious glances, the sunlight glistening upon the tips of their pointed spears.

Something was amiss.

SWOOSH!

In one horror-stricken moment, Agabus was rocked off his feet as the heavens opened, parting like the world's most enormous set of curtains and flooding the entire entourage below with radiant light—a light so *white*, so *pure*, so *holy*, so *penetrating*, that Agabus was certain it had cut right through him, slicing through body and spirit, joint and marrow. Exposing his filth-encrusted heart and every secret sin he harbored deep within his soul. Laying bare his glaring hypocrisy and selfish ambitions. And frightening him to the very core, filling his entire being with the most fearsome sense of dread he had ever known.

Risking a glance toward the front of the caravan, he saw Saul of Tarsus stagger to his knees, grasping his head in his hands as if in a fit of bitter agony. And then the blinding light intensified in power, soaring over the sea of moaning, terror-stricken travelers, frightened beasts, and wheeled conveyances like a pulsing, undulating flood.

Certain his eyes were forever destroyed by the shocking blast of light, Agabus trembled violently, attempting to make himself small and hiding his face against the cold paved stones of a Roman road.

God of Heaven, have mercy! his heart cried out in terror as he awaited the striking death blow sure to come.

For he knew with utter certainty that he was not fit to stand before a holy God.

***

Saul of Tarsus

"Saul, Saul, why are you persecuting Me?"

Shuddering uncontrollably, Saul of Tarsus cowered upon the road, oblivious to all but the blinding, heart-stopping light enshrouding his trembling form and the powerful voice from heaven washing over him like a flood of thundering waters. There was something unsettlingly familiar about that deafening voice from the heavenlies addressing him by name in his beloved Hebrew tongue...

Who but Almighty God is capable of displaying such matchless power? Saul realized, and yet, had he dared to contemplate a divine encounter with the God of creation, it certainly would not have unfolded this way.

Why are you persecuting Me?

Powerless to calm his own violent trembling, Saul considered the confusing question ringing through his mind like a loudly tolling bell, his brows drawing together in perplexity.

He, Saul, persecuting God on High? Was he even capable of such a feat?

And suddenly, unexpectedly, another thought crossed his mind—a thought almost too impossible to entertain. Perhaps he, Saul, was confused about the God he thought he served. For if *this* was God Almighty, then perhaps he was terribly misguided in his conception of Adonai. The God he had served all his life would have commended his faithfulness and valiant efforts and applauded his unswerving perseverance! But *this* God... *This* God was demanding an account for sins committed against Himself!

Upon his knees and squinting against the staggering light engulfing him, Saul shuddered to think of what might become of him for his apparent violation.

Questioning his own wisdom for the very first time in his young life, Saul whispered in a fear-soaked voice, "Who are You, Lord?"

Nothing on this earth could have prepared Saul

for the booming response that met his ears.

"I am Jesus of Nazareth, whom you are persecuting."

Jesus of Nazareth. Saul was certain his heart stopped beating in his chest. Pushing himself up on trembling elbows and wincing through the blinding pain, he gazed heavenward, desperate for even a fleeting glance of the One who spoke.

Far above him, enshrouded in majestic clouds that glistened and reflected the dazzling light of His holy presence, was the vague form so like that humble Carpenter from Nazareth, and yet so *changed*, so glorified, so resonating with power and authority from on high that Saul was forced to turn his face away. But not before he saw the outstretched hands, reproving and yet...gently beckoning.

The hands marked with the unmistakable scars of the Romans' iron nails.

Shuddering uncontrollably, Saul buried his face in trembling hands, his breath coming out in short, frantic puffs.

He had been *wrong*. So deeply, terribly, unmistakably wrong! Even as his mind argued against the downright impossibility of the matter and the seeming injustice of it all, the glaring evidence before him proved far too difficult to deny.

Jesus of Nazareth was, indeed, the Son of God. And just as He had promised, He had ascended to Heaven to be seated at the right hand of His Father.

Then Jesus spoke again, His tone saturated with grace and empathy, shocking Saul to his very core. "Saul, it is hard for you to kick against the goads."

Mouth agape, Saul marveled at a shocking revelation.

Jesus *saw* his inner struggles. And Jesus *under-*

stood.

The stunning realization was like a punch in the gut, and yet somehow a welcome one. Images of a furious black ox kicking against the goads until glistening trails of red blood glittered upon his legs flashed through Saul's tortured mind. Jesus had been watching him on that quiet farm road, the Spirit of God gently prodding him to take notice.

Like that stubborn, uncomprehending beast, he, too, had been resisting the goads designed to prod him in the right direction, to guide him down the path that must be taken to ensure an abundant harvest.

Setting his jaw in determination, Saul resisted the fear engulfing his entire being. He could not perish by the wayside, lost in sin and stubborn unbelief. This couldn't be the end!

"Lord," he breathed, his typically robust voice sounding weak and cowardly in his own ears. "What do You want me to do?"

"*Arise.*" The powerful voice resonated within Saul's heart and soul with searing heat, kindling a new type of fire in his breast. "Go into the city. There, you will be told all things which are appointed for you to do."

Shielding his eyes with a quaking hand, Saul sought a glimpse of the commanding figure in the skies, to no avail. The blinding light had grown far too intense, burning through his retinas with unbearable potency.

Then Jesus spoke again, and Saul wondered if his heart would burst within him at the sound of a voice surpassing the deepest of thunders. "Saul, I have appeared to you for this purpose, to make you a minister and a witness—both of the things which you have seen and of the things which I will yet reveal to you."

He, Saul, a minister and a witness? To the gospel of *Jesus Christ*? Heart pounding frantically in his chest, Saul pondered the impossibility of that awe-inspiring pronouncement. Such a calling would surely promote trials and hardships of every kind. His colleagues would be utterly dumbfounded—and very likely, murderous—when they learned of his defection. And what of the men, women, and children whom he had already committed to prison—or worse? Surely he wouldn't be welcomed or accepted by the church after the fierce persecution he had inflicted upon them.

And then another thought crossed his mind, a thought nearly too terrible to ponder.

He, the infamous hunter, would soon become the hunted. In one earth-changing, heart-stopping moment, the predator had become the prey.

His would be a life of danger, suffering, and fierce opposition. The prestigious life he had painstakingly built for himself would be utterly shattered. His flawless reputation, forever marred. His unrivaled scholarship, laughed upon. His wealth and riches, meaningless.

Grasping throbbing temples in his hands, Saul wondered if he could bear it.

And then, as if reading his very thoughts, Jesus spoke again with gentle fire, penetrating Saul's anxious heart and troubled mind like a soothing balm.

"I will deliver you from the Jewish people, as well as from the Gentiles, to whom I now send you—to open their eyes, to turn them from darkness to light, and from the power of Satan to God, that they may receive forgiveness of sins and an inheritance among those who are sanctified by Me."

To the Gentiles? Shocked and repulsed, Saul resisted the urge to argue aloud. It was almost too much to bear! To be called to his own people would prove challenging enough. But to intermingle with filthy dogs, unclean Gentiles? To dedicate his existence to saving godless, undeserving heathens? He would be rendered ceremoniously unclean for all eternity!

And yet, his heart was moved by Jesus' compassion and the urgency of His calling.

To turn them from darkness to light, and from the power of Satan to God, that they may receive forgiveness of sins and an inheritance among those who are sanctified by faith in Me...

Drawing a ragged breath into heaving, burning lungs, Saul bowed his head to the ground until his forehead touched the smooth gray stones of the Roman road. Feeling exhausted and utterly drained, he realized in amazement that he had already made his decision.

Follow Me. The call to action reverberated through his heart and mind, impossible to dismiss or deny.

What else could he do but embrace this incredible, unlikely calling from on high?

***

Agabus

Just as suddenly as the glory of the supernatural had descended upon the quiet road, the blinding light vanished, leaving the entire entourage to wonder about their sanity.

Splayed upon the well-paved road, Agabus could feel the coolness of the stones soaking through his worn clothing, chilling him to the bone. Shuddering and quaking like a frail, trembling leaf being whipped about in a violent wind, he slowly, uncertainly, lifted his head.

It was like the calm after a storm. A quiet blue sky. Billowing white clouds drifting lazily across the heavens in tranquil oblivion. Chirping birds. A still breeze. Dust settling upon the road, having been stirred by the prancing hooves of frantic beasts mere moments earlier.

A perfect calm.

As his heart rate began to resume its normal pace, Agabus exchanged nervous glances with his traveling companions, all of them scattered upon the road like cowering, frightened mice. He imagined they were all secretly pondering the same question: Dare they proceed forth after such a shocking, unexplainable encounter?

"*No!*" Saul, still at the head of the caravan, bellowed out, his voice echoing and bouncing off the nearby mountains.

Heart picking up speed again, Agabus wondered what terror must lie ahead to invoke such a response from their fearless leader. As several guards rushed toward Saul, Agabus found himself pushing past his comrades and rows of mule-drawn carts, hurrying toward the distraught Pharisee.

He *had* to know what had happened. He'd seen the flashing light and heard the deep rumble resonating with the power of a thousand roaring waterfalls, and yet he was unable to discern the words or understand the message.

But somehow, Agabus knew Saul must have received a divine revelation. And he could not rest until he discovered what it was.

Reaching the front of the caravan, he found Saul still on his knees, grasping his head in his hands. Several guards encircled him, exchanging looks of caution and confusion.

"My eyes," Saul was groaning, tightening his grasp upon aching temples. "My eyes."

Bending to catch a closer look, Agabus' heart sprang into his throat at the sight that met his gaze.

He had never seen anything like it. For mere moments before, Saul's sharp, predatory eyes had roved about the desert landscape, unblinking, dark, and merciless.

But now, the eyes of Saul of Tarsus were dull and clouded like a blind man's, his unseeing gaze haunted as one who had stared death in the face and nearly succumbed to its terrors.

"I see nothing," Saul breathed, his shoulders heaving in fear and confusion. "I am blind. I am *blind*!"

Covering his mouth with a trembling hand, Agabus wondered if the Pharisee had been struck blind by God Himself, a judgment upon him for the sins committed against the innocent men, women, and children of the Jerusalem church.

Would the same judgment descend upon those who now aided Saul in his mission of death? Was he, too, in danger?

"Damascus looms upon the horizon," one of the guards spoke gruffly, interrupting the disturbing course of Agabus' thoughts. "We'll have far better luck entering the city than turning back now."

"Yes, we *must* enter the city," Saul agreed, his

tone boding no argument. "We cannot turn back. We cannot!"

"You," the guard barked, giving Agabus' shoulder an especially rough shove and propelling him toward Saul. "Take him by the hand and lead him on the road."

Blinking in surprise, Agabus stared at Saul, still crumpled on the road. Surely the proud and pompous Pharisee would refuse to be helped along by an inferior colleague!

But to his great surprise, Saul stretched forth a trembling hand, rather like a helpless child.

Heart pounding in his chest, Agabus grasped Saul by the hand, helping him to his feet. He could hear the whispers rippling through the caravan as his associates debated about Saul's fate and the bizarre happenstance upon the road. He knew Saul could hear it, too. He could only pray the dangerous man was humbled rather than enraged.

As the straggling caravan resumed its unimpressive pace, Agabus dared to lean in just a bit closer to Saul, wondering if he would regret voicing the question upon his lips. "What happened, my lord?" he asked in a breathless whisper, fully expecting a violent reprimand.

Instead, the Pharisee turned his blind and haunted gaze upon him, his features etched with fearful resignation. "I saw Jesus of Nazareth. He is alive. He is Lord."

Stunned to his very core, Agabus recalled the last conversation he had shared with Mary before his departure.

"*Agabus,*" Mary had spoken with great conviction that night in the Upper Room. "*I have told you be-*

fore, and I shall tell you again. I am praying for you without ceasing, that—"

Agitated, Agabus had rudely interrupted her. *"I know, I know,"* he had insisted, pacing the room like a madman. *"You're praying that God will reveal Jesus as Lord to me, beyond any shadow of doubt. I know."*

"And He will." Mary had only smiled, further frustrating him.

"But how?" he had demanded in disbelief.

"We must wait and see."

Shaking his head in awe, Agabus pondered Saul's shocking confession. He had expected to go down to his grave long before hearing such an unbelievable proclamation from the enemy of Christ.

I saw Jesus of Nazareth. He is alive. He is Lord. He is Lord.

Considering the parting of the heavens, the dazzling light, and the thundering voice from on high, Agabus realized that Mary's faithful prayers of many months had been answered.

In the most miraculous way.

CHAPTER 30

Tabitha

Joppa

No cure. No cure. No cure.

The graceless physician's ill tidings pounded in Tabitha's mind like the anxious rhythm of war drums beating out a battle song.

Leaning forward in the chair stationed by her uncle's sickbed, Tabitha covered Joram's limp hand with her own. She felt utterly helpless to save him.

This maddening sentiment of sheer helplessness was all too familiar for the orphaned widow, arousing painful memories of excruciating loss. Resisting the urge to wallow in her misery, Tabitha set her jaw firmly, blinking back hot tears of anger and grief.

If only Philip had remained in Joppa, she thought, frustrated by the injustice of her situation. *If only he hadn't left.* A single touch from the faith-filled evangelist could have easily healed her uncle. Hadn't Adam's father, Josiah, just experienced the healing power of Philip's prayer? Was it too much to ask the same for her uncle, who would undoubtedly perish in his sins without divine intervention?

Tempted toward petulant frustration, Tabitha pushed unproductive thoughts aside, choosing instead to weigh her present options. Perhaps it wasn't too late to send for Philip. Was it plausible to dispatch messengers to meet him on the road? In her present state of anxiety, she couldn't recall the distance between Joppa and Caesarea. But hadn't Kelila said it wouldn't be a very long trip? For all she knew, Philip and Kelila had already arrived in the highly populated port city. If so, it would prove nearly impossible to locate the young couple until Philip sent word regarding his new whereabouts.

Begging God for wisdom, Tabitha remained stationed at her uncle's bedside like a faithful sentry. Joram hadn't improved one bit since he had collapsed the previous day. If anything, his worsening pallor and shallow breathing indicated a steady decline.

Drawing a shaky breath, Tabitha waited upon the Lord, committing her cause to Him. She knew the entire household waited with bated breath, hoping for an unlikely miracle.

She could only hope and pray that they wouldn't be disappointed.

***

Agabus

Damascus

Saul had previously arranged to lodge with a family friend, a distinguished older Pharisee of Damascus named Judas, who resided with his wife in an opulent house located on Straight Street. Agabus drew a huge sigh of relief when he was ordered to accompany blind Saul to the stately home and commanded by a guard to assist the dazed Pharisee in any way needed. Otherwise, he would have been required to lodge in one of the city's questionable, overcrowded inns as his fellow scholars were forced to do.

Judas' wife, a matronly, silver-haired woman with an impeccable appearance and a gracious manner, had greeted them warmly after they were ushered into the spacious reception hall by a well-dressed manservant. Her husband, Judas—sporting an impressive white beard and the elegant garb of a respected Pharisee—promptly joined her, proving to be every bit as gracious as the smiling hostess. Both were clearly alarmed when, mid-greeting, they noticed Saul's ghostly eyes and vacant stare. Plunging past pleasantries, Saul grimly disclosed that he had been blinded on the road outside the city.

Though the couple responded as graciously as possible, it was obvious both were troubled and confused by Saul's unexplainable malady. Tersely, Saul ordered Agabus to retrieve his trunk from the cart outside. Agabus didn't relish the thought of lugging the heavy trunk to the room which they had been assigned, although he decided that the task would prove more favorable than listening to an agitated Saul trying to convince the old couple about what had transpired on the road to Damascus. He could only pray that they wouldn't be turned away after Saul briefed the elderly couple about the shocking miracle that had transpired on the road. Frankly, Agabus wouldn't blame old Judas should he dismiss

Saul as a raving lunatic.

Sighing loudly, Agabus obliged Saul's request about the heavy trunk, apprehensive about sharing a room with the infamous Pharisee. Saul was bad enough under normal circumstances; now, robbed of his sight and anxiously brooding, Agabus feared his company would prove unbearable. Possibly even dangerous.

Having finally retrieved the trunk with great difficulty from the cart outside the outer court, Agabus was met at the door by the same manservant who had shown them in. Without a word, the servant led the young Pharisee past the reception hall and down a broad, frescoed corridor. Annoyed, Agabus resisted the urge to demand that the insolent manservant relieve him of his burden and carry the trunk himself. True, he didn't rank nearly as highly as Saul, but he was still a respected scholar, for heaven's sake! It was almost unthinkable—him trotting behind a lowly manservant, expected to carry his own load! Had he not been entirely dependent upon Saul for decent lodging, he would have most certainly spoken his mind about the matter!

"Your room, my lord," the manservant flatly informed him with a bored sweep of his arm.

Further peeved, Agabus watched in disbelief as the servant disappeared back down the long corridor without bothering to ask if he required any further assistance. Wondering how such a lovely, hospitable couple had acquired such a lazy servant, Agabus shouldered the trunk with difficulty, passing through a curtained doorway and stepping into a well-furnished guest chamber boasting a large, comfortable bed, plush Persian rugs, and a convenient wooden desk placed against the farthest wall. The chamber was well lit with flickering lamps mounted throughout. Broad, elegantly latticed windows allowed the waning sunlight to stream in pleasantly, slanting across the luxurious, patterned rugs. Huffing his displeasure, Agabus dropped the heavy trunk at the foot of the bed, glad to be rid of the cumbersome burden.

If only he could so easily lay aside the burden weighing upon his soul.

Crossing the room, Agabus paused at the largest window overlooking Straight Street. Stiffly folding his arms over his chest, he pondered all that he had seen on the Damascus road. For in one fateful moment, an entire lifetime of learning had been shattered. The convictions and beliefs that had shaped his worldview since childhood—utterly dashed to pieces. His hopes and dreams of rising to prominence in the academic and religious community—destroyed. That is, *if* he embraced the Way of Mary, Barnabas, the believers of Jerusalem, and their risen Lord, Jesus Christ.

Fleetingly, Agabus wished he could merely dismiss what had happened upon the road. Should he do so, the seamless and tidy plan he had so diligently constructed for his own life could carry on, uninterrupted. His would be a life of ease, wealth, and prestige. He would be esteemed by his people, possibly even commemorated as one of the kindest, greatest scholars of all time. His heart's desire since youth would be his to claim.

Groaning in anguish, Agabus took his head in his

hands. It was hopeless, utterly hopeless.

For no matter how much he might wish to do so, he couldn't deny what he had seen on the road.

And his life would never be the same again.

***

Tabitha

Joppa

Jerking awake, Tabitha realized someone's hand rested gently upon her shoulder. Glancing sideways, she saw Tirzah standing quietly beside her chair, her lovely features empathetic.

"How are you holding up?"

Still groggy, Tabitha allowed herself a moment to process Tirzah's kind inquiry. Since she didn't wish to discuss her present feelings, she thought it best to change the subject. "I can't believe I fell asleep in this chair," she murmured, shaking her head. "I should be watching Joram. Not dozing away."

"You've been 'watching him' nonstop since his collapse yesterday morning," Tirzah reminded her with obvious concern. "It's nearly nightfall, Tabitha. You need rest."

"How can I rest when he is so sick?" Tabitha asked her, her large hazel-green eyes reflecting her misery.

"And how can you care for him without rest?" Tirzah shot back with annoying logic. "Joram has a fleet of servants on the premises, all of them capable of keeping an eye on him. Assign one of them to sit with him for a few hours so you can rest."

"I want to be here if he awakens," Tabitha insisted, shaking her head stoutly.

"Then ask the servant to alert you if he stirs."

"And if he dies while I am gone?"

Tirzah sighed in resignation, seeing that her suggestions were futile.

"Where is Laurel?" Tabitha asked, her gaze flitting anxiously toward the door. "She's not with you?"

"She's with Martha," Tirzah assured her. "I wanted to check on you to make sure you're all right. I've been so worried for you. We all have."

Weary and bleary-eyed, Tabitha's gaze traveled toward her uncle, laying lifeless in his bed. She hadn't dared leave his side since his sudden decline. "I must look like a mess," she finally sighed, impatiently tweaking her tousled braid.

"I'll fetch you some fresh water, a washbasin, a comb, and a change of clothes," Tirzah volunteered, glad to be able to assist her aching friend in some way.

"That would be wonderful," Tabitha confessed, eager to freshen up. "Thank you, Tirzah."

"By the way, Martha is worried sick since you haven't eaten since yesterday," Tirzah added, giving her friend's shoulder a final squeeze. "She is fixing supper for you now and will send it for you when it's ready."

Weakly, Tabitha nodded her acknowledgment. Though she greatly appreciated the kind gesture, her stomach lurched at the thought of food.

"Is there anything else I can do for you?" Tirzah asked kindly, pausing in the doorway before heading out to fetch the promised supplies.

"Keep praying," Tabitha finally answered after a long, painful pause. "That's the most important thing we can do right now. Keep on praying, and don't lose heart."

Nodding her understanding, Tirzah slipped from the still chamber, praying silently even as she went.

CHAPTER 31

Saul of Tarsus

Damascus

Darkness. So pervasive, so still. Engulfing, all-encompassing. Like the darkness eating him alive from within, penetrating his soul and spirit, body and mind. Like the darkness claiming his being, buried in the deepest recesses of his heart—so deep, in fact, Saul hadn't even known it had taken residence within him.

Fear. It was ever-present, overwhelming. Suffocating, never-ending. Descending upon him like ravenous carrion birds, sinking greedy talons deep into his soul.

And regret. Paralyzing, unspeakable regret, unrelenting, debilitating, overwhelming. Saul knew he would be consumed by it. He couldn't bear it. How could he go on?

Lying prostrate on the floor of the lavishly furnished guest chamber in which he now resided, his face in his hands, Saul's heart cried out to a seemingly distant and unfamiliar God.

Who was He, really? Certainly not the vengeful Ruler whom Saul had ignorantly revered all his life. No, this God was incomprehensibly loving, surprisingly merciful. For this God had wrapped Himself in weak human flesh and dwelt among unworthy, wretched sinners, wooing them back to Himself with tenderness and warmth. This was not a cold, austere God enthroned above the heavenlies, far removed from His creation, with cold, merciless eyes roving to and fro about the earth, searching for someone to punish. No, this God had walked among His own, patiently enduring poverty, hardship, condemnation, and eventually, a tortuous death upon a Roman cross. All for the sake of *love*. All for the hope of *redemption*.

Utterly confounded, shaken to his core, Saul wrestled against assailing doubts, desperate to make amends, desperate to find peace. He—the most promising student of the most highly revered scholar of the holiest land on earth—realized in amazement that he knew absolutely nothing about the God he had claimed to serve so faithfully all his life.

The thought was staggering. And far more frightening than he cared to admit.

So, then, who was this God, so unlike the One he had logically constructed in his astute, scholarly mind?

Groaning in inexplicable grief, Saul mourned the loss of all he had ever known, all he had ever wanted. He mourned the loss of prestige, the loss of security, and the loss of swelling self-confidence. And, oh, the loss of his *sight*! To be rendered completely, utterly blind was dreadful, unthinkable, astounding! What kind of future was in store for him now as a helpless blind man? He would become a burden to his family and society, unable to make a living. He would be utterly dependent upon the goodwill of others and the inefficient system established by the religious leaders.

Oh, the religious leaders! He shuddered to think of them. Rather than offering solutions or empathy, he knew his colleagues would undoubtedly cast judgment on him, pronouncing his disability as God's curse for some hidden, unspeakable sin! Some would be shocked, others, amused. Still, others would gloat at his apparent failure and vie for his coveted position. Balking at the prospect, Saul set his jaw in sheer defiance.

And then another dreadful thought, even worse than the others, assailed him, ripping his heart to shreds.

Why, as a blind man, I shall be deemed unworthy to enter the Temple, he realized, his heart pounding frantically in his chest. *I shall be cut off from fellowship with God and my brethren!*

Saul feared his punishment was far too great, his future far too grim.

Oh, God! Oh, God! his heart cried out. *I cannot bear it. How can I go on?*

As if prompted by a gentle whisper, Saul suddenly recalled the poor, the destitute, the blind, the lame, and the maimed—countless men and women with stooped shoulders and hopeless eyes—that he had turned away from the Temple, banishing them from fellowship with God and men. And, for the first time in his privileged young life, Saul experienced the sting of regret, sympathizing with their pain.

Oh, God, forgive me. Forgive me, God in Heaven! Have mercy on my soul!

Were it not for the promises burning in his heart like fire, Saul knew he would have surely succumbed to despair. And yet the words of the glorified and resurrected Jesus rang in his mind like a tolling bell, reminding him that—some way, somehow—God had not dismissed him as a lost and hopeless cause. The Son of God Himself had promised that the Lord would show him what to do once he reached the city.

Saul would have felt much better about his situation had the Lord promised to divulge the details *sooner* rather than later. Already, three days had passed since his fateful encounter with the risen Christ. And he was convinced they had been the longest three days of his entire life, enshrouded in the darkness of blindness, his heart twisting in fearful apprehension.

How long must I wait, O Lord? How long must I suffer this unspeakable agony?

Stretching forth his hands, Saul remained prostrate on the ground, gripping the plush, tasseled rug with numb, wooden fingers. With a sharp pang to his heart, he realized that never again would he see the swirling colors of an expertly hand-woven tapestry, nor the breathtaking beauty of sunrise, nor the blossoming flowers carpeting the hills of early spring.

Recalling his final conversation with his little sister, Leah, before departing from Jerusalem, Saul's soul was further chagrined by the fact that she had, indeed, been *right*. Hadn't she asked him what he would do if God stopped him dead in his tracks?

Releasing another anguished groan, Saul battled against complete and utter despair.

***

Agabus

Anxious for any excuse to escape Saul's intense, smoldering presence, Agabus slipped from the guest chamber, muttering that he intended to fetch some fresh water for the brooding Pharisee. He already knew that Saul would refuse the refreshment. The man hadn't touched food or drink since the supernatural incident on the road and the loss of his sight. Thankfully, his lame excuse went unheeded as Saul remained prostrate and silent on the floor, his grim face buried in the carpets layered near the impressively arrayed four-poster bed.

Padding down the same frescoed corridor he had traveled earlier in the day, Agabus wished he was capable of reading Saul's mind. It was terrifying, watching the broken man lying face-down on the ground, groaning in agony. He couldn't decide if Saul was repenting for the sins he had committed against the church of God, or strategizing a backup plan since his initial assault upon the believers of Damascus had been frustrated the moment he was struck blind outside the city.

It had been difficult not to pry, pressing Saul with questions about his present state. How had he been impacted by the appearance of Jesus upon the road? Was he now convinced that Jesus was Lord, or even more determined to discredit Him and destroy His followers?

For three days, Agabus had waited upon the distraught Pharisee hand and foot, attempting to foresee his needs before they arose but failing miserably. It would seem he made a lousy servant. But who could blame him? He was accustomed to being served, not the other way around! Unfortunately, he'd had very little practice in the art of servanthood.

Rounding a corner, Agabus wondered if it was acceptable to slip into the kitchen and help himself to a cup of water. Perhaps he should locate a servant and request permission. He knew better than to return to Saul's room empty-handed, for then Saul might accuse him of shirking his duties and simply making excuses to leave his charge.

"You are Agabus, yes?"

Nearly jumping out of his skin, Agabus jerked around to see old Judas posed comfortably on an elegantly upholstered couch gracing the farthest wall.

"My lord," he said quickly, bowing his head in respect—not to mention, apprehension. Pinned in place by Judas' intelligent gaze, he felt rather like a schoolboy caught dodging his lessons in Torah. "Please forgive my intrusion, sir. I came to fetch a cup of water for—"

"Saul has finally broken his fast?" Judas inquired, lifting heavy brows in relief.

"Well, um, no. Not exactly," Agabus admitted, nervously wringing his hands. "But I hoped to entice him with some refreshment. He has endured many weeks of hard travel, and I fear this fast may prove detrimental to his health."

"You are a good aide for Saul," Judas remarked

with a nod of approval. "He should be grateful. Worthy help is difficult to come by."

Flushing in agitation, Agabus resisted the urge to point out that he was a respected scholar, not *hired help*!

"It is late," Judas observed, his bearded face contrasted by shadow and flickering lamplight.

Clearly, not late enough, Agabus thought, peeved. He had hoped the master and lady of the house would have long since retired for the night. He assumed dawn was mere hours away. "Something must weigh heavily upon my lord's mind," Agabus dared, hoping to divert the attention from his own late-night wanderings. "For you to remain up at this hour."

"Indeed." Judas nodded slowly, stroking his impressive white beard. "You are quite perceptive."

Wincing, Agabus wondered if the old man paid him a sincere compliment or merely mocked him.

"Saul's account about what happened upon the road proves troubling, indeed," Judas continued, leaning forward on the couch. "Please, take a seat," he added, gesturing toward an opposing chair.

Balking inwardly, Agabus obliged, slowly lowering himself onto the chair. Though the sitting area was comfortably and luxuriously furnished, he hadn't wished to trap himself in a midnight conversation with a complete stranger! To make matters worse, he was far too familiar with Judas' type—an aging scholar harboring time-honored wisdom, eager to converse and debate for the mere sake of it. And, undoubtedly, he would relish every moment of it.

Yet, Agabus, in his agitated, frazzled state, was

in no mood to converse long into the wee morning hours, discussing the mysteries of the universe and the haunting secrets of the unknown. He was beginning to regret his hasty decision to wander down the hall under the guise of seeking a cup of water. He certainly wouldn't make that mistake again.

"The incident upon the road, resulting in Saul's sudden, unexplainable loss of sight," Judas began, leaning back on the comfortable couch as if settling in for a nice, long chat. "You were a witness, I presume?"

"I was," Agabus admitted, trembling inside. Should this respected leader among the local Pharisees question him about the supernatural encounter, he could very well find himself in deep trouble if his response failed to please the notable elder.

"And what did you see?" Judas asked him, his wise old eyes appearing to gaze into his innermost soul.

"Everything Saul told you today..." Agabus stammered, clasping trembling hands in his lap. "It happened, my lord, just as he explained to you."

"You were not present when Saul disclosed that information," Judas reminded him with a hint of suspicion. "How can you confirm it if you did not hear it?"

"My lord, Saul was deeply shaken by the encounter upon the road," Agabus said quickly, feeling the sweat soaking through his elaborately stitched tallith. "I am confident he would have spoken truth about the matter."

"And I, as well," Judas mused, thoughtfully dragging weathered fingers through his beard.

Agabus simply waited, assuming there was far more safety in silence. He could only hope, anyway.

"Young man," Judas continued, his leathery features appearing almost ghostly in the lamplight. "For many years, I earnestly sought the Messiah. I longed to see Him walk the earth before I was called to rest with my fathers. Even a mere glimpse of His majesty would have satisfied the longing of my soul."

Agabus sat just a bit straighter on his chair, intrigued despite his fluttering nerves.

"Naturally, I heard the rumors about a miracle-worker—from *Nazareth*, of all places—a Man reputed to heal the sick and even raise the dead. And yet, like the rest of my skeptical colleagues, I dismissed the rumors as little more than fanciful hearsay. But then His following began to grow at an alarming rate. Troubled by all that I was hearing, I wrote to a trusted old friend, Gamaliel, in Jerusalem. And I found myself further puzzled when he neither confirmed nor denied the Man's divinity. This, more than anything else, gave me pause."

Agabus stared at Judas in surprise. He had often pondered Gamaliel's telling silence regarding Jesus of Nazareth. It was even rumored that the world-famous rabbi had discouraged Saul from seeking vengeance upon His disciples, appearing grieved by his star pupil's unwavering obsession with destroying followers of the Way. Could it be possible that Gamaliel was sympathetic toward the believers' cause? Dare he even hope?

"And now, *this*," Judas went on, shaking Agabus from his whirling reverie. "I have known young Saul all his life. I attended Bet Midrash with his father. I would trust the word of both father and son without hesitation. And Saul's testimony of a blinding light upon the road and the appearance of a risen and *liv-*

ing Jesus Christ, clothed with power and authority from on high, interceding on behalf of His followers..." Old Judas shook his head in wonderment, his voice trailing off as he pondered all that had been revealed to him. "And if that isn't enough," he added with a chuckle of fascination, "there were dozens of witnesses to confirm Saul's report, not to mention the fact that a perfectly healthy young man was rendered instantly blind."

Agabus stared at the elderly scholar in disbelief, marveling that he would even consider...

"What is it, young man?" Judas asked him unexpectedly, sending his heart racing yet again. "This troubles you, yes?"

"Respectfully, my lord," Agabus managed, his palms sweating in the most unpleasant manner. "May I ask...ah, well, do you believe the testimony of Saul of Tarsus, which you heard today? Do you believe this Jesus of Nazareth to be the promised Messiah? The One we have long awaited?"

Judas smiled faintly, leaning forward in his seat. "I believe the most important question, young man, is this: Do *you*?"

Blinking in near panic, Agabus only waited, his breath coming in short, heavy puffs. Should he confess his newfound belief in Jesus Christ as Savior and Lord, Judas could very well report him to the Sanhedrin. He could be punished, flogged, arrested, or worse!

Recognizing the younger Pharisee's painful inner struggle, Judas' fatherly features softened. "Agabus," he said kindly. "I am an old man. I have lived my life. Should I believe Saul's testimony and confess my faith before the elders of our nation, what have

I to lose?"

Shifting uncomfortably in his seat, Agabus considered the grand house in which Judas resided, the gracious wife who clearly adored him, the fleet of servants waiting upon him, his coveted position of power and authority, not to mention the treasure troves of expensive finery filling every nook, cranny, and corner of his rich abode. In Agabus' opinion, Judas had very much to lose, indeed.

"But *you*," Judas informed him, his thumb pressing thoughtfully against the dimpled chin hidden beneath his snowy white beard. "You have much to lose. You have your entire life ahead of you. Your career has just begun. You have yet to experience the ecstasy of taking a beautiful young bride nor known the incomparable joys of fatherhood. Some, indeed, would argue that a profession of faith on your part would, in fact, cost everything."

Agabus swallowed hard, his throat going dry. The old man spoke truth; he had no doubt about that. He could only wonder at the intensity of his pronouncement, the challenge in his tone.

"So the real question, my friend, is this," Judas finished, an air of finality in his tone. "If you believe this Jesus of Nazareth to be Lord, what, then, shall you do?"

CHAPTER 32

Saul of Tarsus

Damascus

"Agabus!" Saul ground out, his heart pounding furiously in his chest. His entire body had suddenly broken into a cold sweat as his senses tingled in warning. Something wasn't right. Perhaps his safety was in question. "Agabus!"

Irritated beyond measure, Saul wondered what could possibly be taking his assistant so long in the kitchen. Agabus had slipped out nearly an hour ago, muttering some weak excuse about fetching a drink of water. For three days now, the blundering Pharisee had hovered over him like an annoying mother hen. And yet, now, when he was actually *needed*, he had disappeared! Peeved, Saul resolved to note the young Pharisee's incompetence on his professional record.

Gritting his teeth in frustration, Saul attempted to push himself up on his elbows, and yet, it was as if some powerful force beyond himself pinned him in place. Frightened, Saul wondered if he was about to be struck dead by the hand of God Himself.

And then a light flashed through his mind behind his closed eyelids, filling his entire consciousness with a presence so powerful, he shuddered in fear.

A *vision,* he realized, grasping at the thick carpets in near panic and burying his face in the bristly fabric as fear consumed him. He wondered if he was prepared for yet another display of matchless power, in his present state. Had he sight to guide him, he would have been tempted to hide under the bed or jump out a nearby window.

And then Saul saw the form of an older man, clear as day, strolling along Straight Street with a purposeful gait. His gaze kindled with holy determination, possibly a hint of apprehension. Undoubtedly, the busy street bustled with activity, but the vision seemed to center upon that one unfamiliar form as everything in the background faded into undulating oblivion. Calmly, the older man approached the gatekeeper of an opulent house towering over the busy thoroughfare.

"I am Ananias," the man spoke, and his voice sounded faint and somewhat garbled, as if he spoke through a long, echoing tunnel. "I have come seeking one Saul of Tarsus."

Catching his breath in amazement, Saul waited, every nerve ending afire, completely enthralled by the strange vision, wondering what it meant...

***

Agabus

Stumbling back down the corridor like the walking dead, Agabus pondered his conversation with Judas, deeply shaken. For far too long, he had suspected that Jesus of Nazareth was, indeed, who He claimed to be. And after the appearance of Jesus Himself to Saul upon the road, Agabus could no longer deny the truth of it.

And yet, he felt worse rather than better. For now, rather than merely suspecting that his life might be turned upside down, he knew with absolute certainty that it would be.

Stealing past the endless rows of mounted lamps, Agabus wrestled with God. Undoubtedly, the Lord had chosen to reveal Himself to him. And Judas' plaguing question rang loudly through his mind, demanding his attention, requiring an answer.

What, then, shall you do?

Pausing amidst the beautifully frescoed corridor, the warmth of the glowing lamps saturating his face, Agabus clenched his eyes shut and clasped trembling hands, seeking aid from the only One who could help.

"Father God, on behalf of Your Son Jesus, I ask for wisdom. I ask for strength. I believe, though it scares me half to death." Drawing a ragged breath, Agabus reluctantly opened one eye, ensuring that he remained alone. Satisfied, he plunged ahead, feeling like an unprepared student facing a daunting exam. "Show me what You want from me. Show me what to do."

Cautiously opening his eyes, Agabus gazed up and down the darkened corridor, half expecting a heavenly being to materialize out of nowhere, bearing divine instructions from on high.

Nothing. Only the quiet crackling of the lamps and the labored sound of his own uneven breathing met his ears. The corridor appeared every bit as lonely as before with the lamplight casting writhing shadows upon the colorfully patterned walls.

Sighing dismally, Agabus proceeded forward, placing one heavy foot in front of the other. It was then he realized he had failed to fetch the promised cup of water. And yet, he didn't dare go back for it now. He didn't want to risk another uncomfortable discussion with the master of the house.

BOOM! It was as if an invisible shock wave barreled through the lengthy hall, knocking him back. Slamming into the nearest wall, Agabus gasped in fear as his entire field of vision was filled with dazzling light. Undulating images, appearing strangely distant, filled his mind, as clearly as if the scene was playing out directly before him.

Heart pounding like the galloping hooves of a warhorse, Agabus realized in awe that he was experiencing a vision. He saw Saul of Tarsus, kneeling humbly before a bearded older man. Agabus imagined there were others present, though he couldn't detect them nor the surroundings through the haze. Gently, the older man placed his hands on Saul's shoulders. "Brother Saul," he spoke, his voice echoing and distant. "The Lord Jesus, who appeared to you on the road as you came, has sent me that you may receive your sight…"

And just as suddenly as the vision had begun, it ceased.

Agabus stood pressed against the wall, quaking in fear. Gingerly reaching up to touch his pounding temples, he wondered at the vision that had been revealed to him.

And then the magnitude of what had just happened hit him full force.

A *vision!* He, Agabus, had just received a vision from the God of the universe! Trembling in amazement, Agabus realized that the Lord had answered his prayer, for his calling had been revealed.

It would seem the Lord had something more in mind for him than spending his days sequestered behind the cold stone walls of a darkened synagogue, penning detailed expositions about the Law.

A *prophet,* Agabus realized in awe, quaking at the magnitude of the revelation.

In the mere blink of an eye, Agabus' occupation of choice had ended, and a new assignment had begun.

A calling far greater than he could have ever imagined.

***

Barnabas

Lying abed, Ananias' eyes snapped open in disbelief. Throwing aside his covers, he sprang from his bed with surprising agility for one of his age.

"Barnabas!" he declared, hurrying down the hall and stubbing his toe on the same stool he had previously tripped over. Grasping his foot in pain, Ananias groaned, wondering why he still hadn't bothered to move the blasted piece of furniture. Who put it there, anyway?

"Ananias?" Barnabas hurried down the corridor, meeting his old friend in the hallway. Though dawn had not yet broken, it appeared Barnabas had been up for hours. His gaze was clear, his light brown eyes reflecting his interest. "Are you all right?" he asked, noting the way his friend now balanced on one foot, wincing as he inspected his throbbing toe.

"I'm fine," Ananias said quickly, releasing his foot and taking Barnabas by the shoulders. "You're never going to believe this."

"Try me."

"I've just had a vision!"

"About?"

"Saul of Tarsus!"

"And?"

"I must go to him at first light." Shaking his head in disbelief, Ananias marveled at all that God had revealed to him. "The Lord Jesus has shown me that Saul is His chosen vessel to bear His name before Gentiles, kings, and the children of Israel."

"It was only a matter of time," Barnabas grinned, shaking his head in wonderment. "Praise our righteous God!"

"You don't seem surprised," Ananias observed, feeling a bit like Barnabas had stolen his thunder. "Saul has been our sworn enemy for years. You couldn't have possibly seen this coming."

"It's obvious the Lord has a plan for that man," Barnabas responded with an easy smile. "Like our father Jacob, Saul has been wrestling against God for far too long. But ultimately, God's will has prevailed."

"In my vision, it was revealed that Jesus Himself appeared to Saul on the road," Ananias mused, forgetting all about his injured toe. "Apparently, he was blinded during the encounter. God is sending me to restore his sight."

"I'm coming with you!"

Ananias nodded, anxious to be off. "You will need a change of clothes."

"A change of clothes?"

"I have been instructed to meet Saul at the house of Judas, one of the wealthiest, most highly esteemed Jews of Damascus," he explained, pointedly eyeing Barnabas' simple, travel-stained robe.

Nodding his understanding, Barnabas flashed a knowing grin. "Have you anything in your closet to spare?"

***

Agabus

"Agabus!"

Agabus rushed into Saul's guest chamber, still reeling from the vision revealed to him in the corridor. Based on the aggravation in Saul's tone, Agabus assumed he was in trouble. Deep trouble. Clearly, Saul hadn't appreciated his long absence.

"Agabus, *get in here*!"

"My lord, I'm here!" Agabus exclaimed, breathless.

"It's about time," Saul retorted, attempting to push himself up on his forearms. Gracelessly, he bumped against the large guest bed and nearly faceplanted. "Hurry! Help me rise."

Rushing to Saul's side, Agabus grasped the Pharisee's elbow, steadying him as he rose upon wobbly legs.

"I've had a vision," Saul murmured, his haunted, unseeing gaze fixed straight ahead.

"And I, as well," Agabus rushed ahead of him. Cringing, he realized too late it might have been wise to hold his tongue.

"You?" Saul asked in disbelief. "A vision?"

"Is that so hard to believe?" Agabus bristled, miffed by his colleague's apparent skepticism.

"A man named Ananias shall restore my sight," Saul told him, pointedly ignoring his question. "I must prepare to meet him."

Agabus stared at Saul in disbelief. "I just received the same revelation!" He didn't mention the fact that the mystery man's identity—the one called Ananias, apparently—hadn't been revealed to him as it had to Saul. That galled just a bit.

"This Ananias," Saul demanded, his cloudy, unseeing eyes roving about in the most unsettling way. "Who is he? Was this revealed to you in your vision?"

"No," Agabus answered slowly, wishing he could have impressed Saul with a resounding *yes*. "Nor to you?"

"Had it been revealed to me, I wouldn't be asking you!"

Agabus grit his teeth in annoyance, weary of Saul's tone. If the man *had* been converted on the road to Damascus, the sanctification process was kicking in far more slowly than he would have liked!

"This Ananias," Agabus ventured cautiously. "Is he a local? Or someone we know from Jerusalem?"

"From Jerusalem? Why? Do you know an Ananias of Jerusalem?" Saul demanded.

"I know at least a dozen men by that name," Agabus returned.

Saul glared in his general direction, peeved.

"What? It's a popular name!"

"I must prepare to meet him. I don't know when he will arrive."

"How may I assist, my lord?" Agabus ground out, hoping he sounded far more gracious than he felt.

"I need a fresh change of clothes from my trunk," Saul commanded with a wave of his arm, attempting to pace about the room but clearly thinking better of it. He had no desire to fall flat on his face. "Find something presentable and bring it to me."

"Yes, my lord." Lifting the lid of the heavy chest, Agabus sifted through layers of finery, feeling slightly envious. Having been assigned to wait upon Saul even before their arrival in Damascus, he hadn't yet found the opportunity to purchase fresh garments for himself.

"Find something for you, as well," Saul ordered tersely. "You smell like road dust and camel's hair."

Amazed, Agabus did a double take. Had the pompous Pharisee truly offered him the use of his prized wardrobe? Grudgingly, Agabus admitted to himself that Saul of Tarsus was, indeed, undergoing a change of heart—despite his overly blunt manner.

"Well?" Saul prompted impatiently, groping for the tall bedpost. Wrapping a steadying arm around the polished wood, he leaned heavily against it, weakened from days without food or drink. "Have you located something suitable?"

"Oh, yes, yes," Agabus stammered, making a hasty selection and lifting the intricate garment from the chest. He supposed it mattered little whether or not Saul would have chosen the prestigious-looking garment himself.

He couldn't see it, anyway.

I suppose there are a few advantages to his sudden loss of sight, Agabus decided, his neatly cropped black beard twitching in a rueful smile.

CHAPTER 33

Tabitha

Joppa

Joram lay upon his bed, still and pale as death.

Leaning forward in her chair, Tabitha clasped his limp, cold hands in hers, her own anxiously trembling. Lips moving silently in fervent prayer, warm tears slid from her closed eyelids, falling like tiny droplets of healing dew upon her uncle's chest.

"Father, please," she pleaded, her chest tightening in fear and regret. "Don't let this man perish without the knowledge of Your Son and His salvation. Father, I beg You, heal this man. Restore him by the power of Your healing presence. He has suffered such grief and loss. Mend his broken heart. Soothe his hardened soul. Heal him, Father, I pray."

Gasping in fright, Tabitha drew back when Joram's cold hands slid from beneath hers.

"What...pray tell...are you...babbling about?"

"*Uncle?*" she gasped, rocketing to her feet in awe.

"You're awake! You're all right!"

"What did I say...about you calling me...that?" Joram managed weakly.

"Oh, my lord!" Tabitha wept, far too relieved to be bothered by his insults. "Praise God. Praise God!" Despite her swelling relief, she couldn't help but recognize that one side of his face still drooped unnaturally, hindering his ability to speak succinctly.

But I suppose there will be time to address any complications later, she decided, brushing aside her concerns. For now, she must take advantage of this blessed opportunity the Lord had presented her to win her uncle to Christ!

"We were all so frightened for you, my lord," Tabitha exclaimed, taking his cold hands in hers. "We thought—"

"Summon my attorney."

Tabitha froze mid-sentence, perplexed. "Your attorney?"

"Isn't that what I said?"

"But, my lord," Tabitha argued, baffled. Had she remained stationed beside his sickbed for days, only to be cast aside after he revived? "I must speak with you about something. It is urgent—"

"As is my command," Joram shot back tersely, looking weak and exhausted. Without lifting his head from the pillow, he demanded shortly, "Do it."

"My lord, please," Tabitha begged him, her heart sinking. "Allow me to speak with you but a moment—"

"After I have met with my attorney," Joram ground out, his voice growing weaker despite his frustration. "Now go! Summon him now!"

Feeling frustrated and defeated, Tabitha realized that her stubborn uncle would remain deaf to anything she wished to tell him in his present state. His mind was fixed upon one thing, and one thing only: meeting with his attorney.

But why? She couldn't possibly imagine.

Nor did she care. All she cared about was convincing Joram to accept Jesus as Lord—before it was too late!

Sighing in resignation, Tabitha nodded in reluctant acquiescence, recognizing that any further arguments would prove futile. She must hope and pray that Joram would be willing to listen after meeting with his lawyer.

"I shall summon him, my lord. But I must speak with you the moment he departs."

"Very well."

With a pounding heart, Tabitha crossed the room, hoping she appeared far calmer than she felt. Mentally formulating a plan, she decided she would locate Eli first. He would know how to contact Joram's attorney, and quickly. She would also ask him to summon the physician, as well. Perhaps the seemingly unhelpful medic could offer more assistance now that Joram had gained consciousness. Next, she would alert the remainder of the household staff about Joram's unexpected progress. Wouldn't they be overjoyed?

And once Joram's attorney arrived, she would wait with Tirzah and Laurel. Her dear friend would readily join her in prayer. And Tirzah's practical manner would help soothe her anxiety as she awaited time with Joram.

Hastening down the hall, she tried not to consider the fact that this might prove to be her last chance to show Joram how much her Savior loved him.

***

Agabus

Damascus

It happened just as foretold in his vision.

Breathless, Agabus stood across the lavishly furnished room, watching in awe as an older believer named Ananias laid his hands upon the blind Pharisee kneeling humbly, broken, before him.

Glancing anxiously about the lavishly furnished sitting area, Agabus noted old Judas leaning forward in his gilded chair, grasping elegant armrests with avid interest. His dignified, cultured wife stood rather stiffly beside his chair, a hand resting lightly upon her husband's shoulder, her soft eyes clouded with uncertainty.

"I heard you had quite an interesting experience on the road."

Annoyed, Agabus glanced sideways at Barnabas, who now stood beside him, having accompanied his friend, Ananias. "You appear changed," he added, speaking just loudly enough for Agabus to hear him, his light brown eyes sparkling with interest. "Tell me, have the prayers of my faithful sister been answered?"

"Aren't they always?" Agabus reminded him, annoyed that Barnabas now had every right to say, *I told you so.*

Barnabas grinned broadly, pleased. But he didn't say *I told you so*, much to Agabus' relief.

"Brother Saul," Ananias said boldly, drawing Agabus' full attention back to him. "The Lord Jesus, who appeared to you on the road as you came, has sent me that you may receive your sight and be filled with the Holy Spirit."

Everyone gasped as something like scales fell from Saul's eyes, dropping to the plush Persian rug below.

"I can *see*!" Bounding to his feet, Saul grasped Ananias by the shoulders, shaking him until Agabus wondered if the old man's teeth rattled. "I can see! My sight has been restored!"

Gauging the reaction of those in the room, Agabus saw Judas shaking his head in awe and chuckling in amusement as his wife drew a trembling hand to her mouth.

Beaming, Barnabas pumped a triumphant fist in the air. "Praise our glorious God! For He has restored far more than your sight this day, Brother Saul."

"Joses, I thought I heard your voice." Turning to face his fellow student and former archenemy, Saul's lips tipped wryly. "I hear you're called Barnabas now."

"I imagine you'll be needing a new name soon, as well," Barnabas grinned.

"First, I must be baptized," Saul declared, his tone leaving no room for argument.

"You haven't eaten in days," Judas' wife spoke up in concern, clearly pondering all she had seen. "You must allow us to prepare a meal—"

"No," Saul interrupted firmly, clearly surprising

his gracious hostess with his uncompromising manner. "I must be baptized—and now! There is no time to lose."

Exchanging looks of utter shock with the others in the room, Agabus marveled at Saul's instant transformation. After being struck blind on the road to Damascus, the fiery Pharisee had become little more than a defeated, shriveled shell of a man, wallowing in agony and despair. But now, his burning zeal had returned full force. Only this time, it kindled with holy purpose rather than dangerous fire.

It would seem that Jesus of Nazareth had finally won over Saul of Tarsus.

"Well?" Saul exclaimed, standing with legs spread and firmly planted, his hands balled into eager fists at his sides. "Can I be baptized, or not?"

Exchanging a knowing look with Ananias, Barnabas lifted his brows in pleased amusement. "I imagine that can be arranged."

***

Tabitha

Joppa

Pacing the hall beyond Joram's opulent bedchamber, Tabitha glanced up, hopeful, as one of the double doors creaked open. Her uncle's attorney, a tight-lipped, meticulous-looking middle-aged man, stepped out rather ceremoniously, appearing very stern and professional.

Swallowing her nervousness, Tabitha crossed the hall to meet the lawyer, anxious to see her uncle.

"I beg your pardon, my lord, but has your meeting adjourned?"

"It has, and just in time, I daresay," the lawyer responded in a clipped tone. "It was a good call, summoning the physician, as well. He is currently tending to your master."

"Has something happened?" Tabitha asked him, alarmed. "Has his condition worsened?"

"Your uncle and I had quite a bit of ground to cover," the attorney informed her, unfazed. "The exertion proved a bit much for him. By some miracle, we finalized his wishes."

"But is he all right?" Tabitha demanded, tempted to take the man by his elegant collar and shake him.

"I'm afraid your master has relapsed," the attorney calmly informed her, placing several sealed scrolls into an expensive-looking bag. "But fortunately, we had concluded our meeting before the incident occurred."

"A relapse?"

"He is currently unconscious, unless the physician has successfully revived him."

"No!" Tabitha gasped, almost frantic. "No, please!" Slipping past the confused attorney, Tabitha burst into Joram's bedchamber, tears streaming down her face, just in time to see the physician standing over Joram's bed, reverently drawing a soft sheet over his head.

Turning around, the doctor sobered at the sight of Tabitha standing frozen in the doorway, her hands clasped over her heart, the color rapidly draining from her face.

"I tried to revive him," the physician explained, almost apologetically.

Staring at her uncle's motionless form outlined beneath the linen sheet, Tabitha's entire being grew cold. "Is he—"

"My deepest apologies, miss," the physician finally said. "He's gone."

"*No!*" Stumbling across the room, Tabitha flung herself down beside her uncle's bed, clasping her hands over his chest and weeping inconsolably.

Why? Her heart cried as tears fell from her eyes, soaking through the soft linen concealing her uncle's lifeless body. *God, why? Why did You let him die? He hadn't yet received You! He will be lost forever.*

Burying her face in her uncle's chest, Tabitha wept as if her heart was utterly broken. Which, she supposed, it was.

Again.

Devastated, Tabitha realized she had failed in her mission. The Lord had called her to Joppa to win her uncle's heart to Christ. And she had failed to do so.

It wasn't supposed to happen this way. It wasn't supposed to end like this.

Discomfited by the tragic scene, the physician picked up his leather bag. Awkwardly clearing his throat, he slipped quietly from the room, leaving the bereaved young woman to sob at her uncle's bedside, utterly alone in her grief.

CHAPTER 34

Tabitha

Joppa

Exhausted, Tabitha lowered herself onto a rickety wooden chair in the dim, narrow passage adjoining the kitchen and enclosed outdoor court utilized by Joram's staff. It had been a long day, laden with sorrow and regret.

She could hardly fathom that Joram's death had occurred that very morning. It was barely dusk, and yet she felt as if an eternity had passed since that heart-stopping moment when the physician had announced Joram's unexpected departure.

Tiredly rubbing her forehead, Tabitha contemplated all that had transpired in the hours since then. With the help of Tirzah, Martha, and several believing widows, her uncle's body had been properly washed, anointed, and wrapped. Shortly thereafter, Adam, Josiah, Phineas, and Simon the tanner had seen to it that he was properly laid to rest. There had been no special service in his honor, no heartfelt ceremony to commemorate his time on earth. After all, who would have attended such an event? Who would have mourned his passing? Joram was a mean, miserly, reclusive old soul, unwilling to lift so much as a finger to help neighbor, relative, or friend. Why would anyone grieve his sudden death?

If anything, the locals were probably relieved that he was gone.

Aching inside, Tabitha leaned her head back and closed her eyes, weary hands resting woodenly on her knees. She had been so certain that the Lord would help her win her uncle's heart for Jesus. He could have been changed, utterly transformed by the Word and power of God.

After all, hadn't she been called to Joppa for *him*?

"Tabitha."

Glancing sideways, Tabitha saw Tirzah poking her head in the doorway, her lovely features pinched with sympathy.

"You have visitors," the potter woman gently explained. "Are you up for it?"

No, Tabitha thought dully. *No, I'm not.* But instead, she managed wearily, "I shall meet them in the reception hall shortly—"

"No, no," Tirzah said quickly, shaking her head in protest. "You've been on your feet all day long. Sit there and rest. I'll send them in."

How can I welcome visitors in this cramped little space? Tabitha was about to argue, but sensing her friend's resistance, Tirzah hurried away before she could do so.

What on earth? Tabitha wondered, slightly

peeved.

But then Adam and his father, Josiah, stepped into the narrow chamber, their broad forms appearing far too large for the cramped space, and Tabitha understood. The men wouldn't have wished for her to make a fuss over them on such a day. They had simply come to encourage her and wish her well.

Rising wearily, Tabitha's hazel-green eyes drifted between the two familiar faces fast becoming dear to her.

"How are you holding up, dear one?" Josiah asked her, his hearty voice even more robust than it had been before sickness had claimed him.

"As best as I can," Tabitha answered honestly, working at a smile.

"Of course, you are," Josiah nodded warmly, his fondness for her evident in his tone. "We have been praying for you."

"Thank you," Tabitha managed weakly, feeling at a loss for words. "And thank you for all your help today. I couldn't have done it without you both."

"If I know you at all, you would have found a way," Josiah told her, exchanging a knowing look with his son. "And you will get through this, Tabitha. The Lord will see you through."

Blinking back tears, Tabitha looked away, determined not to weep. Hadn't she wept enough in her lifetime?

"If you will excuse me, dear one," Josiah said after a moment of strained silence. "Poor Eli is still rather distraught. I should speak with him, if you don't mind."

"Please do," Tabitha nodded, deeply concerned for

the anxious and high-strung overseer. Eli had been utterly devastated by his master's untimely death.

With a gentle nod of departure, Josiah slipped out of the vestibule, leaving Tabitha standing alone with Adam in the narrow space dimly lit by waning torchlight.

"Tabitha," Adam finally spoke, his kind eyes earnestly seeking hers. "I'm so sorry."

Dropping her gaze, Tabitha wondered how much she should say. Her heart was nearly bursting with grief, and she knew this compassionate young man of God would understand.

"Adam," she managed weakly, making a study of her own sandaled feet. "My uncle died without the Lord, and it's all my fault."

"*No.*"

Adam's typically cordial tone was so firm and uncompromising that Tabitha glanced up at him in surprise.

"This is not your fault, Tabitha," he said again, his brown eyes willing her to believe him. "Each of us are granted the gift of free will. You couldn't *force* your uncle—or anyone else, for that matter—to be saved."

"I could have done more—"

"You were completely devoted to Joram," Adam interrupted firmly. "Most women would have been out that door on day one, but you stayed. You remained faithful."

"It wasn't enough."

"You gave it your all, Tabitha," Adam told her, taking a step closer in his insistence. "Don't ever doubt that."

Unsettled by his closeness, Tabitha looked away. How desperately she wished to believe him!

"Tabitha?" Adam asked her gently, his eyes betraying his concern for her.

"I shouldn't have listened to him," Tabitha whispered, her eyes welling with tears. "Joram revived, Adam, just before he died. I was granted the opportunity to share Jesus with him one last time, but he demanded that I summon his attorney, and I obeyed him. I shouldn't have listened to him. I shouldn't have obeyed!"

"And do you suppose your uncle would have listened to you had you openly defied his orders?"

"I don't know," Tabitha finally sighed, defeated. "Perhaps."

"But probably not."

"And now I'll never know."

"Listen to me," Adam said, boldly taking her chin and forcing her to meet his gaze. "Joram's death is *not* your fault. His refusal to receive Christ is *not* your fault. Don't you ever forget that."

Heart pounding furiously in her chest, Tabitha simply nodded, surprised by his insistence. And the unsettling look in his brown eyes.

Sensing her unease, Adam took a small step back, wisely placing a bit of distance between them. "I can't imagine how you must be feeling right now," he told her, his tone filled with genuine empathy. "Losing your uncle so soon after your husband—"

Tabitha's head came up then, her features betraying her shock. How did Adam know about Stephanos' death?

"Philip told me everything when he was here,"

Adam explained, sensing her alarm. "I'm sorry. I don't know what I was thinking, bringing that up right now—"

"No, no, it's all right," Tabitha said quickly, cringing inwardly. What must he think of her, knowing she had intentionally allowed him to believe that she was still married?

She didn't even want to think about it.

"So what will you do now?" Adam asked her, wisely changing the subject. "What will happen to the estate?"

"I haven't the slightest idea," Tabitha answered truthfully. "I suppose Laurel and I will need to find another place to stay."

"And will you stay in Joppa?"

"I'm not sure. First, I must seek the Lord's guidance in this." Heart racing, Tabitha didn't wish to decipher the hope reflected in his eyes. Not now.

"But I am so worried for Joram's staff," she plunged ahead, her deep concern for them coloring her tone. "What will happen to them, Adam? Where will they go?"

"I imagine Joram will have made provision for them in his will," Adam assured her. "Perhaps a pension, of sorts, to aid them until they can find work elsewhere."

Tabitha could have laughed in his face but resisted the temptation to do so. After all, it would be entirely inappropriate so soon after Joram's departure. But she seriously doubted that her selfish uncle could have cared less about what happened to the household staff when he passed.

"Listen," Adam told her, interrupting her anxious

train of thought. "We're all praying for you, Tabitha. God will see you through this. And I'm here for you, whatever you need. You know that."

"Thanks, Adam," Tabitha said, immensely grateful for his kindness.

As the handsome young man slipped out the darkened doorway, Tabitha watched him go, troubled by her contrary emotions.

CHAPTER 35

Agabus

Damascus

Seated beside Barnabas on a hard stone bench in an austere synagogue in Damascus, Agabus listened in amazement as Saul of Tarsus, the church's greatest tormentor, stood upon the speaker's platform, his powerful voice ringing out over the gathering of confused men and women as he boldly proclaimed Jesus Christ as Messiah and Lord.

After his baptism, Saul had finally broken his fast—much to his hostess's relief—and instantly sprang into action, embracing his calling as God's chosen vessel with powerful zeal. Agabus could scarcely believe his ears, and neither could the Jewish men and women huddled around him in the dim, dank synagogue. Whispers rippled through the audience as friends and neighbors questioned Saul's newfound convictions—and his sanity. But far more concerning to Agabus than the congregation's obvious confusion were the threatening glares of the religious leaders as they watched their former ally turned traitor preaching on the platform.

"Did you ever believe you would live to see the day?" Barnabas asked, grinning and leaning in close enough for Agabus to hear his whispered inquiry.

Agabus could only shake his head in puzzled amazement. He had, indeed, lived to witness one of the most unlikely miracles of church history. And yet, if the grave expressions on the faces of the religious leaders were any indication, he couldn't help but wonder if he would live to see another day after Saul finished delivering his sermon.

It had been mere days since Saul's shocking conversion, and already, their enemies were many.

***

Rhoda

Jerusalem

Pausing beneath an ivory trellis laden with twisting vines, Rhoda glanced tentatively over the tall stack of freshly laundered linens cradled in her arms. Despite the winter chill lingering in the crisp, cold air, Mary's inner garden court was a lovely, inviting place with its elegant greenery, richly patterned awnings, curved marble benches, and gilded outdoor furniture.

But today, Rhoda wasn't observing the beauty of the quiet respite. Instead, her eyes were drawn to young Leah, seated still as stone upon a marble bench placed beside a towering wall. Rhoda might have mistaken the girl for a garden statue had she not been radiating nervous energy.

"Leah?" Rhoda dared, wondering when the girl had arrived at the estate. "Are you well?"

"Hello," Leah said quietly, turning tragic eyes upon her friend. "I'm fine."

"But are you?" Rhoda asked her gently, gingerly placing her stack of linens on the nearest marble-topped stand and crossing the distance between them. Taking a seat beside Leah, she tried for an encouraging smile. "You appear dismayed."

"Don't I always?" Leah sighed, her gaze dropping to her lap. Folding her hands nervously, she said, "Here I am, a new believer. I should be spilling over with joy and peace, like you. Like Mary. And yet, all I can do is *worry*."

"It's understandable," Rhoda assured her gently, wishing she were better with words. "Your brother, Saul, has resolved to kill our friends and fellow believers. You worry for him, and for them."

"Mary says God will get Saul's attention," Leah said mechanically, lifting her sober gaze. "She seems so certain that the Lord will prevail in my brother's life. She's hosted dozens of prayer meetings on his behalf. So why can't I have faith like hers?"

"Mary has been walking with the Lord quite a long time," Rhoda said slowly, hoping to comfort her friend. "Faith like that doesn't often happen overnight. One must continue to pray, and trust, and watch the Lord at work. That's how faith grows."

"Stated so simply," Leah sighed, shaking her head. "I suppose that's what I must do—keep praying, keep trusting, keep watching."

Rhoda watched her friend's expression closely,

sensing she was little comforted.

"I hope Barnabas will return soon," Leah added, her dark brows knit together in worry. "Mary must be worried sick for him."

"I don't think Mary worries much for anything," Rhoda reminded her with a small smile.

"When Barnabas returns, he can tell us what happened in Damascus," Leah reminded herself. "I do hope he brings good news, Rhoda. I hope he was able to warn the believers there before my brother arrived."

"I hope so, too." Rhoda nodded, sensing there was more to Leah's concerns than her brother's most recent rampage. "Is there something else?"

Leah looked at her then, her dark eyes welling with indignation. "I cannot marry the man my father has chosen for me!"

Rhoda stared at Leah, blinking in surprise at the typically staid girl's unexpected outburst.

"I won't do it, Rhoda," Leah insisted, vehemently shaking her head. Reaching for her long, straight black braid, she tugged at it anxiously before tossing it rather carelessly over her shoulder. "How can I bind myself to a man who hates our Way with a passion? I've heard the apostles' sermons. To be yoked to an unbeliever is sin."

"To willingly marry an unbeliever is, indeed, sin," Rhoda acknowledged slowly, desperately praying for wisdom regarding the sensitive discussion. "Yet, in your case, I'm not sure you have a choice, unless you run away. And I'm not entirely sure that would honor the Lord, either."

Leah's dark brows knit together in dismay, unwilling to accept her undesirable fate.

"Have you spoken about this with Mary?" Rhoda asked her gently.

"That's why I'm here," Leah nodded. "She wishes to pray with me."

"That's a very wise thing to do," Rhoda agreed. "When we find ourselves in impossible situations, it's important to take our questions and concerns to the Lord. He can make a way in the wilderness, Leah, even when it seems impossible. And I believe He will do this for you."

"But how can you be so certain?"

"I've seen His hand at work many times before."

"In situations like this?"

"Especially in situations like this," Rhoda smiled. "When we can do nothing about our own predicaments, God's glory shines through the most."

Nodding glumly, Leah tried to take Rhoda's encouragement to heart.

***

Kelila

Caesarea Maritima

Caesarea Maritima was unlike anything Kelila had ever seen. Not only was it designated as the seat of Roman government in Palestine, but it also served as headquarters for the Roman troops stationed in the Holy Land. Dominating the sandy white coastline of the shimmering Mediterranean Sea, the predominately Gentile city had fast become a thriving cultural center, boasting lavishly overdone luxury palaces, marble temples flaunting colossal pagan statues, a grandiose seaside theater hosting a dizzying array of entertaining diversions, a hippodrome capable of housing over twenty thousand people eager to bet on the chariot races, and a seemingly endless swash of sophisticated-looking, red-roofed public buildings and houses. The world-famous harbor was indeed a manmade wonder, providing anchorage for at least three hundred mammoth ships. But most impressive to Kelila was the shockingly advanced sewer system buried under the city, which emptied discreetly into the gently rolling tide.

"My, the traffic in this city is unbelievable," Philip declared, pushing the front door open with his back, his arms burdened with hastily wrapped packages, and slipping into the spacious house in which he had arranged lodging. "Never before have I seen a city with its streets so congested." Crossing the threshold, he dropped his armload of recent purchases on the nearest stone counter. Based on the shape of the bulging packages and the clattering and clanging accompanying Philip's hasty deposit, Kelila assumed he must have purchased multiple pots, pans, and cooking utensils. While on the road, they had always made do with one simple cookpot. To shoulder an entire kitchen's worth of cookware would have proven far too laborious for hard travel.

"It's rather like a miniature Rome out there, isn't it?" Kelila commented from across the kitchen. Standing at the wide stone counter located in the cooking space, Kelila turned, paring knife in hand, to further note her husband's purchases. "That's a lot of supplies," she commented with lifted brows. "What will we ever do with all of that when the Lord calls us elsewhere?"

"Actually, that's what I want to talk about," Philip told her, his brown eyes promising.

"About what we're going to do with all those pots and pans?" she asked him a bit skeptically as he joined her.

"No," Philip laughed, taking the paring knife from her hand and setting it down on the stone counter. Tenderly tucking her lush tresses behind one ear, he gazed into her face, smiling warmly. "I have something to tell you."

Heart racing, Kelila searched her husband's mysterious gaze. She'd grown quite familiar with that look. He had an announcement to make, and clearly, it was something important.

"Well?" she asked him, bracing herself for the worst even as she hoped for the best.

"I bought the house today."

"You *what?*" Kelila declared, shocked and appalled.

"I bought the house."

"*This* house?"

"Yes, this house," Philip chuckled, amused.

"But...but..." she stammered, entirely caught off guard. "But *why?*"

"To everything there is a season," Philip reminded her, sensing her mounting alarm. "The Lord did indeed call us to traveling evangelism for a time, but now, I believe that season has ended. It's time to settle down, to establish a home and to focus on outreach in our community."

"But...but *here?*" Kelila managed, wondering if she sounded as stunned as she felt. Try as she might, she just couldn't fathom calling this place home. The breathtaking seaside city was indeed a marvel to behold, but she had imagined settling down to raise their children in a quaint, friendly little town like Sychar—not in a powerful Roman metropolis!

"Kelila?" Philip asked her, puzzled. "You don't appear happy."

Giving her husband a blank stare, Kelila wondered what she should say. She knew she must tread carefully, for it would be easy to fall prey to fragile emotions in a moment like this. She certainly didn't wish to say anything she would later regret.

"Kelila?"

"It's just…" Kelila began, her tone betraying her deep uncertainty. "Well—"

"I thought you wanted to settle down," Philip supplied, clearly perplexed. "Has something changed?"

"No," Kelila quickly assured him. "Nothing has changed about that. I just didn't expect to settle *here*."

"But why not here?" Philip asked her, confused.

"Caesarea Maritima? Really, Philip?" Kelila groaned, striving for calm.

"It's a beautiful city," Philip returned, clearly puzzled by his wife's reaction. "Less than a year ago, you would have loved to settle in a big city."

"Yes, but for all the wrong reasons!"

"I'm confused."

"What of the Gentile influences permeating this region, Philip?" Kelila pointed out, losing patience. "What of the flagrant immorality flaunted upon every street corner? Caesarea Maritima is no place to settle down and raise a family!"

"I couldn't agree more," Philip assured her.

"Well, good," Kelila nodded, thankful he had finally accepted reason. "I didn't think you would insist upon staying—"

"But God has called us to abide here, nonetheless," Philip interrupted her gently. "I know this beyond any and all doubt."

Kelila could only stare at him, frustrated and appalled.

"I don't know *why* God has led us here, nor does it matter," Philip explained, gently taking her hands and graciously overlooking the fact that she stiffened at his touch. "What truly matters is our obedience, Kelila. God has a plan, a good plan. Can you trust that? Can you trust *me*?"

Resisting the urge to respond with a sharp retort that was, in her opinion, well-deserved, Kelila considered her husband's earnest plea. She had long since learned to trust in God's leading, even if she didn't like it or agree with it. And she had also aimed to be a supportive wife, standing beside Philip even when his calling had proven difficult.

And yet this time felt...different.

What if Philip was wrong? What if he had misunderstood the Holy Spirit's leading? After all, this was the life of their *child*, for heaven's sake! Couldn't Philip see how very much was at stake? They couldn't afford to make mistakes, not now. Not anymore.

"How about this," Philip sighed, looking troubled but not defeated. "Why don't you take some time to pray, Kelila. Ask the Lord to speak to you. He desires to reveal His will to you, and He promises He shall be found if you search for Him with all your heart."

Offering her shoulders a gentle squeeze, Philip turned and left the house, leaving her to stand alone beside the counter, agitated and upset.

Turning around, Kelila reached forward and grasped the stone ledge in front of her, her gaze protectively dropping to her bulging belly.

This can't possibly be Your plan, can it, Lord? Glancing over her shoulder, she assessed the lovely house her husband had proudly purchased. She couldn't deny the fact that it was spacious and attractive, with elegantly latticed windows overlooking the sparkling turquoise waters of the Mediterranean. Creamy marble tiles swirled underfoot, and the beautifully crafted marble pillars upholding the high ceiling reflected masterful Greco-Roman structure. The style, floorplan, and fixtures proved both modern and elegant.

Perfect for hospitality, she had to admit, though grudgingly. *But so far from family and friends,* her thoughts roved on, and she was deeply, inexplicably saddened. What was the point of having a grand, lovely house if you were unable to extend hospitality to family and fellow believers?

Annoyed, she seriously doubted they would encounter one single person of decency in this godless city. After all, most of the residents were pagan Gentiles, and the small Jewish minority in Caesarea were so hopelessly tainted by Gentile influence and culture, she imagined the likelihood of winning them to Christ was next to nothing. The chances of encountering a fellow believer was basically nil!

Lord, she prayed, swallowing her pride and her frustration with great effort. *Philip says I should seek You in this. If this is the place for us, then show me. Even one friendly face would prove encouraging, Lord.* Sighing in resignation, Kelila retrieved her paring knife and decided to get back to work.

CHAPTER 36

Tabitha

Joppa

It felt rather like operating on borrowed time.

Joram's faithful staff worked in hushed silence in a somewhat mechanical fashion, all of them wondering the same thing: When would they be ordered to vacate the estate and seek employment elsewhere? Surely it would be soon.

The concern weighed heavily in the atmosphere and upon each of their hearts.

Attempting a cheerful front, Tabitha patiently reminded the troubled staff that Joram might have made provision for them in his will. Perhaps he'd even made arrangements for them to continue working at the estate under the supervision of a designated overseer. Though highly unlikely, it wasn't entirely out of the question, she reasoned. She hoped to learn something about the state of affairs soon, but she was completely unfamiliar with the protocol and legal proceedings involving one's last will and testament. For all she knew, the agony of *not knowing* might even drag on for months.

A persistent rapping upon the broad entry doors resonated through the vast reception hall, jarring Tabitha from her troubled thoughts. She froze at the sudden explosion of sound, dust rag in hand, full of misgivings. Instinctively, she sensed that the fate of the entire household was about to be decided.

"Now who could that be?" Tirzah quipped, seated on the cool floor tiles with Laurel, assisting the toddler with her latest block-building project.

"I'll find out," Tabitha resolved, setting aside her dust rag and mentally preparing herself for the worst.

Slipping past them, Tabitha hurried into the narrow vestibule. Uttering a silent prayer, she opened the double doors with a bit of effort, wincing as blinding sunlight flooded the dim compartment.

"Good afternoon."

Drawing back in surprise, Tabitha's stomach lurched with dread at the sight of Joram's attorney.

Had he come to evict them from the house? What final orders had Joram left behind for his lawyer to enforce?

"G-good afternoon," Tabitha stammered, self-consciously straightening her apron. "I suppose you wish to speak with Eli, my master's overseer—"

"No, I have come to speak with *you*, Lady Tabitha," the lawyer responded in his typically clipped fashion.

Lady Tabitha? Blinking in surprise, she quickly addressed his error. "I beg your pardon, my lord, but there must be some mistake. You see—"

"Come, come," the lawyer tersely interrupted with a click of his sharp tongue. Stepping past her, he said calmly, "We must conference immediately in your former master's study. Please join me."

Wide-eyed and utterly perplexed, Tabitha slowly closed the door behind him. With a puzzled shake of her head, she turned on her heel to follow after the impatient lawyer.

***

"But—but I don't understand," Tabitha gaped at her uncle's stern-faced attorney, dragging in a shaky, ragged breath. "You're saying that my uncle left his entire estate *to me?*"

"You heard me," the lawyer nodded, looking rather comfortable seated behind Joram's massive desk. Shuffling through a thick stack of parchment papers, he glanced up to meet her gaze, almost daring her to argue with him.

"But—but *why?*" she finally managed, faintly grasping the back of the gilded chair before her.

"Perhaps you should sit down, my lady," the attorney suggested, gesturing toward the chair she currently grasped like a lifeline.

Coming around the chair on wobbly legs, Tabitha slowly lowered herself onto the seat, still reeling in shock.

"There," the attorney nodded his approval. "That's better."

"I still don't understand," Tabitha managed, clutching at the elegantly wrought arms of her chair. "Why would Joram leave everything to *me?* He detested me and everything that I stand for!"

"I don't ask questions," the attorney quipped a bit

drolly. "I merely respect my client's wishes and see that they are fulfilled. Now, according to this final will and testament, you are ordered to retain the current household staff—"

"Oh, praise God!" Tabitha breathed, tears of gratitude stinging her eyes.

"Joram has made provision for their compensation," the attorney rattled on, clearly eager to state the facts and leave. "He left you some final instructions, along with a parting sentiment. Can you read?"

"Yes, yes," Tabitha nodded quickly, eager to unravel the mystery behind Joram's mysterious actions.

"Excellent."

Leaning forward to accept the parchment document, Tabitha broke the seal with trembling fingers. Gingerly unrolling the scroll, her eyes flooded with tears at the sight of her uncle's wobbly penmanship. She imagined it had taken every ounce of strength that he had left—along with a great deal of help—to pen his parting words.

Tabitha,

You must wonder at this parting gift of mine. It is the least that I can do, and, frankly, it pales in comparison with the incomprehensible treasure you have revealed to me: Jesus Christ, Son of God, Savior. Who but God Himself could grant a young woman such great love for an old miser like me?

As you oversee the operations of this estate, I request that you administer the ensuing funds toward mission work, as you see fit. I trust you.

My beloved Pennie would be pleased to know our estate now rests in your capable hands.

I shall see you again when the Lord welcomes you home. There, I shall reside in YOUR mansion, for surely yours will be far grander than mine.

Always your uncle,
Joram

Always your uncle. Unable to see past the welling tears blurring her eyes, Tabitha rolled up the parchment scroll, clutching it close to her heart.

He believed! She realized, her entire being so flooded with joy that she wondered if she would burst. *In his final hours, Joram recognized the truth! Oh, thank You, Jesus! Thank You, Lord!*

"I trust that explains his reasoning," the attorney said in his ever-stoic manner. "Now, allow me to review some final details with you before I depart."

***

"You mean, he left everything to you?" Tirzah gasped, appearing completely dumbfounded. "*Everything?*"

"I still can't believe it myself," Tabitha murmured, dazed. "But I don't care about that. What matters is that Joram *believed*, Tirzah. He believed just before he died."

"What do you mean, you don't care about that?" Tirzah demanded, her brown eyes wide. "You *should* care! This is a massive estate. It's a huge responsibility!"

"Joram seems to have worked everything out,"

Tabitha answered, bending to pick up her little daughter. Nestling the toddler close, Tabitha stroked the girl's wispy curls, deep in thought. "Before he became ill, Joram had arranged a visit with a prestigious investor from Greece. Apparently, in his will, Joram requested this man to assist me in the business aspect of daily operations in exchange for a larger return, for which I am exceedingly grateful."

"But what if the investor arrives and refuses the offer?"

"We shall pray for God's will in this," Tabitha answered decisively.

"All right, then," Tirzah grinned, reaching out to tweak Laurel's rosy cheek. "This is surreal, isn't it? Have you even considered what you will do with all this—this—splendor?"

After gently lowering her squirming daughter to the ground, Tabitha slowly straightened, her hazel-green eyes growing round as the magnitude of her situation and the weight of newfound responsibility hit her full force.

"It would seem," she finally said, drawing in a calming breath, "that I have quite a bit of praying to do."

***

Agabus

Damascus

Pausing on the threshold of the humble guestroom in Ananias' home, Agabus placed a hand upon the doorpost, watching quietly as Barnabas neatly tied up the four corners of his worn traveling bag. With the final month of the year fast approaching, the celebratory Feast of Purim would soon be upon them. He imagined the apostle must plan to return to Jerusalem to celebrate the joyous occasion with friends and family.

"Ananias said I would find you here," Agabus observed, his dark eyes serious and shadowed beneath his extravagant head covering. "You're leaving Damascus?"

"It's time," Barnabas told him, turning to reward him with a knowing smile. "The believers in Jerusalem will be overjoyed to learn of Saul's conversion."

"They won't believe it. Not for a second."

"I imagine most will be... optimistically cautious."

"Or downright skeptical."

"Spoken like a true skeptic," Barnabas grinned, receiving a perturbed look from the young Pharisee. "Nonetheless, I must return. The brothers and sisters should know that their prayers have been answered."

"Indeed," Agabus agreed, wondering how many prayers the faithful church of Jerusalem had offered to God on his own behalf. "They deserve to know."

"That, they do."

"I spoke with Saul this morning," Agabus went on, his tone betraying both hesitance and resolve. "He has released me from my duties here. I want to go with you."

"Do you?" Barnabas asked, one brow lifted in question. "Given your new allegiance to the Way, Damascus may prove far safer for you, Agabus. If you return to your own order and they learn of your defection—"

"The believers should hear about Saul's conversion from someone who was there," Agabus interrupted, drawing an approving smile from the seasoned apostle. "I witnessed the miracle firsthand. I saw it with my own eyes."

"Ah," Barnabas nodded in understanding. "You are ready to join us in worship, then? Publicly? Despite the cost?"

"I am," Agabus managed, annoyed by the niggling fears that remained his constant companion. Nevertheless, he knew he must learn to cast his anxieties upon the Lord. From now on, he would go forth with confidence and courage—even if it killed him, which it very well might! But boldness wouldn't happen of its own accord. He knew he must intentionally practice trust and obedience if he wished to cultivate a harvest of blessing in his life. And in his opinion, this was certainly a good place to start.

"All right, then. Excellent," Barnabas declared, his light brown eyes sparkling with amused anticipation. "And I can think of one lovely lady, in particular, who shall prove especially interested in learning of your miraculous conversion!"

CHAPTER 37

Kelila

Caesarea Maritima

Despite Philip's wise suggestion, Kelila did far more stewing than praying.

Less than an hour had elapsed since the evangelist had left his wife alone to pray, and already, the expectant mother had mentally fabricated all manner of disasters that would likely befall them—and their child—should they remain in Caesarea, as her husband seemed determined to do.

Placing a wobbly hand on her ever-growing abdomen, Kelila closed her eyes, overwhelmed. Soon—very soon, perhaps—her child would enter the world. But how could she bear to deliver this baby alone in a strange, unfamiliar city, without the loving, patient aid of her mother and sister? And how could she possibly begin the daunting journey of motherhood alone, so very far removed from her loved ones? Who would help her navigate the newness of being a parent? After all, she hadn't the slightest idea how to raise a child! She needed help!

Nearly beside herself, Kelila tossed aside her paring knife. It clattered loudly on the stone countertop, further agitating her already frayed nerves. She hadn't yet finished preparing the vegetables for the midday meal, but she didn't care. How could she possibly think about vegetables at a time like this?

A gentle tapping on the front door further aroused her ire.

Philip has a lot of nerve, coming back here already, she thought, whirling around to let him in. Taking a step down to stand on the threshold, Kelila considered throwing down the latch rather than letting him in. Coolly adjusting her work apron and taking a calming breath, she pursed her lips together in displeasure as she swung open the door.

"Shalom, my dear, and good day!"

Open-mouthed with puzzlement, Kelila found herself staring into one of the kindest, friendliest faces she'd ever seen. For standing just outside the door was a petite, middle-aged woman with dark brown ringlets peeking out from beneath her creamy white cap, her radiant smile lighting every feature.

"Um, hello…" Kelila stammered in embarrassment. Had the woman noticed her state of agitation when she'd opened the door? Mortified, Kelila attempted to regain her composure in a hurry!

"Hello there," the woman greeted her warmly. "You must wonder why I'm here."

"Why, yes," Kelila nodded dumbly. Suddenly recalling her manners, she quickly stepped aside, opening the door a bit wider and gesturing for the woman to enter.

"Please, do come in."

"Oh, thank you most kindly, but I needn't intrude," the woman replied with a wave of her hand. "This won't take but a moment of your time. I simply wished to introduce myself, as you and your husband have only just arrived."

"Yes, we have," Kelila nodded blankly, perplexed by the woman's unexpected hospitality.

"My name is Adah," the woman went on, and Kelila was surprised to encounter a fellow Jewess so soon. "Being a midwife, I couldn't help but notice your condition, my dear."

"You're a midwife?" Kelila gasped, her tone betraying her disbelief.

"Indeed," Adah supplied, a twinkle in her friendly brown eyes. "And should you need any assistance before, during, or after your delivery, I'm happy to extend my services at no cost. After all, we neighbors must help each other, yes?"

"That is incredibly kind." Tears burning her eyes, Kelila silently repented for her lack of faith. "You say we are neighbors, Adah?"

"Indeed," Adah smiled, pleased. "I'm the house next door."

The house next door!

"You are an answer to prayer," Kelila told her frankly, blinking back hot tears. "I've been worried sick about delivering this baby, especially so far from the aid of family and friends."

"Then you needn't trouble your pretty little head a moment longer," Adah told her firmly. "I've been delivering babies for over thirty years. I could very well do the thing in my sleep if need be!"

Laughing, Kelila marveled at the goodness of

God.

"Truly, I cannot thank you enough—"

"It is my pleasure, dear," the kindly midwife informed her sincerely. "Now I'd best be on my way. But if you need me—for any reason at all—you know where to find me."

"Thank you, Adah. Truly, thank you." Kelila was about to close the door when a thought occurred to her—a thought so outrageous she hesitated to even consider it.

"Adah?" she called after the cheerful woman, hoping she wasn't about to overstep her bounds.

Pausing to swivel around on one heel, Adah arched a friendly brow in question.

"May I ask...well, may I ask what it is that inspires your great kindness?"

Facial features alighting with a peace all too familiar to Kelila, Adah answered forthrightly, "I met a Man once in Jerusalem, when my husband and I journeyed to observe the Passover. His name is Jesus, Jesus of Nazareth. Perhaps you've heard of Him?"

Kelila could only stare at the woman with astonished eyes, completely stunned to silence.

* * *

Tabitha

Joppa

Throwing open the wardrobe doors in Joram's former chambers, Tirzah's brows arched in skepticism as she and Tabitha surveyed the lone item hanging within.

"Joram left you *this*?" Tirzah asked blankly, perplexed.

"According to the paperwork his attorney reviewed with me, yes," Tabitha nodded in confusion.

"*Why?*" Tirzah asked her rather gracelessly.

"I can't imagine why." Stretching out her hand, Tabitha reached reverently into the open wardrobe, gently fingering the satiny folds of Aunt Pennie's wedding gown. "Perhaps he wanted me to have it because I repaired it for him."

"Well, it's worth a great deal of money, I suppose. Maybe he thought you could sell it."

"Oh, Joram would never want me to sell this," Tabitha exclaimed, startled by Tirzah's suggestion. "He treasured it. I couldn't sell it."

"Well, he left you the entire estate, so you won't exactly be needing the money," Tirzah quipped with a wry smile.

The entire estate. Tabitha's stomach tightened at the thought. She'd been wrestling with it all day, still attempting to absorb the reality of the lawyer's shocking announcement. The thought of taking over the operations of an entire seaside manor—not to mention the shipping business funding it—was truly daunting. She couldn't help but wonder if she was capable of such a feat.

"Tabitha, are you all right?"

Drawn back to the present moment by Tirzah's careful inquiry, Tabitha nodded quickly, more to assure herself than her friend. "I'm fine. Just pondering all that must be done over the course of the next few days."

"Thank goodness you have that attorney to help

you sort through all of it. And the investor from Greece—when will he arrive in Joppa to show you the ropes?"

"It could be months," Tabitha responded, praying that the business wouldn't self-implode before then! "Eli believes we can manage until his arrival. He's been overseeing Joram's affairs for years."

"I hope this mystery investor is capable," Tirzah observed, closing the wardrobe doors and turning around to face her friend. "Even more so, I hope he can be trusted. What do you know of him, Tabitha?"

"Next to nothing," she admitted, feeling extremely uneasy. "Only that he's a wealthy investor reputed to have remarkable business acumen and skill. Apparently, he's a mighty figure in the shipping industry."

"Has Eli met him?"

"Only once, many years ago."

"And what are Eli's thoughts about him?"

"Apparently, this man is a rather opinionated and formidable figure." Tabitha met Tirzah's pointed gaze, her own clouded with uncertainty. "Eli suggested that I brace myself. He thinks it's going to be a bumpy ride."

CHAPTER 38

Kelila

Caesarea Maritima

Kelila was ready and waiting when Philip returned from his stroll—and probably quite a bit of praying, as well.

Watching tentatively from her perch in the spacious sitting area, she waited as Philip quietly entered the new house, turning and slowly closing the door behind him. When he turned to face her again, his brown eyes betrayed his hesitation. Undoubtedly, he wondered if his wife would be harboring further resentment after their disagreement.

"Hello," Kelila said a bit sheepishly, lifting a slender shoulder in a manner reminiscent of a playful shrug.

"Hi," Philip smiled, his features relaxing just a bit at her subdued manner.

"Sit with me?" Kelila asked him, patting the space beside her on the upholstered couch—the only piece of furniture they had purchased, thus far. *And very likely the only piece we can afford for quite some time,* Kelila had thought when Philip had brought the elegant lectus home the previous day.

That should have been a tip off, she decided, annoyed she'd missed it. *Philip wouldn't have made such a purchase just to leave it behind to travel on.*

Crossing the room, Philip approached his wife, his soft eyes fondly grazing her rounded belly as he sat down. Taking her hand, he looked relieved when she didn't resist his touch.

"What's on your mind, love?"

"I have a confession to make," Kelila informed him a bit self-consciously, wondering why it was so bothersome to swallow her own pride, even when she knew she had been in the wrong.

Philip leaned in closer, tenderly tucking a strand of dark hair behind her delicate ear.

"Just when I begin to think I've learned to trust God and submit to His will, my resolve is sorely tested," she sighed, her gaze flickering away. "When the Lord called us to traveling evangelism, I wasn't exactly thrilled about it."

"So I recall," Philip grinned, tweaking her rosy cheek.

"But I learned to trust His will," Kelila went on. "I enjoyed every moment we spent in Sychar. Then, God called you to travel alone. Though it was hard for me to accept it, the Lord helped me through it."

"Indeed, He did."

"Yes," Kelila nodded slowly. "And then there was Joppa. And now we've been called here, to Caesarea Maritima. I have loved every moment of this ministry God has given us, Philip. True, there were difficult moments. Painful ones, even. But I eventually learned to trust that His way is best."

Philip only waited, allowing his wife to air her thoughts without interruption.

"But now…" Kelila sighed, cradling the little life within her with trembling hands. "We are bringing this little one into the world, Philip. And I find that it's so much easier to trust the Lord for my own well-being than for the safety and welfare of this child."

"It's perfectly understandable," Philip assured her, squeezing her hand. "It's only natural to be protective of one's own child. I feel it, too."

Kelila looked up at him in surprise. She hadn't considered that he might be concerned, as well.

"When the Holy Spirit spoke to me, revealing that we must settle down in this unexpected and seemingly foreign city… Well, I was troubled—to say the least—at the thought of raising a family here. But then I felt the strongest impression upon my heart, as if the Lord had whispered in my ear, 'Would your little one be safer in a city of your own choosing apart from My will?' And I remembered that the center of God's will truly *is* the safest place to be, and that applies to our children as well."

"I will try to remember that," Kelila sighed. "I was also concerned about having the baby here, so far from family and friends. My time is drawing near, Philip, and I must confess—I'm getting nervous."

"You needn't fear, beloved," Philip told her, tenderly stroking her cheek. "Having a baby is the most natural thing in the world."

"Natural, yes. But certainly not easy," Kelila reminded him. "I've heard horror stories about women in labor. And it's not entirely uncommon for mothers to perish in childbirth. That's what happened to Tabitha's aunt, Pennie. Did you know that?"

"I didn't," Philip answered, watching her with reassuring eyes. "But God will be with you, Kelila. You won't deliver this baby alone."

"That's what I wanted to tell you," she said, thankfulness welling within her at the mercies of God. "After you left this morning, I was furious. And though I should have been seeking God, I fussed and fumed instead. And yet again, even in my faithlessness, God remained faithful. He sent me an angel today, Philip—a kind midwife named Adah who has offered her services. She has promised to help me deliver this baby, free of charge."

"That's incredible, love!"

"And it gets even better," Kelila rushed ahead, wondering why she had wasted so much time doubting the Lord's undeserved favor. "Adah is a fellow believer, Philip! She met the Lord when He walked among us. We are not alone here."

"Praise God." Smiling broadly, Philip cupped Kelila's face in his hand. "His mercies are truly astounding."

***

Tabitha

Joppa

Tiredly crossing the room, Tabitha shivered, her bare feet padding across the cold stone floor of the storage room she had shared with her daughter for nearly a year. Lowering herself onto her threadbare cot, she leaned back slowly, propping herself up with weary hands.

It had been quite a day, laden with difficult decisions and emotional turmoil. Thankfully, Laurel was finally asleep, her fragile back rising and falling in time with her gentle breathing. The household staff had also retired for the night, and Tirzah had long since returned home.

Now, in the solitude of the early twilight hours, Tabitha was grateful for the opportunity to seek the Lord in prayer without interruption. Tucking her legs up underneath her, Tabitha tossed her long braid over one shoulder before folding her hands in her lap.

Oh, Lord, where to even begin? As her gaze swept the small, darkened room, she suddenly realized in astonishment that she was now free to select any suite in the house—*her* house, just imagine—to reside in. The thought was almost too outrageous to contemplate. She couldn't help but feel slightly presumptuous leaving the space her uncle had assigned her to select a more accommodating suite of her own!

Pushing troubling thoughts far from her mind, Tabitha resolved that, first and foremost, she must seek the Lord's will in this new and unexpected venture. Never in a thousand years could she have imagined she would find herself here, becoming the lady of a wealthy seaside estate. Even more daunting than that thought was the fact that she was now responsible for overseeing her uncle's booming shipping ventures, as well.

How on earth could she do it? Was it even possible?

Merciful Father, she prayed, bowing her head in earnest supplication. *I am overwhelmed. How should I proceed from this point forward? Where should I go from here?*

There was simply so much to do, so many crucial decisions to be made. And she hadn't the slightest idea where to even begin.

I must write to Mary first thing in the morning, she decided. *Mary will guide me in the right direction and offer sound advice.* Her circumstances mirrored her former lady's in such a shocking manner it was almost uncanny. Both had lost husbands. Both were forced to raise their children alone. Both had had massive enterprises thrust upon them, virtually overnight. And both were responsible for the operations of a very formidable estate.

First, I shall begin renovations to host the local church here, Tabitha mused, feeling good about making her first major decision concerning the estate. Her uncle had instructed her to utilize her inheritance for the furtherance of the gospel, and this was certainly a logical starting point. She could easily follow the model Mary had instituted in Jerusalem, rotating prayer and worship services throughout the day so all believers could attend without overcrowding the sprawling home.

But what's next, Lord? Please show me the next step. Battling fatigue, Tabitha clasped her hands a bit more tightly, praying fervently for guidance. Though she felt good about her decision to renovate the mansion to accommodate the growing church, she sensed there was something more the Lord desired. The gentle stirring in her spirit was indicative of God at work.

Bone-weary, Tabitha strove for wakefulness, committing her cause to the Lord in prayer. After placing her concerns before the Savior, she eventually curled up on her side, drawing her threadbare blanket under her chin.

A full minute hadn't yet passed before the exhausted young widow slipped into a peaceful state of slumber.

***

Kelila

Caesarea Maritima

Standing at the wide stone counter dicing vegetables, Kelila set aside her paring knife, unexplainably fatigued. Spreading her hands atop the cool stone surface, she braced herself against an unexpected wave of…nausea? Indigestion? She wasn't sure. All she knew for certain was that something didn't feel *right*.

Taking a deep breath, Kelila steadied herself, reached for her knife, and resumed her chopping just as a subtle tightening sensation seized her abdomen.

I'm not in labor, am I? she thought suddenly, perplexed. According to her calculations, it was still a few weeks early for the baby's arrival. Now would be an entirely inconvenient time for the child to arrive! After all, Philip was out consulting with a local carpenter about purchasing furnishings for their new home, which was currently empty.

Oh, my, Kelila thought, alarmed. I can't be in labor! *We can't welcome a child into an empty house!* Not to mention the fact that Adah had just departed several days prior to visit family in nearby Apollonia. Kelila hadn't thought twice about the woman's departure. After all, her services shouldn't be required for several weeks yet!

Or would they?

The sensation settled just as quickly as it had come upon her. Kelila simply stood still, waiting. Would it happen again? Or was she in the clear?

Breathing an enormous sigh of relief after several uneventful minutes had passed, Kelila brushed aside her concerns and resumed her steady chopping.

She must have simply imagined it.

There it is again!

Within moments, the tightening sensation returned, a bit more forceful this time. Tossing aside the knife, Kelila braced herself against the counter, striving for calm.

This can't be happening, she thought, her mind racing frantically. *Lord, we're not ready! This isn't the proper time. Surely You know that, Lord!*

If she had hoped for a response, the only one she received was yet another uncomfortable tightening of her swollen abdomen.

Striving for calm, Kelila contemplated her options. Should she set off to locate Philip, or simply wait for him to return home? It was highly unlikely her labor would progress rapidly since this was her first child. She decided it would be wiser to simply await her husband's return, rather than risking getting lost while attempting to locate him in an unfamiliar city.

Kelila closed her eyes, silently begging God for help. And wisdom.

CHAPTER 39

Kelila

Caesarea Maritima

Kelila thought Philip would never get back.

When he finally did, he remained maddeningly calm.

"You needn't worry, love," he assured her, having helped her settle comfortably on the one piece of furniture they currently owned. Kneeling by her side, her stroked her hair tenderly, smiling. "You're doing fine."

"I don't *feel* fine!" Kelila hissed, grasping her abdomen and wincing in discomfort. Though the contractions were still decently spaced and hadn't yet become painful, she was absolutely certain she'd never been more uncomfortable in her entire life! "What am I going to do, Philip? How can I have this baby without a midwife?"

"The Lord's mother did so, and in a stable surrounded by all manner of beasts, at that."

Well, good for her, Kelila wanted to harrumph. Naturally, Mary, the mother of Jesus, would have birthed a child in a stable in a city far from home without the aid of family, physicians, or midwives!

"Besides," Philip reminded her, sensing his wife's mounting indignation. "It's entirely possible that Adah will return from Apollonia long before our baby makes an appearance."

"Philip, I'm in labor *now*!"

"You're still at the earliest stages, love," Philip assured her, tweaking her cheek. "Remember what Adah told us? You will likely labor for hours, even days."

"Days!" Kelila moaned miserably. She knew the discomfort would only progress from here. The thought of enduring agonizing labor for *days* was unthinkable!

"The Lord is with us, Kelila," Philip whispered, bending to tenderly kiss her forehead. "Trust Him."

"Trust Him?" Kelila blinked at her husband, incredulous. "Forgive me, Philip, but that's easy for you to say! *You're* not the one having to deliver this baby!"

"No, I'm not," Philip admitted graciously. "I didn't mean to sound callous, love."

"Well, you did!"

"Try to stay calm. Think of the baby."

"All I can think about is this baby," Kelila moaned, grasping her abdomen as another tight contraction seized her. "I need a midwife, Philip. I need you to find someone!"

"I'm not sure I should leave you, beloved—"

"Philip, I need you to do this," Kelila pleaded, her heart racing as doubt gave way to fear. "And I need you to do it *now*."

Nodding in resignation, Philip rose from her bedside, praying silently as he slipped out the door and closed it gently behind him.

***

Tabitha

Joppa

Standing upon the rocky coast of the glittering Mediterranean, Tabitha's intense hazel-green gaze rested upon the azure waters below. From her perch upon a high, plunging precipice, she possessed a sweeping view of the Great Sea and sandy white shoreline far below.

She had to admit, it was breathtaking.

Folding her arms over her chest, Tabitha allowed herself a quiet moment with her own thoughts. The household staff had bombarded her with questions all morning, each of them looking expectantly to her for answers.

Answers she did not have.

Entrusting Laurel in Tirzah's care, Tabitha had hastily departed for a much-needed stroll and a breath of fresh air. She needed more time to think. And pray.

How could she have possibly known that this quaint seaside city—entirely foreign to her until recently—would become her home? When she had left her beloved Jerusalem to minister to Joram, she had expected her stay in Joppa to be temporary, at best. She had always planned to return to the holy city, to familiarity, to her former mistress, to her friends, her church.

Her husband's grave.

Reverently lifting her gaze, Tabitha searched the sapphire blue sky smattered with fluffy white clouds as if hoping to discover a divine message scrawled across the heavenlies. While she greatly rejoiced in her uncle's conversion, the fact that he had left her so great an inheritance complicated her future plans.

Oh, Lord, am I even capable of shouldering this burden? she wondered, her heart pounding dully in her chest. *I have always imagined my life would be dedicated to the ministry of the gospel, not to the management of an enormous shipping business and wealthy seaside estate! What is Your will in this, Lord? I am open to Your leading.*

The prayer had scarcely finished forming in her mind when Tabitha was hit by another thought, one was so incredible and yet, so logical, she wondered why she hadn't considered it before.

Glancing heavenward and sharing a secret smile with the One who had formed her, shaping her purpose and her destiny long before the world had even begun, Tabitha spun on her heel and hurried back to the mansion.

***

Kelila

Caesarea Maritima

Feeling increasingly uncomfortable, Kelila was beginning to regret her decision to send Philip out in search of a midwife. How long would he be gone, anyway? Did he intend to search the entire city until he found one?

And what if the baby arrived in his absence?

Groaning in misery, Kelila pushed herself up into a partially sitting position, grasping her rounded belly with shaking hands. The prospect of birthing a child was frightening enough. But to do so alone, without her husband or a midwife present, in a strange city, far from the comfort and assistance of loved ones, was almost unthinkable!

Oh, Lord, she groaned miserably. *Why did I send Philip away? Where is he? Bring him back, Lord!*

As if in answer to her prayer, the front door banged open, slamming against the opposite wall.

"Philip," she moaned, certain she'd never been quite so glad to see him as he stepped over the threshold and hastened to her side.

"How are you feeling, beloved?" he asked, kneeling beside her and stroking back the damp tendrils from her perspiring forehead.

"Pretty terrible."

"Oh, my love." Taking her hand, Philip squeezed it reassuringly. "I'm sorry I was gone so long. Locating an available midwife on such short notice—"

"Did you find one?"

"Why, this home is positively threadbare!" As if in answer to Kelila's question, a rotund Greek woman emerged upon the threshold, her sharp eyes sweeping the house with keen displeasure. "This simply will not do."

"As I mentioned earlier, we've only just arrived in Caesarea—" Philip attempted to explain.

"And how exactly do you intend to care for a

newborn without the most basic of necessities?"

"We thought we would have several weeks yet to prepare for the child's arrival, but—"

"Well, clearly not," the midwife huffed, crossing the room to stand imposingly over Kelila, her hands planted on her hips. "How long have you been laboring?"

"Several hours," Kelila responded weakly, daunted by the older woman's callous manner.

"This your first child?"

Kelila nodded miserably.

"So I thought," the midwife nodded curtly. "If you think this is bad, just wait until the hard contractions start rolling in."

"We're obviously new at this," Philip said quickly, straightening to face the hard little woman before him. "Some encouragement would be helpful and most appreciated."

"It isn't comfort she needs," the midwife retorted, impatiently smoothing her apron. "She needs to know what's coming so she can brace herself."

"In the meantime, what do we need to do?" Philip asked wearily, wondering if it would be best to simply dismiss the negative midwife and attempt to deliver the baby himself.

"Go stoke that fire," the midwife huffed, pointing toward the steadily dwindling flames in the hearth. "And put plenty of water on to boil. If you haven't any clean cloths around, then I suggest you go find some in a hurry."

Nodding his understanding, Philip squeezed Kelila's hand before slipping away to perform the midwife's bidding.

CHAPTER 40

Tabitha

Joppa

"Tabitha, you're a genius. Why didn't *I* think of that?"

"It wasn't me, Tirzah," Tabitha reminded her friend as they convened together in Joram's former office. "I know the Holy Spirit guided me to this decision. It came to me clear as day, just like resounding bells or the penetrating blast of a trumpet."

Dropping into one of the chairs facing Joram's desk, Tirzah grasped the gilded arms, shaking her head in wonderment. "Just think, soon this place will be alive and buzzing with activity. Why, it'll be utterly transformed!"

"That, it will," Tabitha agreed, going around Joram's massive desk. Drawing aside her uncle's thronelike chair, she lowered herself slowly, gingerly, onto it. It felt strange, being seated behind her uncle's desk—now *her* desk. Based on the Lord's most recent revelation to her, she imagined she would soon be spending many hours in this chair overseeing the various operations of a vibrant, full-time ministry, very much like her beloved mistress in Jerusalem. She could scarcely believe the shocking turn of events that had transpired and the unexpected course her life had taken.

"I knew you would use the mansion to host local church services," Tirzah spoke up, interrupting Tabitha's train of thought. "But to renovate this place as a home and refuge for the widows and orphans of Joppa...Tabitha, it's brilliant."

"This mansion is perfect for hospitality," Tabitha explained enthusiastically as her mind flooded with exciting possibilities. "Each of the suites can be transformed to house several widows, along with their children. There is ample space for many families here. In addition to that, we have an entire household staff on call to assist with the needs that will naturally arise, such as laundry, preparing meals, and housecleaning."

"And what about the church?" Tirzah asked her, her brown eyes sparkling with interest as she leaned forward in her chair. "Where will services be conducted?"

"I've decided to utilize the reception hall for that," Tabitha explained, her excitement rising steadily along with Tirzah's. "It's an enormous space. We can knock down the vestibule walls at the entry, as well, to allow for even more space. Once we clear out all the furniture, there will be plenty of room to bring in benches, if needed, and a stand to place up front so the deacons can address the gathering."

"It sounds perfect," Tirzah nodded her support. "And if services are conducted at regular intervals, as they are in Jerusalem, then there will always be enough room for believers to gather. We'll just meet in shifts, rather than trying to fit every believer in Joppa into one service."

"Exactly," Tabitha nodded. "I must speak with Josiah, Adam, and Phineas. As the elders of the church, they will be responsible for organizing church services and spreading the word so our fellow believers are informed about the changes taking place."

"When will you meet with them?"

"I've asked them to join me for supper this evening so we can make plans," Tabitha explained, mentally reviewing everything that would need to be discussed. "They're as eager as we are to get started."

"Perfect."

"There's a lot of work to do," Tabitha observed frankly. "I don't wish to waste any time. This afternoon, I shall assemble the household staff and fully disclose our plan going forward."

"Do you expect them to receive it well?"

"Eli will undoubtedly harbor some reservations," Tabitha admitted. "He's very stringent regarding the faith of his fathers, and I doubt he'll appreciate hosting church services in his home, at first. But I believe he will come around. He may even be won by the faith and conduct of our fellow believers."

"Wouldn't that be something?"

"As for the rest of the staff, I think they'll be very supportive," Tabitha continued, smiling faintly. "Possibly even excited."

"I think you might be right."

Leaning forward in her chair, Tabitha folded her hands on top of the desk, marveling at the wonders about to unfold.

"You know," Tirzah said quietly, her manner growing uncharacteristically gentle. "I know you don't speak of him often, but were Stephanos still here with us, he would be very, very proud of you."

Looking away, Tabitha felt a sharp pang to her heart.

"Tabitha?" Tirzah asked gently, extending a loving hand toward her friend. "Are you all right?"

"I'm fine," Tabitha quickly nodded, biting her lower lip and attempting to swallow the lump forming in her throat. "Actually, I've thought of that many times this morning—how thrilled he would have been to see all of this."

"He would, indeed," Tirzah nodded warmly.

Reaching for her uncle's stylus, Tabitha tapped it on the desk top several times, allowing herself a moment to recover from the unexpected wave of sorrow sweeping over her. Keenly, she recalled a late night many years ago in Jerusalem when she had stumbled upon her dear lady, Mary, weeping inconsolably in her own office. Mary, too, had ached at the absence of her beloved husband, Mark. How he would have rejoiced in his wife's mission and calling in Christ, had he lived!

"You know," Tirzah remarked with a droll little smile, interrupting Tabitha's silent reverie. "You look rather like you belong in that chair."

Glancing up in surprise, Tabitha's wide eyes met Tirzah's mischievous gaze.

"Just don't let all this power and authority go to your head," she teased, her brown eyes gleaming with fun.

Grateful for the comic relief, Tabitha shared a

hearty laugh with her dearest friend, grateful to God for her sweet companionship and support.

***

Kelila

Caesarea Maritima

Time dragged on, hour after agonizing hour, with seemingly little progress. As her labor pains increased with breathtaking intensity and regularity, Kelila became more and more anxious. But far worse than the pain was the deeply niggling suspicion that something wasn't quite *right*.

"Philip," she groaned, weakly reaching for his arm after a particularly miserable contraction. "I don't feel right."

"You're in labor," the midwife shot back, annoyed. "You're not supposed to feel right."

Gritting her teeth, Kelila resisted the urge to react with a stinging retort. She didn't appreciate this midwife's terse bedside manner, not at all. The hard little woman had made her feel like a blubbering fool rather than offering consolation or encouragement as she labored to deliver her firstborn child.

"I'm here, love," Philip assured her, gently dabbing at the perspiration on her forehead with a damp cloth. "You're doing fine."

"Something is wrong, Philip. I'm sure it is," she whispered, lowering her voice so the midwife wouldn't be privy to their private conversation.

"Why do you say that, beloved?" Philip asked her, his brown eyes welling with concern. "Are you in pain?"

Seriously? Kelila almost retorted. What kind of question was that?

"Philip," she responded instead, concealing her frustration with great effort. "I'm *in labor.*"

"Well, yes. I know," Philip quickly amended, clearly flustered. "Naturally, you're in pain. I just meant… well, why do you say something is wrong?"

Crying out suddenly, Kelila bent forward, grasping her contracting abdomen with trembling hands.

Reaching for his wife, Philip helped her brace herself against the pain of yet another hard contraction as the midwife looked on with a disapproving scowl.

It would seem their present discussion would simply have to wait.

CHAPTER 41

Agabus

Damascus

It would be yet another long, arduous journey home to Jerusalem.

Shouldering his pack on already tired shoulders, Agabus decided that the formerly dreaded jouncing, jostling chariot would have proven a far more favorable mode of transportation than his present option: struggling to keep time with the agile and seemingly inexhaustible Barnabas. Not only was the apostle in excellent shape, but he was also a seasoned traveler, accustomed to weeks and sometimes even months of hard travel without reprieve.

Agabus could only hope and pray he wouldn't drop like a fly by the wayside.

"How are you holding up, friend?" Barnabas called over his shoulder, several paces ahead of the straggling scholar. "Faring well?"

Using his shawl to dab at the perspiration on his brow, Agabus tried for a positive tone. "I'm still alive, if that's what you're asking."

"Excellent."

Peeved, Agabus paused amid the road. He had a niggling suspicion that his future would involve a bit more travel than he would have preferred. For the umpteenth time, he wondered if he was actually up to the task the Lord had clearly assigned him.

It was then that he realized his sandaled feet were planted on the very stones upon which Jesus Christ had revealed himself to Saul—and to him.

Overcome with surprise and a deep sense of reverential awe, Agabus turned around slowly, shielding his eyes from the steadily rising sun as it crested the lumbering hills sheltering age-old Damascus now far behind him. The drab surroundings of the cosmopolitan city were characterized by barrenness and dust, and yet, Damascus itself appeared like a verdant green oasis, right there in the midst of a seemingly endless desert. Like a hidden secret, that oasis had been there all along, since the dawn of time. Just waiting to be stumbled upon by the first weary traveler. Waiting to provide nourishment, refreshment, and life.

Rather like the everlasting truth Agabus had finally discovered within the unlikely borders of Damascus. Like a bubbling oasis amidst a barren desert wasteland, the Living Water had been there all along, springing forth unto eternal life for all who dared to partake of it. To receive it. To embrace it.

Releasing a knowing sigh, Agabus raised his eyes heavenward in a silent plea for help, mercy, and guidance. For though he now returned to his native Jerusalem, which undoubtedly remained unchanged since his departure, he himself had changed drastically. Soon, he would set foot within his own familiar city, the same beloved Temple, the same regal stone synagogues and academic libraries. Soon, he would reunite with his peers and his superiors. And yet, he would return a changed man.

Everyone was bound to notice. And he didn't even want to think about what might transpire after that.

"Everything all right, friend?"

Jarred by Barnabas' concern, Agabus turned around slowly to face his travel mate, now far more than just a few paces ahead of him.

"It's just that…" He faltered, his heart pounding as the full realization about where he now stood hit him full force. "This is the place where Jesus met Saul, the place where everything changed."

"Ah, I see," Barnabas smiled knowingly, the lines around his mouth deepening in response. "Holy ground."

***

Kelila

Caesarea Maritima

Night was falling, and yet Kelila's labor dragged on.

Anxious beyond what he'd imagined possible, Philip drew aside the midwife, pausing beside the hearth for a brief whispered conference.

"My wife is concerned, my lady. She fears something isn't right with the baby."

"All new mothers are concerned about that," the older woman shot back tersely. "Labor isn't for the faint of heart. Childbirth is no joke. The sooner she learns that, the better off she'll be."

Stunned by the woman's callous manner, Philip resisted the urge to reward her with a scathing rebuke. Instead, he silently begged the Lord for patience...and wisdom.

"May I ask your name?"

"Agatha."

"Now, Agatha, may I please ask you to consider the fact that perhaps something could be wrong? Perhaps a more thorough examination is in order."

"Are you questioning my methods, Jew?" Agatha retorted, her dark eyes flashing in challenge. "I've been delivering babies longer than you've been living! First-time mothers always have long, painful deliveries. Always."

As if emphasizing the midwife's statement, Kelila released another sharp cry, gasping in pain as another contraction gripped her full force.

Going to his wife, Philip quickly kneeled beside her, grasping her hand as she endured another bout of misery.

"You're doing just fine, love. I'm here."

Inexplicably troubled by the tears dampening Kelila's cheeks, Philip closed his eyes and begged the Lord to intervene on behalf of his wife and unborn child.

***

Tabitha

Joppa

It was late, far too late for office work. And yet, Tabitha just couldn't bring herself to retire for the night. There was simply so much to do, so many arrangements to be made. So many meetings to coordinate, so many projects to oversee.

How could she possibly rest now? How could she ever rest again?

The entire mansion was quiet and still as its occupants slumbered late into the night. Barricaded in her uncle's office and seated behind his large, ornate desk, Tabitha shuffled through stacks of paperwork, most of the documents entirely foreign to her. It had been a busy day, reviewing ledgers with Eli for the purpose of financial planning and budgeting. She had muddled through it somehow, carefully asking intentional questions when she didn't fully understand a concept and desperately attempting to mentally store and file Eli's thorough answers.

Oh, what she wouldn't give to have Mary there with her to guide her through the overwhelming muddle of business-related questions pounding in her head. Though sorely tempted to write to Mary, begging her to visit and guide her through the confusing process, Tabitha had refrained. Mary had her own ventures to oversee and operate, after all. It would be selfish to ask her to put everything in Jerusalem aside to travel to Joppa to help her. She had already written a letter explaining her sudden, unexpected inheritance and accompanying responsibilities. She knew Mary would most certainly write back, offering wise and practical advice.

Sighing, Tabitha neatly stacked a tall pile of parchment documents and slid them across the cluttered surface of the desk. It was becoming too difficult for her tired eyes to decipher the numbers on the page in the glowing lamplight. Perhaps she should attempt to focus on something else, for now.

At least until morning.

Leaning back in her uncle's chair, Tabitha grasped the gilded arms and closed her eyes, contemplating what more could be done before retiring—that is, if she could settle down enough to relax. Her mind was abuzz with ideas and possibilities. Already, a whirlwind of arrangements were underway. Soon, the mansion would undergo a complete and utter transformation as the reception hall was converted into worship space and the remainder of the home was renovated into a house of refuge and a place of safety for the widows and orphans of Joppa.

True, the project before her was daunting. But she fully trusted the Lord to see it through. She had absolutely no doubt that God had led her to Joppa for this very purpose, not to mention for the salvation of her uncle, her dear friend Tirzah, and dozens of others. And now, it was truly thrilling to contemplate what wonders the Lord planned to reveal in the next chapter of her life. She could hardly contain her excitement about establishing a home base for the local church and building a safe place for the needy and destitute of the region. There was no doubt whatsoever in her mind that the Lord had called her to Joppa for such a time as this.

She couldn't wait to watch Him at work!

Let's see, Tabitha mused, mentally reviewing the plans for the following day. *Josiah and Adam have already been recruited to locate capable builders to see to the renovations. And Phineas is drafting a schedule for prayer meetings and worship services. Eli has thoroughly reviewed the books with me, and now I must simply wait for Joram's investor to arrive to provide some valuable insight and business advice.*

Reaching for her uncle's favorite stylus, Tabitha tapped it on the desk a few times, deep in thought. Eli was quite certain that the investor would *not* appreciate Tabitha's plans to utilize the mansion for worship services and charity work. She hoped and prayed he wouldn't oppose her mission and stir up trouble.

Regardless, she knew she must obey the call of God on her life, despite any opposition that might arise.

CHAPTER 42

Philip

Caesarea Maritima

Despite Philip's prayerful entreaties, dawn's slow arrival failed to usher in the birth of his first child. And yet, Kelila's labor dragged on.

Having been relocated to a makeshift bed on the floor near the hearth, Kelila clutched Philip's hand like a lifeline as the midwife grudgingly conducted a more thorough examination, having finally been goaded by the evangelist's insistent request.

Straightening, the midwife wiped her hands on her apron, her expression and body language strangely closed.

"What is it?" Philip asked, stroking Kelila's sweat-soaked tendrils back from her forehead.

"Something's wrong, isn't it?" Kelila gasped, desperately attempting to shut out the overwhelming pain.

"The baby appears to be wedged in a dangerous position," the midwife informed them, her tone blatantly devoid of empathy. "It may be undeliverable."

"What do you mean undeliverable?" Philip demanded, his tone measured.

"Your wife will likely labor this way for days, to no avail."

"No," Kelila cried out, attempting to sit up and grasp her heaving belly. "No, please. There must be something you can do."

"In such instances, it is safest to sacrifice the child for the sake of the mother."

"No!" Kelila dissolved into tears then, her entire being paralyzed with fear and pain. "How can you say that?"

"It's the only way. Unless you wish to perish in childbirth with a long line of others who refused to heed wise counsel."

Taking Kelila in his arms, Philip's heart pounded in his chest like a battle drum. Sickened and exhausted, he couldn't help but wonder at the seeming silence of the God he loved.

And then it occurred to him, so vividly that he was taken aback.

The enemy of his soul did not want this child to be born.

"I am trained to remove the child, should it be necessary—" the midwife went on, rolling up her fitted sleeves as if preparing to do just that.

"It won't be necessary," Philip cut in firmly, certain that this was a specialized form of spiritual warfare they now faced. But he refused to surrender the life of his child. Despite his own steadily mounting fear, he determined to place their situation in God's hands.

"You may go," Philip informed Agatha, his tone boding no argument.

"Surely you won't be so foolish as to—"

"I said, you may go," Philip repeated, wishing he

had dismissed the faithless Greek woman hours earlier. She had only made the situation far worse, seemingly relishing Kelila's fear and pain rather than offering helpful solutions.

"I expect to be fully compensated for my time and services—"

"And you shall be. But, first, I must tend to my wife. Now go."

Surprised by the gentle evangelist's uncompromising tone, the midwife turned and stormed from the house without further argument.

"Oh, Philip," Kelila wept, doubling over in pain. "I can't do this. I can't."

"We're going to pray, Kelila," Philip told her, nearly overcome with anxiety. But he had to be strong for his wife. She was utterly exhausted and emotionally spent, far worse than he.

"I hurt," she whispered, weeping. "I hurt so much."

Oh, beloved, he wished to say. *I hurt for you.*

Cradling her like a small, helpless child, Philip gently stroked her hair, begging his Father in Heaven for the help that He alone could provide.

***

Kelila was fading fast when the front door slammed open unexpectedly. Though she was too far spent to notice the interruption, Philip jerked his head up, fast becoming desperate.

"Adah!" he gasped, never so happy to see another human being in his entire life. "What are you doing here? I thought you were visiting your mother!"

"The Lord awakened me the night before last," she said quickly, rushing to Kelila's side and immediately evaluating the situation with wise, well-trained eyes. "I knew I must return. I hastened as quickly as possible."

Oh, thank You, God. Thank You. Rising unsteadily to greet the woman, Philip suddenly broke down, weeping, as fear mingled with hope and relief battled in his soul.

"Shhh, it's all right." Taking the tall, broad-shouldered evangelist in motherly arms, Adah stroked his heaving back, whispering words of comfort and consolation. "Oh, my poor darlings. What you must have endured."

"The substitute midwife says there's no hope for our child," Philip managed shakily. "She said the baby must be sacrificed to save Kelila."

"Nonsense," Adah huffed, tightening the apron about her trim waist and rolling up her sleeves. Amazed by the peace that the small midwife had ushered into the formerly hopeless chamber, Philip watched as she bent to meet Kelila's disoriented gaze, her calm features alighting with a reassuring smile.

"We serve a God of miracles, dear ones," Adah reminded them, completely unfazed by the former midwife's pronouncement of doom. "Now let's ask Him for one."

***

Tabitha

Joppa

"These men are highly regarded in their trade. They do fine, honest work, and I believe they're a perfect fit for this venture."

"Thank you, Josiah," Tabitha smiled graciously,

warmed by the older man's enthusiasm for the project at hand. "I trust your judgment completely. If you believe these carpenters are fit for the job, then we shall hire them today."

Josiah nodded eagerly, pleased by Tabitha's high praise.

Seated in the mansion's lavish triclinium-style banquet hall, Tabitha offered a meaningful smile to each of the godly men seated at her table—kind Adam, with his cheerful father Josiah, and their faithful friend, Phineas. Eli, who was fast becoming Tabitha's right-hand man, stood at her elbow beside her couch, tablet and stylus at the ready. A simple spread graced the long table, far simpler than Joram's kitchen staff was accustomed to preparing. But Tabitha had already decided that simplifying meals would be a practical and simple way to reduce the cost of living in the elegant seaside mansion. Considering the fact that there would soon be many hungry mouths to feed, she knew she must learn to be an extremely wise steward of every single shekel her uncle's shipping business produced.

"I just want to thank you all for your enthusiasm and support." She smiled warmly, overwhelmed by the dear friends the Lord had brought into her life and home. "Josiah and Adam, you located trustworthy builders far more quickly than I would have thought possible. And Phineas, thank you for coordinating church services in such a way that every believer in Joppa can attend at some point each week."

"It was my pleasure," Phineas assured her. "And services can commence the moment the renovations are complete."

"Wonderful," Tabitha smiled, hoping the renovation process would be swift. "Now if it's all right, I'd like to run an idea by the three of you."

"Anything," Adam assured her, receiving nods of agreement from Josiah and Phineas.

"All right," Tabitha continued, grateful for their willingness to listen and offer wisdom. "As I am preparing this place as a home for the destitute of the region, Eli and I have been buckling down on expenses and putting together a careful budget. As I'm sure you've noticed, my uncle's taste in décor is slightly more, um, opulent, than mine."

The men shared a knowing chuckle, for Joram's garish preferences and absolute insistence upon luxury in his house was almost famous in Joppa.

"Well, in his will, Joram gave me permission to utilize the assets of this estate in whatever way would most benefit the furtherance of the gospel," Tabitha explained. "So, we've decided to greatly simplify the rooms and décor in this mansion. We plan to collect most of the furnishings, artwork, fixtures, and such, and sell these items to garner more savings. What are your thoughts on this? I'm open to feedback and direction, as I sorely need it."

"It's a great idea," Adam said forthrightly, meeting Tabitha's gaze with confidence. "How can we help?"

"Well, as of today, I've instructed the servants to begin gathering items from each room," Tabitha answered, attempting to focus on her response rather than the way Adam's gaze rested troublingly upon her. "We will place everything in storage rooms to be appraised and hopefully sold as soon as possible. I'm just not entirely sure how to locate practical buyers. Have you any suggestions?"

At this, Josiah and Adam exchanged knowing looks, their brows raised in amusement.

Tabitha simply waited, intrigued by their unexpected reaction.

"You're asking if I know anyone interested in purchasing sound goods?" Josiah grinned, folding strong arms across his chest. "I own and operate a seller's booth in Joppa's main business district! As such, I know every merchant on the docks."

Clasping her hands, Tabitha resisted the urge to squeal her delight. Why, she hadn't even considered this welcome bit of news!

"You needn't worry about a thing, dear one," Josiah assured her, exchanging knowing looks with his fellow men in the triclinium. "I'll spread the word and see what I can do."

CHAPTER 43

Philip

Caesarea Maritima

Midday came and went without ushering in the birth of a child.

Though Adah remained cheerful, calm, and soothing as ever, Philip sensed that the midwife's concern was steadily deepening. Stationed like a faithful sentry at Kelila's side, she coached the exhausted and frightened young woman through the painful contractions, praying aloud in between the painful bouts.

"Philip," Adah said, glancing up from her patient vigil and noting his pinched, anxious features. "Why don't you rest a bit? I'll be right here by Kelila's side. You needn't worry."

Though he felt dead on his feet, the thought of dozing off while Kelila was in her present state was unthinkable.

"You need rest," Adah reminded him gently. "I'll

be right here with her, Philip."

"I couldn't, but thank you, Adah."

"I understand," the midwife nodded. "But please, do consider it."

Something about her tone warned Philip that Kelila's intense labor wasn't anywhere near finished, and the thought was unbearable. How much longer could he endure to watch her intense suffering, completely unable to ease her pain?

"Adah, may I have a word with you alone?"

"Philip, no, please," Kelila panted, her eyes growing round with fear at the thought of being left alone. "Don't go."

"We're only going to step aside a moment, Kelila," Adah assured her, gently dabbing her sweat-soaked brow with a damp cloth. "We won't leave you. You can watch us the entire time, dear one."

"Please hurry," she managed weakly. "Please."

Gently drawing the midwife aside a few feet away from Kelila, Philip lowered his voice, anxious beyond imagining. "Adah, I need you to speak plainly with me."

Adah met his gaze with troubled but honest brown eyes.

"Are we going to lose this child?"

Looking away, Adah bit her lower lip, carefully considering her response.

"Oh, God, no," Philip breathed, running a trembling hand through his hair.

"You mustn't lose hope, Philip," Adah told him firmly, touching his arm. "God is here, even now. His will shall prevail."

"The former midwife, Agatha, said we must sacrifice the child for the sake of the mother. Adah, am

I going to lose them both if Kelila continues trying to deliver this baby?"

"It's true that the child seems to be wedged in a difficult position. Most likely, the babe is having great difficulty emerging past the pelvic bone. It happens often when the mother is slender and narrowly built, like Kelila. In this case, I have been completely unable to turn the child. Everything I have tried to do has proven futile."

"What more can we do?"

"We can pray."

"Pray?" Releasing a sigh of frustration, Philip shook his head.

"Yes, pray," Adah told him stoutly. "You are a faith-filled evangelist, dear one. Your testimony has resulted in the salvation of hundreds, possibly even thousands. You of all people know how to pray."

Feeling slightly rebuked, Philip responded a bit sheepishly, "Why is it so much easier to have faith on behalf of others, Adah?"

"It always is."

Kelila suddenly released a sharp cry, drawing them from their conversation. Weeping inconsolably, she begged them to return to her.

"You know who you are in Christ, Philip," Adah cast over her shoulder, hastening to her charge's side. "The Lord has worked mighty miracles through you because you have been a willing vessel. Perhaps it's time to surrender to God's will, to have faith, and to allow Him to work through you on your own behalf, and not merely for the sake of others."

Suddenly ashamed, Philip realized he had, indeed, lost faith. How easily he had trusted God on behalf of strangers and fellow believers! But to trust

God to work mightily in his own life?

O you of little faith, why did you doubt? As the words of Jesus whispered quietly through his mind, Philip was galvanized into action.

God was still in charge. He was still on His throne. He was, indeed, capable of working miracles on behalf of Philip, Kelila, and their unborn child.

Father, forgive me, Philip prayed fervently, crossing the room and kneeling beside his anxiously weeping wife. Firmly taking her hand in his, he met Adah's gaze, who gave him one firm, confident nod.

"Father, in the name of Your Son, Jesus, through the power of Your Holy Spirit, hear me."

Kelila's weeping increased along with her pain, but Philip was not deterred.

"The enemy of souls has come against us, Lord. Only You know why he doesn't want this child to be born. But You are greater, Lord. And by the power of Your name, I command this child to move and to be brought forth!"

Placing a hand on his wife's bulging abdomen, Philip declared with authority, "In the name of Jesus Christ, the Son of God, may it be so."

Beneath his hand placed firmly upon Kelila's rounded belly, Philip felt a very distinct, unmistakable movement.

Still seated across from Philip on Kelila's opposite side, Adah's eyes grew round with awe.

"The baby's coming, Philip. Praise God, it's time!"

CHAPTER 44

Tabitha

Joppa

Stepping gingerly into the lovely bedchamber once treasured by her aunt, Tabitha's gaze swept the elegant room in fascination. This room had long since drawn her with its feminine grace and soft touches, so unlike the rest of the mansion which Joram had so garishly outfitted after his wife's passing. The furniture was comfortable and lovely and thoughtfully arranged. Tabitha admired the canopy bed with its graceful curtains and plush pillows, as well as her aunt's old vanity set and gilded mirror gracing the opposite wall. She especially delighted in the way the curtains fluttered in the cool sea breezes from the open balcony. The entire chamber was filled with the calming scent of the sea.

This is where we shall stay, Laurel and I, she decided, feeling a certain closeness toward a kindhearted aunt she had never known but truly admired. The storage room she had previously occupied would need to be utilized along with the rest as the mansion was outfitted to house dozens of women and children. And this room, centrally located on the upper floor amidamidst the remaining suites, was perfectly suitable for her. She would be right in the midst of the guests residing in the mansion, easily accessed and not aloof or far removed, as some ladies of elegant manors tended to be.

Allowing herself a final sweep of the lovely chamber, Tabitha decided she would leave the room entirely as it was. After all, Joram had carefully preserved it to honor the memory of his beloved wife. And Tabitha had far too many tasks at hand to bother with redecorating her own room.

It was perfect, anyway.

Gently leaning against the door jamb, Tabitha folded her arms knowingly, a soft smile playing about the corners of her lips. Instinctively, she sensed that Joram would be pleased she had chosen to abide here. She couldn't help but imagine that her Aunt Pennie would have been pleased, as well.

***

Kelila

Caesarea Maritima

Basking in the glow of joyful motherhood, Kelila cradled her perfect little daughter in the crook of her arm, overwhelmed with gratitude toward God and the deepest sense of wonder.

"You are perfect, little one," Kelila whispered,

amazed by how tiny and fragile and still the infant appeared as she slept, safe in the arms of her mother.

Seated on the comfortable couch in the sitting area of her new home, Kelila marveled at all that had transpired in the last few days. While her labor and delivery had proven terribly traumatic, she knew she would gladly do it all over again if it meant bringing this precious little one into the world. Mere days old, her baby girl was a living, breathing wonder—undeniable evidence of the tender mercies of God.

"I'm back!" Philip announced loudly, swinging open the front door and emerging with an armload of groceries from the market.

"Shhhh!" Kelila hissed, pointedly glancing down at the sleeping babe in her arms. "You'll awaken her, Philip."

"Sorry," Philip whispered, carefully depositing the groceries on their newly acquired table before gently closing the door behind him. Tiptoeing toward Kelila in an exaggerated fashion, he lowered himself onto the opposite side of the upholstered couch.

"She's beautiful, isn't she?" Kelila whispered softly, stroking the baby's silken cheek.

"*You're* beautiful," Philip told her, his brown eyes soft. "May God be praised. He brought forth our precious daughter and preserved the life of my beloved wife."

"God is faithful."

"He is, indeed."

"What do you have there?" Kelila asked curiously, hoping their whispered conversation wouldn't awaken their slumbering daughter.

"A letter," Philip grinned, playfully waving the

sealed parchment scroll in the air.

"A letter?" Kelila repeated blankly. "From whom?"

"Most likely from Ephraim and Adorina. Before we left Joppa, I sent word to them that we would be relocating to Caesarea Maritima."

"Oh, Philip!" Kelila exclaimed, momentarily forgetting to keep her voice low. Quickly correcting her tone with a sheepish little smile, she added, "Will you read it to me?"

"I don't know. It might wake the baby," Philip teased, his eyes sparkling with fun.

"Philip!"

"All right," he grinned, carefully breaking the wax seal and unrolling the stiff parchment. "Ah, yes. This is definitely Ephraim's script," he nodded, scanning the first few lines with a fond little smile. "Though, undoubtedly, it was Adorina who told him what to pen."

"Oh, how I miss them!" Kelila sighed, rocking the sleeping babe in her arms. "How Adorina would have delighted to meet this little one."

"Perhaps, someday, she will."

Blinking back bittersweet tears, Kelila nodded in hopeful agreement as Philip began to read. Eager to savor every word written by her dear Samaritan friends, Kelila listened with rapt attention as Philip recounted the couple's description of the growing church in Sychar and the new synagogue-like structure in which they had begun to host services. In her typically no-nonsense fashion, Adorina updated Philip and Kelila on the lives of all the dear friends they had grown to love during their time spent in the quaint Samaritan village. But Kelila was most interested in Adorina's final sentiment, addressed specifically to her. With tears in her eyes, Kelila listened as Philip read, and she could almost see Adorina's dark eyes and fervent features burning brightly, speaking to her husband, Ephraim, in her low alto voice as he captured her words upon the page.

> *Kelila, my wonderful friend, I must thank you for something you brought to my attention shortly before leaving Sychar. Perhaps you may not even remember it, for it was a casual conversation we shared that day. But as we spoke, you asked me if I had forgiven my father—the man who hurt me so deeply. For years, I blamed him for the negative, resentful feelings I harbored toward my heavenly Father. However, I now realize that it was wrong to nurse such bitterness against my earthly father. After much thought and prayer, I have made a conscious decision to forgive him. True, there are still moments when I remember the pain, the hurt, and the betrayal involved in my relationship with him. But when rebellious, unruly feelings rush in, I simply relinquish them to God.*
>
> *Thank you, Kelila, for bringing this matter to my attention. It is a blessed relief to know that I am right with God in this. I cannot thank you enough, beloved.*

"Oh, Philip," Kelila whispered, overjoyed for her friend. "Adorina finally has peace about a matter that has plagued her for many years. I'm so happy for her."

"It sounds like you played a crucial role in bringing her to that realization," Philip smiled proudly, reaching out to squeeze her knee.

"It was clearly the Lord, not me," Kelila pointed out. "I do remember asking Adorina if she had forgiven her father, and, frankly, her reaction startled me. I'd never seen a trace of bitterness in her eyes, until then. Obviously, it was the Lord who worked on her heart, gently drawing her into right relationship with Him in this area."

"Praise our merciful God for His patience toward us."

"Yes," Kelila agreed, turning a loving gaze upon the precious little bundle in her arms. "We must write them back, Philip, and tell them all about this sweet girl, our little miracle, heaven-sent."

"God must have mighty things in store for this one," Philip mused, stretching out a hand to stroke the rosy, silken cheek of his sleeping daughter. "The enemy did everything in his power to prevent her arrival. And yet, the will of our God prevailed."

"Praise His glorious name," Kelila whispered, tears of happiness and relief stinging her dark eyes.

"Indeed."

"Our sweet little Nessa," Kelila smiled through her tears, bending to kiss the soft infant cheek and savoring the sound of her newborn daughter's beautiful name upon her lips. It was, in fact, the perfect name.

Nessa, meaning *miracle*. And a miracle she was, indeed.

In every imaginable way.

CHAPTER 45

Mary

Jerusalem

The lamps were burning late into the night in Mary's quiet office library. Posed staidly behind her massive desk, Mary shuffled through piles of parchment documentation, far too focused on her work to feel the weight of exhaustion. It was a habit of hers, sequestering herself within the tranquility of the bibliotheca long after the rest of the household slept. Here, she was granted the gift of uninterrupted quiet hours, time to study, time to think, time to pray, and time to review the stacks of financial ledgers and paperwork piled high upon her desk.

An unexpected shadow slanted across the entryway, followed by another one.

Slowly, cautiously closing the opened ledger on her desk, Mary lifted her gaze, her gray eyes scanning the perimeter of her office.

"Greetings, beloved."

"Barnabas!" Mary cried, springing to her feet and rushing around the side of her desk, graceful arms outstretched.

Emerging from the sea of brightly painted pillars framing the entrance, Barnabas rushed his younger sister, wrapping strong arms around her and swinging her off her elegantly sandaled feet.

"Oh, Barnabas, you're safe! You've returned!"

"I told you I would."

"Praise God!"

A second figure emerged from the shadows then, moving slowly, stiffly.

Drawing back from her brother's embrace, Mary's gaze landed on an exhausted and somewhat frazzled-looking Agabus.

"Agabus!" Mary exclaimed, warmed by the sight of him. "You look dead on your feet."

"I *feel* dead on my feet," he quipped with a wry smile. "The trek from Damascus to Jerusalem is no joke."

"Certainly not a journey for the faint of heart," Barnabas grinned, amused.

"I told him we should turn aside for the night, get some rest, and resume our journey home in the morning," Agabus pointed out, adjusting his wrinkled, travel-worn head covering with an air of annoyance. "Your delightful brother here insisted that we keep moving."

"We were so close to home," Barnabas reminded him with a playful slap on the back. Ignoring the Pharisee's cringe, he added, "There was no reason to tarry."

"Personally, I consider brigands, robbers, zealots, and thieves preying upon senseless travelers poking around in the dark a perfectly reasonable reason to tarry."

"We came here straight from the road," Barnabas informed her, beaming. "We knew you'd wish to see us, Mary, after so long a journey."

Intently watching the men interact, Mary folded her arms, noting her brother's twinkling eyes and faint, hidden smile. And there was something different about Agabus, despite his characteristic grousing. As if deep down, where it most mattered, he suddenly possessed the inner peace he'd earnestly sought for so long.

"Agabus," she said knowingly, her light gray eyes pinning the young man in place. "Is there anything you wish to share with me, sir?"

Exchanging a somewhat mischievous look with Barnabas, Agabus folded his hands calmly before him, meeting Mary's intense gaze with candor. "You will recall our last conversation before I left Jerusalem to reach Damascus with Saul of Tarsus, yes?"

"Of course," Mary nodded. "You were quite distressed. I assured you that I would continue praying that God would get your attention, that He would powerfully reveal Himself to you beyond any shadow of doubt."

"Well," Agabus grinned, receiving a hearty slap on the back from Barnabas. "Your prayers have been answered."

"Oh, Agabus!" Mary cried, her heart swelling with joy so great she could scarcely contain it. "Praise God!"

"Indeed."

"I want to hear all about it," Mary insisted, going around her desk and settling gracefully in her chair as if preparing herself for a nice, long chat. "Tell me everything, Agabus. How did it happen?"

The two men standing before her exchanged yet another knowing expression, their eyes dancing with amusement.

"About that," Barnabas grinned as he and Agabus situated themselves in the chair facing Mary's desk. "We have news for you, Mary. And now you shall see why we couldn't wait to come to you, despite this midnight hour."

"Yes," Agabus conceded with a wry smile. "It involves your longtime pal, Saul of Tarsus."

"I'm glad you're sitting down," Barnabas added, stroking his tidy beard with an air of bemusement. "Are you ready for this?"

Glancing back and forth between the two unlikely comrades seated before her—her brother, a bold, outgoing Levite, and her dear friend Agabus, a timid, overcautious Pharisee—Mary's suspicions were instantly confirmed. Heart soaring, she knew beyond any and all doubt that God had answered the prayer of her heart, her prayer for Saul of many years.

"Dare I suggest that our one and only Saul of Tarsus has finally seen the light?" Mary mused, willing herself to remain calm and composed despite the excitement coursing through her veins.

"Ah, my dear Mary," Barnabas replied, receiving a knowing chuckle from the young man seated behind him. "Saul has certainly seen the light, literally. In every sense of the expression."

"Oh, thank You, God!" Mary nearly wept, clasping her hands over her chest in overwhelming gratitude. "He is faithful, my brothers. So faithful!"

"His tender mercies far surpass our human understanding," Barnabas smiled, pleased to witness his sister's joy and relief. "For not only has Saul accepted Jesus Christ as the Messiah of all mankind, but God has called him to bear the beacon of hope to all the world. Saul is God's chosen instrument, and he shall proclaim the light of the gospel unto the ends of the earth."

"Already, we ourselves have witnessed him take up this calling with gusto," Agabus added. "Saul has been proclaiming Jesus Christ as Messiah among believers in the very synagogues he previously sought to destroy."

"Oh, Barnabas. Agabus. Will we ever comprehend the marvels of our God?" Cupping her face with slender hands and shaking her head in awe, Mary allowed herself a moment to fully absorb the wondrous announcement and to praise the Lord for His overwhelming goodness as the deepest sense of gratitude flooded her entire being like the gentle waves of a calm and quiet sea.

For by the mighty hand of God, the sworn enemy of Jesus Christ and His beloved church had miraculously become their greatest advocate. Oh, how the enemy of souls must be trembling in rage, even as the angels in Heaven rejoiced!

CHAPTER 46

Tabitha

Joppa

The seaside mansion was alive with bustling activity as servants rushed about to and fro, laughing and chattering in steadily mounting excitement as they performed the bidding of their newly acquired yet already beloved mistress.

Downstairs, the rapping, tapping, hollow sounds of heavy construction echoed and bounced off the elegantly frescoed halls as the vestibule walls were removed and the vast reception hall was renovated to host local church gatherings.

Upstairs, the servants fluttered from room to room, cleaning, dusting, arranging furniture, and seeing to the final touches on each room. Traveling the mansion's long upper corridor and nearly bursting with excitement and gratitude, Tabitha paused in the first doorway, eager to gauge the progress of each newly prepared bedchamber. Leaning against the elegant doorpost, Tabitha folded her arms and tilted her head to one side as she evaluated the improvements, pleased.

It had proven to be quite a job thus far, redoing every single suite on the upper floor. And yet, slowly but surely, Tabitha's vision for the mansion had come together as she worked tirelessly with the household staff to empty the massive rooms of excess furniture, artwork, trinkets, fixtures, and baubles. The storage rooms below were fairly overflowing with items to be bartered or sold, even though Josiah had already unloaded an exorbitant amount of valuable merchandise to various merchants at the docks. The proceeds from Josiah's sales had allowed Tabitha to make practical purchases to furnish the suites, and she was incredibly pleased with the results. Despite the fact that the garishly overdone bedchambers had been greatly simplified, the newly improved suites were cozy and inviting, each one housing several beds to accommodate multiple families per room, if needed. Carefully stocked with fresh linens and warm blankets, each room also boasted plush, inviting rugs and practical yet attractive furnishings. Sheer linen curtains framed the open windows, fluttering in the cool sea breezes and allowing for plenty of fresh air and sunlight to flood each room. Tabitha had also insisted upon including a miniature washroom in each suite, providing fresh cloths and a large pitcher with an accompanying washbasin. She was especially pleased with the neat little wooden bins brimming with handcrafted toys which she had lovingly placed in each suite. Undoubtedly, the orphans who would soon be flocking to her mansion would've never laid eyes upon such lovely toys, much less owned any for themselves. She absolutely couldn't wait to see the wonder reflected in their eyes when the needy children settled into their new home.

Everything was finally coming together, and Tabitha couldn't be happier. Even as the entire household scampered about in eager preparation, the lovely seaside estate resounded with a calming sense of peace. Tabitha knew, without a doubt, that she was walking in the will of God.

Gingerly entering the room, Tabitha stepped past the new furnishings and slipped out onto the balcony—a lovely hanging structure overlooking the towering city walls and crashing blue waves upon the rocky shore. Resting her hands on the elegant wrought-iron railing, Tabitha leaned forward into the breeze, closing her eyes as the salty air kissed her flushed face in the most refreshing way. Heart nearly bursting with anticipation, she imagined this new home as a cheerful place brimming with the laughter and chatter of dozens of happy children. This would, indeed, become a safe place, a refuge, a haven from the unexpected storms of life. And who could possibly relate to those who had suffered such battering storms better than she? For even at her young age, Tabitha had experienced immeasurable loss. And yet, the Lord had shaped her sorrows into something beautiful. Her compassion toward those who had experienced suffering and hardship was unrivaled, fueled by having experienced her own great losses.

Lifting her face to bask in the faint winter sunlight, Tabitha opened her eyes, awed by the wide blue sky and the oceanic beauty of her surroundings. All of it spoke with resounding clarity of her Maker, the One who had shaped not only the heavens, the earth, the skies and seas, but also the days of her life and, ultimately, her destiny.

Soon, this place will become all it was meant to be, Tabitha thought, sharing a secret smile with her Creator. *Precious Lord, thank You for bringing me this far. I cannot wait to fully embrace Your calling. And wouldn't my dear Aunt Pennie have been so thrilled to see all of this unfold? The earnest prayer of her heart was that, someday, this mansion would become a refuge for the needy and destitute. And You have brought it to pass, Lord.*

Shaking her head in awe, Tabitha watched as a majestic white gull soared high overhead, releasing a gusty cry as if in agreement with her thoughts.

Clasping the railing and leaning as far as it permitted, Tabitha smiled to herself, marveling at the faithfulness of God.

Wouldn't her dear Aunt Pennie be thrilled to know that the fervent prayer of her heart had been realized over three decades later? She could scarcely comprehend the wonder of it all!

***

Leah

Jerusalem

Quaking inside, Leah responded to Mary's summons with a swelling sense of dread. She knew it must be urgent, for a messenger had arrived on her doorstep at the crack of dawn, announcing that

Mary of Jerusalem had requested an audience with her as soon as possible. Instantly, a horrid premonition had settled over Leah. For, instinctively, she had known that Mary's unexpected summons involved her wayward brother, Saul.

Oh, God, she'd thought, overwhelmed with fear and dread. *What has he done now?*

Standing tall in her typically stoic manner, Leah now paused at the pillared entryway of Mary's impressive office library, steeling herself for whatever news might await her. Drawing a somewhat quivery breath, she tucked a wayward strand of long, straight, raven-colored hair behind one ear, her dark eyes glittering with resignation. She knew that the impending meeting would prove serious, indeed. Why else would Mary summon her amidst the household's frenzied preparations for Purim, which would commence at sunset? The matter was obviously quite urgent for Mary to do so.

"Leah, what a pleasant surprise!"

Glancing over her shoulder, Leah saw Rhoda hastening across the courtyard, arms outstretched for a friendly embrace.

Turning reluctantly, Leah allowed her friend to take her in soft arms, though she remained stiff and pensive despite her best efforts to relax.

"Something is wrong," Rhoda observed, drawing back to study her friend's pinched features at arms' length.

"Mary summoned me early this morning," Leah told Rhoda frankly. "I'm worried it's about Saul."

"I heard that Barnabas returned late last night, along with his friend, Agabus," Rhoda confirmed. "There's a sense of excitement in the air, though I haven't the slightest idea what it's about. Perhaps it's simply relief over Barnabas' safe return. I know Mary was quite worried about her brother."

"If Barnabas has returned from Damascus, then Mary's news must be regarding my own brother," Leah guessed, her heart sinking. "Oh, Rhoda, if he succeeded in his hateful mission and destroyed innocent followers in Damascus, I don't know what I'll do..."

"I could be wrong," Rhoda ventured cautiously. "But I have a distinct impression that Mary bears welcome news. She arose early this morning and immediately sequestered herself in the bibliotheca, even forgoing her breakfast. Though we haven't yet spoken today, I sensed her excitement as she hastened down the hall. I've since learned that an announcement is to be made this evening when the believers gather to usher in the Feast of Purim at sunset."

"What kind of announcement?" Leah asked tentatively, her stomach churning unpleasantly.

"I'm afraid I cannot say," Rhoda confessed. "I shall undoubtedly find out this evening, along with everyone else."

"Very well," Leah sighed, steeling herself once again as she prepared to enter the intimidating office library. "I suppose there's only one way to find out."

CHAPTER 47

Leah

Jerusalem

Stealing steadily past the rows of painted marble pillars standing like silent sentries guarding the dimly lit bibliotheca, Leah held her head high despite the anxiety churning within her soul. The regal office library was dimly lit at this early hour, with mounted lamps burning and casting a faint orange glow upon the frescoed walls as curling whisps of smoke rose steadily toward the vaulted ceiling.

Approaching the front of the impressive chamber, Leah was surprised to find not only Mary regally seated behind her massive desk, but her brother Barnabas, as well, standing at her elbow.

Leaning eagerly forward, Mary's hands remained folded delicately on the top of her desk as Leah drew before her, waiting expectantly. The girl's dark eyes darted back and forth between the two, warily questioning.

"Greetings, dear sister," Barnabas spoke warmly, his light brown eyes lighting upon the small figure standing before his sister's desk.

"Greetings," Leah answered cautiously, her intense gaze traveling from Barnabas to Mary. Noting how brother and sister exchanged a knowing, hidden smile, Leah knew a brief moment of relief. Perhaps Mary had summoned her to reveal welcome news, after all, as Rhoda had suggested.

But just as quickly, Leah's heart dropped like a stone.

Oh no, she realized, heart pounding furiously in her chest as a dreadful thought took shape in her mind. *Saul is dead. That's why Mary has summoned me. Something terrible must have happened to him. Otherwise, Barnabas would have surely been arrested along with the other believers in Damascus.*

Attempting to talk herself out of the possibility, Leah reminded herself that Rhoda had been quite certain that Mary's news was welcome. And yet, Leah was little encouraged by the thought, for surely the demise of the church's greatest enemy would be great cause for rejoicing! Perhaps that's why Mary and Barnabas appeared so relieved, so at ease.

"It's my brother, isn't it?" Leah dared, meeting Mary's gaze with glittering dark eyes.

"Yes," Mary nodded, her sheer blue head covering resting gracefully upon her silken brown hair and cascading over her slender shoulders.

"He's dead, isn't he?"

"Dead?" Mary repeated blankly, turning to cast a questioning glance over her shoulder toward Barnabas, who merely shrugged his broad shoulders in response. And then a thought seemed to occur to her, for a joyous smile graced Mary's aristocratic features as she nodded her head in confirmation. "Yes," she added carefully. "Yes, your brother is dead."

Bowing her head in overwhelming sorrow, Leah wondered at the uncharacteristic glibness of Mary's tone. True, Saul had caused the church nothing but terror and misery for far too long. Even so, Leah was stunned that Mary and Barnabas would rejoice over the demise of a lost soul, however wicked he might have been.

"I repeat, your brother is dead, but not in the physical sense," Mary clarified, interrupting Leah's anxiously tumultuous train of thought. "Saul is now dead to sin, but alive to God! For Jesus Christ Himself appeared to your brother on the road to Damascus, Leah. And by His grace, Saul has become a fellow believer, a new creation."

"What's more," Barnabas added, his eyes alight. "Saul has been charged to carry the glory of the gospel unto all the nations as a chosen instrument ordained by the hand of God Himself."

Stunned into complete and utter silence, Leah stared, wide-eyed and openmouthed, at Mary and Barnabas.

"Your prayers for your brother have been mightily answered, Leah," Mary continued as Barnabas smiled broadly beside her. "Yet again, God has shown Himself faithful."

"But…" Leah stammered, scarcely able to breathe, for her heart was nearly bursting with shock…and relief. "But, *how*? My brother—he *believes*?"

"He has become a champion for the gospel," Barnabas assured her, dropping a hand to rest casually on his sister's shoulder.

"I can't believe it…" Leah murmured under her breath, dazed.

"Believe it, dear one," Barnabas grinned. "When God has set His sights upon a lost soul, He'll move heaven and earth to reach him. Which is exactly what has happened in the case of your brother, Saul."

"We plan to announce the miracle of Saul's conversion tonight during our evening service," Mary explained, her gray eyes resting warmly upon the astounded young girl before her. "However, as his sister, we felt that you should be the first to know."

"Is he still in Damascus?" Leah finally asked, the shock settling just enough that she felt capable of voicing coherent questions. "When shall he return to Jerusalem? I want to see him."

"Saul himself doesn't know when he will return," Barnabas told her with a rueful smile. "He's now being led entirely by the Spirit of God. And wherever the Spirit leads, Saul intends to follow."

With a slow nod, Leah attempted to process this shocking bit of news. How could she have possibly guessed that the brother who zealously persecuted the church and scoffed at the existence of a triune Godhead would someday be fully committed to being led by the Holy Spirit?

"But there's more, dear sister," Barnabas added warmly, his light brown eyes sparkling with promise.

Leah glanced up at him then, her dark eyes conveying her disbelief.

After exchanging one last, knowing look with Mary, Barnabas turned his attention upon young Leah, smiling warmly. "Before I left Damascus, your brother spoke with me about an urgent matter, one that concerns you, dear one. Thus, I have an important message to deliver to you, a message that cannot wait."

Wondering at the urgency in Barnabas' typically easy tone, Leah stood still as stone, heart pounding, as she awaited the apostle's unexpected revelation.

***

Rhoda

Anxiously pacing the lovely inner court, Rhoda prayed earnestly for Leah. Her friend had appeared inexplicably troubled before slipping into the bibliotheca to speak with Mary. Rhoda hoped the news awaiting her friend would prove to be welcome rather than disturbing.

Wondering if her haphazard pacing would wear out the elegant tiles underfoot, Rhoda was about to consider feigning some reason to join those convening in the bibliotheca when Leah emerged from the pillared entryway, appearing utterly dazed.

"Leah!" Rhoda exclaimed, hurrying to her friend's side and taking her arm.

Leah turned her head slowly, grazing Rhoda's anxious gaze with startled eyes.

"Leah, what happened?" Rhoda nearly demanded, concerned by the young woman's obvious disorientation. "Are you all right?"

"I am free," Leah murmured, shaking her head in complete and utter perplexity. "I'm free, Rhoda."

"You're free?" Rhoda repeated blankly, attempting to follow Leah's train of thought. "What do you mean, free?"

"My entire life has been turned upside down in an instant," Leah muttered in amazement, clearly perplexed. "And yet I've never been so very happy."

Shocked, Rhoda realized that Leah was blinking back tears, and it occurred to her that she had never seen the brave young woman cry before. Not even once. Even now, Leah courageously battled against the tears, refusing to grant them a place.

"Leah," Rhoda spoke gently, feeling rather dense. "I'm afraid I'm not following. What do you mean, you're free?"

Reaching into her simple tunic, Leah produced a narrow parchment scroll bearing her brother's wax seal. "This," she explained, raising the scroll to allow Rhoda a better look. "Rhoda, my betrothal has been dissolved. I needn't marry the unbelieving Pharisee to whom I was engaged. I am free, praise our gracious God in Heaven!"

"Leah, that's amazing," Rhoda exclaimed, throwing her arms around her friend's neck. "Oh, you must be so happy!"

"More so than I can explain."

"Oh, thank You, God," Rhoda breathed, her heart flooding with thanksgiving on behalf of her good friend.

"There's more," Leah informed her, still appearing dazed after her entirely unexpected encounter with Mary and Barnabas.

"More?" Rhoda declared, blinking in surprise.

"My brother, Saul—he is the one responsible for dissolving my betrothal," she explained a bit shakily, still in shock. "He has appointed Barnabas to be my guardian in his absence. But not only that, Rhoda—he has commanded that, should I ever choose to marry, I must wed a fellow believer."

"A fellow believer?" Rhoda blinked in confusion, totally perplexed. "But, Leah, why would Saul command you to marry another believer? He utterly abhors followers of the Way! It wouldn't make any sense at all for him to command you to marry one, unless he somehow recognized the truth for himself..." Voice trailing off in bewilderment, it was then that Rhoda met Leah's gaze and saw that the girl's dark eyes were afire with determination and purpose.

And peace.

The stunning realization hit her like a ton of heavy bricks.

"Wait," Rhoda declared, hesitant to even voice her question for the mere absurdity of it. "Are you saying...are you saying that Saul...did he...?"

Blinking back warm tears and nodding her head with great feeling, Leah confirmed Rhoda's seemingly impossible query.

"Oh, Leah!" Rhoda declared, throwing her arms around her friend once more. "I'm so happy for you! So very, very happy, my friend!"

Sinking into Rhoda's soft embrace, Leah marveled at the tender mercies of God, laughing joyously and even shedding a few liberating tears as she embraced her dearest friend.

CHAPTER 48

Mary

Jerusalem

Strolling the fashionably paved Upper City avenues arm-in-arm with her brother, Barnabas, Mary's bright eyes absorbed the Purim festivities with interest. The well-lit streets were fairly alive at dusk as families with slews of giggling children ushered in the glorified holiday by parading the palm-lined walkways, singing, dancing, laughing, and playing musical instruments in celebration of the patriotic feast.

Purim was a joyous occasion and celebratory in nature, commemorating God's supernatural deliverance during the days Queen Esther in Persia, when she obediently interceded on behalf of God's people and thwarted the evil Haman's plot to destroy the entire Jewish race.

"I suppose we should turn back," Mary sighed wistfully, savoring this coveted moment with the older brother she had always adored. "The believers are undoubtedly already gathering in the Upper Room, and Simon Peter's sermon will soon commence."

"The believers will likely fall out of their seats when I make the unexpected announcement about Saul's conversion," Barnabas grinned, his eyes twinkling with a hint of mischief.

"Without a doubt," Mary agreed, her anticipation building rapidly as the long-awaited service drew nearer.

"Praise our gracious Father for His abundant mercy," Barnabas nearly sang in his deep, lusty tone.

"I have enjoyed this quiet stroll with you," Mary informed her brother with a playful poke to his shoulder, allowing him to guide her over an elegantly arched bridge overlooking a bubbling fountain framed by towering palms, verdant green shrubbery, and curved marble benches.

"And I, with you," Barnabas assured her fondly, proud of his little sister.

Pausing at the graceful crest of the elegant walking bridge, Mary released her brother's arm and leaned forward, resting delicate hands upon the wooden railing and clasping them together in sheer delight. Few things gave her greater enjoyment than observing the beauty of the holy city at sunset, especially during a holiday when the cozy limestone houses and torchlit streets echoed and reverberated with the cheerful sounds of festive music and camaraderie.

"I was worried about you, you know," Mary confessed with a faint smile, her gray eyes sweeping the panoramic sunset view before her. "When you were in Damascus."

"I told you not to worry."

"You might as well have told me not to breathe," Mary shot back with a rueful little smile.

"You and I have long known that God had His sights set upon Saul," Barnabas reminded her, drawing alongside his sister and grasping the bridge's railing with strong hands. "It was only a matter of time. Saul could only resist the Spirit's leading for so long."

"Even so, Saul had to reach a conclusion about the Lordship of Jesus Christ for himself," Mary added, her gaze distant as she contemplated all that had transpired in recent weeks. "God grants each of us free will. Saul could have certainly chosen to resist the Spirit's leading to the bitter end."

"Well, praise God that stubborn man finally saw reason," Barnabas chuckled in amusement.

"A blinding light from Heaven and a blatant confrontation by a Man believed to be crucified, dead, and buried would likely encourage anyone to see reason," Mary laughed. "Even someone as unreasonable as Saul of Tarsus."

"That is, indeed, true," Barnabas agreed with a chuckle.

"How wondrous the feast has proven to be this year," Mary mused, watching as the sun's steady descent upon the western hills cast the entire region in hues of gold. "What better way to commemorate God's miraculous deliverance during the Feast of Purim than by celebrating our own deliverance from our sworn enemy, Saul of Tarsus, and glorifying God for that unlikely conversion."

"Undoubtedly, Saul's conversion shall usher in

a blessed season of peace for the church of God,"
Barnabas decided. "This season of discipleship and
evangelism has proven to be a long, hard road, beginning with the martyrdom of our beloved Stephanos and the violent persecution surging shortly
thereafter. But God has proven faithful, Mary. And
He has seen us through."

"Indeed, He has. But a season of peace, you say?"
Mary murmured, wondering at the beauty of such
a promise. "Will it last, Barnabas?"

"Probably not for long," Barnabas chuckled
frankly. "The church will always have enemies,
Mary. Just as Jesus warned us, the world will no
sooner accept *us* than it accepted *Him*. But for a
time, I imagine we shall enjoy a blessed reprieve,
since Saul of Tarsus was the man responsible for
spearheading the persecution against us. But until
another arises to take his place, I imagine we shall
worship together in peace and safety."

"I cannot even fathom such a thought."

"We must indeed savor every moment and make
the most of it while it lasts," Barnabas told her. "This
is when we double down in our efforts to reach our
fellow Judeans with the light of the gospel, Mary.
We must act now, while yet we can."

"I can only imagine the mighty things God must
have in store for you, Barnabas," Mary told him,
warmed by her brother's driving passion to reach
the lost. "Your love for God and men is truly ex-
traordinary."

"Only time will tell what God has in mind for
each and every one of us," Barnabas mused humbly,
offering his sister his arm. "Well, Mary, I suppose
we should head back. As you pointed out, evening

service is about to commence. Shall we be on our way?"

"I suppose we shall." Taking her brother's proffered arm, Mary smiled wanly, allowing him to guide her across the bridge. For the first time in many years, the way ahead held unspeakable promise and glad tidings borne upon gentle whispers of peace.

Heart soaring with gratitude toward God on high, Mary stepped off the elegant land bridge and into a bright and promising future, heavy laden with joy and peace.

And endless possibilities.

A LOOK AT:
REDEEMED

In a land steeped in ancient mysteries and divine wonders—the Promised Land—a powerful love story unfolds.

Not only does this tale bring to life the enduring bond between Ruth and Boaz, but it also delves into the poignant journey of Adara and Kemuel, a young couple burdened by the heartache of childlessness. In a society where barrenness is seen as a curse, their struggle becomes a testament to the unwavering strength of the human spirit.

As these two couples' lives become entwined by the providence of God, they witness firsthand the depth of His redemption and the boundless reach of His grace.

Immerse yourself in this Biblically-inspired story of hope and discover the relentless power of faith, love, and redemption.

AVAILABLE NOW ON AMAZON

ABOUT THE AUTHOR

Rachael C. Duncan is a passionate follower of Christ. Her goal is to reach as many people as possible for the sake of Christ and His kingdom. She believes that God has gifted each of His children with different gifts to be used to strengthen the body of Christ and fulfill the Great Commission. (Matt. 28:19-20; 1 Cor. 12)

Rachael was blessed to be raised in a strong Christian home, and she accepted Jesus Christ as her Lord and Savior at a very early age. Since then, she has determined to live her life in accordance to His Word and to share the love of Christ through the gift of writing.

Rachael has been passionate about writing since she was a small child. She especially loved writing plays and short stories. At the age of fourteen, she wrote her first play, which was performed as a dinner theatre production by a local school.

She has been actively involved in both women's and children's ministries for over a decade. Currently, she enjoys teaching a weekly girls' Bible study, writing plays for a local homeschool group, and participating in local ministry outreaches for women and children.

Rachael currently resides in Texas with her husband and their first "child"—a playful rescue puppy named Riley! In addition to her writing, she is an enthusiastic "keeper of the home" and "helpmeet" as well as being actively involved in ministering to the women and children God has placed in her life. (Titus 2:3-5; Gen. 2:20-23)